WORRY STONE

The Camerons of Tide's Way
Book Six

Skye Taylor

SandCastleBooks.net

Praise for Skye Taylor

"Skye Taylor's **Worry Stone** is a deeply emotional tale. Authentic and evocative, this love story between a veteran and a one-time war protester makes us appreciate the healing power of love. I loved it!" - Eve Gaddy, National Bestselling author of Heart of the Texas Doctor

"**Keeping His Promise** - A compelling tale of love, compassion and being true to your heart." - NY Times and USA Today bestseller, Caridad Pineiro

"Falling for Zoe is a deftly plotted and delightful story of family, of real life, and love, and trying to do the right thing. **Falling for Zoe** is a romantic gem." - Cheryl Reavis, Best selling, award-winning author

"Bravo Zulu for **Healing a Hero**, filled with turmoil, tenderness, and painful secrets from the past. Will Gunnery Sergeant Philip Cameron have to choose between the Corps and the woman he loves?" - Heather Ashby, author of the Love in the Fleet series

"In **The Candidate**, Matt Steele could be the White House occupant we all wish for, running a strong campaign with a platform the country sorely needs. But Steele's past comes back to meet him in a way he never imagined, via a photograph and a stranger. In a time when an honest candidate is almost a myth, Steele has the option of being true to his past, or saving his political career, but who will be hurt in the process? An enjoyable read that will renew your sense of patriotism." - C. Hope Clark, Bestselling author of the Carolina Slade and Edisto mystery series

Is love enough to heal a soul-wounded Marine?

Sandy Marshall has been rescuing and healing injured creatures all her life, so it's nothing new when she jumps to the defense of a Marine recently returned from a war zone who's being heckled by a fellow student. But when she falls in love with Nathan Cameron, she discovers that bringing home a soul-wounded Marine just might break her heart.

Cam wasn't planning on getting involved with anyone until he put the war firmly behind him and got his life back on track, but the hope and sunshine Sandy brings to his troubled heart is as unexpected as it is irresistible.

Will Sandy's love be enough to bring Cam back from the edge of despair and convince him to get the help he so desperately needs? Is his love for her strong enough for him to pull his life together and be the man she believes in?

The Camerons of Tide's Way Novels

Falling for Zoe

Loving Meg

Trusting Will

Healing a Hero

Keeping His Promise

Worry Stone

Loving Ben (Short Story)

Mike's Wager (Short Story)

Also by Skye Taylor

Iain's Plaid
(a time travel romance)

The Candidate

In Memory of:

CPT John Scott Parker
US Army Ret.

And in honor of:

All the men and women who served in all branches of our military in an unpopular war, sacrificing their youth, their innocence and for far too many of them, their lives. In particular, my childhood friend, Tony - LTJG Carlton P. Miller Jr. USN who was lost at sea while returning to the USS Ranger after a successful mission somewhere between North Vietnam and the Gulf of Tonkin.

This is a work of fiction. Names, characters, places and incidents are either the products of the author's imagination or are used fictitiously. Any resemblance to actual persons (living or dead), events or locations is entirely coincidental.

SandCastleBooks
    St. Augustine, FL
    Print ISBN: 978-1-7322287-3-3
    Copyright 2019 by Skye Taylor
Published in the United States of America

Skye Taylor enjoys hearing from her readers.
    Visit her at: www.Skye-writer.com
Cover design by Carrie Richter
    Images used on cover under license from Shutterstock.com
    Interior design by Skye Taylor
    Anchor Natis76/Dreamstime.com

CHAPTER ONE

January 2014 - Tide's Way, North Carolina

"DAMN!"

Nathan Cameron sat back on his heels as the phone rang for the third time. He ran an impatient hand through his disheveled silver-streaked blond hair as the insistent ringing continued.

Cam frowned. His wife wasn't where she should be, which was in the kitchen scrounging up some lunch. And answering the phone. She'd volunteered to run the floor sander back to the rental place for him so he could finish the last coat of lacquer, but she should have been back by now. Abruptly the ringing cut off.

Sighing, Cam surveyed the expanse of shining floor. It looked even better than he had anticipated. Sandy was going to love it. He dipped his brush back into the can.

The phone began its shrill summons again.

"Sonofabitch." A hint of resignation colored Cam's mumbled cuss. He balanced the brush on the rim of the can, shoved himself to his feet and rushed toward the kitchen. The strident peal continued. He snatched the phone off its charging station.

"Cam here," he barked.

"Nathan Cameron?" A soft voice ignored Cam's irritation.

"You got him!" Another damned sales call! Cam strove to curb his impatience. "Look, I'm kinda busy." As he scanned the kitchen for some sign of his wife's return, he let the phone drift away from his ear.

"Cam!" The soft voice rose, a hint of urgency replacing the calm. An eerie stab of premonition set Cam's heart to thudding ominously. He pulled the phone back to his ear.

"This is Dr. Jorgenson at New Hanover Regional Medical Center. This is Cam from the EMT squad, right?"

Cam nodded mutely, then forced a croaking assent from his suddenly paralyzed throat. Jorgenson sounded familiar. He must have run into the woman before. As a volunteer EMT, he'd met most of the doctors at the New Hanover facility.

"Your wife has been in an automobile accident."

Shock swept through Cam like a rip tide. He clung to the phone with a desperate, white-knuckled grip and fought to find his voice. A horrible vision of her broken lifeless body flashed through his mind. His chest constricted, and his vision went suddenly black. *Oh, God, NO! Not . . .* He grabbed for the counter to steady himself.

"She's conscious and asking for you, but she's going to need surgery very soon. I have a team getting prepped."

"I'll be there in five." Cam dropped the phone on the table, already on his way toward the back door.

Wintery air cut through his worn chambray shirt as he stepped outside. He shivered. Rushing into the garage, he grabbed an old leather flyer's jacket off a nail by the door and shoved his arms into it. He shivered again. He tugged the door to his truck open, fumbled through his keys, then hoisted himself onto the seat and slammed the door.

The key wouldn't fit into the ignition because his hand wouldn't stop trembling.

"Damn!" He almost wept with frustration. Finally, the key slid into the shaft, and the engine purred to life. *She'll be okay. She has to be okay.*

He jerked the stick into reverse, and the truck lurched out of the garage, perilously close to taking out a doorframe. Cam stomped on the brake and brought the vehicle to a bucking halt.

Get a grip. Cameron. You aren't gonna do anyone any good if you rack your-self up, too. He closed his eyes and willed the trembling and panic away. Slowly, he released his death-grip on the wheel and took a deep breath. Then, with a calm he was far from feeling, he backed the truck into the street.

Every minute felt like half an hour as he fought to keep the truck from slithering off the road. When had the freezing rain begun? *If I'd known, I'd never have let her go out in it. I'm a pigheaded jerk. I just had to get the damned floor finished today. And for what?* If he'd taken the truck, she would be home and the Buick would be in the garage. She'd have been safe. Anger and helplessness fought in his raging thoughts. And guilt.

Fifteen minutes later Cam finally skidded into an empty space in the emergency lot off Wrightsville Ave. He leapt from the truck and ran blindly across the parking lot, almost colliding with a departing ambulance. As Cam stumbled to catch his balance, the driver shook his head in disgust. Cam waved a hasty apology, not even taking the time to notice if it was someone he knew.

He slid up to the automatic door and cursed again when it didn't open fast enough. Then, after a journey that seemed to have taken a lifetime, he strode into the emergency room and up to the admissions desk.

"My wife's here somewhere. Dr. Jorgenson called?"

A harried looking woman whose name Cam couldn't recall looked up from the sheaf of papers in her hands. "Cam?"

"My wife," he repeated.

The woman stood up to stretch over the counter and point. "Trauma Room One. First door on the right. Oh, Cam. I'm praying for her."

"Thanks." Cam said over his shoulder as he moved away. He'd brought too many people here over the years. Just never one of his own.

As he dashed into the room marked Trauma One, a familiar young woman in green scrubs intercepted him. "I'm glad you're here." The I.D. dangling around the woman's neck read *Dr. Danielle Jorgenson.*

"My wife?"

"Cam, I'm so sorry." She cleared her throat and became professionally cool. "We need your signature, and I'd like to explain what we'll be doing."

Cam grabbed the clipboard and scribbled his name while Dr. Jorgenson went on in a brisk voice. He tried to pay attention. Tried to absorb the details of the procedure Dr. Jorgenson outlined, but his frightened mind refused to focus. No wonder they didn't let doctors treat their own family members. It was hard to find the emotional distance required to make rational decisions.

"I trust you, Doc. Do whatever you have to do," Cam muttered huskily when she finished speaking. "Just . . ." He pressed the clipboard back into the doctor's hands, his eyes focused on the gurney behind her. "Just do your best."

Sandy Cameron looked small and horribly vulnerable with IV tubes taped to the back of her hand and a monitor bleeping rhythmically above her head. Her face was so pale that a faint blue network of veins showed beneath her skin. Streaks of blood matted her blond hair, and a nasty gash oozed on her forehead. A pile of bloody clothing that had been cut from her body lay in a heap at side of the room, but he refused to look at them. There was urgency in the air. And apprehension. As he moved toward the only woman he had ever loved, it was like a waking nightmare. Fear churned in his gut.

She reached out to him, the snaking red tube trailing away to a nearly empty plastic sack of blood. He reached for her. It took all the control he possessed to still his shaking fingers. Even more to force the corners of his mouth into a smile of reassurance.

"I'm s-sorry," she whispered through bruised lips. " I w-wasn't p-paying . . . I m-messed up the car."

"Never mind the damned car." Her hand felt like ice. "All I care about is you."

"I love you, Cam."

"I love you, too," he replied with a catch in his throat. Words he'd uttered so often, in so many ways over the years took on a sudden urgency. The look in her eyes stopped his heart cold. He'd seen that look before. A life time ago, he'd seen that look of calm resignation. Of acceptance.

Her eyes fluttered shut.

He panicked. "Open your eyes. Dammit, open your eyes and look at me. You're gonna be okay. Y'hear me? Listen to me!"

Her lids lifted. Slowly. Tiredly. The look remained. Tinged with pity.

"Hang in there, sweetheart." Cam spanned her face with both hands and gently kissed her battered mouth. "You gotta hang in there. I need you."

Her eyes rolled back into her head. The monitor shrieked. Someone shouted, "Code!" Immediately, the room filled with people.

A nurse tugged at Cam's jacket. "It would be better if you waited in—"

"I'm not going anywhere," Cam interrupted.

With a hand on his shoulder, the nurse urged him out of the way, but didn't make him leave.

Someone jerked the sheet back and half a dozen hands went to work. Paddles were applied, then her body jerked violently. The line on the monitor leapt. Leapt again, then settled back into a more regular pattern, and some of the tension left the shoulders of the people hovering over the table.

"Call the OR and tell them we're on the way," Jorgenson ordered with authority. She yanked the stainless steel rail into place. An intense looking intern shoved a gleaming metal post into a bracket on the gurney, and then transferred the IV bottle and the sack of blood. The orderly was already pushing the stretcher out the door.

Cam followed them into the hall, hurrying to keep up.

"I'm still here, sweetheart. Ya hear me?" She had to know he wasn't ready to let her go. It wasn't her time.

The elevator doors opened with a hiss, and they all surged into it: the doctor, the orderly, the intern, the gurney and Cam. Cam jockeyed for position. He reached for his wife's hand.

"Hang in there, sweetheart." Had her hand moved in his? He wasn't sure. Her eyes didn't open. He tried to will his own strength into her battered body. She had to fight back.

The doors rolled back again, revealing the sterile world of the surgical floor. Pale green walls, spotless grey floors, everything else gleaming bright and coldly white. For the first time in his life, Cam hated the antiseptic smell of it. Hated the feeling of helpless panic it engendered in him.

The orderly and the intern rolled the gurney out of the elevator toward a set of swinging doors. Jorgenson hurried past, swinging her hip around the corner of the stretcher.

A new nurse appeared at Cam's side. "You'll have to wait outside, Mr. Cameron."

He had to let the doctor do her job. But a frantic need made him cling just a moment longer. He bent and kissed his wife again, this time on the mouth. "Don't give up, sweetheart. Fight." Her eyes flickered open for a fleeting moment.

As they rolled her away from him, Cam raised his voice. "I love you." Then the doors swung shut and left him gazing through a small square window. The gurney disappeared around a corner.

"Mr. Cameron." The nurse tapped his arm. "There's a family waiting area just down the hall."

Numbly, Cam followed the woman down a short hall and through another set of swinging doors to an opening on the right. A typical waiting room, furnished with comfortable looking, though worn, easy chairs and a small sofa. A television loomed in the far corner and a coffeemaker sat on a small counter beside a tiny sink and a stack of disposable cups. Beyond a table littered with magazines, a picture window looked out over the suburban neighborhood and the University campus beyond.

"Can I get you anything?" The nurse hesitated in the doorway. "Juice or a soda."

He shook his head.

"There's a phone if you need one." She gestured toward a low table just beyond the sofa. "It's a direct outside line, but you can use your cell here, too."

"Thank you."

The nurse nodded and left. Cam thought about the calls he should make. But, what would he tell them? He couldn't think.

He crossed to the window. The streets looked slick and freezing rain clicked against the window pane. Cam shoved his hands into his pockets and pressed his forehead against the cool glass. He fought back tears and the terror that threatened to engulf him. His fingers closed around a small smooth stone. A stone he had carried in his pocket for over forty years. It was polished and smooth and warm from his body. A worry stone, Sandy had called it when she'd found it on the beach. A lucky worry stone.

"You keep it in your pocket, and when you're worried about things, it's like a talisman." Her lilting voice echoed down over the years.

He hadn't believed it then or since, but he'd kept the stone anyway, because it had been her very first gift to him. Not much had distracted him from his self-absorbed world of pain during that first year of their life together, but the smooth little stone had reminded him of her belief in him. When things had been at their worst, her love and stubborn loyalty had been enough to keep him glued together. She had been enough. She had been everything. She *was* everything.

And he needed her still. With a gut-wrenching intensity that couldn't be put into words.

"Please, God." Cam barely recognized the frightened, pleading voice as his own. "Please, don't let her die."

The window glass had warmed where his skin touched it. It felt as warm as the little stone in his pocket. Hot tears swamped his eyes, and he stopped fighting them. "Don't let her die," he pleaded as the tears began to slip down his cheeks. His fingers tightened around the tiny stone, and memories of how it all began crowded into his heart.

CHAPTER TWO

AUGUST 1970 – UNIVERSITY OF NORTH CAROLINA, WILMINGTON, NC

SANDY MARSHALL PLEADED with the registration clerk. She should have come last week when registration opened, but she hadn't expected the class to fill up.

"Are you absolutely, positively sure it's full? I really, really need this class." She tried to keep the desperation out of her voice. She couldn't afford another semester past this one.

"I can put you on the waiting list?" The registration volunteer looked decidedly uncomfortable.

"You don't understand." Sandy leaned toward the youthful volunteer and lowered her voice as if she were sharing a very personal secret. "If I can't get into this class, I can't graduate next spring. I haven't got enough money to pay for another semester, and I have to take this class to graduate."

The volunteer shuffled through his papers once more, glanced apprehensively at her, and then gave in. "Okay, stick your name in here." He pointed to a space below the last name on the first page.

"They'll see the mistake, but they won't be able to figure out who to bump."

Relief flooded over her. "Thank you, soooo much. You don't know how much this means to me." She scribbled her name in the space indicated, then gave the young man a beaming smile of thanks.

"Yeah, well . . ." He fidgeted, his gaze shifting side to side, then past her. "Just . . . just don't say anything, okay?"

Sandy made a gesture of zipping her lips, gave the volunteer another winning smile, then turned away and slammed into a wall. A wall that turned out to be the hard-muscled chest of a tall, solidly built man who had been waiting behind her in line.

"Oops! Sorry, I . . ." Her gaze flew up to the startled face looming above her. A jolt of unexpected electricity ripped through her. Her heart hammered wildly. Her mouth went completely dry.

"Not a problem." The man's piercing blue eyes flickered over her with brief interest, then he stepped past her, his attention already focused on the registration desk.

Sandy couldn't decide what disconcerted her most, his curt appraisal or her own astonishing reaction to the momentary, impersonal contact. Never in all her life, had she experienced such an immediate and staggering physical response to a man. Nor been so coolly dismissed.

She backed away, unable to tear her gaze from his broad-shouldered, indifferent back and close-cropped blond head. He was lean and deeply tanned, and there was something about him that reminded her of her brother. The reminder of Tony sliced through her.

Tony was still missing in action in Vietnam.

She preferred to remember the easy-going big brother he'd been before he'd joined the Army, but other, more recent memories were stronger. The deeply-tanned, tautly-fit soldier who'd stepped off the plane three years ago with such an adult air of confidence had been serious and troubled and rarely laughed, and nothing like the brother she'd known all her life who called her String Bean. The brother who would have laughed at the idea of volunteering for a second tour.

Sandy banished the troubling memory of Tony and returned her attention to the man she'd run into who now bent over the registration table. *I wonder if that sun-bleached hair and tanned skin were acquired in Vietnam?*

The man's closely trimmed hair accentuated the strong column of his sun-browned neck. The broad shoulders, slim hips and long legs cased in khaki slacks were impressive, too. Maybe he was a surfer? Or a lifeguard? She couldn't see his face, but the long golden lashes and chiseled masculine cheekbones made her heart beat a little faster.

Without warning, an arm slipped around Sandy's shoulders, jolting her from her rapt study of the man at the registration table.

"Hiya, Honey. Get your classes all settled?" The man hugging her with such disagreeable familiarity was the biggest jerk Sandy had ever known.

Bud Wilson thought he was God's gift to women. A star running back on the varsity football team, Bud had become accustomed to the fawning adoration of the entire cheerleading squad and half the co-eds on campus. Somehow, he had managed to convince himself that Sandy enjoyed playing hard to get and he persisted in his annoying pursuit of her in spite of her continued refusals.

She jerked away, flushing with irritation at his conceited intimacy. "I'm not your Honey, Bud." She glared at the man towering over her.

"That could be fixed." Bud grinned smugly. He tilted his head toward hers with obvious intent.

"What part of the word 'no' don't you understand?" Her patience was wearing thin.

"You know you're just playing hard to get." Bud winked. "But I like my women feisty."

"I'm not playing anything, Bud. Now back off."

Bud swooped in and gave her a moistly unpleasant smack on the mouth before she could turn aside. When his self-satisfied smirk grew wider, Sandy's disgust at the very unwelcome kiss blossomed into revolt. She slapped him, shocking herself even more than Bud.

"Bitch!" An angry flush surged into Bud's face, but it didn't hide the rapidly reddening handprint on his cheek. The interchange had begun to draw attention. Was the crimson staining Bud's cheeks anger or embarrassment? Her own face felt humiliatingly hot. She couldn't believe her appalling lapse of manners.

"That's no way to speak to a lady." A deep North Carolina drawl cut into the taut standoff.

Realization that the drawl belonged to the man she'd just been admiring made her wish she could just disappear altogether.

"Stay out of this." Bud spat the words toward the source of the interference, but his angry glare remained glued on Sandy. His nostrils flared as he made a grab for her wrist.

The man knocked Bud's hand away with a swift easy gesture. "This guy bothering you, Ma'am?"

Could people actually die of mortification?

"I told you to butt out." Bud whirled toward the interloper. He had to look up and that fact clearly infuriated him even further. His eyes flicked over the bleached hair and near-gaunt leanness. Then, slowly, his expression changed to one of scorn. "Shit! Now, would you look at that? A living, breathing, pot-head, baby-killer!" Bud spat. "We don't much take to your kind around here."

Sandy gasped. Even Bud had noticed the indefinable difference that separated this man from the other students. Suddenly, she understood the other things about him that had brought Tony to mind. The things that had soldier written all over them. She had seen, but hadn't registered the military haircut. Now she noted the erect posture and squared shoulders. The air of competence.

The soldier flinched, and seemed to pale beneath his tan.

Sandy's gut tightened with outrage, instantly eclipsing her embarrassment. Everyone had a right to their opinion about the war in Southeast Asia. Even Bud. But he couldn't know for sure that the stranger had been in Vietnam. And whether he had or not, the man had come to Sandy's defense as a gentleman, and he didn't deserve Bud's scorn for that.

"Leave him alone, Bud." She made a move to step between the two men.

Bud ignored her, rudely pushing her aside. He jabbed the taller man's shoulder with two fingers and made a spitting sound. "Why don't you take yourself somewhere where people aren't so particular? Or, how about back to the jungle where you belong?"

"Bud, stop it."

The soldier said nothing.

"Not so brave without an M-16, huh?" Bud jabbed again.

"Make love, not war." Someone chanted inanely. Another voice joined in.

"How many innocent civilians you kill? Huh?" *Jab. Jab.*

A muscle twitched in the soldier's jaw. His restraint was impressive. His big hands were clenched, white-knuckled, at his sides. His startlingly blue gaze was both tense and vulnerable. And pained.

The same kind of pain she'd seen in Tony's eyes when he thought no one was watching. Disillusionment and hurt. She had a desperate need to protect this man from Bud's malicious idiocy.

Her gaze caught on the name embroidered across the left breast of his jacket and a totally crazy idea leapt into her head. Audacious and fraught with embarrassing possibilities, but...

"You better shut up while you've still got a choice, Bud." This time Sandy did step between the two men. "Come on, Cam. Let's get out of here."

"You know this baby-killer?" Bud's voice rose in contemptuous disbelief.

"Since forever. And he's not a baby-killer. He just did his job. One you probably wouldn't have the guts for." Sandy lifted her chin and looked the soldier straight in the eye. "I'm really glad you made it back in one piece, Cam. Now I can kill you for not writing like you promised. You didn't even send me a postcard."

Bud's sputtering outrage and the scandalized stares of the fawning group surrounding him gave Sandy a perverse feeling of satisfaction. Everyone must be thinking she was a traitor to the cause, to everything she'd been protesting about for the last two years. What this would do to her reputation, she didn't know. Even more startling, she didn't care. Something about this stranger felt more compelling than her disgust over the war and what it was doing to the young men who were sent to fight it.

She placed a hand on the startled soldier's forearm and tiptoed to plant a bold kiss on his tanned, smooth-shaven cheek. "How come you didn't call me when you got home?"

· · ·

CAM STIFFENED at the woman's touch. The fleeting snatch of satisfaction at the goggling incredulity on the son-of-a-bitch's face dissolved into confusion. Who was this woman? He couldn't think straight through the haze of fury clouding his brain.

"I don't think we've . . ."

"Boy, have you got a lot of explaining to do." She cut him off and linked her arm through his." Are you finished here?"

"Yes, Ma'am, but . . ."

"Ma'am? Good grief, Cam, I'm not your mother." She threw her head back and laughed. She was the most beautiful woman he'd ever seen. The tousled blond curls framed a pretty heart-shaped face with a generous mouth that curved up appealingly at the corners. But it was her bright hazel eyes that caused his heart to skip a beat. They were warm and expressive and right at the moment they were full of fire and trying to send him some kind of wordless message.

If she really was the friend she was pretending to be, he'd have written to her every day he'd spent in that hell-hole. And he damned well would have called her the minute his plane touched down in the good old U.S. of A., too.

But he didn't know her. And he didn't know what she wanted from him. Maybe she just meant to set him up for further humiliation. He tried to withdraw his arm from hers, but she tightened her grip and dragged him through the crowd toward the door.

"Thank you," she said in a suddenly husky voice as they crossed the polished foyer of the student center.

"For what?" There was bitterness in his voice, but he was still too angry to control it. "For creating a scene?" He should be thanking her for preventing him from destroying the arrogant bastard. Frustrated rage roiled uncomfortably in his gut. He felt so out of place. He had nothing in common with these people. Not their idealism, nor their innocence. He should have skipped the whole idea of adding a couple management courses to his resume and just gone back to working for his uncle.

"For telling Bean-brain to leave me alone. I don't think anyone's ever told him 'no' in his life. Except me." She shoved the outer door open and towed Cam through it.

The crowd of protesters had thinned since he'd gone into the building, but the ex-soldier still ranted about the war as Cam's rescuer dragged him down the stairs and steered him toward a path that appeared deserted.

Sunlight flickered down through the tossing branches of the trees that shaded the campus. A capricious breeze tugged at his clothing and began to cool Cam's anger, but did nothing to clear the dazed sense of having fallen down Alice's rabbit hole. He looked down at the pretty young woman still clinging to his arm and tried to recall what she'd just said. Something about that jerk being told no.

"Besides, Bud started it," she observed, coloring slightly. She glanced back over her shoulder, then returned her intense hazel gaze to his face.

"It's time someone taught him some manners," Cam suggested. He shivered. It was barely September for Pete's sake, but he still felt cold half the time. He hunched his shoulders inside the lightweight jacket.

"Bud doesn't like getting turned down. Anyway, thanks for coming to my rescue. I'm just sorry he took his bruised ego out on you."

"It's nothing."

"Of course it's something," she countered immediately, the pink deepening. "Especially since it got you noticed. You probably wish you never said anything. Right?" She looked at him with something suspiciously like sympathy coloring her amazing eyes.

"It's nothing," Cam repeated. He didn't need pity either. Especially not from this naive little coed who probably didn't even know where Vietnam was, let alone what really went on over there.

"Well, it meant something to me, and I'm trying to thank you." She smiled in spite of his unfriendly set-down. The pink had receded, and Cam thought again that she had to be the loveliest woman he'd ever met. She smiled, and a dimple appeared. "Why didn't you punch him out, anyway? Considering all the outrageous things he said to you, I wouldn't have blamed you for making an even bigger scene."

"If I punched every anti-war asshole who insulted me, I'd land myself in a heap of trouble." The kind of trouble he didn't need. He just wanted to be left alone.

"I suppose," she conceded. "But it sure would have been fun to see

Bud get decked." She smiled, and her eyes danced with merriment. "Anyway, now that we've met . . ."

"We haven't met. Not officially, anyway." He tried to distance himself from her disturbing closeness. His hurt was too fresh, too raw. He felt defensive and suspicious in spite of her guileless smile. Perhaps, because of it.

"You rescued me from Bud's disgusting attentions. That's all the introduction I need." She tilted her head, letting it rest against his shoulder as if they were lovers.

Giddy with the roller coaster ride of emotions, Cam stared down at her, at a loss for words. *What I'd really like is to kiss your sassy little mouth and see if it tastes as sweet as it looks. You've got invitation written all over you and you're making it hard to remember I'm a gentleman.* When the breeze ruffled her blouse, he caught an unintended glimpse of smooth, creamy skin curving enticingly into the edge of a lacy pink bra. *Jesus!* He shut his eyes abruptly and turned his head away. His heart thudded, and it was difficult to draw a full breath.

He shoved his hands into his pockets before he did anything he shouldn't. "I don't even know your name."

Abruptly, she moved away from him. He should have been glad for the stress relieving distance, but he wasn't. The warmth and scent of her body lingered.

"I'm Sandy. Sandra Anne Marshall if you want it all." She curtsied with elaborate formality. "I'm from Lanford, New Hampshire and," she hesitated a moment, then hurried on. "I'm a senior and I plan to teach when I graduate and I'm on the yearbook staff. I'm a really terrific person, I'm a Red Sox fan and my favorite player is Carl Yastrzemski."

"My kind of woman," Cam blurted before he could stop himself. She was confident and sexy and inviting him to forget his miserable frame of mind.

"Your turn." Sandy thrust a hand toward him, palm up.

Without thinking, Cam took the hand she offered. Instead of the expected handshake, her slender fingers laced themselves through his and a wave of desire and forgotten emotions raced through him.

"My turn for what?" he croaked, trying to catch his breath and take command of his thoughts.

"Does everyone call you Cam?"

"Everyone but my mother." He forced himself to look into her sparkling eyes instead of down the enticing V of her crisp white blouse. "She calls me Nathan."

"So, what's Cam short for?"

"Cameron."

"What are you studying? Did you really just get back from Vietnam? You come from around here?" She peppered him with questions.

He ran a hand over the top of his bristly butch. "I grew up here in Wilmington. My whole family is from here." Family that had welcomed him home with as much enthusiasm as this woman put into gaining his acquaintance. Family that didn't seem to understand his moodiness or his desire to withdraw into his own little world of pain, any more than Sandy Marshall did.

"So, what do you want to be when you grow up?" She changed the subject hurriedly, maybe sensing his desire to retreat.

"A construction engineer." This was an easier topic. "I spent my first four years of college more or less just getting by. Just didn't want to believe I was a grown up yet, I guess. I wanted the good times to go on forever." He hesitated, shrugged, then added, "But they didn't, and now I've got to make up for lost time."

"But you're already in construction." She gestured to the logo embroidered beneath the nickname on the breast of his jacket.

"My uncle's company. I've worked for him off and on since I was old enough to hold a shovel.

"So, what branch of the military were you in?"

"Marines." Maybe the clipped answer would put a stop to further probing.

"So you owe me."

"I owe you? For what?" Apprehension stirred in his gut.

"For rescuing you from Bud." Her grin widened even more. "Actually we sort of rescued each other from the jerk, but if I promise not to mention him again, how about dinner?"

CHAPTER THREE

"Oh, Natalie." Sandy groaned theatrically as she threw herself across her roommate's bed and rolled onto her back. "He's the most gorgeous man I've ever met."

Natalie turned her head and scowled. "Who, Michael? Please tell me you aren't letting him sweet-talk you again."

"Michael is yesterday's news." Sandy frowned as she recalled the uncomfortable farewell scene with Michael at the end of last term. Their decision to split up had been pretty one sided. Michael had wanted something she didn't feel for him. He'd been hurt and angry, and she'd been sorry for him. Just not sorry enough to make any promises. "We broke up before the summer. Did you forget?"

"Yeah, that's what I thought, but I never know about you, and if he acted hurt and wormed his way back. . . Well, never mind. So, who are we talking about?" Natalie put her pencil down, shut her notebook, and then turned in her seat to face Sandy.

Natalie O'Sullivan was Sandy's best friend and confidant. They shared a room, their clothes and their deepest secrets, but the similarities between them ended with their height and build. Sandy sported an unfashionably short crop of tousled blond curls and Natalie had a long unruly mane of flaming red hair tumbling around her shoulders.

Natalie was as shy as Sandy was outgoing and complained constantly that it just wasn't fair that Sandy hardly ever had to study and got straight A's while she had to practically chain herself to her desk just to get passing grades.

Above Sandy's bed hung an autographed poster of Carl Yastrzemski with a schedule of games thumbtacked next to it. Natalie thought baseball was as boring as watching grass grow. Sandy loved running. Natalie considered that activity as unfeminine as a smelly locker. The slender redhead loved to eat, anything and everything, and explored new and different cuisines with relish, while Sandy ate whatever was put in front of her without thinking too much about it. But somehow, after having been thrown together in their freshman year, they had become the best of friends.

"So who's the lucky guy this time?"

"It's *the* guy."

"*The* guy?" Natalie plopped down on the bed next to Sandy, crossed her legs and planted her palms on her knees. Her carefully shaped brows rose expressively. "Tell all."

"He's a Marine. And I think he's been in Vietnam, but he wouldn't talk about it."

Natalie's eyebrows lifted. "And just how does a Marine fit into your protest schedule?"

"He doesn't, of course. But that's not the point." Sandy rolled over and sat up. "He's tall. He makes even me feel petite. He has shoulders like you wouldn't believe and the bluest eyes I have ever in my life seen. He's got the nicest smile, and there's something about him that makes me want to tear all my clothes off and throw myself at him."

"Sandy!" Natalie sounded genuinely shocked.

"I swear. I've never felt like this before." *Like maybe I'm coming down with something!* Sandy crossed the room to the borrowed birdcage on the corner of her desk and checked on its occupant.

"It's time to set that guy free." Natalie said.

"But I just met him," Sandy protested whirling back to face her friend.

"I meant the bird. His wing has been healed for weeks now. He belongs outside." Natalie shrugged. "But never mind that, now. How did you meet this poster-boy Marine of yours?"

"You'll never believe it."

"Try me," Natalie challenged, settling in for all the details.

"I kind of kissed him and pretended I'd known him forever."

"*Kind of* kissed him? How do you *kind of* kiss a guy?"

"I only kissed him on the cheek. That's not really a kiss." Sandy's face felt suddenly warm. *I wish I'd kissed him on the mouth.* Now, she was a little breathless and warm.

"I see. And you've never even seen him before?" Natalie's eyebrows disappeared under a curtain of red bangs. "What on earth were you thinking? What did he do?"

"Well, I sort of took him off guard. I think he might have been too distracted to do anything."

"Can you blame the guy? Think of it . . . a beautiful woman he's never met walks up in the middle of . . . Where did you say you were when you kissed this guy?"

"Registration."

"Right! A beautiful woman walks up and kisses him, bold as brass, in a front of a room full of people for no reason he can guess. Any red-blooded man would be distracted!"

"But it wasn't me who distracted him. I mean . . ."

"And you think being kissed by a ravishingly pretty stranger isn't distracting?"

"I'm not that pretty," Sandy protested.

"And I'm not Irish."

Sandy laughed in capitulation. "Okay, so I'm pretty and I'm a stranger, but really, Bud Wilson was the problem. He offered to let me reconsider being his girl. And I said *no* for the umpti-umpth time. Only Bud wasn't listening, as usual, and I slapped him."

Natalie gasped. "You slapped Bud? In public? You Yankees might behave that way but here in the south? It's just not done."

"Bud gave me a disgusting, slobbery kiss," Sandy defended herself. "What all those other girls see in him I can't imagine. He makes me want to puke, and I'd finally had enough. But then he made a grab for me, and Cam stopped him."

"Who's Cam?"

"That's what I'm trying to tell you. Are you going to listen or ask questions?"

"I'm listening." Natalie pressed her lips together.

Sandy returned to Natalie's bed and plopped down. She recounted the scene at the student union while Natalie, true to her word, refrained from interrupting.

"So I rescued him," she finished, settling back into Natalie's pile of colorful pillows.

"Hold everything." Natalie held up one hand. "Tell me what I'm missing here. You said this guy was a Marine, right?"

Sandy nodded. *I bet he's gorgeous in his dress blues! I wonder if I'll ever see . . .*

"So how come a Marine needs rescuing? I mean . . ."

"You had to be there . . ."

Natalie held up her hand again. "If he really is a Marine . . ."

"But he . . ."

"Let me finish." Natalie shook her head sadly. "You're always on a mission, Sandy. For as long as I've known you, there's always some injured or mistreated critter you feel a burning need to save. And I can understand, most of the time anyway, but a Marine? Good grief, Sandy, I'd have thought any Marine worth his salt would be more than capable of defending himself against a blowhard like Bud."

"I'm sure he could. If he'd wanted to, he could have made Bud seriously regret starting the whole ugly scene." That aura of tightly leashed power had emanated off Cam in waves as he'd faced his tormentor. But there had been that look of unfathomable pain, and the sharp stab of empathy that had driven her to come to his defense. "Cam didn't fight back because he lives by a different code of conduct than Bud does."

"My God, Sandy. This isn't like bringing a puppy home. This is a man. A man you know nothing about."

"I know he's the sexiest guy I ever met." *Sexy with an enormous capital S!* "Something about power held in check is a major turn-on. At least for me."

"You're hopeless!" Natalie shrugged, then got off the bed and walked toward the window.

"Wait 'til you meet him." Sandy rolled off the other side of the bed and headed toward the closet. "Then maybe you'll understand. You want me to see if he has any brothers that are unattached?"

Natalie rounded on her, blushing furiously. "Don't you dare!"

"Just offering." Sandy ducked into the closet, rummaged through the hangers, and then came up with a navy blue linen dress. "What do you think of this?"

"For what?" Natalie came back to sit on the edge of the bed.

"For tonight. He's taking me out to dinner."

"He didn't waste much time, did he?"

Sandy grinned. "Actually I asked him."

"You are incorrigible!"

"What do you think about the dress?"

Natalie tipped her head to one side. "What kind of impression do you want to make?"

"The right one." Sandy held the classically-styled dress in front of herself and studied herself in the mirror. *This is important. The most important thing in my life.* "This is the guy I want to make a woman of me. It's time I joined the sexual revolution."

"Sandy! You just met him!" Natalie's face registered shock and maybe a little disapproval

"I know." Sandy sighed.

"He could be dangerous," Natalie warned darkly. "Some of these guys come home acting pretty weird, you know."

"He's not weird. He's gallant in an old fashioned sort of way. Maybe it's a military thing, but probably just southern gentleman stuff."

"If he's old fashioned, maybe he won't be all that into women's lib and free love. A Marine just home from Vietnam is a zillion light years from the love-fest of Woodstock, you know."

"Then I'll have to change his mind."

Natalie shook her head "Unbelievable! That's what you are, girl. Totally unbelievable. I just hope you know what you're doing." She turned her attention back to the blue dress. As she smoothed the wrinkles of her own well-worn, tie-dyed skirt over her slender knees, she tilted her head to consider Sandy's question.

"Too prim," she finally pronounced.

"Too prim?" Sandy surveyed herself in the mirror again.

"Well, not if you're auditioning with his mother, maybe."

"Yikes! Not that." Sandy tossed the blue dress on the bed. "What should I wear, then?"

"You could attract a man's attention in ratty jeans and a paint smock, but if you want this guy to sleep with you, I guess you've got to do a little better than that."

"In spite of this feeling in my gut that I can't explain, I don't really intend to throw myself at him. At least, not on the first date."

Natalie snorted. "Seems to me like you already did that." She glanced at the blue dress with a frown. Then her expression brightened. "What you want now is to impress him with your softer side, right?"

Sandy nodded.

"How about that silky pink dress my Mom sent me."

"You've never even worn it." Sandy fingered the soft folds of the beautiful pink dress hanging on Natalie's side of the closet. She had coveted it as soon as she'd seen it.

"And I never will. Not with this hair. Mom refuses to admit she gave birth to a raving redhead, and she continues to buy me things that would look great on her, but just awful on me." Natalie got to her feet and crossed to the closet.

"How many times have I got to tell you, red hair doesn't mean you can't wear pink?" Sandy asked pulling a fold of the soft fabric under Natalie's chin and considering the effect.

"Don't waste your breath." Natalie dragged the garment off its hanger and held it up against Sandy's white blouse and dark slacks. "It'll be perfect. Soft and enticing . . . and something he can't resist touching. That is the image you want to portray, right?"

"Yeah," Sandy agreed dreamily. In her mind, she could see herself dancing in Cam's arms, a vision in pink silk that he couldn't tear his gaze away from. Or keep his hands off. A blush stole up under her collar.

"Then it's a done deal. Now let's see what we can find for your feet." Natalie dove back into the closet in search of a pair of matching shoes.

CHAPTER FOUR

Maybe Cam shouldn't have agreed to take Sandy out to dinner. It felt too much like a date, and he wasn't ready to date anyone. He was still trying to get used to being home and putting his life back together. He was jumpy and inclined to withdraw into himself when the world got too intense. He wasn't fit company for a nice girl like Sandy Marshall but she'd never understand that.

His altruism wavered as she came down the stairs after his arrival at her dorm had been announced. The soft pink dress hugged her curves and made his blood pump a little harder. Perhaps a simple dinner date was something he could pull off without hurting her or embarrassing himself. It wasn't like he was committing to a relationship or anything permanent. Maybe it would be fun hanging out with someone who just plunged into life without worrying about the future or brooding over the past.

He'd chosen a restaurant on the beach, away from the noisy, crowded downtown that put him on edge. Away from the campus and the demonstrations. Besides, they served great seafood.

"Ever been here before?" he asked as he pulled into the parking lot. The place looked like it had been there since the island was first settled. Certainly for as long as Cam could remember. Its cedar shingled roof had bleached out to silver years ago and the fieldstone walls were tucked into the dunes where it appeared to have weathered everything the Atlantic Ocean could throw at it.

Sandy grinned at him. "Nope! I didn't even know a place like this existed out here. I thought it was all surfer bars and hamburger joints."

"I think it predates surfer bars and hamburger joints. My grandparents used to come here." He climbed out of the car and circled around to open her door for her before she could hop out on her own.

"An officer and a gentleman," Sandy said as she swung her feet to the ground and stood.

Cam grunted in denial, but placed his hand at the small of her back as he guided her toward the door. His fingers tingled with the warmth of her body and he almost pulled his hand back.

Once inside, a white-jacketed maître d' led them through a low-ceilinged, candle-lit room to a table by the window. Sandy took the seat being held for her and glanced out the window overlooking the beach and the endless parade of waves breaking and running up the sandy shore toward the restaurant.

"Let's go for a walk on the beach after dinner."

Cam followed her gaze. "Uh. Okay. I guess." Seemed like a dangerously romantic thing to do, but how was he supposed to get out of it gracefully? He studied her for a long moment. She was so young and so carefree. Something he'd been about a hundred years ago. He couldn't recall the last time he'd gone for a moonlight walk on a beach with a girl.

A wide smile grew on her face. A smile that held a hint of something that rang warning bells in Cam's head. But then she picked up her menu and the feeling passed.

The waitress came a moment later, turned the heavy water glasses over and filled them. "Are you ready to order? Or do you need another few minutes?"

Cam looked at Sandy. She immediately ordered a steak, medium rare with a baked potato and broccoli. Cam hadn't even looked at his menu, but he ordered the special of the day and handed his heavy gilt-edged folder to the waitress.

"How did you end up at a school in Wilmington all the way from

New Hampshire?" Maybe getting to know more about her was a mistake, but they had to talk about something.

"It seemed like a good idea at the time. My boyfriend was going to UNC. His father grew up somewhere around here and it was his dad's alma mater. They had a good liberal arts program so why not?"

"What happened to the boyfriend?" Surely she wouldn't have wangled dinner with him if she was in a relationship with someone else. Would she? He'd given in to her audacious suggestion because he hadn't thought of any way out of it, but he wasn't keen on poaching another man's property.

"He moved on to someone else." She wagged her head with a smile, making it clear her heart wasn't broken, or at least, if it had been, she was over it. "It was for the best, really. Do you have . . . anyone special?"

"No," he answered a little too curtly. "I've—I've been away."

"In the Marines. What was it like?"

"Being in the Marines?" He tensed.

"Being in Vietnam."

"Who said I was in Vietnam?" He glanced around the busy dining room wishing he could think of something else to talk about.

Her blonde brows rose. "Are you telling me you weren't?"

The waitress returned with their salads giving Cam a reprieve.

A short reprieve.

"You *were* over there. Right?" Her fork poised over the salad, her amazing hazel eyes pinned him, waiting for an answer.

"I was." He shoved a forkful of salad into his mouth so he wouldn't have to elaborate.

"My brother didn't like to talk about it either."

Cam's heart jerked. He'd pegged her as a carefree woman with nothing more serious to worry about than wangling her way into a class that was already full. But she had a brother who had been there. That changed things.

Her cheerful expression clouded over. "He got heckled when he was home, too. I think that's part of why he went back. He's MIA."

"Oh God. I'm so sorry." Cam reached across the table to cover her free hand with his. "That's got to be hard." Harder than losing a brother? Maybe? Tom was gone forever, though. There was still a chance her brother would turn up. He patted her hand again and sat back.

"T-Tony meant to be a priest. Instead he decided he needed to go fight a war so he volunteered, and they turned him into a medic."

"How are your parents taking it?" His mother would be praying over her rosary beads all day if he'd gone missing. His father probably wouldn't have been much better.

"My Dad died three years ago. My mother left when I was a little kid."

Chagrinned, he pushed his salad bowl aside. Showed how wrong he'd been, making snap judgments about her based on her cheerful, outgoing personality.

"I'm even sorrier." How did she stay so bubbly and positive? "How do you bear it? Being all on your own?"

Her hazel eyes glinted with what might be tears. He needed to change the subject. For both their sakes.

"I don't really have a choice, do I?"

He shrugged. "I guess not."

"We were close, Dad and Tony and me. He never remarried and I was always worried that mom left because of me and Tony. I don't think she liked being a mother very much." Sandy shut her mouth with a snap. As if she'd said something she hadn't meant to reveal.

"That's harsh," Cam said softly, touched by her difficult past more than he wanted to be.

"I can't believe they sent your brother back since he was all the family you had."

"I didn't think he'd have to go again, but I guess good medics are hard to come by. And he volunteered to go. I was so angry with him."

And no doubt felt guilty about the anger now that he was missing. Cam's bad humor since returning seemed out of proportion. He'd lost a brother, but he still had his parents and the rest of his siblings. He had his health and all his body parts which was a lot more than some of the men he'd fought with had.

"So," Sandy said jerking him out of his inner reflections. "Tell me about your family. I've paraded all my skeletons." She put a slice of cucumber into her mouth and began chewing.

"That could take all night."

"I've got all night." She smiled encouragingly, then speared a cherry tomato.

Sandy's half eaten salad was pushed to the side as a thick steak, running with pink juice was placed in front of her. The waitress removed Cam's empty salad plate and set a savory dish of rice, chicken and vegetables in its place.

"Are you really going to eat all that?" He gestured at her plate doubtfully. Where did she put all that food on that slender sexy frame?

Sandy wagged her steak knife in Cam's direction. "Every bite, so don't get any ideas about sharing."

She was so much more complicated than he'd thought. Somehow she'd been able to absorb repeated tragedies and still present a cheerful face to the world. And find the courage to put herself between him and the obnoxious Bud that afternoon, and challenge him to reward her with a nice dinner. If only he was in a better place right now. Settled and willing to get into a relationship. She'd be everything he was looking for in a woman.

"So, what about your family?" she urged as she cut into her steak.

"There's seven of us: George, Linc, Beth, Susan, Abby . . . and me."

"But that's only six."

Cam hesitated. "Tom was killed in Nam."

"Now it's my turn to be sorry." Sandy reached across the table, and tried to lay her hand over his.

Cam moved his hand away, and grabbed his glass. "It's nothing," he muttered, bringing the glass to his lips. Even after all these months Tom's name filled him with guilt and regret.

Sandy withdrew her hand, and a slight flush rose to her cheeks. Before good manners could reassert themselves, and have him babbling out more than he wanted to share, the corners of her mouth turned up in a teasing smile. "So, you're the baby of the family, then?"

Cam breathed in relief at the change in the direction of their conversation.

"Yeah. I'm the runt."

"Right, and I'm the jolly green giant." She dug into her potato.

"You wouldn't believe it to look at me now, I suppose, but I really was a runt. Linc used to call me that all the time. He still does, in fact."

"And you believed him?"

"What else could I think? All my brothers were over six feet. I barely made five feet ten when I graduated from high school, and I didn't weigh more than one forty soaking wet. My mother used to assure me I'd catch up, but I didn't really believe her until it happened. By then I was in the Marines, and it didn't matter anymore."

Cam watched her cut another juicy morsel from her steak. "So, how's the steak? Worth defending with a knife?"

"You bet." She answered, popping it into her mouth, and chewing with relish. "So, I guess all your brothers and sisters are married, and there are a bunch of nieces and nephews?"

"All but Abby. She's finally getting married next month." A safer, easier topic.

"Finally?"

"According to my mother, good southern matriarch that she is, Abby is a genuine old maid. Abby's a doctor and if she'd followed my mother's advice, no doubt, she'd have been divorced before she hung up her shingle. Actually, if she'd listened to my mother, she'd have given up the idea of being a doctor altogether and settled down to produce another half dozen grandbabies and sip sweet tea on her veranda with her lady friends."

"So, your mother's a little old-fashioned. That's not a bad thing."

Caught by the note of envy in Sandy's voice, Cam realized he'd never given much thought to the benefits of being part of a large family and having a mother who could always be counted on to be there for them. Sandy's growing up had been hugely different from his own. He guessed it must have been hard for a girl to grow up without a mother. Even though all his sisters argued constantly with their mom, he knew they could always count on her love and support.

"Maybe not," he conceded. "But, she's a *lot* old-fashioned. Her entire life has been Dad and us kids. She married Dad right out of high school, and she worries about everything."

"She sounds wonderful. You're so lucky." Sandy pushed her empty plate away. "My mother left so long ago, I forgot what it feels like to have one. I don't even know if she's still alive."

"Jeez, now I've really put my foot in it."

"It's nothing," Sandy parroted his own dismissive catch phase with a dimpled smile. "Will you take me to meet your Mom some day?"

Alarmed, Cam didn't answer her question. Taking her to meet his mother would be tantamount to making a commitment. He hardly knew this woman, in spite of the ease of their conversation. And commitment filled him with dread. He wasn't ready for that kind of relationship, never mind the emotional intimacy it would bring.

"How was everything?" The waitress asked, startling them both.

"Great," Cam answered, thankful for the regular interruptions the waitress' diligence provided.

"Would you like to see a desert menu?" The woman offered.

Cam glanced at Sandy with lifted brows. When she shook her head, he turned to the waiting woman. "Just the check, thank you."

"You weren't kidding about the steak," Cam teased as Sandy's empty plate was removed. "Where do you put it all?"

Sandy patted her flat stomach. "Right here. You aren't going to forget your promise are you?" she said as he dug through his wallet and took out several bills.

"What promise was that?"

"To take me for a romantic walk on the beach . . . in the moonlight."

CHAPTER FIVE

ROMANTIC? MOONLIGHT? WHEN HAD HE PROMISED ANY SUCH thing? Cam's gut churned with conflicting emotions. He'd enjoyed the meal and her company, and truth be told, was reluctant for the evening to end, but a romantic walk on the beach? In the moonlight? That sort of thing led to places he didn't want to go. Actually, he did want to go there, but not with her. He wasn't that kind of guy.

"I need to stop at the car first," Sandy said smiling up at him with a mischievous glimmer in her eyes. She lifted one foot and considered it. "I borrowed these shoes so I don't want to get them sandy or wet."

She slid from her chair and reached for his hand, urging him toward the door to the parking lot.

Cam followed Sandy to his borrowed car with mixed desires warring in his gut. He wanted to flee. And he didn't want to. He was a mess.

He unlocked the car and stepped back while she tucked her purse under the seat. Then, she ordered him to turn his back.

"I'm ready," she announced shutting the car door with a flourish.

He glanced down at her bare feet and frowned. He'd stood just inches away while she had been removing her pantyhose and shoes. Desire stirred in his loins.

"First one to the beach wins."

Wins what? he wondered, as Sandy dashed across the parking lot. By the time he'd removed his own shoes and followed her around the restaurant to the beach, she was dancing across the sand with her arms outstretched.

He wriggled his toes in the sand and watched her. *She has the most incredible body.* And every inch of it showed to breathtaking advantage in the soft pink dress that clung with such tantalizing elegance. He might be emotionally battered, but his sex drive was alive and well. He'd have to be careful or he'd be in over his head before he knew what hit him.

Sandy twirled in his direction, her hand reaching for his. Her short silky curls blew merrily about her face, and a flush stained her cheeks. Her eyes sparkled, and her cherry-red lips parted slightly. She looked like the woman of his dreams. Except there was no place for a woman in his life right now.

"Come on." Sandy grabbed his hand and tugged. "Let's go wading."

"It'd be a shame to get your lovely dress wet," he managed to say in a reasonably normal voice. On top of the uneasy feeling still throbbing through his being, a vision of the dress, soaked and clinging even more suggestively than it already did, ran through his mind.

"We won't get wet, I promise," Sandy wheedled, towing him toward the hard-packed sand and gently lapping waves. "And thank you for the compliment."

"Not a problem." Not a problem, my foot! He felt like he was standing on a precipice about to fall off.

They waded in and out of the sheen of seawater skimming its way up the beach, hands linked, as the moon rose out of the sea, and began to spread a river of sparkling silver across the water. It was as romantic as he'd feared. Every bit of him hummed with awareness of just how desirable she was, while his brain tried frantically not to notice.

"I love the beach. Don't you?" Sandy peered up at him.

The breeze tossed her curls into even greater confusion around her face. She was so unselfconsciously pretty she took his breath away.

He nodded in answer.

"It's just about my most favorite place to be." She looked at him seriously for another moment before turning her gaze back toward the curling waves. "Lanford, New Hampshire is a long way from the sea so it was kind of a novelty when I first started school here. I go to one beach or another whenever I can catch a ride." Her gaze came back to his, and she grinned as she kicked up a spray of water that sparkled with moonlight.

"The ocean is my happy place. Sometimes it's peaceful, like tonight. Sometimes it's angry, with huge crashing waves. But whatever mood it's in, when I'm hurting, I always feel better after I've listened to the surf for a while. You ever felt that way?"

Abruptly Cam was transported to another world and another time. To a far different beach half way around the world. And a night spent staring out over the tropical waters of the South China Sea. An invisible fist clutched painfully at his heart with the memory of that other beach. The beach at Da Nang that had been so close and yet so far from the war that had robbed him of so much. Filled with anguish and anger, he had shouted himself hoarse until the calming rote of the waves had begun to soothe his shattered soul.

"Yeah, I have," he answered softly. He shook his head to banish the unwanted memory.

"I spent a week at the beach in Salisbury, Massachusetts when my father died. And I spent a lot of time at a quiet little beach up in Tide's Way after I got the news about Tony." Sandy offered.

She stopped walking, and Cam stopped with her, forced to turn to face her with their hands still entwined. She looked up at him, her eyes wide and intense. She had her own difficult memories, he realized, and not necessarily any less painful than his own. Then she shrugged slightly and a smile began teasing the corners of her mouth.

"Besides, it's . . . it's romantic. Don't you think?"

He swallowed hard, returning her suddenly mysterious gaze. His pulse sped up. Then her gaze slid away from his, and the bottom fell out of his stomach.

Balancing on one foot and clutching his hand, Sandy wriggled one toe into the damp sand. She stooped to pick something up. In the fading light, it glistened wetly when she held it up for him to see.

A small round stone, tumbled smooth by the action of the sea. Sandy pressed it against her cheek for a moment then held it out.

"It's a worry stone."

"A worry stone?" Cam asked as he took it from her. The tiny stone felt glossy as he rubbed his thumb over its polished surface.

"A lucky worry stone considering where I found it." She grinned at him. "In Maine stones like this are everywhere. In fact, some beaches are all stones and no sand. Not so much here in North Carolina, though. So that makes this a lucky, worry stone."

"Besides being pretty, what does a worry stone do?

"You touch it. You know, hold it or whatever. Keep it in your pocket, and when you're worried about things, it's like a talisman." She stepped closer, her gaze locking on his again. She peered intently up at him as though she were trying to see into his soul.

The scent of her drifted around him with seductive mystery. An intoxicating mixture of spring flowers, mystery, and woman. It suggested so much and promised things he hadn't dared to believe in for a long time.

"Is it supposed to make worries go away?" His voice sounded peculiar.

She shrugged one shoulder. "My dad had one. I've no idea where it came from, but for as long as I can remember, he carried it in his pocket. He said he liked the way it felt, all warm from his body, and when he was anxious he rubbed his fingers over it. "

A small sad smile flitted over her features.

"Perhaps I should give it back . . . You look . . . anxious about something." He held the stone out. Maybe she was thinking of her dad being gone and that's what had brought the sadness to her face. He wanted, more than he'd ever wanted anything, to take this woman into his arms. But he wasn't sure he should.

"You keep it," she whispered as she closed his fingers around the stone. She flattened her palms against the front of his sport jacket, and stepped closer. So close that pink silk and the soft flesh beneath it brushed teasingly against the backs of his hands and sent another shock wave of desire rocketing through him.

"I'm only anxious that you're never going to kiss me."

· · ·

SANDY ROSE UP onto her toes and turned her face up to Cam's. He didn't seem inclined to take advantage of her invitation so she slid her hands around his neck and leaned into him. Her heart raced. She wanted to feel his mouth on hers more than she'd ever wanted anything. Why was he hesitating?

"Kiss me, Cam," she whispered.

The blue of his eyes wasn't visible in the moonlight, but the intensity of his gaze touched her insides with a longing she'd never felt before. What was he waiting for?

The dimple in his cheek became more pronounced for a brief second, and then disappeared, and finally, when she thought her heart would burst with anticipation, he dipped his head toward hers.

His mouth felt as cool as the sea in the dusky evening air. Fleeting and chaste. Not what she ached for or expected. She parted her lips, inviting more. His lips warmed and began to explore the contours of her mouth. She sighed and tightened her arms about his neck. An irresistible wave of longing poured over her with the suddenness of a summer thunderstorm.

The arm resting loosely about her waist went taut and a moment later Cam pulled the full length of her body firmly against his own. His free hand wandered over her shoulders and down her back, caressing the softness of the dress Natalie had promised would catch his attention. He groaned as his mouth took possession of hers.

Like the first time she'd ever been kissed, Cam's kiss awed and excited her. But she was a woman now, not barely fourteen. The desire racing through her veins wasn't that of an innocent young teenager either. And Cam wasn't a bumbling kid. He was a man. Grown up and experienced. He certainly kissed like he was experienced.

Their tongues danced together as flashes of heat and fire obliterated the cool night air. Even the sea surging around their ankles had lost its chill. An unfamiliar hardness pressed into her belly arousing even more excitement and yearning. Her ears rang, and desire washed over her with appalling abandon. If this was what sexual liberation was all about, she wanted more of it.

The drumbeat of unfamiliar music filled her ears and if Cam hadn't held her clamped against him in an uncompromising embrace she would have crumpled into a quivering pink heap on the damp sand. There wasn't a solid bone left in her, only tingling nerve endings, a thudding heart, and earth-shattering fireworks!

Don't stop, Cam. Please don't stop. Her body hummed with sensations in places a long way from her mouth and with more urgency than she had ever experienced. *I want . . . Oh God. I don't know what I want.*

Abruptly Cam lifted his head. His breath came in ragged gasps, and his eyes were wide and dazed looking. Sandy stared back, her own eyes feeling as big as his, and her breathing just as harsh. She couldn't tell if it was her heart or his that pounded so furiously between them.

As the clamor in her head began to recede, it was amazing to find the sea still docile, and the rising tide still eddying wetly about their ankles. The moon shone with complacent permanence and the stars winked as they always had - and yet everything had changed.

CHAPTER SIX

"So, did he live up to your expectations?" Natalie gave Sandy a nudge.

"Who?" Sandy murmured, still half asleep and trying to hang on to a wonderful dream featuring a handsome soldier and a tryst on the beach.

Natalie plopped down on the edge of Sandy's bed. "Who? Was it that unmemorable you don't even recall going out with the guy?"

The bed bounced, and the vision of the soldier disappeared. "What time is it?" Sandy mumbled.

"Is memory loss an effect lust has on a normally rational woman?"

"What memory loss?" Sandy let go of the last wispy remnants of her dream and rolled over to peer up at her roommate through dream-fogged eyes.

"You forgot to set your alarm. You missed your morning run. You missed breakfast. And, if you don't get a move on pretty soon, you'll miss your first class."

"Oh, no!" Sandy sat up with a jerk. "I was supposed to meet Cam. He must think I forgot. Oh, Natalie, he'll think I don't . . ."

"He called."

"Cam called, and you didn't wake me up?" Indignation and disappointment had her scrambling for her clothes.

"He told me not to. He said he'd see you around."

Sandy flopped back onto the bed appalled that she had missed her breakfast date with Cam. A date she'd pretty much had to pry out of him. In spite of the earthshattering kiss, he'd seemed reluctant to commit to anything when he'd dropped her at the front door of her dorm.

What if we don't happen to run into each other?

"Oh yeah," Natalie added as she gathered up her books. "He said 'No problem.' Whatever that means."

YEAH, right! No problem! Cam's fingers toyed with the little stone nestled in his jeans pocket. If it was no big deal, why couldn't he concentrate on anything else?

"I shouldn't have called," Cam muttered, a bleak feeling settling into his gut. "Maybe it was just a sympathy date." This was what he wanted, after all. No commitments. No one to worry about besides himself until he could pull his life back together.

But that kiss! He'd kissed girls before without having his world shattered. Kissing Sandy had been something else entirely. He'd lost all control and all sense. He'd kissed her like a drowning man. He'd still been reeling from the aftershocks when she suggested meeting for breakfast and he'd agreed. He'd even been looking forward to it.

Then his night had been as troubled as always. It had started out okay with the pleasantly arousing memory of the way she'd molded herself into his embrace and accepted the hungry desire he hadn't been able to disguise. But when sleep finally came, he'd been back in Nam. A long way from Sandy's bubbly optimism and sexy enthusiasm.

Maybe it was better if he didn't see her again. Or at least not right away. Perhaps this neediness would go away. Maybe next semester or a year from now he'd be in a better place. Be a better man.

He shifted uneasily on his stool in the *Code Seven* watching his brother Linc rinse coffee mugs and line them up on a folded towel beside the little sink under the polished oak bar. Linc owned the *Code*

Seven, a cop hangout that was half bar, half coffee house. He served a basic breakfast, a varied short order lunch menu, and a single item house special in the evening, and he had no shortage of customers. Cam had come because he was famished and knew Linc would feed him since he'd missed breakfast at the frat house and given up waiting for Sandy at the dining commons.

He'd waited for what seemed like hours, his stomach growling, watching for Sandy, but she hadn't come. When he'd finally given in and called, Sandy's roommate had told him Sandy was still sleeping and offered to wake her up. He'd told the woman, Nancy he thought her name was, that he'd see Sandy around.

Maybe it was Nadine? Cam tried to recall if Nancy or Nadine or whatever her name was had sounded encouraging?

Now he wasn't sure what he was supposed to think. Clearly Sandy hadn't had any problem sleeping so maybe last night hadn't been as life changing for her as it had been for him. Maybe she wasn't as eager to see him again as she'd sounded last night when he took her back to her dorm A woman as gorgeous as Sandy must have dozens of men vying for her time and attention. What made him think one date with him would have turned her world on its ear?

Maybe she kissed all her dates like that. Maybe it meant nothing. "Maybe it was just a sympathy date," he muttered a second time.

"A sympathy date?" Linc peered up at Cam, his brow furrowed.

"After what happened at registration yesterday."

"What does registration have to do with whether it was a sympathy date or not? For that matter, what in hell is a sympathy date? And since when did you have any trouble impressing women?"

Linc dried his hands on the towel tucked around his waistband and folded his arms on the bar.

"There was an anti-war rally going on outside the hall where registration was taking place. I was kind of on edge anyway, but then some dickhead got fresh with Sandy. I said something to the asshole, and then he started calling me names."

"If you called him an asshole, what'd you expect?" Linc shook his head in mock sorrow.

"I didn't call him anything. I just suggested he treat her like a lady."

"And that translates into a sympathy date?"

"Not exactly," Cam admitted. Then he told his brother the whole story. "So she might have just taken pity on me. She's got a brother in the Navy who's MIA and from things she said, her brother had a hard time when he came home between tours."

"A lot of women have brothers in the military, and a lot of them have been in Vietnam, and I bet it ain't easy for any of them when they come home. Doesn't mean their sisters accept dates just because they feel sorry for a guy who lived through the same thing their brothers did," Linc argued reasonably.

"But she didn't show up for breakfast," Cam answered, still torn by the conflicting conviction that he wasn't in a good place to get involved with anyone and the desire to kiss Sandy again.

"Didn't her roommate say she overslept?" Linc countered. "I suppose *you* never slept through the alarm before?" Cam began to shake his head, but Linc hurried on. "Give her the benefit of the doubt, Runt."

"Don't call me that."

Linc reached across the bar and knuckled the top of Cam's head. "Runt!"

"Linc . . ." Cam glared at his brother. "If I wanted grief . . ."

"Sorry, Cam, but you're acting like a runt. You had a date with a woman who gave every appearance of having had a good time last night. Stop being so down on yourself. You're a nice guy any girl should be happy to spend time with. Don't go working yourself into a flap just because she missed breakfast this morning. Call her this afternoon and ask her out again. If she says no, which I highly doubt, then at least you'll know where you stand. If she says yes, then you didn't have a problem in the first place."

Everything Linc said made sense. If only Cam was sure he had any business pursuing her at all. He hadn't dated since before Nam, and he'd been different then. He wasn't the easy-going jock he'd been before the ugliness of war had left its indelible mark on him, and he wasn't sure any woman would ever want the man he'd become. Even Sandy, once she got to know him better.

"Thanks for the advice, Linc." Cam slid off the stool. "And the breakfast."

"No problem."

"That's my line," Cam retorted, a half smile tugging at the corners of his mouth. Linc was the best of brothers, even if he did call him Runt to get a rise out of him. And he served up a dynamite breakfast.

Cam pushed the street door open and a small, black head popped into view followed by the rest of Linc's youngest son.

"Hey there, Sammy." Cam scooped his four-year-old nephew into his arms for a bear hug.

"Hi, Uncle Cam!" The little boy giggled.

Cam put the boy down and ruffled his silky hair. "What are you doing here?"

"Mom sent me," Sammy replied. "I'm supposed to stay with Dad while she gets her hair cut."

"Free labor," Linc laughed lifting the hinged section of the bar to allow his son entry.

"Make him pay you, Sammy," Cam called after his nephew, as the boy flew through to the kitchen to greet the short order cook.

"Good luck," Linc said going back to his work. "I can't wait to meet this woman who's got you in such a twist."

Cam waved without answering, and then let himself out onto the street and headed back toward campus. He had paperwork to get squared away. If he passed Sandy's dorm and happened to see her, maybe he'd stop. If he didn't, he'd consider that the answer to his conflicting instincts.

CHAPTER SEVEN

Sandy hadn't 'run into' Cam in more than two weeks. Maybe she'd been wrong about him being *The One*. This last semester before she began student teaching was pretty busy, but that hadn't stopped her from thinking about him and looking for him everywhere. She'd turned down four perfectly nice guys who'd asked her out because she just couldn't drum up any interest in them. How long was this yearning desire going to last before she gave up and moved on?

As she walked into the Student Union with two classmates, her eyes roved over the crowd as they always did. Always hoping for a glimpse of his tall frame or a glint of sun-bleached hair. She sucked in a breath of surprise and stopped dead in her tracks when she saw him, hands on hips, studying the bulletin board on the far wall.

"Sandy?" One of her friends looked back to see why she'd stopped. "You coming?"

"Um . . . I just remembered something. Catch you later." Sandy turned on her heel as if to leave the building. Her classmate nodded and followed the other woman into the bookstore.

Sandy moved closer to the bulletin board. It was him.

He was glaring at a poster for the anti-war rally downtown on

Saturday. The rally she had promised to speak at on behalf of soldiers, like her brother, who were missing in action.

Cam jerked away from the board, his mouth clamped into a hard, uncompromising line. Should she approach him? Or not? He looked angry. But if she didn't grab him now she might never get another chance.

"Cam?" she called out.

He whipped around, his eyes wide and startled. Then his gaze sharpened.

"Cam." She crossed the tiled floor in a hurry. "Where have you been? I've been looking for you everywhere."

He smiled briefly when she finally caught up to him and his dimple flashed. "Couldn't have looked *every*where. I haven't exactly been hiding."

"It seemed like everywhere." Her pulse raced as she stood there looking up at him, remembering the way he'd made her feel that night on the beach. "I don't even know if you're living on campus or with your family. I never saw you at breakfast, so I didn't know where to find you."

"Well, now you've found me. I—" He broke off and looked away. His jaw worked like he was trying to come to a decision about something. Maybe he wasn't as glad to see her as she was to see him. When he looked back at her a tug of war seemed to be waging in his expression.

If she didn't say something right now to keep him here, she might regret it. "It's your turn, you know."

His brows rose. "My turn for what?"

"To ask me for a date." There. Bold as brass, but it couldn't be helped. One of them had to get things started. "I'm sorry I stood you up for breakfast, but I promise it won't happen again."

"Not a problem," he muttered. He fidgeted with the zipper on his windbreaker.

"I'll have a problem if you don't ask me out." She tilted her head and smiled at him.

"You might have a problem if I do."

It was her turn to raise her brows. "Why's that?"

"I'm . . . not like the other guys around here. I'm . . . " He fidgeted some more. "I'm not very good company sometimes." He sounded grim.

"I thought you were very nice company."

"I'm not always in a gentlemanly mood."

Sandy lifted her chin not sure how to respond.

He raked his fingers through his short, bleached strands of hair. "Look, Sandy. I'm still working on how to live like a civilian again. I'm not always that nice. Sometimes I even scare myself. I don't know what you expect from me, but whatever it is, I probably don't have it to give you."

"Can we at least talk about it?" She was desperate. Why she was so certain this man had to become part of her life, she wasn't sure, but if she let him, he was going to walk away and she'd never find out.

"You're not going to let this go until we do. Are you?"

She shook her head, but gave him her warmest smile.

He sighed, then nodded toward the coffee shop.

When they were seated in a booth with his back to the wall and two tall fizzing vanilla cokes on the table between them she took a breath and plunged in, anxious to breach his defenses before he could circle the wagons.

"How do you know I want something you can't give me?"

He shrugged and took a sip of his drink.

"How do you even know I want something?" she persisted.

"Women always want something."

"You are in an ornery mood today, aren't you?"

"I told you I'm not always nice."

Sandy nodded her head from side to side. "Well, you're right about wanting something. I want another date. With you."

"I like a woman who says what's on her mind and doesn't beat around the bush."

"Good. Because I usually say whatever comes into my head. Sometimes it gets me in trouble. Some folk aren't all that happy about bald honesty. Especially in this part of the country. Or so I've discovered."

"It's different in New Hampshire?" His dimple appeared again.

"Us Yankees are a lot more direct than you southerners." Something it had taken almost two years of college before she finally managed to get the hang of. "It took me awhile to realize 'bless her heart' isn't a compliment and my mouth gets me in trouble sometimes."

"My temper gets me in trouble."

"Your temper?" She stared at him waiting for the punch line. He didn't seem like the kind of man given to outbursts of temper. Especially not after the careful control he'd kept on his anger the day Bud had taunted him at registration.

Cam closed his eyes as an expression very like pain crossed his face. When he opened them again the expression was gone and she was surprised by the bright, mesmerizing blue she hadn't fully appreciated before. It had been too dark in either the restaurant or on the beach. Now she felt like she was drowning in clear blue pool.

"I'll try to behave if you'd like to show me that beach you were talking about on Saturday."

Saturday! Sandy swallowed around the lump in her throat. That was the one day she couldn't go to the beach with him. She had a speech to give. For Tony's benefit.

She shook her head slightly and his expression immediately clouded.

"It's okay if you're not free," he began.

"Oh, Cam. I would love to go to the beach with you, but I have to go downtown on Saturday. I've got this thing I just can't get out of."

"I understand," he mumbled picking up his coke and chugging it.

"No. It's . . . there's a . . . meeting of sorts. I . . . well, I have to go because . . . well, because . . ."

"Not a problem," Cam cut her off.

"Sunday?" she asked, holding her breath.

He hesitated so long she wanted to reach out and shake him. Then he finally nodded. "Sunday it is. After church."

CAM STRETCHED out on his too short bed and folded his hands behind his head. Remembering the feel of her lips touching his. Of her hand resting lightly on his shoulder. The scent of spring flowers that hovered around her. There was something very special about Sandy Marshall. And about the way she made him feel.

She made him think about things he dared to want, but couldn't have.

What am I doing, getting involved with a nice girl like Sandy?

Sleep and exhaustion tugged at him. He fought it, remembering instead, the way moonlight looked in Sandy's hair. The way the ocean tumbled and splashed around their feet as she bent to pick something up. Remembering the way she'd held out the little stone for him to see. Remembering . . .

THE CORPSMAN ASSIGNED to Cam's platoon had a photo of his new baby. He thrust it toward Cam. "Ain't he just cuter than a puppy dog?" Jenkins didn't look old enough to be a new father. He didn't look old enough to be out of high school, never mind a corpsman with more than eight months of action behind him. "I can't wait to get home and hold that little tyke in my arms and introduce him to his Daddy. Five more months, LT. Just five months, and I'll have him snuggled right here." Jenkins made a cradle with his arms and rocked an imaginary baby.

"It must be tough being half way around the world. Missing your wife and all. And not being there when your son was born." Cam handed the photo back, envious that this youthful corpsman had a family back home waiting for him.

Cam had plenty of family. Just not anyone special. Not a wife counting the days until he returned. Nor a son waiting to meet his father. Not even a girl-friend. He'd seen Jenkins reading the letters his wife wrote, his face soft, his expression yearning. Often his eyes filling with tears. What would it be like to have someone that special in his life?

"Yeah. It's tough." Jenkins gazed at the photo longingly. "I just wish I could hold my son right now. He's almost a month old already, y'know."

"Well, he'll be old enough to smile back at you when you get home. Maybe that'll make the wait worth it."

"I guess," Jenkins agreed, not sounding convinced as he tucked the photo into the lining of his helmet. "You got any kids, LT?"

"You got any kids, LT?"

Jerked from his nightmare, Cam bolted upright in bed. Christ, was he ever going to stop dreaming about that damned corpsman? Cam's heart pounded so hard it hurt. He gasped for breath and fought for sanity.

He flung himself out of bed and turned the light on. Staring around the small room, he suddenly felt claustrophobic. He yanked the door open and rushed down the hall. The fraternity house was dark, and everyone was asleep.

Cam slowed his pace, trying desperately to regain control. He crossed through the living room, passed the furniture and the television set to the windows. For a long time, he prowled from one window to the next as his heartbeat returned to normal, and the memory of Jenkins fate faded into the general horror of his tour in Vietnam.

Finally he returned to his room, but no way could he go back to sleep. He turned on his desk lamp and opened his site management notebook. His gaze caught on the doodle in the margin. *Sandy Marshall*. He smiled as her image edged out his nightmare. He picked up his pencil and drew a heart around her name.

Then he frowned. In just seconds, he obliterated the heart beneath an elaborate geometrical design. *I can't get serious about her. I shouldn't be seeing her at all, never mind getting serious. She should be hanging out with guys who aren't loaded down with enough guilt to sink a battleship.*

Cam flung the pencil down and shot to his feet. He paced angrily back to the window, Jenkins face in his head again.

It should've been me that got blown up.

CHAPTER EIGHT

As the rattle of applause greeting her introduction died out, Sandy climbed onto the impromptu stage set up in Hugh MacRae Park where a raucous Anti-war rally was being held. She curled her fingers over the top of the podium as if its solid support would make the next half hour easier. She tried to ignore the butterflies in her belly along with the smell of pot in the air and the insistent chanting.

What was I thinking when I agreed to come here today? Why did I think these fanatical anti-war protestors would care about the soldiers who didn't ask to be where they were? All they want is out of Vietnam at any cost! I should have known. I was one of them until Tony went MIA.

She surveyed the mass of faces, looking for at least one friendly face to focus on. Most of those close to the stage were attentively waiting for her to speak, but others on the fringes of the crowd that spread across the lawn and spilled into the street beyond the park still ranted noisily about making love, not war. Annoyed drivers tooted their horns at the stragglers, adding to the noisy confusion.

Sandy had come for Tony. She wanted this avid, angry crowd to understand the possibly negative outcome for the thousands of soldiers still listed as missing in action should the United States pull out precipitously. The realization that most of these bigoted protesters wouldn't care about Tony or any of the others made her angry.

A flare of determination replaced the butterflies in her stomach. She needed the anger to get her through this. Enough anger so she wouldn't care what they thought of her. *But they're going to hear my story, whether they like it or not.*

"Ladies and Gentlemen," Sandy began.

"End this war! End this war! End this war!" the chant began at the back and rolled forward like the wave at a baseball game. Posters with slogans spouting similar viewpoints waved like metronomes.

"Ladies and Gentlemen," Sandy spoke again, louder this time. "Thank you for allowing me to speak to you today about the plight of our men being held as prisoners of war and those listed as missing in action."

Closed fists punched the air, and boos erupted.

"We want peace."

"Make love, not war!"

"Get us out of Southeast Asia!"

Sandy remembered an earlier rally when she'd been part of the crowd, booing and shouting at a speaker who had questioned Hanoi's lack of honesty about POWs. *God, I was so naïve. And just as rude.* Disgust at her earlier, blind self and this mob of closed-minded protesters made her grit her teeth with resolve. She rapped her knuckles sharply against the mic and kept it up until most of the ranting stopped.

"When my brother was on his first tour in Vietnam, I was right out there with you. I wanted the war over so he could come home, and I wish it had ended before Tony got sent back. He would have preferred not to go, but he didn't feel he had a choice. The soldiers who are fighting this war aren't the ones making the decisions."

"Baby-killers! Baby-killers!"

"Tony was a medic, not a baby-killer." *Is a medic. Is, is, is!*

"What about the slaughter of innocent villagers?" a belligerent young man with a tie-dyed rag tied around his long hair and beads spilling down his chest screamed.

"Tony is a medic. Now he's missing in action."

"Maybe he's at the Hanoi Hilton where he belongs!" Mr. Tie-dye retorted.

It felt like someone had punched her in the stomach.

"He is a medic," she repeated through clenched teeth. "He didn't kill anyone."

"He shoulda stayed home, then." Tie-dye hooted derisively. Others joined in the taunting.

Sandy tried to ignore them. "Since Tony has been missing, I've come to realize that it's not that simple to just end the war. What will happen to him and others like him if we just pull out without making provisions to get them back?'

"They get what they deserve!" Now the heated response came from several places.

"They don't deserve to be abandoned," Sandy countered, slapping her palm against the podium in anger and frustration.

"They didn't belong there in the first place," came the instant reply.

"Soldiers go where they are sent."

"He could have gone to Canada."

"Soldiers follow orders, even when they don't want to."

"We want peace! We want peace! We want peace!" Hand clapped in time to the chant.

"What about my brother?" Sandy screamed in frustration.

The hissing and booing rose to a crescendo.

Sickened by the intolerance and precipitously close to tears, Sandy gave up. She couldn't compete with the narrow-minded clamor. This crowd came to vent their anger, not listen to her. What a fool she'd been. *Yeah, Sandy good luck changing the world.*

She shoved the mic away in disgust and stalked to the back of the platform. "I can't do this anymore," she told the organizer. She jumped down and elbowed her way through the uncaring mob. Hurt, anger and frustration boiled inside her as she stumbled away from the cacophony of outraged voices. No way would anyone ever rope her into another such scene.

For the first time since she'd gotten involved in the protest movement, she began to realize there were darn few moderates among them. They were just a pack of fanatics who probably didn't personally know anyone who had fought or gone missing. They had one agenda, and it didn't matter who got hurt. As she stormed across the park toward College Road, words she never used aloud jumbled their way around inside her brain. Crude words like the ones they had directed at her. *Dumb-asses! Pea-brained idiots! F-ing potheads!* Maybe they couldn't get their brains around the problem because they were too stoned to think at all.

Why did I think I could make a difference? Tony thought he could make a difference by going back to Vietnam, and look where that got him? What was I thinking?

Her outrage and frustration had finally given way to tears. Tears for Tony. Tears for herself. And tears for all the other young men gone missing and the families who waited and prayed and hoped. Prayers and hopes unlikely to see happy endings if radical mobs like this had their way.

Sandy stopped and dragged her sleeve across her eyes dashing the unwanted tears away, then realized she'd just passed the bus stop. She did a U-turn and hurried back to stand at the curb and wait for her ride back to campus. She didn't feel like talking to anyone so she was thankful to be the only one waiting.

She was sick with disappointment. She'd wanted to do something for Tony's sake. She had thought she could make them see there were other things to consider. Suddenly the memory of Cam and the ridicule he'd had to put up with at registration shoved its way into her consciousness.

Oh, my God, how much more heckling has he had to put up with that I don't know about? Tony told me he got spit on at the airport when he was in uniform. What if that happened to Cam too? What am I doing here?

What would Cam think if he found out where she'd been? She'd been deliberately vague when he invited her to spend the day at the beach with him. She felt guilty. Guilty and unfaithful. Cam seemed so sympathetic when she'd told him about Tony, but he wasn't likely to be so understanding about her getting involved with this bullheaded, anti-military crowd.

A sudden fear of how Cam might interpret her involvement gripped her. He might be completely turned off. *Please, God, don't let him find out. At least not until I can explain. None of these rabble-rousers are worth jeopardizing my friendship with Cam. Not the missing soldiers. Not the organizer who insisted I come today. Not even Tony. Oh, God, not even Tony. But Tony isn't here, and Cam is. What if Cam needs me? If he's fighting demons like Tony, maybe I can help. I can be there for him. I can be understanding in a world that doesn't care. I can love him whole again.*

I can love him whole again!

Suddenly the park, College Road and the bus stop she'd waited at so often before seemed like they were totally alien. Sandy gazed around at the familiar scene as if she'd never seen it before. Her heart beat loud in her ears, and she sat down abruptly on the graffiti covered bench.

I can love him.

The bus pulled in and stopped, but Sandy remained where she sat.

"I love him."

Sure, she'd told Natalie that she was going to marry him and marriage implied love. And the fireworks that night on the beach had been a revelation, too. But she'd never actually said the words out loud. But there it was.

"I'm in love with Cam."

Crazy, head over heels, in love. And I could have been with him right this minute instead of getting heckled for trying to do a good thing.

"You planning on waiting until the next bus, miss?"

The bus waited with its doors open, the driver's hand on the door lever. She jumped to her feet. She mumbled an apology as she hustled up the steps, then made her way to the back where there were empty seats.

I'm in love with Nathan Cameron! All the way down College Road toward home, she savored this new knowledge, her heart swelling almost painfully.

I'm in love with Cam.

CAM SQUIRMED, self-consciously aware of the intimacy being forced on him by two unknown women who'd plunked themselves down beside him in the TV room of Sandy's dorm. One of them was clearly on the make. He wished Sandy would appear to rescue him. Natalie had assured him Sandy would show up in time for the game, but the first pitch had already been thrown, and she still hadn't returned.

He had come on a whim. Drawn by an unexplored need to see her. But maybe he shouldn't have. He definitely shouldn't have accepted the invitation to join the ladies in the parlor while he waited.

Natalie had been silent on the subject of where Sandy had gone. As evasive as Sandy when she'd told him she wasn't free to go to the beach today. Where had she been that neither woman wanted him to know? He wondered, with a sinking feeling, if it had anything to do with the poster he'd seen on the bulletin board in the lobby. One of the speeches was supposed to have been about MIAs. That would have interested Sandy. And been more than enough reason to turn his beach date down. She was understandably worried about her brother.

Cam tried to ignore the women as he considered the inexplicable hold Sandy had gained on him in such a short time.

To be honest, he admitted ruefully to himself, his first attraction to Sandy had been entirely physical. Ogling her neat little backside as she bent over the registration table, he'd felt a definite stirring of interest. Mere interest had given way to unabashed admiration when she'd stood up to the taunting idiot in Cam's defense, her pert, sexy breasts rising and falling rapidly with her agitation. Then there'd been that tantalizing peek down the front of her blouse while she laughed up at him. It had all been more than enough to arouse any man with eyes in his head.

But getting to know her, the woman beneath the body, had deepened his appreciation to something a whole lot more than just sexual interest. There was something sincere and intriguing about this woman. Something about her that dogged his every thought. Made him want to be with her every spare minute.

It amazed him that his macho self-sufficiency had been so quickly and easily punctured. How had it happened? It was even more disturbing to wonder where this relationship, if that's what it could be called this early on, was going. Sandy was the kind of girl you treated with respect. Like the boss' daughter or the girl next door. Dating her without getting serious would be close to impossible.

And serious with a girl like Sandy meant commitment. This was not high school. He couldn't give her his class ring to wear on a chain around her neck, take her to the sock hops and neck at the drive-in movie. Sandy was a woman who would be thinking longer term than that and he was in no shape to offer more. He was an emotional train wreck.

Unwilling to pursue that line of thought, Cam dragged his attention back to the game and watched the Chicago pitcher wind up and deliver another strike to the Red Sox batter. Sandy claimed her favorite player was Yastrezemski, but he wasn't playing today, so maybe she wouldn't be in such a hurry to get back to watch the game.

"So, Cam," the brunette on his left purred. "Where'd you get that delicious tan?"

"From the sun," he answered discouragingly. He kept his gaze on the TV.

"Funny man." She leaned closer, one breast thrusting provocatively past his elbow to plant itself against his chest. "You like to surf?"

"Surf?" Cam asked, momentarily puzzled and more than a little distracted by the suggestive press of feminine flesh against his chest and arm. *What has surfing got to do with anything? Oh, yeah. Surfing. Tan. They went together. Clearly the mess in Southeast Asia had never occurred to this little airhead.* "Ah, no. I don't surf."

"Lifeguard?" She didn't give up easily.

Cam lurched to his feet, brushing off her clinging fingers. "Nope, not lifeguarding either." *Christ! Could she be any more obvious?*

Miss Brunette pouted prettily. Pretty if you liked that sort of coquettishness. He didn't. It wouldn't have worked on him even if Sandy hadn't been his reason for being here. Eager to escape, he navigated his way though the maze of overstuffed chairs and sofas to the archway and out into the hall. He took the front stairs three at a time. And then he saw her.

She skipped a few steps, then twirled once before resuming her way up the sidewalk. Cam stopped and watched her happy progress toward the dorm. His heart rate sped up. Wherever Sandy had been, she appeared pretty pleased with life. He had a sudden painful thought. What if she'd been with another man? Should he disappear? Or should he step into her path. Without realizing he was making a choice, he did the latter.

"Yikes!" Sandy jerked to a halt, her face coloring swiftly. "You . . . you surprised me! I didn't . . . didn't expect to see you."

"Obviously." A wave of disappointment slammed into his gut. What had he expected anyway, dropping in unannounced like this when he knew she had other plans? "Maybe I shouldn't have come," he muttered.

"I'm not . . . I mean, it's not . . . I'm glad you came," she babbled disjointedly.

His gloom lifted immediately. "I'm glad, you're glad." *How inane. Get a grip Cameron. You're not a teenybopper.* "I thought you might try to catch the Red Sox game on television so I came over to join you."

"Did you really want to see the game? We can watch the end of it if you'd like. Or maybe do something else."

"No. I mean. I just thought . . . I wanted to see you." It felt like she'd given him a gift. Actually, she had. The gift of her time and undivided attention. Wherever she'd been earlier, right at this moment she gave every appearance of wanting to be with him. He wanted to take her for a walk, put his arm around her shoulders and feel her snuggle into him. "I thought maybe we could go for a walk."

"Oh, let's." Sandy hesitated, then reached out and slipped her hand into his. "How about the wildflower forest?" She stood partially facing him, swinging their arms back and forth, with her fingers laced through his.

"Wildflowers?" he parroted, his mind more on the intimate feel of her palm pressed against his own.

"And trees, and birds and ferns and dragonflies. It's a fun kind of place that feels like you're in the middle of the woods but you're still right here on campus." She turned and drew him with her across the lawn and around the corner of the dorm.

"I found it quite by accident one day when I was out running." She chattered enthusiastically about this forest place as they walked down a street lined with trees and busy with traffic. Cam half listened, his own mind torn between the pleasure of just being with her and nagging curiosity about where she'd been earlier.

"So, how did your morning go?" Curiosity won out.

"Not so good," Sandy answered after an awkward hesitation. Her smile faded and a parade of expressions crossed her face. Indignation. Anger. Hurt. Then she brightened. "But my ride home was . . . enlightening."

"Enlightening?"

"A revelation actually." A teasing smile touched Sandy's lips.

"Oh!"

"You don't want to know who I was thinking about?"

"Only if you want to tell me," he lied.

Sandy made an abrupt turn off the sidewalk and onto a dirt path. She didn't say anything as they walked deeper into the unexpectedly woodsy area. More paths branched off in several directions. She hesitated at the junction, with a finger to her lips, deciding which way to go, he supposed; while he concentrated on figuring out how to get her to tell him what, or maybe *who*, she'd been thinking about without coming right out and asking.

"Oh, look, Cam! A fairy house!" Sandy dropped his hand and ran a short way down one path where she fell to her knees.

Cam hung back, admiring her trim form and the body-hugging jersey that showed it off to such ravishing advantage.

"Come see it."

He moved to her side, then squatted to inspect the creation nestled in the hollow of a big pine tree's roots.

Someone had taken a lot of time to create the little house complete with a slice of bark for a roof, tiny stones outlining a path, and twigs stacked up to form walls that even sported miniature windows.

"It's a fairy cottage," Sandy informed him, twisting to look up at him. "Isn't it cute?"

"Yeah," Cam answered, his breath catching in his throat. He straightened up, and Sandy followed slowly, her gaze never leaving his. He started to reach for her hands, but instead he spanned her waist with his own and drew her to him. "But not as cute as you."

Sandy smiled briefly, then sobered. "I'm too tall to be cute." Her voice sounded erotically raspy.

The kiss began almost as chastely as it had the night on the beach, but quickly changed. Sandy pressed herself against him as eagerly as he welcomed the feel of her sexy body molding itself to his. Their mouths were hungry, demanding.

Sandy's hands slipped beneath his windbreaker, encircling his waist. Her fingers splayed over the flat of his back, the heat of her palms seeping through his shirt. Cam let go of her waist and cupped her face with both hands. *Surely she doesn't kiss everyone like this!*

Eventually, he had to come up for air. He lifted his head and opened his eyes. Her face, still cradled in his hands was so close to his, he could see tiny reflections of himself in her eyes turned dark with desire.

"Dare I hope I'm who you were thinking of on the way home?" he finally found the courage to ask?

"Did you think there might be someone else?" The teasing tone was back.

"Is there?"

She shook her head slightly, the teasing gone as quickly as it had come.

Cam let out the breath he'd been holding and circled her with his arms. Sandy dropped her head to his shoulder, her face turned in against his neck.

"I feel like we've known each other for months instead of just a couple weeks." Her breath wafted warmly past the collar of his shirt.

"Kind of hard to believe. Huh?" he whispered back, laying his cheek against the riot of blonde curls.

"It's really crazy." Her voice sounded full of wonder. "You know? If I hadn't found out I'd need that extra class at the last minute, I'd never have gone to the Student Union that day. We might never have met."

"Scary thought," he muttered. Already he didn't want to consider his existence without her in his world, but the strength of that attraction frightened him. He wasn't ready.

"But it happens like that sometimes," she said, giving him a squeeze. "A friend of mine calls chances like that God's incidences."

"God's incidences?"

Sandy lifted her head to look up at him. "Yeah, you know. God's incidence, rather than a co-incidence. Like God arranged it. Like he meant for us to meet."

"Maybe." *More likely it was just dumb luck. If God had been involved, surely he'd have introduced Sandy to someone a whole lot more suitable than Cam would ever be.*

"Well, however it came to happen, I'm glad." Her mouth widened into the generous grin that welcomed the whole world to join her.

"Me, too." Cam felt his own face break into a crazy grin. *She's so incredible! What can she possibly see in me?*

"Really glad?" Sandy tiptoed to kiss him. A fleeting, teasing kiss.

"Really," he replied, his voice husky. When she kissed him again, he tightened his embrace and covered her mouth with his.

How long they stood there in the hush of the woods, wrapped tightly together, driving each other mad with sexual excitement, Cam had no idea. But eventually, he came to his senses. He could think of only one ending to this kind of necking.

Sandy was a nice girl. Not the kind of girl you screwed without a thought to the consequences. You took girls like Sandy home to meet your mother. You married girls like Sandy. He sobered abruptly.

He put his hands on her shoulders and stepped back. "Maybe we should be getting back?" He struggled to bring his breathing under control. "Before I forget you're a lady."

Sandy pouted. Nothing like the brunette back at the dorm, but clearly not happy with his having ended the embrace or putting a stop to an activity both had more than enjoyed. Then her mouth quirked up in a come-hither smile.

"Are you always so chivalrous, Cam?"

CHAPTER NINE

Cam blinked hard, fighting gritty exhaustion. He swept his gaze first right, then left. It was nearly dusk, and they were hurrying to get back inside the wire before dark, but just because they were almost back to the base didn't mean they could be any less vigilant.

"Psst! LT?"

Cam glanced back at his radioman. "Yeah?"

"I got a bad feeling in my gut."

"I've had a bad feeling in my gut ever since I got to Nam." Cam put one muddy, worn boot in front of the other. Concentrated on staying alert in spite of his fatigue. His worst fear was missing a tripwire or stepping on a mine.

"Something's off," Corporal Miller insisted, nervously scanning the same thick vegetation that had Cam on edge.

A ripple of alarm ran up Cam's spine. He held up a hand signaling his squad to halt. The kid liked to whine, but he had a sixth sense about things.

Cam peered intently into the dense green jungle. The rest of the men did the same. Everything seemed eerily quiet. Not even the familiar chattering of animals.

"Jesus Christ," Miller swore in a hushed whisper and crossed himself.

Then Cam saw them. Four men, sprawled amid the foliage beside trail.

Americans. Army, by the uniforms. What the hell were Army doing here? In Marine country?

Cam stepped carefully off the trail. He felt suddenly vulnerable. His skin crawled as if he were being watched. A fresh flood of perspiration added itself to his already sweat-soaked fatigues. He bent over the first man, forcing himself not to turn away from the mangled bloody chest, and felt for a pulse. Nothing. Heart still thudding with dread, Cam moved to the next body.

"Corpsman up!" Cam shouted, urgency suddenly outweighing caution. Then softer, "Get the Captain on the horn. This poor bastard's still alive." Cam moved to the third man, but he was gone. Same for last guy. Dead before they hit the ground, Cam thought, grimly noting their massive head injuries and the stench of death.

Cam returned to the soldier with the pulse just as the Jenkins crashed through the brush. The corpsman fell on his knees beside the soldier who tried to talk, but only managed a panicked yelp. His fingers clawed at the dirt. Blood trickled from the corner of his mouth.

"What have you got?" Captain Seymour appeared at Cam's side. Took in the injured soldier and growled a sigh of distress.

Jenkins grabbed the wounded man's shoulder and started to turn him over. The soldier's eyes widened in terror, but still no words came. In the next instant, Cam spotted the booby trap.

In a split second that seemed to last a lifetime, the Captain saw it, too, and reacted. He flung himself across the doomed soldier's body, screaming for everyone to hit the deck.

Cam drove his shoulder into the cluster of men who'd swarmed up behind him for a closer look, bowling them over like tenpins. The detonation was deafening. Shrapnel peppered his unprotected flesh. Stinging. Sharp. Pain stabbed viciously into his eardrums. Shreds of leaves and branches fell like rain. Then unearthly silence.

Dazed and nearly deafened, Cam staggered to his feet.

One of the Marines Cam had knocked down sat up and blanched. "Jesus fucking Christ!" Then he turned away and puked.

Cam lurched toward the carnage. His stomach heaved. Words died in his throat.

The captain's eyes stared lifelessly through a mask of blood. His chest had been torn to shreds. His organs spilled out onto the dirt. His body severed nearly in half. He'd made the ultimate sacrifice to save his men.

The booby-trapped soldier was nothing but bloody pieces of barely identifiable body parts splattered over everything in the clearing, including Cam and the men he'd tackled to safety. But where was the corpsman? The new young father? Cam scrambled through the growing gloom.

He found Jenkins ten feet away, thrown against a tree. The corpsman's arms, arms that had ached to hold his new son, were gone. His helmet had been shoved half off his head. His eyes were wide with uncomprehending shock.

Cam yanked the field dressing from the corpsman's helmet and pressed it against a bleeding stump. "Stay with me, man!" He groped around for the corpsman's medical kit. "Jenkins! Look at me! For Christ's sake, get a chopper in here on the double." Cam screamed to Miller. He grabbed another field dressing and jammed it against Jenkin's other stump.

"You're gonna make it. Don't give up on me, Jenkins. You fucking hear me?"

Jenkins looked sadly into Cam's eyes. "I never got to hold my son."

CAM SPLASHED cold water into his face, trying unsuccessfully to wash away the fragments of his nightmare. He pressed his palms into his aching eyes, then stared at himself in the mirror. His eyes were red and puffy. He'd been crying in his sleep again. Something he never gave in to while awake, but over which he didn't seem to have any control when he slept.

The shocked, sad eyes of the young corpsman haunted him more than anything else he'd seen in Nam. It had been his fault. He'd called the corpsman up to tend the wounded soldier without looking for booby traps. He knew about the vicious tricks the enemy liked to play. If he'd checked first, he'd be dead instead of the captain. Or missing his arms, like the young father who'd only wanted to get home and meet his new son.

As they'd lifted the corpsman into the chopper, Jenkins, drifting and dopey on morphine, had insisted it wasn't Cam's fault. But it had been. His thoughtless haste had cost that young man his arms and the chance to hold his baby. And it would always haunt him. He didn't deserve to have sons. He didn't deserve to be alive. He could never have children. He wouldn't be able to bear the guilt.

Cam hung his head over the sink, unable to look into his own eyes anymore. He needed to pull himself together. He was expected to show up at church in an hour and for dinner at his parents' house afterward.

He'd come home from the war and his family acted like everything should be back to normal. They seemed to expect him to be as he'd always been. But he couldn't find his way back. He was a haunted, broken, emotional mess. Only one person had managed to pierce his gloom and find a remnant of the eager young man he'd once been. Sandy. And he was more afraid of dragging her down with him than he'd ever been for himself.

He should stop seeing her before things got really serious. But he didn't want to. Meeting her for breakfast felt like having the sun come out after months of rain. The despair that hung around him after a night filled with horror parted like the clouds when he saw her hurrying toward him, sassy blond curls bouncing, and her smile wide with joy. Sitting across from her, watching the excited play of emotions and thoughts flitting across her features while she talked filled him with such hope. Hope that maybe he *could* feel normal again. *One day.*

It didn't even matter what she talked about. It only mattered that she eagerly shared bits and pieces of her life with him. Telling him stories about her growing up. Sharing her enthusiasm for life. Her dreams and plans. Sandy was so full of energy and brimming with happiness. It was a lure he just couldn't resist.

Cam glanced back at the mirror and was surprised to find a smile on his face. *She's so good for me*, he thought. *If only I wasn't so bad for her.*

CHAPTER TEN

SANDY DASHED ACROSS CAMPUS, LATE AS USUAL, AND HURRIED UP THE stairs. Having breakfast with Cam had very quickly eclipsed running as the focus of her morning routine. She couldn't ever remember being so happy. Or so eager to start her day. Well, okay, admittedly, she still had a hard time rolling out of bed the first time her alarm went off. But once she'd gotten up, she couldn't wait to see Cam again.

The sight of him leaning casually against the Dining Commons railing, his blue eyes radiating pleasure took her breath away. She loved the way Cam dressed. He looked like a model in a Brooks Brothers' catalog as he lounged against the railing with his khaki clad legs crossed at the ankles. She especially loved the way his broad shoulders filled out his crisp white shirt. *I never thought dress shirts were all that sexy, but on Cam . . .* She hurried up the steps and kissed him good morning.

Cam led the way inside, then through the line loading up his tray while Sandy took the bare minimum and contemplated the best way to fix her current dilemma. Getting out early to go running had been a challenge in the first place. Now it would mean getting up before it got light. No way did she want to give up having breakfast with Cam, but she really needed to get back to running or she would soon become a blimp. Especially since Cam's idea of a reasonable breakfast included enough food for an entire platoon of Marines.

Or . . . Another possibility popped into her head as they found an empty table, sat down and began to eat. *Maybe I could get Cam to go running with me? Then again . . . Maybe not. Maybe he hates running as much as Tony.* Tony claimed that the absolute worst part of military life was the odd notion that the only way to get from point A to point B was at a dead run, preferably with someone screaming in your ear and seventy pounds of gear on your back. Tony vowed, quite vehemently, that when he got out of the Navy he would never run again, not even to catch a bus. Maybe Cam agreed.

Sandy rearranged several uneaten pieces of French toast on her plate. She watched Cam as he mopped up a lake of syrup with a half a slice of French toast folded onto the end of his fork, then brought it to his mouth. He ate like he hadn't eaten in weeks. And he ate that way every day!

"How can you consume so much food and still be so . . . so trim?" she asked with more than a touch of envy. Cam had filled out some since the first day she'd set eyes on him, and the gaunt hollowness had begun to leave his face, but he still looked amazingly fit. "Didn't they feed you in the Marines?"

"Believe it or not, bad as everyone claims this stuff is, Dining Commons food is a huge improvement over the slop we got in the chow hall. And you don't even want to know about C-rats. But, if it makes you feel any better, I can't keep on like this much longer."

"Well, I shouldn't think so."

"And not just eating like a pig, either. I've gotta stop dawdling over breakfast every morning, too." The bald statement brought Sandy's heart to a standstill.

She searched his eyes for a hint. He lived at Delta Tau. Cheaper, more independence, better digs, he had told her. And better food. He'd been breakfasting at the commons just to be with her. *Please, God, let it be the food that palled on him and not me.*

"Mind you." He winked. "I like starting the day with my own personal ray of sunshine. It's just that I haven't had a chance to get in a run since we met. I've gotten so out of shape I'd probably crap out on the first mile."

Sandy's heart began to beat again in double time. *I'm his personal ray of sunshine?* Then, "You - you *like* to run?"

"You got something against running?" Cam's blond brows bunched into a comical look of dismay.

Sandy shook her head. "Not me. It's just that . . . I thought maybe. . ." she let her words trail off.

"It's one habit I picked up in the Marines worth keeping. One of my weirder obsessions if you listen to Linc. He thinks I'm nuts." Cam rolled his eyes.

"Jeesh, Cam. You might have mentioned this *obsession* before." She tried her best to look disgruntled, but couldn't control the bubble of laughter.

"What? And scare you off?" Cam got up grinning, and gathered up their trays.

"Never happen!" Sandy grinned back. "And here I am, afraid to talk about *my obsession* with running 'cause I'm afraid you'll think I'm a tomboy or something. Natalie insists it's totally unladylike to get all hot and sweaty running around campus when I could be getting my beauty sleep. Those are her words."

Cam snorted. "You don't need extra beauty sleep."

"Thanks. I think." *I hope that's a comment about my appearance, and not disapproval of my habitual tardiness when it comes to meeting him for breakfast.*

Cam glanced at her over his shoulder. "So, you're really a runner?"

"I am."

"That's cool! The Corps got me hooked. What's your excuse?"

"Do I need one?" Sandy followed him through the crowded dinning hall.

Cam shrugged. "Nope. Don't guess you do."

"So when? When do you run, I mean?"

"Used to run before breakfast." Cam stopped in front of the row of plastic tubs next to the dining hall exit to sort the cups and plates and silverware, then tossed their trash into the barrel at the end. "But that was before I met you."

"Me, too." *Maybe this was going to work out after all.* "I was on the track team in high school, and we always ran after school, but when I got to college I didn't go out for track, and afternoons just never seemed to work out. So I run in the morning. Or I did." She made a face.

"Running wakes me up and gets my day off to a good start. Of course . . ." As they trotted down the stairs and into the warm August sunshine, she had to hurry to keep up to Cam's long strides. "Of course, lately, having breakfast with you feels like an even better way to start my day. But, I guess being in love is supposed to be like that."

Cam lurched to a halt, and Sandy tumbled into him. "Being in *what?*" He sounded appalled.

"I said . . . it's . . ." She looked up at him, her laughter evaporating. "I'm . . . I love you, Cam."

His gaze bored into hers, intensely blue and slightly stunned. She hadn't meant to blurt it out like that. "I didn't mean to tell you yet. Or maybe not at all. Not unless you said it first, but . . ." Her heart raced in panic. *Oh, God, what was he thinking?*

"I'm afraid." Cam sounded as breathless as she felt.

"Afraid?" Her whole world held its breath. "Of me?"

Cam shook his head. "Of *me*. Of whatever this is between us. It's all happened so fast. I'm not . . ." Cam stopped mid-sentence and swallowed hard.

Not what? Not in love with me? Not even thinking about loving me?

"Not what, Cam?" Her heart hammered painfully, dreading his answer.

"I . . ." He swallowed. Swallowed again, Adam's apple bobbing. "I think I'm falling in love with you, too."

"You only think?"

"I know I'm falling in love with you, but . . ."

Suddenly Sandy's chest didn't feel big enough to hold all the feelings squeezing into it. "But what?" Her throat was so tight it hurt.

Standing so close, yet not touching, the air between them hummed with tension and something more.

"Sometimes I feel like we've known each other forever. Then, I'm afraid I'll wake up one morning and find out you were only a dream," he said quietly, his face taut with some emotion she didn't understand.

She slid her arms about his waist and hugged him hard. "I'm not a dream, Cam. I'm real. I know it's been kind of fast and all, but . . ."

As Cam's arms closed around her, the stack of books he'd been carrying tumbled carelessly onto the gravel pathway. Her world spun in dizzy circles.

She stared up into the endless blue of Cam's eyes, and waited for him to kiss her. When he did, she opened her mouth immediately, wanting to drink him in and make him part of herself. Stars exploded, and she couldn't seem to breathe, but it was wonderful. She was right where she wanted to be. Held so close she could feel the lean hardness of him even through the layers of clothing that separated them.

A blinding rush of inexpressible yearning blotted out their surroundings. Sandy abandoned herself completely to the whirling, consuming thing that made every nerve ending in her body feel like it was on fire. She ached. She felt weightless. She felt . . .

Abruptly, Cam thrust her away and held her at arms' length. She gaped at him in surprise, gasping to catch her breath. "Wow! That was better than fireworks."

The fingers Cam shoved through his bristling hair trembled. "I'm sorry. I forgot where we were." His voice didn't sound any steadier than his hand.

"I kinda like it when you forget." Sandy's voice sounded husky and not like her own. She was as shaken as Cam looked, but she didn't care if the whole world watched. She snaked one arm about his neck and tried to pull his mouth back down to hers. Someone whistled suggestively.

"Sandy, please," Cam whispered in urgent agitation. "What will people think?" He blushed.

Astonished at the flood of dull red rushing up under Cam's tan and into his sun-bleached hair, Sandy released him. He stooped to gather up the forgotten books, then took her hand and dragged her down the path, away from the crowded Dining Commons walkway. Sandy took a dozen skipping steps to keep up.

Cam always seemed so self-confident, so unruffled, even when idiots like Bud Wilson taunted him about having fought in Vietnam. This new aspect of Cam's personality unnerved her. The pink ears and the sudden diffidence were so unlike the man she thought she knew.

"Do you care so much what people think?"

"I don't know." Cam appeared to think about it. "Yeah, I guess I do. Besides, that's not the way I was brought up to treat a lady. Especially not one I care about."

Sandy's heart skipped a beat. "I'm honored you care enough to consider my reputation, Cam, but this is the seventies. It's not like when the nuns used to brainwash us about sex and sin when we were in high school. It's all about love-ins and 'if it feels good, do it.' Nobody much minds what we do as long as we don't hurt anyone else while we're doing it."

Cam looked at her sternly for a long moment before responding. "I mind."

"But everybody I know . . ."

"I'm not everybody you know." Cam's face settled in uncompromising lines that gave Sandy an uncomfortable feeling in the pit of her stomach.

"That's why I love you, Cam. Because you *aren't* like anybody else. Except . . ."

"Do you *like* me?" The question pierced her with its ferocity.

"Of course, I like you." *You think I kiss just anyone like that?*

"Just the way I am? Without trying to make me into somebody I'm not?"

The intensity in Cam's eyes and voice began to feel more than a little scary. "Of course I like you just the way you are. How could I love you this much if I didn't like you?" Her voice trembled.

Cam reached for her and pulled her back into his arms, pressing her face into the warmth of his chest. One big hand caressed the back of her neck.

"I'm sorry, Sandy. I didn't mean . . . I'm being a jerk, and I'm sorry." He swallowed, and she felt the effort. "It's just that what I feel for you isn't . . . " He swallowed again. "I'm not just trying to score with the prettiest girl on campus or angling to get you into my bed. What I feel for you is special."

He thinks I'm the prettiest girl on campus. And special. This time, Sandy's heart missed several beats. *Special enough for a forever relationship? I know I'm falling in love with you.* But his voice had wavered on the word special, and Sandy sensed doubt in him. What they had *was* special. She had known it from the very first. But her certainty didn't leave room for doubt, so she didn't understand his. What exactly did he mean by special?

Sandy gave Cam a quick, hard hug, then stepped out of his arms. Maybe he just needed to learn to relax a little, and go with the flow.

"What if I want to be angled into your bed?" She struck what she hoped was a provocative pose.

Cam gulped and didn't quite manage to keep a flash of desire from darting into his eyes. "You don't mean that," he said after a pause.

Sandy hesitated. She'd been kidding. Hadn't she? Yet the look in his eyes, so quickly hidden, had started something buzzing inside her.

She liked to think of herself as a liberated woman. Not a bead-wearing, pot-smoking hippy, of course, but free of the stifling morality her parents' generation had preached. Free to express her love with everything she had to give a man. Not that she would tumble into bed with just anyone. In fact, she had never wanted to before now.

But with Cam . . . Her heart zipped into overdrive, and her breathing became decidedly odd.

Maybe she hadn't been kidding.

Except that Cam still stared at her with a dampening mixture of disbelief and reproof. Finally, her gaze dropped from his. "No, I guess not," she mumbled, confusion and uncertainty edging out sexual excitement.

"Sandy?" Cam lifted her face with a knuckle beneath her chin. "It's not because I don't want to. Or because I don't find you attractive. Quite the opposite."

She tried to nod, but Cam held her chin firm. "Then, why, Cam?"

"IT'S . . ." Cam sighed heavily. He didn't know how to put his feelings into words. He was acting like a freaking choirboy, but he had reasons. Reasons that had nothing to do with wanting her or not.

Classes had begun and the paths crisscrossing campus were deserted. Though his eyes were intent on Sandy's face, he was aware of the emptiness around them. He could kiss her now with all the hunger he had in him without tarnishing her reputation or his own.

Except that kissing her wouldn't be enough. Not nearly enough.

"Let's play hooky." Sandy suggested unexpectedly.

His heart leapt, eager yet alarmed. "And do what?"

Sandy grinned at him mischievously. She hadn't forced him to explain why he didn't want to take her to bed, but she had something else in mind. Alarm bells went off in his brain.

"And go running. We can pack a picnic and take it to my special beach up in Tide's Way. We can run 'til we drop, then eat until we're stuffed."

Cam glanced past her at the vacant campus. The beach would be just as deserted, but if he ran himself into the ground, maybe he could kill this raging ache in his groin and get control of the situation again. He wanted to spend every free minute with Sandy, he just didn't want to sleep with her. Or rather, he did want to. He wanted to make love to her with an intensity that grew more difficult to fight every time they were together, but no way he could let himself give in to that temptation. Sandy wasn't the kind of girl who slept around no matter what she said about love-ins. She'd expect some kind of commitment . . . the kind of commitment he didn't know if he'd ever be ready for.

"Please, Cam? Let's do it? It'll be fun. I've never played hooky before."

"O--kay," he agreed, reluctantly. She looked so eager and so unutterably appealing. How could he say no?

CHAPTER ELEVEN

A stitch caught in Sandy's side as she struggled to keep up with Cam. She had never run in soft sand before, and it was harder than she had thought. Her calves burned, and her lungs were ready to explode. Cam made it look like a walk in the park, and she suspected he was taking it easy, letting her keep up. If he wanted to, she'd be eating his dust, no doubt.

Finally, they made it around the point, and onto hard-packed sand where ocean waves ran boisterously up Anchor Beach. Pride be damned! Sandy gave up, detoured back to dry sand and dropped onto her hands and knees, clutching her now aching side. When she could breath again without gasping, she rolled onto her back and smiled up at Cam.

"Hey Marine, you didn't crap out after all."

"So, I exaggerated." He stood, bent at the waist, hands on his knees, head lifted to look at her. His shirt was damp with sweat, but he gave no other sign of having run hard. He smiled slightly, then sank gracefully onto the sand at her side, drew his knees up to his chest and gazed out at the sea.

Sandy watched the breeze tug at the fabric of Cam's t-shirt and admired the muscles outlined beneath the damp patches that clung to his body. *I wonder how those muscles look without the shirt? I wonder what it would feel like if I didn't have a shirt on either? And he pulled me into his arms until my breasts pressed against that hard muscled chest? And his calloused hands skimmed all over my bare skin?* God, she was breathless all over again!

Cam twisted to look at her over his shoulder. He was grinning. "Loser has to go back for the lunch."

Heat rushed into her cheeks and she sat up in a hurry, glad Cam couldn't read her mind. "Winner - goes," she countered, unable to disguise the catch in her voice.

"Still winded? I thought you said you were a runner?" He got to his feet and reached a hand down to her. "Sorry, I'm teasing. That was a tough run. How about we both go?"

Sandy put her hand in his and let him pull her to her feet. They followed a path that led back through the dunes and past the old anchor that gave the beach its name, ending where they had parked Linc's battered old Rambler. Cam dug a blanket out of the trunk and leaned in the rear window to grab a large paper sack with the Code Seven logo on the side.

Sandy led the way back to the beach tapping the anchor on her way by. "It's supposed to bring good luck," she explained over her shoulder.

Cam juggled the bag and blanket and tapped the anchor, copying her. "Whatever," he muttered. "I think you bring your own brand of luck wherever you go." He winked at her.

I'm not sure how to take that," Sandy replied skipping a step. Was he talking about her personally or luck in general?

Cam shrugged, apparently not planning to elaborate and they walked back onto the beach in companionable silence. Cam spread the blanket out and invited her to join him.

"Linc sure knows how to pack a good lunch," Sandy observed as she began removing the contents of the paper sack and arranging them on the blanket.

"What makes you think Linc packed this stuff?"

"You did?" Sandy looked up at Cam in surprise. She looked at the logo on the bag, then back at Cam.

"Well, I didn't actually make it," Cam admitted. "I just cadged it off Linc's short order cook."

Sandy laughed, then asked, "So, what will you have, Mr. Mooch? The fried chicken or a tuna salad sandwich?"

For a while, they sat munching hungrily, gazing out over the blue water and rolling waves. She felt happy and carefree and very content. She wished she could spend the whole day every day with Cam. It didn't really matter what they did, just being with him made life seem perfect. She couldn't recall ever having this feeling of ease with a man before. Of not having to make small talk. As if they were just good friends.

I wonder if Cam will ever think of me as a friend? A real friend, not just a girlfriend? Sandy suddenly remembered the pointed question Cam had asked her that morning. *Do you like me? Just the way I am?*

Of course she liked him. Admittedly, she still had a lot to learn about him. And in spite of her babbling on over breakfast every day, he still didn't know everything about her either. Perhaps friendship takes time. More time than falling in love. Friendship, she reflected as she considered her relationship with Natalie, meant knowing a person really well, understanding what made them tick and loving them in spite of, or perhaps because of, the imperfections. That was ground she and Cam hadn't explored yet. They'd been too busy falling in love in the short time since they'd met.

She turned to watch Cam as he gazed at the ocean while he devoured his sandwich. His eyes squinted slightly against the glare, as if he were searching for something. She wondered what he was thinking about.

He'd grown up in the area, yet didn't seem to be nearly as in love with the sea as she. Or maybe that was just familiarity. She wondered suddenly if he enjoyed living close to the ocean or if he'd be anxious to be off. To the city, perhaps? Or someplace a long way inland?

As she folded the waxed paper from her chickenand tucked it back into the bag, Cam turned his head and winked at her. Her heart did its little jig of pleasure at the already familiar gesture.

"A penny for your thoughts?" Cam touched the back of her hand lightly with his fingertips before reaching for a second sandwich.

There were a thousand things they didn't know about each other yet. Maybe where they wanted to live after graduation would be a good place to start.

"I'd like to live close to the beach after I graduate. In a little out of the way place just like this. A place where kids could grow up safe and have fun at the same time. I love the idea of having a big family, too. How about you?"

Cam finished chewing, then swallowed. "Well, I already have more than enough in the way of family, but I think I'd enjoy living somewhere near the ocean. I always have and it would seem strange not to."

"I meant I'd like a house full of children. My own children, not just nieces and nephews and cousins. Although, I'd enjoy those, too."

Cam glanced at her, his eyes bluer than usual and with an oddly penetrating expression in them. "What, no husband?"

"Of course, a husband." The blue eyes grew more intense. "A husband *and* children." The thought of Cam in the roll of husband and father gave her a warm fuzzy feeling. A warm feeling that suddenly became more intense. She lowered her gaze to the blanket between her feet. If she returned that discerning blue stare, he might see the longing in her eyes. He would know she meant him.

"What if your husband isn't so eager to fill this house by the beach with kids?"

Sandy's gaze jerked back to his in surprise. His question caught her like a punch to the solar plexus. She had never considered the possibility that Cam wouldn't want children. Was he talking about himself? Or just asking in general terms? She was crazy in love with this man, but if he didn't want children . . . She swallowed hard. What an impossible decision, to choose between the man she loved and the house full of children she'd always dreamed about. "I guess we'd have to talk about it, then." She hesitated. "How about you, Cam? Do you like children?"

"Of course I like kids."

"But do you want to have children of your own?"

Cam rolled one shoulder in a vague non-answer. "So tell me more about this house near the sea."

Why the reluctance to answer her question about children? She searched his face, looking for a hint, but he returned her gaze with an unreadable expression. Maybe he'd just gotten used to being a carefree bachelor and hadn't really given much thought to having a family. Sandy filed it away for a later conversation and answered his question.

"Not a huge house. Just one big enough for . . . Well, big enough for however many would be living in it. But I want it to be near the beach. I love walking on the beach."

"So I've noticed." Cam winked again.

"Don't you like the beach?"

"I like it fine when I'm with you. But I'd like a place to keep a boat." He finished his sandwich and brushed his hands against his shorts.

"What kind of boat? A motor boat or a sailboat?" Now they were getting somewhere. Cam liked boats.

Cam pulled the top of a bag of potato chips open and offered it to her. "Maybe both?"

Sandy raised her brows and took a handful of chips. "Both?" Really liked boats, it would seem.

"Well, I know I like to fish, but I'd think I'd like to learn how to sail, too."

"Haven't you ever been sailing?"

For a moment, Cam didn't answer. He returned his gaze to the bay. "Only once."

"And?" Sandy prompted.

"I got to know a guy in Nam . . ." Cam's voice sounded oddly hushed. "An old man who had a strange little boat with a sail. One evening he took me out in it. He had a couple fish lines out, and we seemed to slip through the water so easy, like a shark on the hunt. When the sun set everything turned orange, then purple until finally there was no color at all. It's the most peaceful feeling I ever remember." Cam shook his head and glanced at her with an attempt at a smile. "Seems hard to believe such a peaceful place could exist in a hell hole like Nam. Huh?"

Sandy returned his serious, introspective gaze. Cam reached across the blanket and took her hand in his. Then he tugged her closer. She scooted across the blanket and rested her head against his shoulder.

She didn't think anyplace on earth could have been more peaceful than right where she sat at this very moment, but his description conjured up a whole new picture of Vietnam. Far different from anything she'd imagined or seen on television.

"What was it like?" She dared to ask, speaking softly, trying not to break the mood.

"What was what like?"

"Vietnam."

Again, Cam paused. His hand tightened on hers, and he didn't answer right off. He upended the nearly empty bag of potato chips into his mouth and chewed thoughtfully. Then he finished off his can of soda.

"Vietnam was hot. You would not believe how hot it could get," he finally began in an abruptly breezy tone. "The tarmac at the airport got so hot I think you could have cooked eggs on it. Your clothes were almost always soaked with sweat and it felt good to get wet when it rained. Unless we were out in the bush, most of the places I spent any time in were noisy, crowded and dirty. Probably why it seemed so incredibly peaceful in a tidy little boat that made almost no noise, with a man who didn't talk because he knew only a few words of English, and I knew even less Vietnamese. And we were far away from . . ."

This time when he stopped talking, Sandy knew he wouldn't finish what he had been about to say. Sadness had come into his voice, and he'd broken off sounding almost gruff. Tony hadn't liked to talk about the things that made him prowl about the house in the night and gave him nightmares either. Was it an attempt to shield their women from what they had lived through? Or a macho thing? A man's way of pretending he could take all the mayhem war could dish out?

"Anyway, that's why I'd like to learn how to sail." Cam pulled her hand into his lap and laced his fingers through hers. "How about you? Isn't there something you'd like to try that you've never done before?" The introspective tone had left his voice, abruptly shutting her out. For those few minutes while he talked about Vietnam, it had been like she was peering into his soul. Seeing the vulnerable man beneath the cool exterior. But then he'd closed a door on her.

"Cat got your tongue?" Cam elbowed her teasingly.

"No. I was just thinking." Sandy lifted her head from his shoulder to look at him. She wanted to ask him what the war itself had been like, but she knew he wouldn't tell her. At least not right now. "I think it might be fun to hike the Appalachian Trail. Not just parts of it, but the whole thing."

"Well, that's probably a lot more likely than learning to sail. It'll be awhile before I can afford a boat. You going to drink the rest of that soda?"

Sandy handed him her can. She wasn't much of a soda drinker anyway. "There's a boat club across on the mainland not far from the bridge. They race a couple times a week. Maybe you could find someone who needs a crew who'd be willing to take you on and teach you the ropes."

"I saw it on our way out here." Cam tossed the second empty can toward the edge of the blanket, then flopped onto his back. "Funny, it's been there all my life, and I never even thought about sailing before." He laced his hands behind his head.

"I think they race on Wednesday evenings and on the weekends. Sunday afternoons, I think. One of the girls in my dorm comes up every chance she gets. She's dating a guy who lives somewhere near here." Sandy shoved the rest of her chicken back into the bag, then laid down next to Cam. She turned on her side and put one arm across his chest. "Maybe we could learn together?"

"Maybe. It's an idea anyway." Cam closed his eyes.

Sandy settled her head on his shoulder and began tracing the anchor printed on his shirt with one finger. "Cam?"

"Umm?"

"You could kiss me now. There's no one here but us and the seagulls."

Cam's blue eyes popped open again. "I could, couldn't I?"

Sandy held her breath, waiting for him to put words into action. His eyes were a brilliant electric blue. *Must be the sea and the sky together that makes them that color. I love his eyes. I wish he'd kiss me.*

He rolled onto his side and brought one hand down to cradle her face. "I wouldn't want to take advantage of a lady."

"Don't think of me as a lady. Think of me as a woman."

The piercing blue gaze flickered down to her bosom then back to her face. "It's a little hard to think of you as anything else."

The heat that flooded over her had more to do with her sudden awareness of the fact that he'd become aroused, than the intensity of his bright blue eyes. "Think of . . . me as . . . a woman who loves you." She strained to bring her mouth closer to his.

"A very desirable one." The huskiness in his voice only added to the excitement building inside her. Just before his lips finally met hers, she wondered fleetingly if a woman's desire showed as obviously as a man's.

His mouth tasted sweet and cool from the soda. His tongue teased her lips apart. Sandy arched into him, giving herself up the swirling exhilaration of his closeness. The unmistakable evidence of his desire pressed into her belly. Her breasts tingled, and a pulsing fist of heat began to grow in her groin.

As Cam's hand roved over her back, pulling her closer, Sandy sighed with pleasure. Her insides felt like a river of fire. She slid her hand under his t-shirt, felt the warm, hard muscles of his chest. She wished he'd put his hands under her shirt, too. Wished he didn't have such an antiquated idea of how a gentleman should behave. She reached behind her and groped for his hand. Hesitated a moment. Maybe she shouldn't.

Then she grabbed his hand and dragged it around to her front. Felt the heat of it burn through her shirt for a delicious fleeting moment.

Cam flung himself onto his back. He brought his forearm up to cover his eyes. "Jeezus, Sandy, what are you playing at?" He was breathing harder than he had at the end of their run.

"I wasn't playing."

"Yeah, you were," he contradicted softly. He peered at her from under his arm. She couldn't tell if he was angry or embarrassed. A niggling puddle of apprehension settled into her stomach. Heat flooded her cheeks.

He took his arm away from his eyes. "Sorry. I didn't mean to embarrass you. It was my fault, too."

"You're not turned off?"

"Jesus, no! What gave you that idea?" His eyes widened.

"But, I love you, and . . ."

"Well, I love you, too." He reached for her hand, brought it to his mouth and kissed her knuckles. "Except I'm trying to behave myself. I'm trying to remember that you're special, and I want to keep it that way. But I'm only a man, Sandy. Not a saint."

"I don't think I would love a saint."

He laughed then, and the knot of tension in her unwound. "Good thing for me, then, isn't it? I'm a long way from being a saint."

Sandy gazed at Cam, studying the handsome face drawn taut with determination. He closed his eyes again, and his thick blond lashes fell against his cheeks making him look years younger. She reached up and trailed her finger over his cheekbone. "I've never loved anyone this way before."

"What way is that?"

"I mean . . . no one ever made me feel the way you make me feel." She let the back of her finger slip down over the stubble on his cheeks, entranced by the way the sunlight caught in his beard like golden specks of water.

"Nice to know . . ." his voice faded off.

Sandy studied him for a while longer, then stretched up and kissed him lightly on the lips. He didn't kiss her back.

"Cam?"

She kissed him again.

"Cam?"

His breathing had changed. His chest rose and fell with the gentle regularity of sleep. His face was completely relaxed, and the boyishness became even more pronounced. He must have been really tired to fall asleep so quickly and easily.

A little disappointed, Sandy curled up next to him and put her head on his shoulder. Then spent several minutes wondering what it would be like to wake up every morning and watch Cam while he still slept? And know she could reach out and touch him any time she wanted? And he would be free to respond?

The last of the afternoon sunlight faded into evening as Cam slept. Sandy watched the sun go down, then noticed the first creeping fingers of chilly night air. Cam slept on. She shivered. Reluctant to wake him, knowing he'd probably be on his feet in a heartbeat and ready to return her to the dorm immediately if she did. She reached for the edges of the blanket and drew its soft warmth up around them. She settled closer drawing his free arm across her waist. A nap on the beach with the sound of Cam's heart beating in her ear would be so perfect. She could pretend for a little while longer.

CHAPTER TWELVE

"JEEZUS!" CAM SCRAMBLED TO HIS FEET. "WHAT TIME IS IT?"

Jerked awake by Cam's abrupt departure from the cocoon of blanket and the resultant rush of cold air Sandy blinked and sat up, gazing groggily around at the night-dark beach.

She felt oddly excited and very disoriented. She peered at her watch in the dim light of a very new moon. "A quarter after ten, I think."

"Shit!" Cam cussed loudly, then muttered something else she couldn't make out under his breath. It didn't sound very complimentary, and he seemed to be directing it toward himself. He began gathering up the discarded soda cans and cramming them into the bag. "Sorry for the lousy language. I've gotta get you home before curfew, and it's gonna be close."

Sandy's muscles felt stiff and cramped, but the rest of her buzzed with inexplicable expectancy. She must have been dreaming something really pleasant, but for the life of her, she couldn't recall even a snatch of it with Cam's simmering impatience distracting her. Reluctantly, she got to her feet and began folding the blanket.

Cam grabbed it out of her hands and tossed it over his shoulder. "C'mon."

He hurried toward the car, leaving her to follow. Confused by Cam's anxious haste and uncharacteristic cussing, Sandy stumbled after him. What had gotten into the man? He flung the picnic stuff in the back seat and opened her door for her, then hurried around to the driver's side of the car.

All remnants of the eager excitement she'd woken with were gone. Blown away by Cam's strange behavior. "Did I do something wrong?"

Cam put the car in gear. It lurched into reverse. "Of course not." He glanced briefly in her direction before returning his gaze to the road and slamming the car into first.

"Then, what's the problem?"

He hunched forward in his seat, both hands clenched on the wheel. "No problem. It's just that you're going to be late."

"I'm not Cinderella, Cam. Nothing will happen to me if I don't get home before they lock the door."

He glanced at her again, his mouth set in a harsh line. "It wouldn't look good."

"We're back to that, I see," she snapped, impatient with his excessive concern about what other people thought and hurt by his lack of concern for how she felt.

Cam drove in grim silence.

"Come on Cam. No one is going to think any less of me because I get back a little late. Half the dorm comes in late, for Pete's sake. It's summer still, and the curfew is a joke. And it's not like we were doing anything wrong, anyway."

Cam grunted, but didn't reply.

A HALF HOUR LATER, he still hadn't said anything. What could he say? It's not like he could apologize for something she hopefully didn't know about, and he wasn't about to enlighten her if he were that lucky. He pulled to the curb in front of her dorm. If he looked at her, he'd see a hurt look on her face.

"I wish you'd tell me what's wrong." The hurt was in her voice instead.

He stared through the windshield. "Nothing's wrong." *Nothing I know how to fix.*

"It sure doesn't feel like nothing's wrong."

"It's just late is all."

"Aren't you even going to kiss me goodnight?"

He couldn't avoid looking at her any longer. When he turned, her eyes looked just as hurt and confused as he'd known they would. His heart ached at the distress he was causing her, but he didn't know what else to do. He wanted to haul her into his arms and kiss her until the hurt look left, but he didn't dare touch her right now, because it wouldn't stop there. He gave her a rueful smile.

"Sorry. I'm being a jerk again, aren't I?" Careful not to touch anything else, he leaned toward her and touched her lips briefly with his own. "Better hurry. Your housemother's getting ready to lock the door." He reached past her and opened the car door.

"Will I see you for breakfast?" Sandy asked as she climbed out of the car. "Same time? Same station?" She rested her hands on the open window of the car door and searched his face for some explanation of his sudden, inexplicable withdrawal.

"Wouldn't miss it for anything." For a long moment, Cam stared at her from the gloom of the darkened car. Then he reached across the seat and put his hand over hers. "Thanks for . . . for a really fun day."

"Yeah, it was fun."

CAM TOOK his hand away and turned the key. As the engine roared to life, Sandy stepped back onto the curb, then watched until the tail lights disappeared. *This morning he tells me he loves me, and now he barely even talks to me. What has gotten into him?*

Hours later, tossing restlessly, and unable to sleep, Sandy was still asking herself questions for which she had no answers. *What did I do wrong? Why had Cam become so remote? Did I say something? Do something?*

He wouldn't even have kissed me goodnight if I hadn't begged like a pathetic loser.

Sandy replayed the entire afternoon in her head, looking for a clue. She thought about their conversation. Maybe she'd made him uncomfortable talking about husbands and children. The piercing look he'd given her had been unreadable, but he hadn't seemed angry. Maybe when he'd voluntarily shared his sailing experience, she had been too pushy, asking him about Vietnam? She had sensed his reluctance and stopped asking more questions. But not, now that she considered it, before he'd already shut her out by changing the subject.

But, he hadn't seemed angry with her then, either. Before he'd fallen asleep, they'd snuggled for a while, and he'd been truly turned on. She knew that for a fact because his running shorts hadn't done much to hide the evidence. He had accused her of playing games with him, and she assumed he meant teasing, but she hadn't meant to tease. Besides, they had been laughing over some nonsense about Cam not being a saint after that, so that couldn't be why he behaved so oddly when they woke up hours later.

A well of despair seemed to open inside her, filled with an aching sense of rejection. With breakfast still hours away, she felt sick with uncertainty. Tears came finally. Slow, smarting tears that soaked her pillow and made her eyes ache.

Please God, let it just be a misunderstanding. Please let everything be right again in the morning.

CAM STARED up into the darkness of his room. Outside, he could hear an occasional voice, muted and far away. It was late, but he could still hear activity in the house. Other Delts coming in late, making arrangements for the morning, using the john, the clink of empty beer bottles being collected, television muttering in the background. Same as every night. Yet, nothing was the same.

He wasn't the same.

A month ago he hadn't even known Sandy existed. Now he couldn't think about anything else. It had all happened so fast. Breakfast every morning. Studying at the library. Watching the Red Sox on television. Dating whenever they could. Calling her on the phone just to hear her voice. Sandy had given him a reason for living again, but the word love had never entered his mind until today.

Yet it had been there, else it never would have popped out of his mouth with such ease, because it wasn't a word he used lightly. In fact, he had never told a girl he loved her before. Not even when he'd been a hormone driven teenager with the same steady girlfriend for his entire senior year.

And what happened to not getting serious? This isn't fair to Sandy. I can't help loving her, but I can't be what she wants me to be either.

Cam closed his eyes, and a collage of images chased each other through his mind: Sandy's hazel eyes, sparkling with happy tears when he reluctantly admitted that he loved her. Her flushed face with a sun-lightened curl of hair escaping from a garishly colored sweatband at the end of their run. The gentle look of empathy when he told her anything about Vietnam. The impish grin that turned her mouth up at the corners when she teased him. The way her eyes darkened with desire when he kissed her.

Damn, he had a hard-on just thinking about her. He flung himself onto his stomach, disgusted and disappointed with himself. He had believed he could control his lust. Sandy had no idea what she did to him. She was so pure and so wholesome. So trusting. None of this was her fault. It was his, and short of not seeing her any more, he didn't know what to do about it.

He realized now that thinking he could keep his hunger for her in check had been a foolish conceit. A fiction that had been shattered when he'd woken in the dark to discover that what had seemed like an erotic dream was appallingly real.

A tantalizing fantasy of Sandy nestled in the crook of his arm, sighing with pleasure while he fondled her breasts. Beautiful breasts that fit his palm perfectly with their ripe warmth.

Then he'd woken abruptly. Sober, shocked and very aroused. His hand shoved up under Sandy's shirt and somehow inside her bra, cupped around her breast. Her nipple hard and erect against his palm. Almost as hard and erect as his dick. He'd violated her unguarded trust in him.

Then, though she had done nothing to deserve it, he'd been unforgivably rude to her on the way to the car and heartlessly silent most of the way home. He had barely kissed her goodnight. And the wounded look of confusion on her face when he had just about kicked her out of the car haunted him more than all his other transgressions. Tomorrow he would have to apologize and find a way to explain.

But how could he explain his outrageous behavior? And, even if he could, then what?

Sandy made it sound so simple. She loved him. And that meant offering him everything she had to give: mind, body and soul. Especially her body. She hadn't said a word about commitment, but it went without saying. Cam wasn't a virgin, but Sandy surely was, and he suspected that if she gave herself to him she meant it forever.

He rolled onto his stomach and for a disorienting moment, had a flashback to Nam. Back to a grungy poncho liner and a willing young Vietnamese woman named Thuy lying pliant and naked beneath him. God help him, he hadn't thought about Thuy in months.

In the quagmire of mud and strife of Vietnam, he had fought valiantly against the temptations of the flesh his parish priest had so persuasively warned him to avoid. Cam had been saving his soul from eternal damnation. Death was too close and too quick to take chances. He'd tried not to even think impure thoughts and had suffered a good deal of ribbing from his fellow officers for his restraint.

Until the night he found Thuy in his bed. Too surprised and too tired to resist, his surrender had come easily. He'd never been with a woman until that night and entering her had been like sliding into a whirlpool. He hadn't had time or the wits to think about the sin he was committing. Or who had set him up.

The following day Thuy had moved into his hooch without asking permission. Not that she would have understood if she had asked and he had tried to explain why not. Her name, he had found later, meant lotus, and she had been as bright and durable as the flower she had been named for. She had cleaned his clothes and shared his food. And she had given him her body. Unholy moments of desperate forgetfulness in the midst of hell. She had asked for so little in return.

For those few short weeks they had needed each other, but he had not loved her. And Thuy had not loved him.

Sandy did.

Why such an angel should have picked him of all the men who

swarmed around her to fall in love with was a mystery he would never understand. An expectation he could never live up to.

Although she hadn't shared it with him, he suspected she might be involved with the anti-war movement, which made her attraction to him even more inexplicable. Sandy was an innocent in so many ways. Except for her brother's MIA status, she was untouched by the unending nightmare. She couldn't begin to know how horrendous it really was. She didn't know about the hopelessness and the rage. Or the dark side of men. The dark side of him.

Sandy had fallen in love with the man Cam pretended to be and wished he still was. The man he so desperately wanted to be again. She couldn't know, nor understand, the black things that curled themselves around his soul. The guilt and the regrets. The things that woke him in the middle of the night in a cold sweat. Things Thuy had been born knowing.

Thuy's dark eyes had reflected the pain and terror that crippled his own heart. They were gentle, almond eyes filled with the resignation of generations. Eyes that had seen too much and suffered more. Thuy hadn't loved him, but she had understood.

Sandy never would.

Sandy believed in happily ever after. Something Cam didn't know if he was capable of anymore. She needed him free of the demons that haunted him. Free of the darkness that sometimes overwhelmed him with hate and self-loathing. She needed a man who could give her life. She needed a man with an untroubled soul and a whole heart.

He had only his love to offer and even that was flawed.

Now that he had admitted it to her and, more importantly, to himself, the intensity of that love scared the crap out of him. Her enthusiasm and passion renewed him, made him feel things he hadn't thought he would ever feel again, but the fiery sexual heat that threatened to burst into a full-blown conflagration scared him even more.

Her fresh and honest sexuality, and her obvious desire to explore it with him made his own raw need hard to fight. Lust burned in his gut, and it would be so easy to give in to the heady passion she provoked. Too goddam easy! But, making love to Sandy would mean marrying her, and marriage terrified him. The intimacy of it terrified him. He wouldn't be able to hide from her or from himself. He wouldn't be able to pretend that everything was fine. Or give her the one thing her heart desired most. Kids! A house full of them!

But God help him. He desperately wanted to go on seeing her. Her zest for life had begun to restore his sense of purpose and enjoyment. Cam buried his face in his pillow. Maybe it would have been better if they had never met. *God, help me. I love her, but I'm afraid I'm going to end up hurting her. Please, God, what am I meant to do?*

CAM OPENED eyes that felt as if they were lined with sandpaper. Rain pelted against his window and ran down in thick twists, collecting on the sashes, splashing onto the sill. A good day to sleep in, he thought groggily. Good thing it was Saturday.

Abruptly, he rolled onto his elbow, and peered at the alarm clock. Nine fifteen. And it wasn't Saturday. It was Friday. *Holy shit!* He leapt from the bed and snatched his slacks off the back of his desk chair. He'd missed his class. And he hadn't been at the dining commons waiting for Sandy like he'd promised, either. *Wouldn't miss if for anything! Right!*

Cam thrust one leg into his pants, hopped about on one foot, caught his balance and then got the other leg in. He pictured the disappointment on her face when she dashed up the walk, peering from beneath the brim of her ridiculous yellow sou'wester and didn't see him waiting. He pulled a clean shirt off a hanger and put it on. He could see her, huddled beneath the meager overhang, watching for him, waiting for him, trying to keep her smile in place as she began to realize he wasn't coming.

Grabbing his old leather jacket off a row of hooks, Cam made for the door.

"Want an umbrella?" Jack, a fellow Delt, looked up from the book in his lap as Cam rushed through the common room. "It's raining cats and dogs."

"I won't melt, but thanks anyway." Cam waved over his shoulder and plunged out into the rain.

By the time he got to the library, rain had plastered his hair to the top of his skull and soaked his pants and shoes. He dashed up the stairs and squelched his way to the back corner where he and Sandy usually holed up to study after their classes. No Sandy. Hastily, he canvassed the rest of the rambling structure, but saw no sign of her anywhere. He had been positive she would be here. Waiting for him with a pouting look of disappointment, but still willing to forgive his absence at breakfast. Maybe even willing to forgive his rude behavior last night.

Cam asked the librarian. The woman was apologetic, but she couldn't remember if she had seen Sandy that morning or not.

She's angry with me about last night. That has to be it. I certainly gave her plenty of reason to be angry. I've gotta find her and apologize.

Cam descended the wide granite steps with a grim sense of purpose, oblivious of the continuing downpour. He began a methodical search of the campus. On his way to Sandy's dorm, he detoured through the student union, but didn't see her in the lounge, the book-store or in any of the booths in the coffee shop. Not at the convenience store between the student union and her dorm, either. Or at her dorm.

Every place he looked and didn't find her, his desperation grew. Where was she? Please don't let her be that upset with him. His heart ached with growing apprehension.

Cam hurried uptown to the Cup of Joe. Sandy thrived on coffee. Cup of Joe was her favorite. The place was deserted with the exception of two uniformed policemen perched on stools eating donuts while they flirted with the waitress.

Having exhausted every possibility he could think of, Cam wandered aimlessly back over the campus. It seemed like every place he looked there was a sparkling memory of Sandy to taunt him, but no sign of the woman herself. His leather jacket was no longer keeping him dry, and he began to shiver.

Was I so unforgivably insensitive that she's avoiding me? Well, if that's the case, I brought it on myself. I hurt her, and I knew I was doing it. What the hell did I expect? His heart felt like it was in a vice.

Is this your answer, God? Is our relationship meant to end like this? Were Sandy and I never supposed to meet or fall in love in the first place? Maybe my boorish behavior last night cured her of what might have only been an infatuation on her part.

Cam jammed his hands into his pants pockets and hunched his shoulders against the pelting rain.

She's better off without me. She's a beautiful, spirited, loving woman who deserves a whole lot better than an emotional cripple with so many hang-ups that I can't even get past worrying about what people will think if I kiss her in public. Never mind sleeping with her. I'm such a loser. I've managed to fuck up the best thing that ever came my way.

Cam shivered violently. His teeth chattered, his eyes ached, and he couldn't recall ever being so miserable. Not even in Vietnam. He stared up into the rain feeling the loss like a blow. Feeling like his heart was breaking. The rain continued to pour. Fat cold drops that quickly numbed his cheeks, but couldn't numb the ache inside his chest.

CHAPTER THIRTEEN

SANDY RAISED HER HAND TO KNOCK ON THE HEAVY OAK DOOR, THEN lowered it again. With a pang of doubt, she stood back and gazed up at the once grand façade. Light from several windows spilled out into the night illuminating the elaborate old-fashioned trim, but not the faded and peeling paint. Delta Tau Delta looked like most of the old fraternity houses. Noble and neglected.

But inside, she knew, it would be warm and comfortable. A haven full of masculine pride that had nothing to do with cracked windows and deteriorating woodwork, and everything to do with the camaraderie and tradition of an all male establishment.

Misgiving clutched at her heart. *Cam might not want me here. He didn't come looking for me so maybe he doesn't even want to see me, any more. What if he's angry I've come? Maybe I shouldn't have come. But, he told me he loved me, and he couldn't have been lying. Cam doesn't lie.*

During the walk across campus, she had practiced her apology. The whole misunderstanding was all her fault, and she needed to apologize. Maybe there was still hope.

Only now that she had arrived, she began to think that coming to his frat house to confront him wasn't the smartest idea she'd ever come up with. Maybe she should go home and try calling. But what if he wouldn't come to the phone? Maybe, she should at least try calling first. She turned to leave.

Abruptly, the door opened behind her, and a shaft of brilliant yellow light caught her in its glow. She halted, one foot on the top step, and glanced over her shoulder. An enormous man with shaggy brown hair stepped out onto the porch. Taller than Cam and made to look even taller by the tight cut of his black bell-bottom jeans. He grinned, and his teeth gleamed whitely in his shadowed face.

"I don't suppose you've come to see me?" He chuckled, a deep friendly sound. "I wasn't expecting female company, but I wouldn't be turning it down."

Sandy turned to face him, not quite certain how to respond.

He chuckled again. "Oh, it's you, Miss. Marshall. Sorry. I didn't recognize you right off. Cameron's got all the luck. He's just watching the game. Go ahead in." The man jerked a thumb over his shoulder. Then, he skirted past her and took all four steps to the ground in a single stride. In another instant, the night had swallowed him up, and Sandy stood alone in the bright rectangle of light from the still-open door.

Now she had to go through with it.

She stepped into the room, and tugged the heavy door closed behind her. The relaxed bodies of a dozen men sprawled along an enormous leather couch and several matching chairs, all heads directed towards the television set on which more men grappled for possession of a football.

Sandy cleared her throat. No one heard her. Her chest felt tight. *I am so totally out of place.*

Cam faced away from her, slouched down with his head tilted back against a bunched up pillow. He didn't know she was here. If she fled right now, she might get away without him ever knowing she'd come.

A skinny redhead in sweat pants and a t-shirt with the sleeves ripped out erupted from the couch, shaking his fist at the TV set. "Bullshit! That ain't no goddammed penalty!"

"Asshole ref." A beefy man with the look of a linebacker aimed a pointed finger toward the set glaring hotly. "Game's rigged. He's seeing things."

Another, older gentleman, seated in a comfortable well-worn recliner suddenly noticed Sandy's presence. He slammed the footrest down and popped to his feet.

"Guys . . . Uh, guys . . . GENTLEMEN!" He raised his voice and finally got their attention. "There's a lady in the house."

Twelve pairs of eyes swiveled in her direction with varying degrees of surprise and appreciation. *Oh, God, I really shouldn't have come.* Her head felt suddenly light and the room began to swim.

Cam scrambled off the couch and hurried toward her. His feet were bare and he wore his favorite jersey with the globe and anchor of the Marine Corps on the front. His jeans were faded and torn and fit with more comfort than style. He looked sexy as hell, and she had a hard time breathing normally.

For a brief moment, his eyes lit with eagerness, and she thought he might sweep her into his embrace like nothing had happened. Then embarrassment took over.

"Hi Sandy." His voice sounded guarded and tight.

Sandy forgot the speech she had prepared. Forgot she had come to apologize. She wanted to throw herself in his arms. Except Cam had thrust his hands deep into the pockets of his jeans, and he looked totally unapproachable.

"I . . ." She cleared her throat. "How come you never called?" Tears surged into her eyes, stinging and sharp. She gulped back a sob that threatened to engulf her. "If you didn't want to see me any more, why didn't you just tell me?" The sob got away from her. Then another.

Cam yanked one hand from his pocket and patted her shoulder awkwardly.

I'm creating a scene. Men don't like scenes. Where's my pride? I'm acting like an idiot in front of all these men, and I'm embarrassing Cam. But she couldn't seem to pull herself together.

"I meant to call, but . . ." Cam slid his hand to the back of her neck and mussed her hair, a little less awkward, but still obviously uncomfortable. Another gut wrenching sob worked its way up her throat. Hearts didn't really break, but it sure felt like hers was breaking right now. *If only he'd put his arms around me and tell me everything will be okay.*

"Come on, Cameron. We're trying to watch a game here. Besides, the lady looks like she could use a little privacy. Take her to your room or something, for Chrissake."

CAM HESITATED. He had been grieving for three days, unsure if Sandy even wanted to see him again. Doing his best to convince himself she would be better off without him. Trying to accept her being gone from his life, and forcing himself not to call her.

But she had come to him.

Sobbing and hurt, yet reaching out. He wanted to crush her into his arms, and kiss away the tears, apologize for all the anguish he'd caused. But not here. Not with an audience.

He moved his hand to her elbow with uneasiness nagging at his conscience. One of his fraternity brothers had some project spread out on the table in the dining room and all the lights were on. No privacy there. Cam steered Sandy past the men sprawled around the television set trying to pretend they didn't notice her distress. With a steady stream of guys coming and going to get beer or snacks, the kitchen would be no better. It would have to be his room. He led her down the short hall, opened the door and ushered her inside, careful to leave the door ajar.

What should I say? I'm sorry doesn't seem like enough. Not after the way I treated her. Guilt and regret ate at his soul. *I should have called her.*

Sandy dashed her sleeve across her face, brutally removing the tears from her eyes. She turned to face him, and he heard another gusty intake of breath. Now that he didn't have an audience, he wanted to pull her in his arms and promise her anything, but she hugged herself, her arms crossed tight across her chest like a barrier. When he'd seen her standing there in the front hall, his heart had soared. He should have ignored his fellow Delts and scooped her up in an embrace so thorough she couldn't have misunderstood his joy at seeing her. He should have kissed away her tears and begged her forgiveness. But he'd missed his opportunity.

"Sandy. I'm sorry."

Sandy glanced around the room, at the shabby oriental carpet covering the floor. At the bed made up so tight it would have passed inspection in boot camp. Her gaze swept across his desk where his books were lined up with meticulous precision. Pens and pencils corralled neatly in a mug with a missing handle. Once a Marine, always a Marine. What was she thinking?

PAIN SQUEEZED SANDY'S HEART. *Falling in love with me didn't follow Cam's plan. He probably had it all worked out to a nice tidy schedule. Take the courses he needed to get into construction management, get his career off the ground, save up a little money, maybe buy a house. Then fall in love and get married. I simply happened along at the wrong time, and he doesn't know where to fit me into his life.*

A dignity she didn't know she possessed rallied in her brain.

"Why didn't you tell me if you thought we should slow things down a little. I'd have understood." *A colossal lie, but he didn't have to know that.* "I just don't like getting stood up."

"I never stood you up."

He looks miserable, but dammit, so am I, and it's all his fault! "You promised you'd see me at breakfast. *'Wouldn't miss it for anything!'* Remember? Only you never showed up. What do you call that?"

"I overslept." His voice sounded husky and uncertain.

"You never oversleep!" She retorted, her anger gaining strength.

"Not usually." He held his hands out, palms up. "But—"

She cut him off. "You could at least have met me at the library after class."

"I went there first, but I couldn't find you."

"I waited for you." Her dignity slipped. Tears began to flood her eyes again. "I went there. You couldn't have looked very hard."

"Even the librarian didn't remember seeing you. I—"

"I went everywhere looking for you, Cam," she rushed on, not giving him a chance to defend himself. "I went to the Student Union. And Cup of Joe. Like, everywhere. I even went to your brother's bar. You weren't anywhere."

"I checked all those places. We must have kept missing each other," he offered, shrugging as if his shirt was too tight. His bright blue eyes looked pained but she ignored this obvious sign of his distress.

"Then why didn't you call me? You could have called. You could've come by the dorm. You know where I live, and it's been three days. Three whole days. I deserved an explanation, don't you think? A goodbye at least?" Her voice rose on each sentence, and she hated the shrillness of it, but she couldn't control it.

Cam reached out and gently closed the door.

Of course! He's worried about what his fraternity brothers will think, God damn him! . . . Damn him, damn him, damn him!

The sharp spurt of anger overrode her pain, and she welcomed it. She needed the courage it gave her. She needed more strength than she possessed to wish him a good life and walk out the door.

"Right! Shut the door! Wouldn't do to have anyone overhearing us! What would they think?"

"Sandy, please —"

"You're always telling me you're not good enough for me, and maybe you've been right all along, but I've been too stubborn to listen. But I'd never have figured you for a coward, Cam." She squared her shoulders and kept talking. If she talked fast enough, he wouldn't have a chance to say the heartbreaking things she couldn't bear to hear. "So, have a nice life. I'm guessing you don't want me around to share it with you."

Her heart shattered into a zillion pieces. Sandy reached blindly for the doorknob. Before her hand could close around it, Cam caught her wrist and dragged her around to face him.

He was strong, and his fingers hurt. His eyes looked haunted and more than a little frightening. She felt breathless. Confused. And ready to bawl.

"I never said I didn't want you around. But I thought it happened that way for a reason. I thought it was for the best." Cam's voice had a harsh edge to it she'd never heard before.

"Best for who?" she managed to ask around the lump in her throat.

"You . . . Me . . . Us," he floundered, and let go of her wrist. "For you most of all."

"Well, you thought wrong." She hiccoughed and glared at him. "It isn't best for me because I love you. You hurt me, Cam."

The blue eyes that met hers were filled with anguish. Burning with emotions Sandy couldn't comprehend. He closed his eyes, and she could see the muscles jumping in his temple as he gritted his teeth and tried to bring whatever raged inside him under control.

Sandy hesitated. "I thought you loved me, too."

Cam's arms closed around her lifting her hard against his chest. She felt weightless and fragile. When he brought his face down to hers, his mouth was hot, brutal and demanding. The hunger in him shocked her. It felt like he wanted to devour her.

Her head swam as she gave herself up to his ruthless kiss. Suddenly, the yearning that only Cam had ever awakened in her exploded into life. She clung to him. A searing wave of sensation burned its way through her.

"How . . ." she gasped when he finally lifted his mouth from hers and released her. She staggered a little. Her knees felt like Jello. "How could you just give up on us? On what we had going between us?"

"I don't know." His voice sounded as if his throat hurt.

"Didn't you mean it when you said you loved me?"

"God help me, yes. I do love you. More than is good for either of us."

Sandy jerked away so she could look him in the eye and ask him to repeat what he'd just said. Instead, her heel caught in a rent in the carpet. Her knees, already wobbly, buckled. She grabbed for Cam, and fell, pulling him with her. They toppled onto the tautly made bed, and Sandy ended up spread-eagle with Cam on top of her.

She giggled nervously with the excitement that raced through her at the sudden intimacy of their positions. Something flickered hotly in Cam's eyes.

"We shouldn't be here like this," Cam muttered huskily as he began to push himself up.

"I know," she agreed breathlessly, pulling him back down. He loved her after all. Relief flooded through her.

"We're playing with fire, you know." He braced himself on his elbows as his big hands framed her face.

She nodded mutely. This time his mouth was tentative and gentle. As if in apology for his earlier violence. But then passion flared. is tongue swept between her lips. She opened her mouth, and welcomed the exhilarating swirl of desire. Making up was sweet beyond anything she could have imagined. She drowned in an intoxicating mixture of relief and passion.

When Sandy became aware of the hard, unmistakable evidence of Cam's arousal pressing into the softness of her belly, the yearning thing inside her blossomed out of control. She whimpered in pleasure and wriggled beneath him.

Cam yanked his mouth away from hers. "Jesus! No! We can't do this, Sandy." He scrambled to sit up. "I want you too goddamned much."

"I want you, too." She couldn't think past the cacophony in her head. Or the knowledge that he wanted her as much as she wanted him. She sat up and then swung her leg over his, straddling his thighs, her face and body just inches from his.

"Sandy, please."

Abandoning any shred of modesty or caution, Sandy yanked her jersey over her head, and flung it into the corner.

"Jesus, Sandy." The exclamation exploded out of him.

She reached behind her and unclasped her bra, let it slide down her arms and tossed it after the shirt.

"Jesus, Mary and Joseph," Cam swore with a groan. "We gotta stop this before we can't."

In spite of his protest, his hands came up to cup her naked breasts. A shower of jittery anticipation added itself to the other unbelievable things going on in her body. She deliberately ground her crotch against his erection.

Cam dropped his hands away from her breasts, and clutched at her hips. "You need to get up," he said through gritted teeth.

The desperation in his voice made Sandy freeze. He felt hot and hard beneath her, and either he throbbed or she did. *Maybe both of us.* Abruptly, he lifted her off him, dumping her back onto the bed.

For a disoriented moment, Sandy stared at Cam feeling rebuked and frustrated. He sat stiffly, hands clenched, eyes squeezed shut, sucking air into his lungs with noisy gulps, and blowing it out through his nose.

Sandy's own breathing felt ragged, and everything in her pulsed with a fiery ache. She wanted him to make love to her. And she knew he wanted her, too. She hesitated, heart pounding with indecision. Then she reached over, and unzipped his jeans.

CHAPTER FOURTEEN

CAM CLUNG DESPERATELY TO SHREDS OF SELF-CONTROL THAT WERE unraveling at the speed of light. Sandy was driving him out of his fucking mind. He'd never been so turned on in his life. He felt dangerously reckless. He wanted to take her and to hell with the consequences. But she was an innocent. A virgin, for God's sake! He couldn't. He shouldn't. He gasped for air. Grasped at restraint. Tried in vain not to envision the perfect shape of her breasts. Or the warm heavy feel of them in his palms. Need raged insistently in his groin while reason fought for control.

Then Sandy fumbled at his waistband and unzipped his jeans, shocking him into immobility. Before he could react, she touched him. *Jesus, God! I can't . . . We can't . . .* Her hand closed around him. Lust fizzed up with the inexorable determination of beer being poured into a glass. He was lost and he knew it. *Shoulda stopped long before it got this far. Shoulda never closed the fucking door! Jesus, that feels good!*

Cam sagged in defeat and let her stroke him. Her fingers were cool and tentative, yet they felt so mind-blowingly right. Her touch unbelievably erotic. *Why the hell have I been fighting this? Fighting her? Oh, God, that feels so fucking incredible.* He opened his eyes and watched her.

Sandy experimented, intent, careful. *Way too late for careful,* some sniggering demon suggested to his conquered conscience. Ignoring it, he studied her face in the light from the desk lamp while waves of hot desire rolled over him like a tsunami, swamping any resistance he might still have possessed. Then she looked up into his eyes, and her hand stilled.

Uncertainty spread across her features. "Am I doing it right?"

Hastily, he removed her hand and scrambled off the bed. Sandy's face crumpled.

"You were doing it way too right, sweetheart." He bent to kiss her worried forehead. *And in another minute, I'd have gone off like Vesuvius, embarrassing me and shocking the hell out of you.*

Her shoulders relaxed, and she smiled, her head tipped to one side. Christ, he couldn't remember ever being this hard or this close to the edge. *Please, just let me do this right. Don't let her be sorry come morning.*

He yanked his t-shirt over his head and kicked his way out of his jeans. He jerked the chain cutting the desk lamp and bent to remove what remained of her clothing. Damn, his hands were shaking! He might explode if he didn't get inside her in about a half a minute.

"You're sure about this?" *Can I stop if she says no?*

But she didn't say no. She fell back onto the pillow and watched him from half closed eyes. Bedroom eyes. Another wave of desire slammed into him. Not that he needed anything more to push him past caution. *Damn, she was beautiful! And sexy as hell.* Long slender legs, narrow waist, a feminine flare to her hips. And those breasts . . . those perfectly-shaped, beautifully-ripe breasts that filled his hands just right. His breath caught in his throat, and need thundered though him.

She stretched naked and unabashed before him, watching him from those seductive bedroom eyes. Then she lifted her arms toward him.

"Come to bed, Cam."

He tugged the blankets out from under her and stretched out next to her on the cool sheets, leaving a couple of very hot inches between them. He studied the curve of her cheek, the shadow of her lush lashes and the slightly parted lips, already swollen from his earlier, brutal kisses. Then he traced each with his forefinger. He wanted to roll on top of her and drive himself into her right-fucking-now. God, had he ever wanted a woman so much?

"You are beautiful."

"So are you," she answered with a little smile.

He chuckled at her absurdity. "Men aren't beautiful. Especially not me." He thought of the ugly shrapnel wounds peppering his back, and some of the urgency faded. *Thank God!* Now that he had stopped fighting what had probably been inevitable from the beginning, he wanted her first time to be as satisfying as he could manage. He couldn't avoid hurting her, but at least he could get control of himself. Enough control not to act like an animal.

"Of course men can be beautiful." Sandy splayed her fingers across his chest, then nuzzled him with her nose, and finally kissed the curly patch of hair in the middle of his chest. "You *are* beautiful. Just like David."

"David!" Cam drew back in consternation. *I could have sworn she was a virgin!*

"Michelangelo's David." She giggled. "You know? The statue in Italy? He's very sexy. Just like you." Again, that lowering of eyelids. That expression that promised so much.

"You've seen this statue?" Cam swallowed his chagrin.

"Of course. And he has very nice legs and lots of bulging muscles and . . . and other things. Cam had never seen a statue endowed with an enormous erection, and he doubted this David statue could be any different. "I see," he murmured, not really seeing at all, but glad for the distraction that had allowed him to get a grip on himself.

Sandy tipped her face up and tweaked his chin with one forefinger. "Did you think David was a man from my past?" she teased.

"No," he lied, with a quick kiss on the tip of her nose. Then, to forestall any further discussion of men from her past, he bent his head and captured her mouth with his. Sandy was his now. He banished the thought of anyone else touching her from his mind.

She's mine. He kissed her and ran his fingers over the contours of her collar bone. *She's mine.* He caressed her breasts. He played with the nipples until they grew hard, and she began to make small noises of surprised delight. *No one has ever touched her like this before. Just me.*

. . .

SANDY COULDN'T BELIEVE how incredible Cam's touch made her feel. His strong, calloused hands were so gentle, yet they made the most amazing things happen to her. When he fondled her breasts, her whole body leapt with unbelievably intense sensations.

She pressed her head back into the pillow and whimpered helplessly.

What was happening to her was so new and so much more than she'd ever imagined. But it felt so right. And Cam was the right man. He was meant to be her lover. The lover who would make a woman of her.

"I love you, Cam."

"I love you, too," he mumbled, his mouth hot around her breast. Then he dipped his hand between her thighs. She gulped in surprise. It felt scary and exciting at the same time. Everything he did to her felt so good. Too unbelievably good.

"Do you still want to do this?"

She parted her legs, answering his question without words. Her body strained toward him. *Make love to me. Please, make love to me.*

"Are you sure?" he asked again, his voice gentle. "You can stop me if you want to. I don't want you to have any regrets."

Sandy jerked her head from side to side. "I . . . I won't regret . . . anything. I promise. Just . . . please . . . Don't stop now!" She ached with an unfamiliar, overpowering need. Every part of her throbbed. Her lips. Her nipples. The place between her legs where the heat of his hand burned into her. "Please."

When Cam touched her again, she trembled uncontrollably. Her back arched. Her fingers clutched convulsively at the sheets. The strange noises she heard were her own, but she couldn't stop them either.

Then abruptly, everything imploded with an unexpectedness that took her breath away. She tumbled through time and space. Here and yet not here. Shuddering. Astonished. Euphoric.

When she could think again, her head still spun, and her heart still galloped like a runaway horse. What just happened? One minute she'd been soaring and everything had been so incredibly intense. In the next, she'd been in free-fall. *If that's what a climax feels like, it's way beyond incredible.*

Cam smiled, his eyes twinkling down at her. "Well?"

"Well, what?" Her mind reeled.

"Did you like it?"

"Like it?" Good God, *like* sounded way too mild for what she'd just experienced. "I thought there would be more," she answered honestly, her thoughts still whirling in astonishment. "I thought . . . I thought you would be . . . inside me."

"There is more, and I will be." He kissed her softly. "I just wanted you to know how good it can feel first. Before . . ."

"Before what?"

"Your first time is going to hurt."

"Well, yeah, everyone knows that."

Cam rolled over into the space between her thighs. He supported himself on his elbows, his fingertips touching her face. His breath came in jagged gasps, and his hands shook. "I really wanted to make this last a whole lot longer, sweetheart, but I don't think I can." He brushed his lips over hers. "Are you still sure?"

"I'm sure," she answered, breathless and eager. She bent her knees then gasped at the astonishing sensation of his body touching her so intimately. "Oh my God, Cam!" Delirious anticipation filled her.

"I'm not God, and this is going to hurt." He sounded worried as he fumbled between them with one hand.

"I don't care." She gazed up into his face, so close to her own. He frowned. "Please." She tugged at his hips.

"I love you," he murmured, his voice husky and deep. He slipped both hands beneath her buttocks. They were warm and large and held her firmly in place as his mouth claimed hers.

Then he entered her with one horrible tearing thrust.

The sharp searing pain erased every trace of excitement. She wanted to close her legs and make Cam and the pain go away. She wanted to scream at him to stop. But she couldn't do either. As tears of shock ran down her cheeks, she forced herself to be still. She gulped back a sob. She had to let Cam finish what she had started.

. . .

CAM MEANT to take his time, but he couldn't hold himself in check after all. With no way to soften the tearing, he drove into her quickly. He felt her instinctive recoil, but was way beyond stopping.

He plunged home again and again. Then, incredibly, she wasn't resisting him any more. Even through the urgency of his drive for release, he felt her relax and begin to move with him. Tentative at first. Then, with growing enthusiasm. Until, miraculously, she met every pounding thrust. Her fingernails digging into his back.

Just when he thought nothing could possibly feel more sensational, Sandy wrapped her legs around his thighs and uttered his name in a husky growl. He came apart in the space of a heartbeat. Shattering! Splintering into a thousand shards flying everywhere. He clung to her like a lifeline while shuddering waves of mind-blowing climax went on and on. And on.

A lifetime later, as the fragments came together bit by bit, he still clung to her, his face pressed into the soft damp curve of her neck.

Never in his life had an orgasm been so sweet or so profound. "Unbelievable," he gasped as the intensity began to fade, and his heartbeat slowed to something nearer normal. Un-fucking-believable!

CHAPTER FIFTEEN

SANDY WOKE DISORIENTED. IN A STRANGE ROOM. AND SORE. SORE
in places she'd never been sore before. Making love had been incredible. More than incredible! Cam had been so worried about hurting her. Like he had any choice! It was a rite of passage, and she'd been eager for it.

With a sudden pang of alarm, she wondered how Cam would feel this morning. Before things had gone too far to turn back, he had given her a chance to change *her* mind. More than once!

He'd been so in control and so concerned that I might regret losing my virginity. I was so out of control, it never occurred to me that he *might regret having sex with* me. *But it should have. Yeah, maybe, I didn't come here to change his mind about sex. But that doesn't excuse my behavior. I was way out of line.*

Nice girls don't show up at a man's fraternity house without an invitation. And they don't make a scene in front of his friends. They most definitely don't accompany a man to his bedroom and close the door. Oh my God. What is Cam going to say when he wakes up?

Suddenly guilty and anxious, Sandy removed Cam's hand and slid to the edge of the bed. Without the warmth of his hand, her breast felt cold. *What if I've ruined everything?*

"Sandy?" Cam's sleep husky voice halted her escape.

"G-good morning, Cam." Her heart thumped painfully. Apprehension gathered in her chest like a cloud of angry butterflies.

"Good morning to you, too." He reached out and drew her back. His body felt big and warm and reassuring. "You weren't going to sneak out on me, were you? I thought only guys did that kind of thing?"

She flipped over to face him. Might as well get it over with sooner rather than later. "You aren't angry with me?"

"Angry? Why should I be angry?"

"For seducing you."

"Oh, sweetheart." He cradled her cheek with one hand. The lengthening hair on top of his head stuck up in endearing spikes. "How could I be angry?"

"Disappointed, then?"

"And why on earth would I be disappointed after having the best sex of my life with the woman I love?"

Tears prickled in her eyes. *He acts as if I did nothing wrong. Nothing that didn't inescapably complicate his life.*

"Because I behaved like a whore?"

He winced. "You behaved like a woman in love. I'm just lucky to be the guy you're in love with." The teasing twinkle had gone from his eyes. "Sandy, you mean more to me than anything."

"But you didn't want . . ."

"But nothing. It takes two to make love, sweetheart. I'm just as much to blame for last night as you are."

"But I teased you into it."

"And I let you." Cam bent his head, and covered her mouth with his.

For a few delicious moments, Sandy reveled in the reassurance his kiss offered, but doubt persisted. She broke off and tilted her head back to see him better. "I've complicated everything."

"I love you. And you love me. The rest will work itself out. We'll make it work."

She laid her head back on his shoulder, and toyed with the patch of curly hair in the middle of his chest. "I wish I didn't have to go to class this morning."

"What time of the month is it?"

"It's almost the end of August. Why? What does that have to do with cutting class today?"

"I meant . . . " Cam cleared his throat. "Um . . . when did you have your last period?"

Startled by this unexpected question, Sandy craned her head to face him again. "I don't remember. Why?"

"What if . . ." He broke off looking startled and anxious. "What do you mean, you don't remember?"

"Well, I don't write it down or anything, and I'm not very regular."

"Damn!" He pulled away from her. "I need to get some rubbers before we . . . before . . . we screw things up any more than we already have."

He regretted it. She knew it. "I've messed everything up, haven't I?" She just knew he'd regret having given in to her scandalous behavior.

"We'll get married." He touched her cheek with the tips of his fingers.

"You don't want to get married."

"I never said I didn't want to get married."

"You implied it." Now she felt like crying. This wasn't the kind of proposal she had dreamed of.

"I just didn't feel like we were ready for that kind of commitment. I didn't say I never wanted to get married."

"You said you were afraid."

"I *am* afraid. I'm afraid I won't be a very good husband. I'm afraid of a lot of things. But

none of that matters."

"It matters to me." Sandy pulled herself out of his embrace and sat up. "I don't want to get married just because you feel we have to on account of we slept together."

"Then what do you want?" A concerned frown pulled his blond brows together.

"I want us to be in love. I want to feel like we have a romance going on." The euphoria she'd awakened with evaporated.

Cam's frown disappeared. "We *are* in love, sweetheart."

There was a knock at the door. "Telephone, Cam."

"Jeezus!" Cam froze. "Who is it?"

"Your sister, Abby."

"Tell her I'll call her back."

"She said she's on her way out the door, and it'll only take a minute."

"Abby always did have rotten timing!" Cam muttered sounding frustrated. He scrambled off the bed and scooped his jeans out from under his chair where he'd kicked them in his haste to get them off the night before. He dragged them on without any undershorts, shrugged himself into the T-shirt he found on the bedpost and headed for the door. "Be right back," he whispered before turning the knob.

After the door had closed behind Cam, Sandy glanced at the clock again. She needed to pee, but she wasn't sure where to find the bathroom. And even if she did, more than likely, it would be occupied. With men! She should go back to the dorm. She needed a shower, too. She hesitated. Torn between waiting for Cam to return so they could finish their awkward discussion and getting dressed and going back to her dorm, putting the discussion off until later.

They had a lot to talk about. Not a quick discussion, either. Issues that they had some serious differences over and, in retrospect, should have sorted out before they became lovers. Of course, she wanted to marry Cam. She'd wanted to marry him since the first day they met. But she hadn't come here to trap him, and she didn't want him offering marriage just because he felt he had to.

Unhappy with the turn the morning had taken, she got out of bed and began hunting for her discarded clothing.

Cam still hadn't returned by the time she finished dressing, so Sandy scrounged on his desk for a scrap of paper to write him a note. A notebook filled with management exercises lay open. He'd scribbled her name in the margin with what might have been a heart around it before he had disguised it with elaborate geometric patterns. A smile tugged at the corners of her mouth in spite of her anxiety, She tore out a clean page and began writing.

. . .

CAM CROSSED himself as the tiny window slid open. "Bless me, Father, for I have sinned. It's been . . ." Cam had to clear his throat. A throat tight with guilt and apprehension. "It's been two months since my last confession, and I . . .I have lusted in thought and deed."

Lusted! The word made it sound so sordid. But it hadn't been. It had been anything but! Making love to Sandy had been incredible. *What am I doing here?* With a suddenly desperate desire to get it over with and get out of this box before it closed in on him, Cam raced through a litany of lesser sins. The act of contrition stuck in his throat. He barely listened to the priest's absolution. He crossed himself again and rushed from the confessional.

He didn't stop to say the penance he had been given in his head-long dash to get out of the church. *Later*, he promised God and himself. He strode through the door and into the grassy courtyard that huddled in the shelter of the massive old church. Sunlight burst on him. He took several agitated strides about the small yard, and the claustrophobic feeling began to recede. Sweat ran down his sides soaking his shirt in spite of a cooling breeze.

Until today, the confessional had always brought him a sense of peace and rightness with God and the world.

"Is everything all right, my son?"

Cam jerked around in guilty surprise.

The old priest stood a few feet away, his hands folded over the buttoned front of his cassock. Father Joseph had been at St. Mark's all Cam's life. Had baptized him, tutored him through his First Holy Communion and confirmation, and sent him off to war with a tiny bible and a bigger blessing. This wise old man knew more about Cam than just about anyone else. He knew most of the evil things Cam had ever thought or committed.

"Everything is fine, Father."

"And that is why you rush out here as if the devil himself were after you?" Father Joseph's gaze was penetrating in spite of its gentleness.

"How long does it take to get married in the church, Father?" Cam ignored the question in the kind old eyes.

"At least three weeks if the banns are to be read. Do I know your young lady?"

"I can't wait three weeks."

Father Joseph sank onto an ancient stone bench whose legs were stained with lichen. "Come and sit, Nathan. Tell me why the urgency. Tell me what is chasing you."

Cam hesitated. Obviously, Father Joseph had not been on the other side of the confessional window or he would not be asking such questions.

"I love her, Father. And I want to marry her."

"Time is a wonderful thing, my son. You should be sure to take enough of it to get to know this young woman, and she you, before taking such a serious step. How does she feel? Is she anxious to wed so soon also?" Father Joseph patted the bench again, and moved over to leave more room.

Reluctantly, Cam sank down beside the priest. At least this way he would not have to look into the unsettlingly discerning eyes. "She doesn't want me to feel like I have to marry her," Cam admitted truthfully. "But she loves me."

"Then why do you feel such a need for haste?"

"I . . . We've been intimate."

"But if you have confessed your sin, God will understand and forgive you."

"Yes, but you don't understand, Father. I . . ."

"I understand a great deal more than you think. I admit I am an old man, but not so old that I have forgotten what it felt like to lust after a woman. A vow of celibacy does not remove the temptations of the flesh."

"But what if I got her pregnant?"

But, I didn't think about that last night, and now there's a very real possibility it could have happened. Oh, God, what if I did get her pregnant?

Jenkin's face swam before Cam's eyes and guilt swamped him as it always did when he remembered how desperately the youthful new father had wanted to hold his own son. And never would – *because of me. I don't deserve to have a son. Please God, I'm so totally unworthy.*

"It rarely happens as easily as you might think," Father Joseph said gently.

"But it could have." Cam cringed. "It . . . was more than once."

"I see," the old man conceded slowly.

"Is there no way to avoid the three weeks?"

The priest laid a gnarled old hand on Cam's knee. "Nathan, please bring your young lady to see me. We will talk, the three of us, and decide what is best for both of you. Will you do that?"

What choice do I have? I won't go to a justice of the peace. Cam nodded.

"Have you discussed your plans with your mother and father?"

Cam shook his head uncomfortably. "Not yet."

"Your parents might surprise you. They, too, were young once, and they love you. They would be hurt to find out you didn't feel you could go to them with your concerns."

Father Joseph patted Cam's knee again, then got arthritically to his feet. "You didn't tell me your young lady's name."

"Sandy. Sandra Marshall."

The old man toyed with the cross dangling on his chest. "You and Sandra need to discuss this, Nathan. Discuss what has happened in your relationship and what should or should not happen in the future. Listen to each other. Listen to your hearts. Bring her to meet your parents, if you have not already done so. Then, come to see me. Together, please." He tucked his hands into his voluminous sleeves. "And don't forget to talk to God. Everything happens in His time. You must trust Him."

Cam watched the old man until he disappeared into the shadows between the church and the rectory. *I already talked with God, but the answers weren't very clear. And I talked to Sandy, too, and her answers aren't any clearer than God's. But I love her. I've gotta make this right.*

CHAPTER SIXTEEN

———

THE BLACK VELVET BOX CONTAINED A BEAUTIFUL DIAMOND solitaire Cam had picked out after leaving the church. Two dozen pink and white sweetheart roses lay scattered in Sandy's lap, and two crystal flutes were nestled in the sand next to a chilled bottle of champagne. Even Mother Nature had him setting the scene with the shimmering light of a new moon dancing across the ocean.

"Will you marry me?"

"Not like this." Sandy's big hazel eyes swam with unshed tears. What was he doing wrong?

"You want me on my knees?" He rolled onto his knees. "Make me the luckiest of men, sweetheart. Say yes and be my wife."

She shook her head.

"What did I forget?" He felt like he couldn't breathe.

"Y-you didn't forget anything. Everything is . . ." She swept her arm in an arc, taking in the roses, the champagne, and the ring. "It's all perfect. Except . . ."

"Except you're telling me *no*?" He felt like he'd been sucker-punched.

"I don't want us to get married because of last night."

Cam flopped back onto his butt. He stared at the glittering ring in his hand for a long moment, then shut the little box with a sharp click and shoved it into his pocket. Then he sat with his wrists resting on his up-drawn knees, his hands hanging limply. He kept his gaze fixed on the tumbling waves as they broke and ran up the beach.

"Why?" He finally asked. "I thought you loved me."

"I do love you." She ground the heels of her hands across her cheeks. "But I won't marry you just because you think you have to ask me because we slept together. Feeling obligated isn't a good reason to get married."

"I'm in love with you." Cam shot her a sideways look. *Admittedly, this morning it had been more about honor. About doing the right thing. I'm an officer and a gentleman, for Christ's sake, and I know what's expected of me.*

But now there's a lot more to it than that. Letting her walk out of my life just isn't an option anymore. No matter how scared I am. "Being in love isn't a good enough reason?"

"Marriage is about more than falling in love and having sex. And you don't have to marry me just because you took my virginity."

"That's not the only reason. You're smart, and beautiful and you're fun to be with. I want you to be around for the rest of my life."

"I want you to be around for the rest of my life, too, but . . ."

"But what?" He knew he sounded curt and frustrated, but his heart was breaking and she didn't seem to notice.

"Have you considered what your parents are going to think?"

"This isn't about my parents. It's about you and me."

"Family is important, Cam. Your parents care about you, and you can't pretend their feelings don't matter. You haven't even introduced me to them yet. If we rush into marriage, they'll think the worst of me. They'd be hurt, and they would have every reason to resent me. You don't know what it's like not to have a family." She hiccoughed.

He wanted to pull her into his arms and hold her until they got this stupid misunderstanding behind them. But her body language told him to keep his hands off.

"You don't know how it feels . . ." She hiccoughed again, "when you don't belong anywhere."

"But you would belong. You'd belong to me. And if my parents think the worst of anyone, it'll be me." *And if you're pregnant, it'll be me they blame, not you.*

"And how would that make you feel? Knowing your parents were disappointed in you?"

"They'd be disappointed in me if I *didn't* marry you." He ran an impatient hand through his bristling hair. If his parents knew about last night, they'd be insisting he make things right. "You don't know my family, sweetheart. Even if we eloped, they'd hustle us off to have the marriage blessed in the church, and then act like it was all their idea. They would go out of their way to make you feel like you're part of the family." He stared at her, hoping to see a change of heart in her expression.

"I don't even feel like I'm a part of you, sometimes. It's like there's this door you slam anytime you feel me getting too close."

Cam jerked back at this bald statement. How could she feel like that? He'd told her things he'd never told anyone.

"You *are* part of me now."

"Why now? Because we fucked last night?"

Cam flinched as if she'd hit him. "We made love!" His eyes hurt with the sudden pressure of unshed tears. "And yes, you're part of me because we made love."

"Marriage isn't just about making love . . ." She stared out at the water, refusing to meet his gaze. "It's not just about romance and being in love, either. It's about being there for each other. For better or worse. It's about not being able to imagine going through life without each other there to share it, and—"

"But I *want* to share my life with you." At least he hoped he did.

"It's about trust." She went on as if he hadn't interrupted. "It's about trusting each other no matter what happens. It's about sharing the bad things as well as the good."

"I do share things with you."

"Not everything." She finally looked at him. There were tears in her eyes, too.

"C'mon Sandy. There are some things a guy just doesn't discuss with his girl."

"What about his wife? "

"I dunno. There are some things . . ."

"You're afraid of marriage."

Okay. She had a point, but he wasn't about to admit it. He forced a half a grin onto his face. "It's a macho thing. Guys are supposed to act like marriage is a trap."

"I'm not that gullible, and you're not acting. If you can't be honest with me, then −"

"I *am* being honest with you," he pleaded.

"Sometimes you get this look in your eyes. Like you're about a thousand miles away. Like there's so much sadness inside you that you can't bear it. I want to be there for you, Cam. But when I ask you what's going on in your head, you say it's nothing. And when you get angry for no reason I can see, you won't explain why. And that's nothing compared to the way you clam up whenever the subject of Vietnam comes up. However awful it was, it's part of who you are, and it won't ever not be. If I'm going to be your wife, I want to know all of you, not just the stuff you feel like showing the rest of the world."

Cam looked away. He ran a hand over his face and stared down at the blanket between his feet. He heaved a ragged sigh, glanced at her again, then back at the blanket. He bit the inside of his cheek, then looked out over the water. The tumult raging in his chest was about more than her turning down his proposal, but he wasn't ready to admit it even to himself.

"Please, Cam. Don't shut me out."

When he finally found his voice, it sounded strained and uncertain.

"When I'm sad or angry − especially when I'm angry, I probably *am* a thousand miles away, and I don't like to talk about it because . . ." He stopped. His hands clenched until his knuckles turned white. Then he relaxed them, spreading his fingers wide and stared at the backs of his hands.

"When I was in Nam . . ." he cleared his throat. "Sandy, I've seen things a man should never have to see, and I've done things no one should ever be asked to do." He swallowed hard, then glanced at her again. "Something got broken in here" He jammed an angry thumb into his chest. "Sometimes I feel very violent inside, and I don't like myself very much. I'm afraid, if you knew about those feelings, you wouldn't like me either."

"But you'll never know if you don't give me a chance."

"It's not that easy. I —"

"Try honesty. Just tell it like it is. I'm a good listener, and I promise not to judge."

Cam reached out beyond the edge of the blanket and grabbed a handful of sand, then let it slip between his fingers. He did it several more times, then dusted his hands together, and rested them on his knees again. "So, what do you want to know?" How much would he have to reveal about his miserable self to get her to change her mind?

"You don't have to tell me your whole life story right this minute. Just don't shut me out when you're hurting, because if you're hurting, then I'm hurting, too, and I want to understand."

"I don't always understand why I feel the things I feel. And some things aren't explainable. You just had to be there."

"Then, if you can't explain it, just let me hug you instead of pushing me away. Maybe I need to be hugged more than you, because it frightens me when you look like that."

"I'm sorry. I didn't realize . . ." He'd had no idea how his preoccupation had impacted her.

"Well, now you do." Sandy leaned toward him and put a hand on his thigh. "So we'll be honest with each other. Okay? No matter how we're feeling? Even when it's not easy?"

"Since we're talking about honesty, how come you haven't told me about your involvement with the Anti-war movement?" He hadn't meant to say that. Hadn't meant to ever let her know he knew.

Sandy yanked her hand back.

"Were you ever going to share that part of your life with me?"

"Of course."

"When?" Why was he pushing this? Now, of all nights?

"I . . . Cam, you don't understand."

"Then explain it to me. Tell me why you participated in the protests. Explain why you couldn't tell me about the peace rally downtown a few weeks back."

. . .

SANDY TOOK A STEADYING BREATH. *Cam's right. Openness is a two-way street.* She dropped her bunched-up skirt back into her lap and smoothed it out. She glanced sideways at him.

He studied her face. Obviously waiting for her answer.

"It started when Tony first went to Vietnam," she began, meeting his gaze. "I just thought if the war ended, Tony would come home. He's the only family I have left."

"That's perfectly understandable, so I don't get why couldn't you tell me about it?" He gazed at her intently, his expression unreadable.

"I didn't think you'd approve."

"It's not for me to approve or disapprove. But, has it occurred to you that ending the war without insisting on provisions for finding our MIAs first could jeopardize any chance your brother might have of ever coming home again?"

"Of course, it has. That's why I went to the rally." She felt suddenly testy that he considered her too naive to see that aspect of the political wrangling. "I didn't go as a protestor. I went to explain about our MIAs and POWs. Not that anyone listened, but I tried. And, I promise you, I'll never go to another protest."

"You don't have to make any promises to me, Sandy. I'm not asking you to give up something if you believe what you're doing is right. I'm just pointing out that you haven't been totally upfront with me either."

"That's the only thing I haven't told you about, and you didn't ask or I would have." His inscrutable expression made her feel even more defensive.

"What about Bud Wilson?"

"What about Bud?" Her voice squeaked with surprise.

"What's he to you?"

"He's nothing to me except a pain in the neck."

"He seemed awfully familiar the day we met. A man doesn't usually act that way without some encouragement. And he keeps implying stuff every time he runs into me."

Sandy couldn't believe Cam would even suggest she might have had a relationship with Bud Wilson. Of all people! A sharp retort leapt to her lips, but she bit it back and tried to explain in a reasonable voice. "Bud never really believed I wasn't playing hard to get."

"Did you ever go out with him?"

Sandy shot to her feet scattering roses everywhere and stalked toward the sea. She splashed through the sheet of water running up the beach, marched through shin-deep froth, plowing deeper, not caring that the salt water might ruin her new skirt. She glared at the previously romantic moon.

"Sandy, I'm sorry." Cam had followed her down the beach. She refused to turn around. "Please, come out of the water."

"Why should I?"

"Sandy, I'm sorry if I sounded like a jealous idiot.

Sandy looked at him over her shoulder. "How could you think, even for a minute, I would date an egotistical boor like Bud?"

"Because I *am* a jealous idiot. I'm jealous of any man who's ever touched you. I envy the first boy you ever kissed. I hate all the horny teeny-boppers who made out with you in the back seat of a car while they tried to cop a feel. And I resent any man who's ever held you in his arms, and danced with you. I'm jealous because I'm crazy in love with you.

"The only thing that doesn't make me sick with resentment is that I know I'm the first lover you've ever had. And, God damn it, I want to be the *only* man you'll ever sleep with. I know I'm not nearly good enough for you, but I love you. I love you so much I feel sick to my stomach at the thought of losing you. I'll probably make your life miserable if you let me, but if you aren't a part it, then my life won't be worth living. Please, Sandy. You've gotta give me another chance."

Stunned by Cam's gut-spilling honesty, Sandy turned toward him, but her feet seemed mired in the sand, unable to move. Cam held his hand toward her, palm up. Then, when she still didn't move, he came to her, ignoring the jumble of breaking waves soaking his neatly pressed slacks.

He reached for her hand and pulled it to his chest, pressing it flat over his heart.

"Please, Sandy. You're breaking my heart. My life won't mean anything if you aren't in it. Please take a chance on me. I don't deserve you, but I need you desperately. I –"

Sandy pressed the fingers of her free hand against Cam's lips to stop the flow of anxious words. Nothing had prepared her for this outpouring, and she felt humbled.

Cam! Strong, capable Cam. Calm under pressure. Disciplined. A man who had lived through a hell she could only imagine, and yet because she had asked, he had dropped all his defenses.

Cam, vulnerable in a way she hadn't realized until this moment. He hadn't wanted to become sexually involved, but her persistence had worn him down. A private person, he resisted sharing his problems, but when she had pushed him, he had bared his heart to her. She felt more than humbled.

After they'd been intimate, and he offered marriage, she had demanded romance. When he gave her romance, she told him there was more to marriage than flowers and being in love. So he gave her his soul. His hurt and uncertainty showed plainly in his eyes.

"You remember . . ." Her voice wobbled. Her eyes felt way too big. "You remember the stone I gave you?"

"The lucky worry stone?" Cam rummaged in his pocket with one hand, found the stone and offered it to her.

Sandy touched it, still warm from nestling against his body. "You worry about all the wrong things." She looked up at him and tried to focus through incipient tears. "There's never been anyone this special in my life before you. And believe me, you're a whole lot more than just special. I'm not going to stop loving you if you aren't perfect."

"I'm not even close."

"Neither am I." The corner of her mouth lifted in a small, rueful smile. "You asked me if I liked you the other day, and I said of course, I liked you. And I'll still like you when things aren't perfect. Even when you feel ugly inside. Even when you don't like yourself. I'm not going to love you just when everything is fine. I care about all of you. I especially care when things hurt you."

"Oh, God, I'm not worth –"

Sandy plucked the stone from his fingers and shoved it back into his pocket. "You're worth everything to me."

He pulled her into his arms and cradled her head against his chest, his hand gently raking curls away from her face. Sandy wrapped her arms about his waist and listened to the steady beat of his heart.

"So will you give me another chance to convince you we should get married?" he asked after several long minutes, his question rumbling quietly beneath her ear.

She tried to nod, but found she couldn't with his palm pressing her face into his chest and his head bent to hers, his cheek hard against the crown of her head.

"How about if you come as my date to my sister's wedding next Saturday? I'll introduce you to my parents."

CHAPTER SEVENTEEN

As Sandy came out of the bathroom, Natalie tucked a bookmark in the novel she had been reading and set it aside. "I thought you said you and Cam patched everything up."

"We did." Sandy reached behind her to shut off the bathroom light, then busied herself rummaging through her dresser drawer, pretending to hunt for her pajamas.

"Then why do you look like someone just ran over your dog?"

Sandy shrugged, but didn't turn around. She fought back tears she didn't want Natalie to see. By some miracle of chance, Natalie had been home visiting her mom the night Sandy had been with Cam so there hadn't been a need to concoct an excuse to explain her absence, something eagle-eyed Natalie would have seen right through. Natalie would be thoroughly scandalized if she knew what Sandy had done. And how could she explain her current predicament without revealing the whole sordid truth?

"I'm fine. Really, I am."

"Hey, this is Natalie here. Your best friend? Remember me? I know you and I know something's wrong."

Sandy found an oversized t-shirt with Yaz' number 8 on the back and pulled it over her head, then shut her drawer and moved toward her bed. Sandy tried for a smile of reassurance but failed.

"It is about Cam, isn't it?" Natalie's voice was gentle and concerned, and suddenly Sandy couldn't keep up the pretense. The tears overflowed, and sobs worked their way up her throat. She pulled up the hem of her t-shirt and mopped her eyes, but the tears wouldn't stop.

"I never thought loving someone would be so complicated."

Natalie sat down next to her and handed her the box of tissues. "What'd he do this time? Was it something he said? Something he didn't say?" Natalie's questions had a sharply defensive tone to them. She wrapped her arms about Sandy and began rocking her. "Please don't tell me you just found out he's already married or something equally hideous?

"He . . ." Sandy hiccoughed, jerked her head from side to side, sobbed, then hiccoughed again. "He asked me . . . " hiccough, " . . . to marry him."

Natalie let out a gasp. "He what?" She dropped her arms and sat back. "So why are you bawling like he broke your heart? I thought you wanted to marry him?"

"But I thought he asked for all the wrong reasons. I got the feeling he didn't really want to be married, and only asked because I trapped him into it. So I said no."

Natalie yanked a half a dozen tissues from the box and shoved them at Sandy, then folded her hands in her lap. "I think you better start at the beginning because I know I'm missing something. Back before classes began you rushed in here gushing like Old Faithful because you met the man of your dreams, and you announced that you were going to marry him. So he proposes, and you turn him down because it's for all the wrong reasons? I don't get it."

"I thought he asked me only because he thinks he has to. Marry me, I mean. Because . . . because . . ." Sandy felt a flood of heat prickling its way up her neck and into her face. She stared at the tissue she was methodically shredding in her lap. Then cleared her throat. "B-because I . . . because we did IT." She waited for Natalie's gasp of disapproval, but it didn't come.

"Give me a break, Sandy." Natalie seemed intent on ignoring the bombshell Sandy had just dropped. "I've seen the way that man looks at you. No way on earth he doesn't love you. He lights up when you walk in the room, and he can't keep his eyes off you. If you ask me, he acts an awful lot like a man in love."

"I know he loves me. That's not the problem."

"Then what is, for Pete's sake?"

"He didn't want to be married."

"But he proposed."

"You don't understand."

Natalie shook her head. "No, I guess I don't. So explain it to me. If he really doesn't want to get married, why on earth would he propose?"

She didn't want to tell Natalie this part, but there seemed no way to around it. Sandy swallowed hard. "I went to his frat House the night you were at your mom's. I know I shouldn't have, but I needed to see him. I wanted to know why was avoiding me." Sandy hesitated, remembering the startled, but eager look that had leapt into his eyes when he first saw her standing in the doorway with his fraternity brothers watching them. And the very different look that flooded those same blue eyes with desperation and desire as he jerked her into his arms once they were in his room, and she'd threatened to walk out forever. That look had told her, as nothing else could have, how much he wanted her. That look, so filled with heat that it doused all of her anger and started an answering fire in her.

"And . . . ?"

"And . . . " Sandy bit her lip, then took a deep steadying breath. "We ended up in bed."

"The bounder!" Natalie surged off the bed, every angle of her body telegraphing outrage. Maybe Natalie hadn't heard her before? Or maybe the word *it* hadn't been graphic enough?

"It was my fault." Sandy jumped to Cam's defense.

"Oh, and I suppose you're going to tell me he didn't take advantage of you?" Natalie snorted.

"Well, actually . . ." Sandy felt herself turning painfully crimson. She couldn't look Natalie in the eye. "Actually, *I* pretty much seduced *him*."

Natalie went totally silent for so long that Sandy finally dared to sneak another quick glance at her. The horrified look she had expected to see wasn't there. Natalie frowned. Still not believing, maybe? Or not understanding how Sandy could have done such a thing?

"It didn't start out that way," Sandy hurried to explain. "But it just kind of ended up with me being way out of control and . . . well . . . one thing led to another and we . . . we made love. So now he thinks he has to marry me."

"Is that what he said?" Natalie came back and perched on the edge of the bed again.

"Not exactly. He said he loved me and together we'd make it work, but . . ." He'd said a lot more on the beach. But that had come after the ring had gone back into his pocket and even when she thought they'd worked their way through all her arguments, he hadn't offered it again.

She told Natalie the rest of the story. Of course she left out most of the really personal things Cam had told her, but she recounted enough so Natalie had a pretty good idea what had happened.

"So, I turned him down, and he's still got the ring."

"But he's taking you to his sister's wedding and introducing you to his parents. That sounds pretty positive to me."

"I know, but . . ."

"But nothing. A man like Cam doesn't introduce just any woman to his mother. Trust me. He said he couldn't bear to think about a future without you in it. Of course, he'll ask again. Think positive. And if I were you, I'd think real hard about the reasons you said no when you really wanted to say yes."

THINK POSITIVE! *Easy for Natalie to say. She wasn't the one on the verge of meeting Cam's parents with a major guilt complex hanging over her head.* Sandy's thoughts were as uncomfortable as her current position wedged between the end of the pew and a very large lady wearing an enormous hat and way too much perfume. The lady's rump made the space even tighter when she leaned across her husband to scrub a spit-dampened handkerchief over the face of a boy of about seven. She finally finished cleaning the little boy's face and shoved the hankie into her ample bosom just as the organ changed from uninspired back-ground music to something promising action.

Sandy turned in time to see Cam pass the end of her pew with a pretty middle-aged woman on his arm. He looked so tall and handsome in an exceedingly flattering tuxedo with his blond hair gleaming in the candlelight. The cut of his jacket accentuated his broad shoulders, and the muted stripe down the side of the trousers made his legs look even longer. Sandy's heartbeat quickened.

Cam grinned down at the woman at his side and patted her hand where it rested in the crook of his elbow. A short and willowy woman, with her still-mostly-blond hair coiled in a long braid around her head like a crown with a pillbox hat perched on top.

Cam's mother. Sandy's heart raced uncomfortably. The little woman smiled up at Cam as he seated her, then she grabbed his lapel and pulled him down to whisper something in his ear. Cam chuckled, then kissed her on her powdered cheek with easy familiarity. *It's definitely his mother! She's going to hate me. She's probably the kind of mother who thinks no woman is good enough for her son?*

Cam moved toward the front of the church to stand next to the line of ushers already in place. His eyes searched the church, then his gaze met Sandy's. He winked. Her heart jumped with a little jolt of electric pleasure, but then it contracted with uneasy apprehension.

Since their emotion-charged night on the beach, Cam had behaved as if the night in his room had never happened. He hadn't made a single reference to that night or the night that followed it. Except that every time they were together, the atmosphere felt super-charged with sexual tension. He must have felt it as well, but he'd been very careful not to be alone with her where things could get out of hand again. And he hadn't repeated his proposal.

Sandy had bought into the concept of sexual freedom long before she met Cam, but now that it had become more than just an idealistic viewpoint, she felt guilty. The more time she'd had to think about how it all happened, the more ashamed she felt. Her thoughts kept returning to Cam's steadfast effort to keep their relationship chaste and her own equally determined campaign to explore new territory. And she hadn't played fair.

It mortified her to remember how shamelessly she had behaved. How provocative she had been. She had ignored Cam's feelings entirely. She looked down at her hands twined tightly in her lap. Soon he would introduce her to his parents, convinced in his heart that he had sinned against his God and dishonored her. Willingly accepting the blame and expecting his parents' disappointment should they learn the truth. He hadn't wanted to be in this position.

Sandy looked up again and caught Cam staring at her with an unsettling look, as if he could read her mind. Her heart began to beat erratically. His gaze probed hers, steady, unsmiling. She couldn't glance away. The sudden, overwhelming memory of his hands touching her bare skin as he whispered words of love roared through her mind. A flush of desire made her want to squirm. *Does he have any idea how badly I want him to make love to me again? In spite of everything?*

Then the organ began the wedding march with a flourish, and Cam's attention turned toward the back of the church. Sandy closed her eyes and sighed.

CHAPTER EIGHTEEN

"THIS IS THE NICEST WEDDING I'VE EVER BEEN TO," SANDY confided to Cam's sister with an envious sigh. She and Beth stood at the edge of the dance floor watching the beaming bride laughing happily up at her new husband. "Abby is so beautiful and so lucky," Sandy added wistfully.

"They make a lovely couple." Beth agreed. "I don't think I've ever seen a man more head-over-heels in love than Adam. He hasn't left her side for a single minute. On my wedding day, I distinctly remember having to hunt Dick down when it was time for us to take our formal departure." As she spoke, her giant of a husband danced past, trying to shorten his steps to match those of his eight-year-old daughter.

Sandy felt like an outsider despite everyone's efforts to make her welcome. She could see the love in this family, the shared history and sheer enjoyment in each other. From Cam's slightly dotty, eighty-one-year-old grandmother down to the toddler, Tommy, Jr., there was a sense of solidarity and genuine respect. Exactly the kind of family Sandy had always longed for and never had. Beth didn't know how enormously lucky they *all* were.

"Dick seems like a wonderful man." Sandy tried to swallow her envy.

"He is," Beth agreed with a comfortable sigh. "And I love him dearly, but I still don't think he ever looked at me quite the way Adam looks at Abby." Beth laughed, then turned to look at Sandy. "Or for that matter, the way Cam looks at you."

Sandy's breath caught in her throat. "D-do you really think so?"

Beth hooted, then glanced across the dance floor. "Just look at him! God, if that's not a man wearing his heart on his sleeve, then I'm a toad. With everyone watching, even! That is just so very unlike our inscrutable little brother." Beth squeezed Sandy's arm as Cam made his way toward them.

Is Beth telling tales of my misguided youth?" Cam snaked his arm about Sandy's waist as if determined to prove Beth's earlier claim.

"Wouldn't you like to know?" Beth teased her brother, then widened her eyes at Sandy in a conspiratorial way.

Cam made a *tsking* sound as he led Sandy onto the dance floor. "I'll have to keep you two safely apart until I've had a chance to tell my side of the story." Then he took her into his arms and swept her into the dance. "So, what were you talking about?"

"Just Abby and Adam." Sandy felt more than a little breathless. She had worn the pink dress again, remembering the warmth in Cam's eyes when he'd complimented her on it. And as she'd removed it from the hanger and slipped it over her head, she'd smiled, knowing, that *this* time, she *would* find out what it felt like to dance with him. But whatever she'd imagined, the reality was even more magical.

Cam was a superb dancer. He made her feel small and light as air as he deftly swept her around the floor to the haunting strains of a waltz. The music and the man were intoxicating. So much so that the guilt and shame she'd been carrying around for the past week seemed a lot less overwhelming. Not nearly as overwhelming as Cam himself.

"So, what about Abby and Adam?" Cam prompted.

"Just what a perfect couple they make."

Cam glanced over his shoulder. "Well, almost perfect. Too bad Adam has two left feet." When Sandy stifled the strangled sound that caught in her throat, Cam turned back to her. "Abby's going to have sore toes for a week."

"So where did you learn to dance so well, Mr. Cameron?"

"Mom made us take lessons." Cam grimaced. "I hated it. At least at the time, but it paid off. You're impressed, right?"

"Somehow, I never pictured a soldier as the kind of guy who would be such a great dancer."

"What? You think Marines never have to play the gentleman? What do you think we do when we aren't crawling around in the mud with a gun?"

"Well, drinking beer maybe?" she retorted with a laugh.

"Okay, we did our share of that, too. But I was stationed at the embassy in Germany for two years. Occasionally, I was expected to gear up in my mess dress and do the pretty at some embassy function or another. Often that included dancing."

"What's *mess* dress?" Couldn't possibly be what it sounded like.

"My formal uniform, the most formal one the military has. You'd probably like it, but I felt like a monkey in it."

"I probably would if you looked even half as great as you do in a plain old rented tuxedo." Too bad he was out of the military. She might never see him in this mess thing.

"I paid good money for this, I'll have you know." He put a little distance between them and glanced down at himself. "Rentals never fit right. At least, not on me. So I had one made that does."

Sandy took her time assessing him, enjoying the color creeping up his cheeks and wondering if he was thinking about the same thing she was which didn't involve a tuxedo, or any clothes at all.

"I've had to participate in so many weddings that it just made more sense to have my own. But of course, you realize that it's the man who's wearing it, and not the tux?"

"Well, of course!" Maybe his thoughts were in the same place as hers had been. She ducked her head to hide the matching color rising in her own cheeks.

The waltz ended, and Cam dropped his arms, stepping back from her and executing a formal bow. "I need some fresh air." He gazed over the sea of chairs and tables toward the door. He touched his fingers lightly against Sandy's back, guiding her off the dance floor.

"Me too," Sandy agreed breathlessly. The way Cam had held her for those last few moments of the waltz had filled her with longing. A longing she feared everyone could see. Ever since Beth had commented on Cam's uncharacteristic behavior, Sandy felt like everyone in the room must be watching them and speculating. Assessing her and her relationship with Cam. Wondering what kind of woman Cam had fallen for.

His parents had been so gracious when Cam introduced her. His mother inquiring about her studies, her family and her home, while his father smiled warmly at her. Had they seen in Cam's eyes what his sister Beth had seen? Could they see deeper? They were his parents, maybe they would guess at more than Beth had.

"You're awfully quiet all of a sudden." Cam ruffled the hair on her neck as they threaded their way through the tables. "Anything wrong?"

"It's nothing," she parroted his favorite disclaimer and turned her head to smile at him. Her throat felt tight, and she shivered at the casually intimate touch of his fingers against her skin.

"Cold?"

"N-not really."

Cam shrugged out of his tailored jacket and slipped it around her shoulders in spite of her denial. Instantly cocooned in warmth from his body and the lingering hint of his aftershave, she felt sheltered and cared for. He opened the door to the dark night outside.

A cluster of young men leaned against the wall smoking, little orange dots marking their location. The hum of their conversation was rowdy and masculine. Cam hurried Sandy past them toward the front of the church. When they reached the shadowy privacy of the deserted front entrance, he pulled her back into his arms.

"Have I told you recently how much I love you?'

She tipped her head back to look up at him. "I love you, too. And I love your family. Everyone is . . . so friendly and such fun."

"My parents really liked you."

"I wonder if they'd still like me if they knew the truth?" Sandy hadn't meant to voice her guilt so bluntly. She hadn't meant to mention it at all.

"They only want for me to be happy, and *you* make me happy."

Except that she'd turned down his proposal, and things had felt awkward even when no mention was made about it.

"You weren't too happy with me last week."

Cam's intent gaze seemed to search deep into her soul for a long time before he spoke, his voice sounding as if the words were being dragged from somewhere deep inside with great reluctance.

"Before we met, my life seemed pretty bleak. God felt a long way off. Like He didn't care anymore. And I didn't care either. I didn't believe in the light at the end of the tunnel because I couldn't see it. You know?"

She didn't know. She had never known that kind of hopelessness and despair. She shook her head, not certain how to answer. In the space of a few moments Cam had gone from teasingly cheerful to introspective and sad. What kind of roller coaster of emotion was he riding?

Cam leaned his elegantly tailored butt against the stone wall and drew Sandy into the space between his thighs. She put her hands on his shoulders and searched his eyes. She didn't know what to say.

"Remember our first date, when you talked me into a walk on the beach? And you gave me that silly little worry stone?" Cam rummaged in his trouser pocket and produced the now familiar stone. He turned it over in his fingers several times, then shoved it back into his pocket. He looked away from her, toward the wide, stone steps where a graceful statue of the Madonna stood.

"You asked me if I thought you were silly for feeling as if the ocean brought solace when you were down. And I couldn't help remembering another beach a long way from here. I didn't want to remember. It hadn't seemed very comforting to me. At least not at the time. It was at a place called Da Nang. I was on R&R there when I found out my brother had been killed."

Sandy thought she detected tears clinging in Cam's thick lashes, but he ducked his head, and she couldn't be sure. She wanted to gather him into her arms and hold him tight. She wanted to protect him from the pain and make everything right again. But this pain came from somewhere deep inside him. A place she hadn't yet been and might never understand.

"The beach was the only place I could go to be alone with the rage that consumed me when they told me about Tom, but it didn't bring me much in the way of comfort. I screamed myself hoarse. I screamed at Charlie. I screamed at the Army for sending Tom back there. Tom had already done his year, and he had a wife and a new baby son. He should have been home with them, and I hated everyone for his being dead. Even Tom. Most of all, I hated myself for being alive."

Sandy understood the grief, but not the guilt. It wasn't Cam's fault his brother had signed up for another tour of duty in Vietnam any more than it was her fault that her brother Tony had gone back. Nor could Cam be blamed for surviving.

"I'm glad you did come home. Otherwise, we wouldn't have met." She reached out to touch his bent head. "And we would never have fallen in love."

Cam leaned forward and buried his face against her breasts. She ran her fingers through his hair and tried to think what she ought to have said. She wished she could see into his mind. After awhile, he lifted his head and looked into her eyes again. "That's what I meant when I said you make me happy. I never thought I'd ever feel that way again, but then you came along and – just when I never expected it, life is worth living again. I don't deserve you."

"Everyone deserves to be loved. Besides, deserving hasn't got anything to do with it. I loved you from the very first moment I saw you."

"Well, that makes two of us."

Sandy pulled away with a nervous laugh. "That's *so* not so." She felt humbled that he had trusted her enough to share something so personal and painful with her, but she didn't know what to say to him. She had asked for his honesty, begged him not to shut doors in her face, but now she realized Cam wasn't the only one who felt uncomfortable with such heart-wrenching revelations.

She played with Cam's bowtie, straightening it and patting it flat. "You just about ignored me the first time you saw me." Teasing was so much easier.

"I did not."

"Did so."

"Didn't." He tickled her, his smile returning.

"Did." She wriggled. "I almost ran you down, and all you said was,

'It's nothing.' You wouldn't ever have noticed me again if I hadn't thrown myself at you."

"You win. I fell in love the second time I saw you. When you kissed me, bold as a sailor home on leave, in the middle of the student union and told everyone you'd known me forever."

"Well, I'm glad we got that straightened out." Suddenly sobering, she stood very still, her mouth just an inch from his. "Kiss me, Cam."

"That's another thing I like about you." His lips touched hers for a brief electric moment. "You always tell me right out what you want." He kissed her again, at length.

Sandy ran her hands up his chest. She knew all the smooth, hard muscle and warm flesh beneath the silky fabric of his dress shirt and the way it made her feel, and in spite of her conflicted guilt, she wished they were somewhere else. Anywhere else besides the front entry of a church. Somewhere she could pull the bow out of his tie and remove those glimmering black studs, then bury her face in the sexy thatch of hair in the middle of his chest.

Cam's hands roamed over her back, then cupped her buttocks and pulled her closer. She felt him hard against her stomach and groaned, surprised at the wanton, husky sound of her own voice.

Abruptly, Cam lifted his head and dropped his hands. "What am I thinking?" he muttered to himself.

"That I'm shameless." Sandy offered uncertainly.

"I'm worse, and I should know better."

"You said it takes two," Sandy reminded him, her face hotter than ever.

"Okay, we're both shameless." He chuckled. A raggedly amused sound. "You really need to marry me and make an honest man out of me."

"Is that the only reason?" The question popped out before she could stop it.

"No, sweetheart. It's not the only reason." He pushed her away, and she had a momentary pang of fright that he meant to withdraw his offer for good this time. Instead, he took both her hands in his and looked into her eyes with sudden seriousness. "Marry me and make me happier than I ever deserved to be. Marry me because I can't bear it if you don't."

She searched his eyes in the dim light of the lamp by the church door. Her heart running about a thousand miles an hour. *Don't mess it up this time with dumb arguments, you ninny. You wanted to marry him a month ago. You still want to marry him. Just tell him yes for Pete's sake.*

He dropped her hands and reached toward her, but instead of taking her into his arms, he dug into the inner pocket of his jacket, still draped around her shoulders. When he withdrew his hand, he held the engagement ring he'd brought to the beach an eternity ago. He found her left hand and raised it. With the ring poised between his thumb and fingers he looked at her, his eyes soft and serious.

"Will you marry me, Sandra Anne Marshall? And love me no matter what? Will you let me love you for always?"

She tried to say yes, but her voice didn't work. She nodded mutely and watched through gathering tears as he slipped the ring over the third finger of her left hand. Her hand shook when he let go, and the diamond blurred into a thousand shards of reflected light as tears began to spill down her cheeks.

Cam brushed the hot moisture away with his thumbs. "Hey, what's with the tears? This is supposed to be a happy occasion." He drew her into his arms, and rocked her against his shoulder.

"I am happy. Truly, I am," Sandy whispered. Her heart felt like it had swollen to twice its normal size and meant to squeeze itself out between her ribs. He'd given her a second chance. She didn't deserve it, but he'd given it to her anyway.

"Tell me you love me." His words were husky and a little uncertain.

She lifted her head to look at him. His blue eyes looked almost black in the dim light. "I love you."

Cam slanted his head to kiss her gently on the mouth. A long sweet kiss that argued his love for her even more persuasively than the passionate one they had just shared. Then he drew back and studied her with a thoughtful expression furrowing his brow.

"When should we get married?"

"Whenever," Sandy whispered through her emotion-clogged throat.

"How about next month?" Cam responded as he pushed away from the low wall and straightened to his full height. He pulled her into his embrace, lifting her off the ground, leaving her breathless and excited.

"Next month sounds good to me."

This time his kiss was even longer and a lot more sensual. His hands caressed her shoulders and her back before circling her waist. She felt every sinewy inch of him, his thighs, his hips, his chest. His mouth. Thoughts about rings and weddings fled and something more immediate took their place.

"I wish we could go to the beach."

Cam's mouth lingered against hers. "Why?" He kissed her again.

"I want you to make love to me, Cam."

Sanity and common sense returned with a thud. "Good God, what am I thinking." Cam stepped back, putting distance between them. "Perhaps we should go back in?"

"I suppose." She knew she sounded wistful, but couldn't shake off her lustful thoughts.

"Don't you want to show off your new ring?"

Sandy gazed down at her dress and tugged it into place. "Do I look a mess? I don't want your parents to think badly of me."

"You look like a woman who's been thoroughly kissed, but my parents will blame me." Cam took her hand in his. "Besides. I just proposed, and you accepted. They'd expect us to seal the deal with a kiss or two."

He led her back around the corner of the church and toward the flickering cigarette lights about the parish hall door.

"Will they be shocked?" Now she felt even more nervous than when he'd introduced her to his parents.

"Why would they be shocked?"

"Because we want to get married so soon?"

"They'll be happy for us," he assured her, squeezing her hand. "Are you going to want a big wedding with all the trimmings?"

"No . . . not, not really. "It's not like I have a mother to help plan a fancy wedding."

Cam stopped walking and dragged Sandy around to face him.

"Maybe not, sweetheart. But if you want a white dress and big party and all the stuff girls like, I want you to have them."

"I want to be your wife." Sandy glanced over her shoulder toward the door where Cam's sister stood, her gleaming satin dress bright against the dark night. "It would be nice to be married here at your church, though. And I'd like to have a white dress, but . . . I don't even have anyone to give me away."

"Linc would love to give the bride away."

"You really think so?"

"I know so."

"Will you ask him for me?"

"Of course. He'll think it's a deal considering you're taking me on, warts and all." He raised the hand that now sported his ring and kissed her knuckles.

"You didn't tell me about the warts. Are you a prince in disguise?"

"Well . . . if you kissed me a few more times . . ." He swallowed a laugh. "On the other hand . . ."

"On the other hand, what?" She giggled breathlessly.

"Why don't we go see if you can catch Abby's bouquet?"

CHAPTER NINETEEN

The moment Sandy appeared, walking confidently down the aisle toward him on his brother's arm, Cam's hard-won composure fled. She looked like an angel in snowy white satin that flowed softly over the perfect curves of her body. Her curls shone with bright golden lights beneath a simple crown of tiny white roses. And the locket, his gift to mark their wedding day, nestled perfectly in the V of her subtly seductive neckline.

She's so incredibly beautiful. So poised and confident. God, I love her so much. More than I thought I could ever love anyone.

His gut churned with apprehension. Waiting almost a month for this day to come had given him more than enough time to consider the enormity of the step he was taking. A step he'd insisted on taking in spite of Sandy's uncomfortably perceptive observation about his fear of marriage.

Father Joseph finished the opening prayers and turned to Cam.

I'm really doing this. Make that we're really doing this. It's not just about me any more. He was breathless and a little light-headed. *It's us from now on.*

Being with Sandy had turned his life around one hundred and eighty degrees from where he'd been just a couple months ago. But, what happened the next time he woke up in a cold sweat? Screaming and scaring the daylights out of her? And God help him if he ever hurt her. She couldn't even begin to guess at the depths of the hateful anger that spun out of control sometimes. *Please, God, let this truly be a turning point. Let all that be in the past. Let me be even half as good for her as she is for me.*

Cam's heart hammered madly and his mouth went dry. "I do." The cool, self-assured sound of his own voice astonished him.

The priest turned to Sandy. "Do you take this man . . ."

Her eyes sparkled up at Cam as she responded. Then Father Joseph placed Sandy's hand in Cam's. *Her hand is solid as a rock.* Cam tried to quell the tremor in his own hand.

"I Nathan Hale, take thee Sandra Anne to love and to cherish. . ." *How could I not love and cherish her? She's all any man could ever want. She's so much more than I deserve.*

Then Sandy repeated after the priest. " . . . for better, for worse."

Cam could almost hear the echo of the ocean that had rumbled in the background the last time he'd heard Sandy say those words. Her gaze held his, and she added a silent, *I love you.*

A sudden sharp-edged jolt tore through his chest. Like the heart-pounding rush of adrenaline that pours through a man's bloodstream in the instant he steps out of an airplane. The plummeting, weightlessness followed just as swiftly.

Only this time, Sandy is my parachute. This wonderful, warm, loving woman who would always be there for him. For better, for worse. Filling the aching holes in his heart and mending the ragged tears in his soul. His sweet, wonderful Sandy. No way did he deserve her love, or her trust.

She still had so much to learn about him, things he hadn't been able to talk about. Might never be able to talk about. Yet what he had shared with her had been accepted with empathy, love and understanding. Sandy wasn't afraid of anything.

SANDY SAW the worried uncertainty hovering in Cam's intense blue eyes. *Is he still afraid?*

Cam had surprised her with his candor the night he first

proposed and in their sessions with the parish priest, but she sensed there was a great deal more Cam had left unsaid. Would she ever know all the dark corners of the hell he had lived through and tried so hard to forget? *Please God, let him learn to trust me with his whole heart.*

Cam's gaze left hers as he fumbled with her hand and then slipped a slim gold band over her knuckle. She glanced down. Her eyes suddenly swam with tears. *I don't cry at weddings.* She blinked hard. *I never cry at weddings, and I'm not going to start with my own.* She blinked again. The matching, bolder band that she would put on Cam's hand wavered through a watery sheen when she reached for it where it lay on Father Joseph's book. As the ring settled onto his third finger, Cam's hands closed around hers. Sandy clung to him. *I'm not the clinging, weepy type. What's the matter with me?*

"We're in it together now, sweetheart," Cam whispered, his lips very close to her ear, his words so soft only she could hear them. "For better and for worse, it's just you and me."

Father Joseph stretched his hand above their heads and pronounced them man and wife. Then Cam swept her into his arms and kissed her soundly to the enthusiastic applause of their family and friends.

"Just you and me," Sandy repeated a little breathlessly when Cam lifted his head and looked down at her. The weepy moment had passed. She gazed up into his sky blue eyes and suddenly her confidence returned. Her heart overflowed with love for this man. Together they could conquer anything. Together, they would . . .

"My turn to kiss the bride." Linc reached past Cam and hooked an arm about Sandy's shoulders. "Welcome to the family, Mrs. Cameron." He kissed her on the mouth, then winked. *He winks just like Cam. How come I never noticed that before?*

Then the rest of the Cameron family crowded in with hugs and congratulations. George, who looked a lot like Linc, but older and more reserved, and didn't wink. And Marik, Cam's father, who did wink at her before he planted a fatherly kiss on her forehead and gave way to his tiny bustling wife.

"Unca Cam," a little voice piped up. Sandy looked down to see

Cam's three-year-old nephew, Tommy Jr., with his arms wrapped about Cam's immaculately pressed trouser leg. "Up," Tommy demanded.

Cam bent and lifted the toddler into his arms. Tommy immediately leaned toward Sandy with his arms outstretched. "Kiss a bride," he announced, very clearly stating his intentions before planting a very wet kiss on Sandy's mouth.

"You don't let anything get by you, do you sport?" George ruffled the toddler's hair. "Come here, Tommy, let's go find your mother."

Tommy grinned with satisfaction and went willingly into his uncle's arms.

"Us, too!" another small voice demanded. Linc's son, Sammy, and his younger brother Seth, looked like little princes in their dark blue suits. Laughing, she bent to accept a kiss from each boy.

"You are very pretty. Almost as pretty as Mommy," Sammy pronounced with solemn sincerity.

"You've got a lot to learn, young man." Linc chided his son. "The bride is always the prettiest lady on her wedding day. Isn't that so, Cam?" Without waiting for an answer, Linc herded his sons away.

"Overwhelmed yet?" A handsome, black-haired man grinned at Sandy with a devilish gleam in his startling green eyes. Sean had been Cam's best friend since kindergarten. She'd known him less than a month, but already she felt like he was her friend as well. He hauled her into an enthusiastic embrace and whispered in her ear. "You look good enough to eat." Then, he transferred his bear-like hug to Cam.

"Congratulations, buddy. You've the luck of the Irish, even if you weren't born to it."

Cam returned the back-pounding hug. "It's not luck, you thick-headed Mick. It's my unsurpassed charm. Speaking of beautiful wives, where's Kathleen?"

"Right here, Cam." Sean's wife of eighteen months stood only five feet three and looked even shorter amidst Cam's tall siblings, but she managed to duck her way through the crowd and slip to her husband's side. "Congratulations to both of you," she said with a gentle Irish lilt, then added, "If this is what the Camerons call a small wedding, I'd hate to see a big one. I thought you said it would just be family, Sean."

"This *is* just family, my love." Sean gave her a quick hug. "Now, aren't you glad you married an only child?" He slanted a wicked grin in Sandy's direction. "I sure hope you knew what you were getting yourself in for."

"Sandy thinks big families are the best thing since sliced bread." Cam reached for Sandy's hand and drew her back to his side. "Now why don't you make yourself useful and get this crowd moving in the right direction."

"Anxious to be getting rid of us already, are ye?" Sean's voice took on a thick Irish brogue. He leaned closer to Cam, but didn't lower his voice before adding. "Too bad if you're feeling a little horny, buddy, but we're planning on a wee bit of a party first."

Cam flushed, and Kathleen jerked Sean's sleeve viciously. "Be nice, Sean." Then she ruined it by giggling.

SEVERAL CHAOTIC HOURS LATER, sitting propped against the headboard of their new queen-sized bed, Sandy remembered Cam's embarrassment and smiled to herself. For nearly four weeks Cam had avoided any opportunity for intimacy. She suspected he must have been more than a little horny, as Sean so crudely put it, and hadn't trusted himself. She certainly wouldn't have been putting any roadblocks in his way. If she'd had her way, they'd have been getting it on without the sanction of marriage or the comfort of a bed.

While she listened to Cam brushing his teeth beyond the half open door to the bathroom, she grinned with anticipation, then carefully arranged the new peignoir that had been a gift from Natalie. The sound of running water finally stopped and Cam came out of the bathroom with his tuxedo trousers folded over one arm, and the front of his boxers tented away from his body. Her grin widened.

Cam hung his trousers, cummerbund and tie on a hanger with fastidious precision, then buttoned the jacket over them. Beneath them, a pair of well worn but carefully shined, black oxfords sat with their heels perfectly aligned. His socks were folded neatly in half and placed across the top.

Jeepers, he's so tiresomely neat, she thought, taking note of the careful arrangement of personal belongings on his dresser, the neat row of shirts hanging in his closet. *I wonder if it's from being in the Marines, or if he's always been like this? He's going to think I'm a slob.*

She glanced around the room at the casual disarray of garments she had tossed wherever had been convenient as she'd taken them off. Only her gown had been carefully hung on a padded hanger, but Cam had done that after helping her with the dozens of tiny buttons that ran all the way down the back of it. She remembered the cool feel of his fingers against her bare skin as he'd undone them and shivered with anticipation.

"Are you ever coming to bed or are you just going to go on playing Suzie Homemaker?"

Cam turned toward her and took a long leisurely look at what her nightgown didn't hide. Then he removed his t-shirt and shorts and deliberately dropped them on the floor.

"Coming to bed, of course."

Suddenly she felt nervous. Really nervous! *Yikes! What's the matter with me? Ever since that first night I've been aching for him to make love to me again. And now that he's finally going to, I'm scared? What's with that?* Her heart raced, echoing loudly in her head.

Cam knelt straddling her legs and looked at her with yearning in his bright blue eyes. He was huge, overwhelmingly masculine . . . and very aroused.

To quell the crazy panic in her gut and stop the mad pounding of her heart, she tried for sassy flippancy. "It's been so long since you ravished me I thought I'd bust waiting for tonight!" A brief spurt of pleasure in the naughty suggestion died when she saw the pained look cloud Cam's face.

"I did not ravish you," he said quietly. He dropped onto the bed beside her, reached to turn out the light, then gathered her into his arms. "I made love to you. It will always be about making love." He caressed her back, his hands sliding silkily over the soft material of her nightgown.

"I'm sorry." She felt chastened by the reverence in his gentle reproof, and the nagging guilt that it was actually she who had ravished him.

"Don't be sorry. Just . . . " His voice sounded husky as his hands moved up into her hair. "Just love me. Believe in me, even when I don't believe in myself. Sometimes I'm not very lovable, but that's when I'm going to need you the most."

His openness disarmed her completely. "I already promised you that." She reached up to trace his cheekbone with one tentative finger. "For better or worse. Remember?"

He captured and kissed her finger. "I remember, but –"

"But nothing." Sandy pulled her hand from his and framed his face. The stubble on his cheeks caused a ripple of desire that short-circuited the tenderness she'd meant to convey. "I love you so much. Please make love to me."

"My pleasure, ma'am."

CAM SAT UP, yanking the bedclothes with him.

"Where's Jenkins?" Cam's head rang with the eerie aftermath of an explosion. "Jenkins!"

"Wake up, Cam."

"I can't find Jenkins." *Too much blood. Too much carnage. Where the hell was the corpsman?*

"Wake up!" Hands tugged at Cam's shoulder. "You're having a nightmare."

Cam struck out at the hands, then stopped himself. He blinked at the shadowy woman in confusion. Slowly the horrific sounds echoing in his brain faded, and he could hear the terrified thudding of his own heart.

"You were having a nightmare," Sandy repeated, her eyes wide with shock. Slowly, tentatively, she reached out to him again. This time he let her touch him. Let her draw him back down. Her voice was gentle and comforting. She rubbed his back in lazy soothing circles. Slowly sanity returned.

The sight of his dead captain's eyes vanished along with the gore and the mutilation and the sounds and smell of the jungle. Their place taken by the quiet dark of his bedroom, in the apartment he shared with his new wife. A zillion light years from the horror of Vietnam.

Gradually the haunting dream lost its grip. "I'm sorry I woke you," he said when he trusted his voice enough to speak. *Christ, I almost hit her!* He felt as shocked as she'd looked.

"It's all right. We're in this together, remember."

"Yeah, right," he answered, still breathless and appalled. *What if I'd hit her?*

"You were looking for someone named Jenkins. Was he one of your men?"

Cam rolled onto his back and reached for her hand. "Thanks for waking me up." He ignored her question.

"No problem," Sandy used Cam's favorite phrase. "Are all soldiers so jumpy at night?"

"I don't know. Most of us, probably. Maybe next time you should just throw something at me first. And stay out of reach until I'm really awake."

"Is there going to be a next time?"

Jesus, I wish I could tell her no. "Most likely," he admitted apologetically.

"Well, at least I'll be prepared. C-can I hug you, now?"

Cam turned toward her and pulled her into his arms. "I'd like that."

She returned his embrace, hugging him hard, as if she could banish the nightmare if she hugged hard enough. In a room filled with the soft sound of their breathing and shadowy shafts of light that filtered through the blinds, Cam closed his eyes and prayed for sleep.

"Since we're both awake anyway . . ." Sandy's muffled voice popped his eyes back open. "I've got a little problem maybe you can help me with."

I thought I was the problem. "Was it something I did? I didn't hurt you, did I?"

Sandy reared up on one elbow. Then she rolled him onto his back and rested against his chest, tracing the cleft in his chin with one finger. "No. Of course not. But I got to wondering . . . After you fell asleep, I got to wondering how I stacked up."

"Stacked up to what?"

"To all the other women you've slept with."

Jeezus! Now he was thoroughly awake. *Where had that question come from?* "There haven't been all that many other women."

"How many is not many?"

Shit! Why does she have to know this? "Just one." It would have been easier to lie and say there had been none, but they'd promised each other honesty. "And there's no comparison. I didn't love her."

Sandy slumped against him, resting her chin on his breastbone.

"Does that bother you?" He pushed a strand of hair behind her ear. Seemed like a strange conversation to be having on their wedding night. Not that it had been a conventional wedding night so far. How many brides woke their brand new husbands from a nightmare and almost got their teeth knocked down their throat?

"I just feel so inexperienced. Like maybe there are things you wished I knew that I don't."

"Good God!" Laughter spurted through him at the unexpected confession and the lingering horror of the last half hour fled. "You've got a lot to learn about men, sweetheart." He lifted his head and kissed her nose. "Inexperience is the very last thing any man I've ever known would call a problem." *The problem will be if she asks me about the other woman. No way I want to try explaining Thuy right now. Or ever.*

"In that case . . ." Sandy pushed herself to a sitting position. She climbed on top of him, straddling him. The warmth of her brought instant arousal. "This seemed to turn you on before. What do I do next? I mean, what would you like me to do?"

"Whatever comes naturally. I'm sure I'll like it." He liked it already.

She moved experimentally, her eyes watching his face intently. He groaned, letting the hot, sweet sensation wash over him. For a few moments, it felt like that first night when she'd unzipped his jeans. When he'd lain perfectly still, just letting her touch him. Letting desire escalate without doing anything to stop it. *God, this feels so good. Too good!*

"Since you asked, I really, really like this."

"Really – Like – What?" she gasped, clearly as aroused as he was.

"You on top." The awakening of Sandy's sexuality was a huge turn-on. She had no idea how much power she held over him.

He reached blindly for the drawer in the bedside table, fumbled around and found one of the foil packets he'd stocked it with. Earlier he'd managed this part without drawing so much attention to the fact, but now, he had to lift Sandy away in order to cover himself. She watched with an odd expression on her face. Perhaps she was thinking of Father Joseph's sermon on following God's plan. Or maybe he was just being paranoid. When he finished, she touched him, frowning.

"Does it feel funny? I mean . . ."

"A little." A lot, actually. But he wasn't taking any more chances on getting her pregnant.

She touched him again. Lightly, curiously, yet sending a raging torrent of need rushing through him. He grabbed her hips and lifted her. Then guided himself in and lowered her slowly. The hot, slick sensation almost made him come. He swallowed hard, trying to contain himself.

"Oh, my God!" Her eyes went wide as she gazed down at him. "You are so big. Bigger than before."

Sudden concern shot through him. "I'm not hurting you, am I?"

"No. It . . . it just feels so . . . so . . . different."

He began to push himself into her, his hands on her hips showing her what he wanted.

"Wow!" she moaned, catching on and beginning to ride him with more deliberate intent.

"Wow yourself," he gasped. His release came fast. He yanked her hips down hard and pressed his head back into the pillows as his world began to come apart. The waves of ecstasy rolling over him were so intense it was almost painful. Then her body clenched around him, and the world shattered completely. She collapsed on top of him, and he wrapped his arms about her while they tumbled through waves of passion together.

They lay twined together for a long time while their heart rates slowed and the world came back into focus.

"That was pretty mind-blowing," Sandy muttered in awe.

In a minute he'd have to go clean himself up, but right now he wasn't even sure he could stand up. He shoved shaking fingers into her silky curls. "You definitely blew my mind."

"Good to know," she agreed dreamily. "I'm glad I'm not the only one without a mind right now."

CHAPTER TWENTY

CAM SLAPPED THE STRIDENTLY BUZZING ALARM AND RAN A HAND over his face. His eyes felt like they had sand in them, and his brain took its time responding to the start of another day. He hadn't managed more than a couple hours of uninterrupted sleep, but he rolled out from under the covers and stood up anyway. He felt unusually depressed this morning. He needed to go running and clear his head.

"Time to hit the deck, Sandy." He reached down to pat his wife's hip through the mound of blankets in the middle of the bed. He was lucky Sandy enjoyed running with him, but he definitely had a hard time getting her rousted out of the sack. No wonder he'd had to wait for her every morning at the dining commons back when they were dating.

"C'mon, Sandy." He knelt on the bed and slipped his hand under the covers to give her butt a squeeze. "Wake up and add a little sunshine to my day. I could use it."

"Mmm." Sandy wriggled, but didn't open her eyes.

This time he scooted his hand around to her breast. "Time to get up, Sleeping Beauty."

She rolled onto her back and opened her eyes. She looked adorable with her hair mussed and her face flushed with sleep. "Didn't I read somewhere that making love uses up as many calories as running?"

"Maybe." His body roused at the suggestion. "But we're going running first." Sandy's half joking search for an excuse to stay in bed had become a familiar routine already. She was getting quite inventive. "We can burn love calories tonight."

Sandy rolled back onto her stomach with a groan. Cam slipped his hand between her legs and teased her until the groan turned sensual. *That'll teach you to put ideas into my head.*

"Later, I promise. Now, hop to!" He got off the bed and headed for the bathroom.

As he brushed his teeth, Cam thought about the exam mark he'd just gotten back. The perfect score astonished him. Partly because he'd never done that well as an undergrad. More because marriage had interrupted his study routine and seriously compromised his self-discipline. But mostly because he'd gotten so damned little sleep. Burning the candle at both ends. *And* in the middle, he thought wryly as he returned to the bedroom and grabbed his running clothes from his bottom drawer.

Sandy sat on the edge of the bed lacing up her sneakers.

"Don't you start your practice teaching this term?" he asked, pulling his shorts on. He supposed running together would become a thing of the past once she had to be at school first thing every morning.

"Not 'till after Christmas," Sandy corrected him as she crossed the room and slipped one hand provocatively down the front of his shorts. "Sure you want to start the day with a run instead of a romp?"

He removed her hand from his shorts. "Don't tempt me."

Cripes, she was insatiable. Enthusiastic, hot and insatiable. He didn't know a single guy who wouldn't be green with envy, but damned if she didn't make it hard to stay focused on anything else. His body's mindless reaction to her didn't help, either. All she had to do was look at him with those sultry bedroom eyes, and he got hard. Unfortunately, she knew it and enjoyed doing it to him. Especially in places like the library while they were supposed to be studying or just as he was getting ready to leave the apartment. "Has anyone ever told you, you're a major tease?"

"Yeah. You." She laughed and detoured to the bathroom. "But isn't that a little like the pot calling the kettle black?" she called back from the other side of the door.

"I don't tease you."

"Oh yeah?" Sandy returned to the bedroom and gave his butt a love pat as she passed him on her way to the kitchen. She glanced at him over her shoulder. "And what do you call what you just did to me before you ran off to brush your teeth."

"That was a wake-up call." Cam followed her through the kitchen and out into the hall. "You didn't seem to be responding to anything else I tried. Besides, it worked."

Sandy snorted and skipped down the stairs and out the front door.

The air felt unseasonably warm in spite of the near darkness. They stretched in companionable silence. When they set off, Cam let Sandy get ahead of him. He enjoyed watching her jog along in front of him a lot more than just staring at the ground as his sneakers ate up the distance. He loved watching the way she moved and the way her short curls blew wild about her head. He especially liked the way her skimpy shorts hugged her tight little butt.

"You're slacking, Marine," Sandy challenged, laughing at him over her shoulder. Then, she broke into a sprint. Catching up with her was easy, but he let her think he tried harder than he did. Most mornings, when they played this game, it cleared away the cobwebs of nightmare and bad humor. This morning it wasn't working.

They'd been married a month, and already Sandy had brought him a measure of peace he hadn't enjoyed since the day before he'd stepped off the plane into the oppressively sweltering heat of Southeast Asia. Married life with Sandy was fun and never dull. The intimacy of marriage hadn't turned out to be as threatening as he'd feared, either. Sandy was patient with the constant nightmares and understanding when he fell into a blue funk. And when they made love, she made him feel like he could conquer anything.

But sooner or later, he had to sleep and no matter how long he managed to put it off, eventually it overtook him along with the terrors he had no defense against.

Last night had been particularly bad.

Cam poured on a burst of speed and passed Sandy easily. "Now who's slacking?" The last three blocks were all up hill and he sprinted all of it, trying to leave the memories behind. But they stayed with him, refusing to be banished. Dripping with sweat and gasping for breath, he arrived at the apartment steps.

He began his cool-down stretches while he kept an eye out for Sandy's bright head to come around the corner.

"Loser gets breakfast," he announced when she finally flopped down on the bottom step beside him. He finished stretching and started for the door. "And last shower."

"Hey, no fair." Sandy skipped her stretches and shoved past him, bolting up the stairs, apparently determined to beat him to the shower.

The water was running, and she had climbed into the tub before he even had his sneakers off. He considered joining her, then decided not to. If he did that, neither of them would make it to class on time, even without taking time for breakfast. He returned to the kitchen and opened the paper to the sports section. He needed a story of triumph. He didn't look up when Sandy appeared and began fixing breakfast.

"What's got you so full of grim this morning?" Sandy whisked eggs vigorously in a cheery yellow bowl.

Cam moved on to the comics page. "Nothing."

"Doesn't seem like nothing." She shoved two slices of bread into the toaster and dropped a pat of butter onto the griddle.

"I'd rather not talk about it." Snoopy had his goggles on and a long scarf wrapped around his neck. For Snoopy the war just seemed like the exciting challenge of outsmarting the Red Baron. Cam wondered if Charles Shultz had ever been to war.

"Why are you shutting me out again?"

Snoopy went out of focus. "It's just the same old nightmare. Worse than usual, is all," Cam mumbled, not looking up.

"Who's Chuck?"

Guilt slammed him in the solar plexus. "An officer I knew."

"You kept calling his name over and over last night. I wondered if he's why you're looking so tired and depressed this morning." She poured the eggs onto the waiting griddle where they hissed and sputtered.

Chuck. Captain Charles "Chuck" Seymour. Cam's commanding officer who'd made a split-second decision that ended his life. *And saved my sorry ass in the process.*

Sandy bent over to toss the egg shells into the rubbish, and her terry robe rode up revealing a smooth curve of enticing bare buttocks. Cam felt himself getting aroused and let it happen. Thinking about getting it on with Sandy beat letting himself brood about Captain Seymour.

"Did he get killed?"

"Yeah. By a booby trap." *That I should have known might be there. Hell, so should've Seymour.*

Sandy slipped a plate of steaming eggs onto the placemat in front of Cam, then put a hand on his shoulder. She waited for him to meet her concerned gaze. "You didn't kill him, Cam. Feeling guilty because he died and you didn't won't bring him back."

Cam snaked an arm about her waist and dragged her down onto his lap. He buried his face in her curls and nuzzled her neck. His hard-on began to throb against her warm bottom. It felt good. Better than good. Better than guilt.

Sandy dropped her head back against his shoulder and turned her face toward his. "The war is over for you, Cam. You've got to let it go."

"It'll never be over. Not for as long as I live." He avoided her gaze as he slid his hands into the opening in her robe. Her breasts were warm in his hands, and the nipples stood to instant attention when he ran his thumbs over them.

"Your eggs," she whispered breathlessly.

"Damn the eggs." He turned her in his lap until she straddled him, then pulled her close.

"We've—got—class." Her voice sounded sexily husky, the words separated by breathy little gasps.

"I thought you wanted to start the day with a romp?" He covered her mouth with his to stop whatever protest she might think to offer.

Several hot and steamy minutes later he carried her into the bedroom and finished what he'd started.

THE EGGS HAD BEEN VERY cold, and Cam had been late for class. His depression returned even before the sweaty flush of sex had cooled, and hung about him, as substantial as his neatly pressed shirt and khaki slacks.

He felt worse about the way he'd treated Sandy. Refusing to talk things through the way she encouraged him to, then using sex to divert her questions. Just because he found it hard to talk about it was no excuse. Sandy was his lifeline back to a happy life, and he had to stop pushing her away when she wanted to help.

Tonight, he promised himself as he doodled her new name in the margins of his notebook. I'll talk to her tonight.

ON HER WAY into the last class of the day Sandy checked the board for her midterm exam scores. She should have been elated by her grades, but their importance paled against her worry over Cam's subtle withdrawal that morning.

He had warned her about his nightmares before they were married. But he'd downplayed their emotional toll. He refused to share their content in spite of her suggestion that talking about them might help dispel their impact. It worked for her when she had a frightening dream, but he didn't agree. He kept telling her that just because he had to live with the horrifying images, he saw no good in ruining her nights as well.

The first time she'd seen Cam's back in the full light of day, she'd gasped, unable to restrain her shocked reaction to the scatter of nasty gouges that marred his smooth tanned skin. Too newly healed not to have been acquired in Vietnam, they must be part of the nightmares. No wonder he woke up screaming. She tried not to think of the pain he'd endured. He didn't stop her when she ran her fingertips over them, but when she asked what happened, he just shrugged and said they were nothing.

He'd taken to leaving their bed soon after they'd made love far too often. Sometimes he prowled around the house, peering out windows into the dark streets. Sometimes he just sat at the kitchen table with a worn deck of cards, laying out game after endless game of solitaire. Occasionally, he'd sit down at his desk and haul his books out to study.

At first, she'd tried to stay awake and wait for his return, but exhaustion always won, so she'd given up trying. She had no idea when he finally returned to their bed and only became aware of his presence when he jerked awake again with wide terrified eyes and gasping breaths. That first night she'd tried to comfort him with a touch, but that just startled him into defense mode, and he'd come close to hitting her. So, now she kept her hands to herself. Kept her platitudes locked inside and waited for him struggle back to sanity on his own. Waited for him to reach out to her, seeking comfort.

Eventually morning came, and they'd head out on a run, an activity he really seemed to enjoy, and usually it seemed to banish the remnants of his night terrors. He seemed more like his old self. At least, the old self she'd met and fallen in love with. She wondered what Cam had been like before he'd been sent to Southeast Asia. Had he been more open then? More carefree?

This morning had been different though. This morning the grim memories had followed him into the daylight. And this time he'd resorted to sex to avoid talking about it. Not that she'd objected too hard. When he'd pulled her down into his lap and slipped his hands under her robe, breakfast, class, nightmares, even the grim set of Cam's jaw had disappeared very quickly under a towering wave of desire. Maybe she wasn't above resorting to sex to avoid facing unpleasant things either?

Father Joseph's advice to put marriage off until Cam had more time to wrestle with his demons before taking on the challenge of building a relationship sturdy enough to weather any storm had been ignored by both of them. Cam hadn't been inclined to consider a delay, and Sandy had been confident that being married to Cam would make helping him easier. She still believed that eventually she'd find a way to reach into his sadness and draw him out, but it was turning out to be a bigger challenge than she'd anticipated.

She kept reminding herself of the words Cam himself had whispered into her ear on their wedding day: *We're in it together now. For better and for worse, it's just you and me.* But it wasn't just the two of them. Ghosts had come home with him from Vietnam. His brother, Tom. Some soldier called Jenkins, who Cam hunted for in his nightmares but never answered her questions about. Now this officer named Chuck who'd been killed by a booby trap. And Cam felt guilty just being among the living.

How did she challenge that? What could she say to convince him that he personally could not be held accountable for the lives that were lost? That he deserved to be alive and to enjoy whatever happiness came his way. He'd done a difficult job that his fellow citizens not only hadn't thanked him for, but had reviled him for instead. He'd done it as well as he could, as well as anyone could ask, but it was over now.

She'd been to the library on her own several times. Looking for books about shell shock, which was a term she'd once heard her father use. Apparently that term came from World War I. Now they called it Combat Stress or Battle Fatigue.

What she'd read about combat stress chilled her. It wasn't just something men suffered from while the fighting was going on. It wasn't like a wound that could be healed before they were discharged. Instead, it followed men home. It festered and disrupted their lives long after the war was over. So many of the things Cam seemed to be experiencing fell neatly into the description: avoiding talking about it, feelings of hopelessness, anger, guilt and shame, trouble sleeping and nightmares. At least he hadn't had flashbacks that she knew of. He didn't abuse drugs or alcohol. And nothing could ruin their marriage. She wouldn't let it. If he tried to push her too far away, she'd fight back.

Sandy squared her shoulders and walked into the classroom, her natural optimism reasserting itself.

CHAPTER TWENTY-ONE

"I wondered if you wanted to go to the New Galway Pub with us on Saturday?" Sandy sat cross-legged on Natalie's bed watching her friend put her hair up on huge rollers. Natalie hated her curls and did everything she could to discourage them. Sandy thought the prickly rollers looked exceedingly uncomfortable but she'd given up trying to convince Natalie that her hair looked beautiful just the way it was. Sandy handed her a vicious looking pin and watched Natalie ram it home with a scalp raking thrust.

"Who's *us*?" Natalie began rolling another long strand of hair.

"Me and Cam, of course. And Cam's friend, Sean, and his wife, Kathleen."

"And I'm like the fifth wheel. No thanks."

"And Kathleen's brother."

Natalie shook her head before Sandy had the added words half said.

"It's not what you're thinking. I'm not matchmaking. Honest."

Natalie turned a skeptical glance in Sandy's direction. "Oh, right. Try pulling the other leg. It has bells on it."

"He's thirty-two, and he has two kids. Why would I want to hitch you up with someone that ancient?"

"Thirty-two isn't ancient. Besides, if he's married and has a couple kids, where's his wife?"

"His wife left him about a year ago for another man. Now she's gone and moved half way across the country, and she took the kids with her. Pat is pretty broken up about not seeing his boys, and Kathleen wanted him to get out a little and have some fun."

Natalie caught Sandy's eyes in the mirror. "Sounds like a set up to me."

Sandy made a face. "You don't trust me."

"I know you."

"Look, the Irish Rovers are only going to be in town for a one-weekend gig. Pat loves the Rovers so Kathleen twisted his arm a little, and he's going. Just because you adore the Rovers, too, doesn't mean anything. There is absolutely no attempt here at matchmaking. Besides, I bet you haven't been out since Cam and I got married. Am I right?"

"Maybe."

"No maybe about it. You spend way too much time studying. I'm not going to take no for an answer." Sandy uncurled herself from the bed and got to her feet. "We'll pick you up around seven. Okay?"

Natalie lowered her arms and turned to face Sandy, her brow furrowed. "I guess, if you promise . . ." She let her voice trail off as she shoved the unused rollers into a bag and picked up the voluminous vinyl cap to her hair dryer.

Sandy kept a smug smile carefully in check. *Thirty-two isn't really ancient and Pat's a hunk, divorced daddy and all. And just maybe he has whatever Natalie's looking for in a man. Whatever she never seems to find in men her own age. I mean, look at me. Cam's seven years older than I am, and I fell for him the first day I met him. And it's working for us.*

"Can you believe who they elected Homecoming Queen?" Natalie interrupted Sandy's train of thought.

It took a moment before Sandy reacted to the change of subject. She shook her head. Frankly, she didn't care anymore. She hadn't even been paying attention to the homecoming plans now that she was a married woman.

"I can't believe that twit Bud's dating got picked," Natalie scoffed.

"She's such a nincompoop."

"But Andrea's against the war, Natalie. It's all political. You knew that." It didn't surprise Sandy that Bud's new bimbo had won the homecoming title, or that she, herself, had been out of the running pretty much from the start. Once she'd gotten involved with Cam, and the student population had begun to question her allegiance to the anti-war faction, she had quickly ceased to be a campus favorite. What did surprise her was how trivial it all seemed now.

"Don't you even care?" Natalie turned an inquisitive gaze her way. Her questioning brows disappeared inside the dryer cap.

"Everything's changed, Natalie. I've changed. I just don't think it matters all that much anymore. I guess I grew up." The depth of Cam's pain and the terror of his dreams had given her a new perspective about life and the really important things. A perspective even Tony's involvement in the war hadn't brought home to her.

"But that stupid little twit," Natalie fumed. She plugged the dryer in and returned Sandy's logic with a mutinous glare.

"Don't let it get to you. There are more important things in life to worry about."

Natalie turned the dryer on. Her eyes told Sandy she wasn't ready let it go so easily. Sandy raised her voice over the whine of the dryer. "See ya Saturday, okay?"

Natalie nodded, and Sandy let herself out. She strode toward the stairs, thinking about Cam and how real the war had suddenly become for her. Everyone talked about how Vietnam was different from other wars because television brought it right into their living rooms. But for her, it had come right into her bedroom. She didn't need visual images of carnage and death to tell her just how awful it was. All she had to do was listen to Cam. Seeing him caught in the grip of terrifying night-mares and watching him struggle with pain so deep it made him scream was the most heart-wrenching thing she had ever experienced.

The sound of Cam's voice always jerked her from a sound sleep to heart-pounding distress. A distress made even more upsetting by the anguish in Cam's words. It tore her up inside because she couldn't see what he was seeing and didn't know what to say or do to short-circuit the nightmare. She'd learned right from the start not to touch him until he was awake, and most of the time, he didn't hear her calling his name. She hadn't been able to bring herself to throw things at him as he had suggested, so she just cowered against the headboard of the bed and waited it out, her heart breaking because she couldn't help him.

Some times he woke weeping, and that hurt even worse. As soon as he realized where he was, he buried his face in his pillow, shutting her out, unwilling to admit to his tears. At least those times she could touch him. Rubbing his back and shoulders, murmuring comforting words, while tears of sympathy ran unchecked down her own face. He never acknowledged her presence until he could roll over and speak to her in a calm, reasonable voice, about something totally unrelated. He never mentioned the tears in her eyes either. She wanted to help him, but he wouldn't let her in and it was tearing her up inside.

"Well, hello, Sandra." Sandy's old housemother prodded the front door open with her shoulder, a brimming paper grocery sack clutched in each arm and a voluminous black handbag dangling from one elbow.

Sandy shook away the unwanted gloom that had settled over her and held the door for the woman. "Hi, Mrs. Hudson. Can I help you with those?"

"Lordy, no." Mrs. Hudson juggled the sacks into a more secure position. "Marriage must agree with you. You're looking good."

"Cam's wonderful." Wonderful to her at least, even if he was hard on himself. "School's going well, and I love being married."

The older woman couldn't suppress the urge to glance at Sandy's stomach. Sandy suspected there'd been a lot of speculation about the suddenness of her marriage to Cam, and it amused her to think how disappointed everyone was going to be when it turned out she hadn't been pregnant after all.

"Well, gotta go. Time to be getting supper on the table for that terrific new husband of mine."

Sandy let the door sweep shut and took the cement stairs two at a time, then, with one hand still on the railing, jerked to a stop.

Bud's twit leaned against the wall grinning at her with a smug look of triumph. Bud sat on the wall beside her with one arm draped about her shoulders.

"Fancy meeting you here." The twit swaggered away from Bud's arm, her hips swaying with over-exaggerated emphasis. "How's it feel not being chosen Homecoming Queen? Bet you thought you had that in the bag, huh?"

Sandy shrugged and tried to step around Andrea. "Congratulations! I hope you enjoy all the hoopla."

"Oh, right. I forgot. You have better things to keep you busy now. What's it like being married to a baby killer?"

"Cam didn't kill any babies." Sandy forced back the insulting reply that popped into her head. Too dim-witted to understand the issues anyway, Andrea only parroted what Bud said, and he probably only took the position he did to avoid looking like he was hiding behind his student deferment. Besides, neither Bud nor Andrea had been there. They had no right to criticize Cam or anyone else who had.

"Marines must be making sissies now instead of men." Bud slid off the wall and joined the twit.

"And just what do you mean by that, Bud Wilson?" Sandy tried to sound unconcerned, but inside she felt sick.

"Your husband seems to have lost his nerve. If he ever had any."

"Cam has a Silver Star."

Bud spat on the sidewalk.

"For valor in combat." *Just shut up*, she told herself. *He only wants to get my goat. Don't let him do it.*

"Where's the valor in murdering a bunch of unarmed civilians?" The corner of Bud's mouth twisted into a nasty smirk. "If he's so proud of what he's done, why doesn't he bother to defend himself?"

"Because your opinion isn't worth the time of day." In spite of her best effort, Sandy felt herself growing hot and angry. She'd seen Bud and others like him bait Cam, and she'd watched the parade of pain and anguish in Cam's eyes as he held himself aloof and refused to rise to their ridicule. She tried hard to stay as cool on the outside as Cam always did.

"And you think your opinion is?" Bud spat rudely on the sidewalk just inches from Sandy's feet. "You're sleeping with the candy-ass. He fucks your brains out until you can't see straight, never mind remember what's really going on in that damned war."

"You better shut your mouth before you don't have one."

Sandy spun around, her heart leaping into her throat. Cam had appeared out of nowhere with a murderous glare in his usually steady blue gaze. His hands balled tightly at his sides. She had never seen him so furious or so formidable.

Bud's fingers tightened into fists, and he lost the negligent slouch he'd affected a moment before. His jaw thrust out pugnaciously. "You gonna make me, candy-ass Marine?"

Cam started to swing. Without thinking, Sandy grabbed his arm and hung on. "Don't do it. He's not worth it."

"Let go, Sandy." Cam didn't look at her. His mouth set in a hard grim line. The muscles at his temples jumped as he ground his words out between tightly clamped teeth. "He can say anything he wants about me, but when he starts insulting my wife, I draw the line."

"Please, Cam." She threw herself between the glaring men. If a fight broke out, Cam would be branded as a wild-eyed, out-of-control vet who'd brought his vicious training home with him. *Please, don't let him hit Bud. Please, God, Cam's not that kind of man.* Sandy's heart seemed to be stuck in her throat. *Don't do it, Cam.*

"Please, Cam." Bud mimicked in a mocking falsetto.

Sandy wanted to smack the condescending look off Bud's face, but that would only escalate this mess. Violence was not the answer. She felt Cam edging past her, and her heart surged even further up her throat. She clutched his arm in panic.

Bud took a step backward. *Now who's the chicken!* Her satisfaction at seeing Bud's uncertainty was fleeting. The muscles in Cam's forearm were rigid under her fingers and he seemed to have grown about six inches taller as he loomed over them all. Hastily, she stepped closer to Bud. Right into his personal space where she could see the strange orange flecks in his irises and smell the sour cigarette odor in his clothes. She thrust her chin out and glared at him. Fear filled her thudding heart. Bud might say something even more outrageous. Cam might explode. She had to stop this. Now!

"You think the sun rises and sets on you, Bud Wilson, but you're dead wrong. You're nothing but a pin-headed, no-good, blowhard. And a punk. You haven't got the brains God gave a flea, and you definitely don't know when to quit when you're in over your head. I don't know what Andrea sees in you, but then, she's as brainless as you are, and there's no accounting for some folks' tastes. So just go crawl back under whatever rock you slimed out of. Go find someone who gives a damn about your ignorant opinions. But leave me and my husband alone!"

Bud gave Cam a lingering, pitying look, then turned on his heel and hurried away without saying another word. *Coward!* Had she said that aloud? But Bud didn't turn back. Andrea tossed her waist length hair over one shoulder with as much scorn as she could cram into the gesture and scurried after Bud.

Sandy didn't dare look at Cam. Didn't want to see that look of grim fury directed at herself. He might never forgive her for interfering. But then she turned, and her heart fell like a stone at the mixture of anger, pain and chagrin that clouded his beautiful, haunted eyes.

Cam opened his mouth twice to speak, but nothing came out. Finally, he found his voice. "What are you trying to do to me?"

SEVERAL HOURS LATER, Cam stood on the stony shore of the river remembering those first shocking moments, when Sandy stood up to Bud. She'd called him names and told him where to go, and Cam had been furious with her. He'd hated the feeling of emasculation. And her hand on his arm, restraining him as if he needed to be controlled. The direction of his rage had appalled him. It appalled him now. He loved Sandy. He loved her more than life itself. But that wasn't what he'd said when he'd finally found his tongue.

Cam fingered a small flat shard of stone, and then hurled it side-armed toward the water. It skipped once, then buried itself in a swirl of the current. He found another and tried again. Three skips this time.

He'd been ready to beat Bud into oblivion. If it hadn't been for Sandy's intervention, he might have, proving Bud's point for him. Bud wasn't a worthy opponent, and he wouldn't have stood a chance. Sandy had been right, Bud's opinion really didn't matter to either of them, but the offensively crude things he'd said to Sandy had finally gone beyond Cam's ability to ignore.

Yet if he had given in to his rage, it would not have ended well. Not for him and especially not for Sandy. He had to get himself under control. He flung another stone out across the slate gray water, his teeth clenched in fury. *That jerk had no business saying such foul-mouthed things to my wife.* Another stone skipped once and dug in with a wet sounding chunk. *Asshole!* Skip. Chunk. *Mean-spirited, small-minded pissant!* Another stone. *Fucking, yellow-bellied, draft dodger!* Skip, skip, chunk!

Cam gave up, shoulder aching from the rage he'd been putting into each attempt. Exhausted, but still angry and tightly wound, he flung himself onto the ground. With his forearms on his knees, he stared out toward the lights on the far side of the river and prayed for peace. It didn't come.

Not so long ago, he and Sandy had sat on their favorite little beach in Tide's Way while she tried to convince him that together they could conquer anything. And after balking at the prospect of sharing any of his pain, he'd surrendered. It had been hard, revealing the little that he had, but he really had felt less alone. By the time their wedding day arrived, he had actually begun to believe that her love would put the horror of the past two years behind him.

Only it hadn't.

What's wrong with me? Why can't I just let it go? No argument that war is a miserable fucking hell. But it's over for me. Nothing will ever bring Tom back. Or Chuck. Or Jenkins' arms. Beating myself up isn't going to change anything, but it will make Sandy's life miserable. So why can't I just let it go?

A guy would have had to be blind not to see the fright in her eyes when she turned to me after she told Bud off. I knew she was upset and at least a little afraid of me, but all I thought about was how I was feeling. It was all about me. What a self-centered prick I am!

The adrenalin pumping through him had, for a few brief moments, banished the feeling of helplessness that had come home with him and lived inside his skin ever since. He had wanted to thrash Bud senseless. But Sandy had stopped him, and he'd taken it out on her.

Cam leaned back and fished in his pocket for the tiny lump of granite Sandy called a worry stone. He studied the rich dark color and fingered the incredibly polished surface. Like watching fish, she said. It was supposed to be calming, like watching tropical fish. He pressed it against his cheek as Sandy had done the night she'd found it and presented it to him.

He wished he could take his angry words back. The wounded look in her worried, hazel eyes should have halted the flood of fury. But he hadn't been looking too hard. He'd just gone on unleashing his own frustrated misery. Letting himself rant, taking it all out on Sandy.

I'm a bigger asshole than Bud.

Sandy loves me. She worries about me. She's the best thing that ever happened to me. Terrific husband I'm turning out to be. I scared the shit out of her, and I hurt her when she didn't deserve it.

Cam hauled back, ready to hurl the worry stone as far into the river as he could. *Dumb, fucking stone.* But he didn't let it fly.

After a moment he let his arm fall. "Nothing helps. Not the sea. Not your little stone. Sometimes, not even you." Cam dropped his head onto his arms. The tight control began to unravel and a shuddering sob tried to cram its way up his throat.

"Damn!" Cam slammed his hand into the sand. "Damn!" He swallowed the sob. His chest ached with it, but he wouldn't let it out. "Damn, damn, damn!" He pounded the sand until his fist felt raw, but the rage didn't leave him.

He rolled onto his feet, shoved the stone back into his pocket, and then stormed back up the beach to the old pickup truck Uncle Bill had given him. When he hoisted himself onto the seat, he looked at himself in the rearview mirror and knew he couldn't go home. Not yet. He'd stop by Linc's place. Have a beer or two, first.

"CAM?" Sandy clawed her way back to wakefulness when she heard a key scrape in the lock of their apartment door. She uncurled from the middle of Cam's big chair, and the afghan slipped to the floor. "You're home. Thank God."

She'd begun the evening rehearsing speeches. Cam couldn't talk to her like that again. Ever. He had no right taking his frustration out on her in spite of her interference with Bud. She wasn't the one who rammed her way through life looking for an argument. Looking for someone to vent on. Next time . . .

As the evening wore on and Cam didn't return, her righteousness turned to worry. *What if there isn't a next time? What if he's in trouble somewhere? What if he's hurt? Or, please God, no, in jail?*

She'd considered calling someone. Linc maybe. But she'd kept her worries to herself until sleep finally overtook her. Now she greeted him with relief winning out over anger. He had come home. Unhurt and, hopefully, not in trouble.

"I thought you'd be in bed." Cam shut the door quietly and leaned against it.

"I was worried." Sandy crossed the floor to where Cam slumped against the woodwork.

"You s-shouldn't have bothered."

He smelled like a brewery. Sandy felt her heart thud with renewed apprehension. "Where have you been?" She hated the sound of censure in her voice, but she'd been worried. Really worried. "You were gone so long."

"I lost track of time." He enveloped her in an unsteady embrace. "I promise not to do it again."

"What? Get drunk or let me sit here worrying about you?" She fought to get free of his arms.

"Both." He nuzzled her ear. "I'm sorry."

Sandy gave in. Glad to have him home, safe and whole, and no longer angry, she didn't want to start another argument. Besides, her body already clamored for something far different.

They left their clothing scattered in a trail from the front door to the bedroom. By the time they reached the bed, she had her legs wrapped about his middle, and Cam was already inside her. Their lovemaking was fiery and furious and over very quickly. Sandy realized Cam had forgotten to use a condom the instant he climaxed. The instant the heat and force of it sent her spiraling into a wild, powerful release of her own. She clung desperately to his sweat-slicked body until the violent explosions settled into dreamy contentment.

Cam fell asleep almost immediately.

And for the first whole night of their short marriage, he didn't wake up in the grip of a nightmare.

CHAPTER TWENTY-TWO

"I'M SORRY ABOUT LAST NIGHT." CAM FINISHED BUTTONING HIS shirt and shoved the tails into his slacks. He tried to remember exactly what had happened when he'd returned home last night. The only clear recollection he could bring into focus was how rough the sex had been and that he'd forgotten to use a condom. The next thing he remembered was waking up with early morning sun in his face, Sandy curled against his side and the sinking feeling that he'd made love to her without protection. Again.

"So you said already," Sandy answered in an oddly strained voice. "Are you blaming me?" She toed off her running sneakers and kicked them into the corner by her dresser.

"No," Cam studied the jumble of shoes in Sandy's corner of their bedroom, then finally looked up to meet her gaze. "I'm the one who got a little drunk."

"A little drunk?"

"Skunked, then." He did remember tearing her clothes off her as they staggered across the living room. She hadn't protested much, and he didn't think they'd even made it to the bed before he was drilling her. *God, I must have been shit-faced. And I promised her it would always be about making love.*

"That wasn't the word I'd have used, but if the shoe fits . . ." She shrugged, then peeled off her sweat-soaked running clothes and tossed them on top of the sneakers before returning her gaze to his. "Are you still mad at me for the scene with Bud?"

"I was never mad at you."

Her eyebrows shot into her tousled blond fringe. "Coulda fooled me."

"I was mad at me. I'm still mad at me, but I shouldn't have taken it out on you." Cam slipped his feet into his favorite loafers and reached to scoop up the change on his dresser.

"Maybe I shouldn't have butted in. You were offended and –"

"You're damned right I was offended. The things he said to you were way out of line. He can say what he wants about me, but—"

"Names can't hurt me, Cam. Don't let him get to you. I'm sorry I interfered. Forgive me?"

"It's probably just as well you did. I mighta put him in the hospital, and that wouldn't have been good." He glanced at his watch and gathered up his books. "For any of us. You especially."

Unselfconsciously naked, Sandy tiptoed to plant a kiss on his mouth. "Forget about Bud. Will I see you for lunch?"

"You'll see me for lots more than lunch if you don't stop parading around nude." Cam tried not to look at her body as he shifted his books to one hand and returned her kiss.

"That would be nice." She let her hand trail down his chest.

"No, it wouldn't. I'd miss my exam." He stepped away from her before he could change his mind and consign the exam to hell.

"Did you leave me any hot water?"

"I guess."

"Tomorrow I get the shower first." Sandy balled up her sweats and dumped them into the hamper. "I never knew a man who took so long in the shower."

"And just how many men have you known well enough to know how long they spend in the shower?"

Sandy grinned, relaxing the frown that had creased her forehead for the last half hour. "Well . . . " The teasing light in her amazing eyes defused his foul mood.

"Well, nothing. You've got nothing to compare to," he teased back.

"Maybe not, but you take forever."

"I like to be clean." The fun went out of the conversation as abruptly as it had begun.

"It only takes five minutes to get clean."

Cam thought of all the days and weeks he'd felt like he might never be clean again. After awhile he'd stopped noticing how rank he was. Death smelled worse. Now, he couldn't rid himself of the compulsion to stand under the shower long past the stage of cleanliness. As if he could wash away memories. This morning he'd been trying to wash away yesterday and his disgusting behavior last night as well.

He struggled to bury his runaway thoughts and keep his voice light and teasing. "Be good, and I'll take you to the movies tonight."

"I'm always good." Sandy ran her hands suggestively down her body.

"You don't play fair." Cam tore his gaze away, then ducked into the kitchen.

"All's fair in love and war." Her voice followed him. He heard her laugh before she stepped into the shower.

"That's about all they have in common," he muttered to himself as he let himself out into the hall. He felt depressed again. And more than a little worried about the possibility of pregnancy. He folded his fingers down one by one and counted. It was more than two months since that night at Delta House.

Surely she'd have told me if I got her pregnant that time. Wouldn't she? Jesus H. Christ, what if she didn't have a period before we got married, and doesn't dare tell me? I wish I knew for sure, but I'm too afraid to ask. But she'd have had to tell me by now! Two months is a long time. Too long not to know for sure.

Crap! This is going to give me ulcers. I really should have stayed away from the booze. Should stay away from it in the future, too, if I can't bring myself to make more intelligent decisions about when to quit.

Damn it! When did Sandy have a period, anyway? Does she even know?

WHEN DID *I have my last period?* The question plagued Sandy all day. She had always been wildly irregular, often going two or three months in between, and not inclined to pay much attention to the days and weeks as they passed. The farther apart, the better. Why ask for trouble? But by now she must be pushing the limit. Even for her.

Cam's insistence that last night had been a mistake had forced her to give the question some serious thought. He'd been apologizing for being rough, but she suspected he was just as bothered about making love without a condom. Could she be pregnant? Every time this prospect popped up in answer to the big question, sweat broke out, and her heart lurched in a queer combination of excitement and panic. *Not possible. Can't be possible. I'm just really late. That's got to be it.*

THE QUESTION still hovered in the back of Sandy's mind as she and Cam walked into the theater with Sean and Kathleen that night.

As Sean helped Kathleen off with her coat, Sandy thought she saw the slightest of curves to Kathleen's stomach and suddenly wondered if it was just Kathleen's natural plumpness. Or had Sandy's preoccupation with the subject made her see things that weren't there? But Sean treated Kathleen as if she were a crate of eggs. And then Kathleen unconsciously cradled her stomach with one hand for one brief moment. *It's not my busy imagination after all.*

"When's the baby due?" Sandy whispered conspiratorially when Sean and Cam had gone off to purchase their tickets.

Kathleen's eyes widened with surprise. "How did you guess?"

Sandy shrugged. "I dunno. Sean's acting awful protective and I just thought . . ."

"We only just found out for sure." Kathleen positively glowed.

Sandy gave Kathleen a quick impulsive hug. "I'm so happy for you. Does anyone else know?"

Kathleen shook her head. "Sean doesn't want to tell anyone just yet. Although, the way he's acting —" She shut up abruptly when the men returned with the tickets.

"What are you two up to?" Cam's expressive blond brows rose as his gaze questioned first Sandy, then Kathleen.

"You forgot the popcorn." Sandy tucked her hand through his arm and dragged him toward the concession.

Through the first half of the movie, Sandy kept glancing at Kathleen who sat on the other side of Cam. She had one hand tucked into Sean's and the other rested on her stomach.

If the men hadn't returned just when they had, Sandy might have confided her predicament to Kathleen. Maybe it was just as well. What would she have said? *Like, maybe I'm pregnant and maybe Cam doesn't want me to be?*

If he didn't, he had sound reasoning on his side. It would be horrible timing. They were just getting used to being married, and they didn't need the added stress of becoming parents yet. Besides, Cam wouldn't be looking for employment until after the New Year. It wasn't too smart to start a family before you had a way to support it. And, she hadn't even graduated, for Pete's sake. But still . . .

"What are you looking at?" Cam whispered in her ear. "The movie's up there."

She stretched up to drop a quick, light kiss on his jaw. "I love you."

Cam turned his head and kissed her on the mouth. It wasn't quick or light. A woman in the row behind them cleared her throat disapprovingly. Sandy giggled and sank down into her seat.

"Now see what you've done." Cam slouched as low as his big frame would let him. He reached over, took her hand in his and dragged it back into his lap. He grinned at her, then rolled his head back to face the screen again.

But it would be nice, Sandy thought, returning her attention to the movie. A baby would be nice. Cam's baby would be especially nice.

"HOW DO YOU FEEL ABOUT KIDS?" Sandy's question stopped Cam in mid-stride. He was prowling about their bedroom putting away his clothing and straightening the things on his dresser. Sandy sat propped against the headboard of the bed watching him.

"What do you mean, how do I feel about kids?"

Sandy smiled up at him with a secretive look in her pretty hazel eyes that made him uneasy. "How do you feel about having them?"

"I haven't thought about it." He ducked hastily into the bathroom. *Liar!*

Before the wedding, Father Joseph had given them what Cam presumed to be the standard lecture about procreation and the role of sex in marriage. The church strictly forbade the use of birth control and children were to be welcomed as gifts from God. His own family a glowing testament to that kind of thinking!

Yeah, right! When God decides to put an end to war so his kids didn't have to die for nothing, then maybe he'd consider it. The idea of his sons having to live through that kind of hell was out of the question.

At least, that's how he justified it in his mind, every time he slipped a condom on. But he couldn't get around the guilt, either.

I let my corpsman go home without any arms, and he'll never hold the son he couldn't wait to meet. I don't deserve to hold a son of my own. Jenkins' fate would haunt me every time I picked the kid up.

Suddenly, Cam was hyperventilating. His fingers clenched around the edge of the sink until his knuckles turned white. He forced himself to breathe slower and relax his grip on the sink. He had to get a hold of himself. He had plenty of justification. He just hadn't explained it to Sandy. Yet.

She raised her voice and asked again, "Wouldn't you like to have children, Cam?"

Cam turned on the water and squeezed a dab of toothpaste on his toothbrush. "Someday," he answered evasively, then shoved the toothbrush in his mouth. He cursed himself yet again for the colossal irresponsibility of making love without protection. He'd vowed it would never happen again.

Sandy had the covers pulled up under her chin and a bulldog look on her face when he returned to the bedroom. "But you like children, right?"

"Of course I like 'em." Cam turned off the bedside lamp and sat down on his side of the bed.

"And you want to have children of your own, right?"

Cam twisted around and took her into his arms, collapsing on top of her. "When the time is right, sure." He nuzzled her neck and she giggled. He found her mouth and kissed her before she could pursue the topic of having babies.

His hand strayed to her breast, and she wrapped her arms about his neck with a gurgle of enjoyment. Passion flared as quickly as it always did, but this time, Sandy seemed anxious to hurry it along, and when he turned away to reach for a condom, she sighed. After a moment she rolled onto her side and snaked an arm about his waist.

"When will someday be, Cam?"

CHAPTER TWENTY-THREE

SANDY'S PERIOD STILL HADN'T APPEARED.

She had no idea when her last cycle had been. Sometime before that fateful night they'd first made love at Cam's fraternity house, but how much before, she just couldn't remember. She hadn't lied exactly, but she had let Cam's hesitantly worded assumption go unchallenged. She had been really late before when she was under a lot of stress. And the last couple months had been a lot more than stressful.

The excitement of their wedding could have been the start of it. Worrying about Cam and dealing with the terrifying nightmares frazzled her nerves. She tried to convince herself that stress explained her lateness.

She checked the meatloaf in the oven and gave the potatoes a stab with a fork. She hoped Cam would show up in time for supper. She gathered up her paperwork, and began to set the table.

If she didn't have to worry about where he was half the time maybe she could relax and her body could get back to normal. He spent hours in the Engineering Lab every afternoon, or so he said. How could anyone spend that much time in the lab? And then he often took off again when she sat down to do homework, saying he would be home in a little while. A little while usually turned out to be very late. Sometimes he didn't even show up for supper in between. It felt like she saw less of him now than before they were married.

Cam stuck his head through the door. "Hey, sweetheart! Know what today is?"

Relief washed over her. He was almost on time for supper and almost sober. As she crossed the room to greet him with a kiss, she tried to think what could be special about today.

"No. Tell me."

Cam produced a bouquet of pink Gerbera daisies. "It's tell-your-wife-you-love-her day." His blue eyes were soft and his grin crooked.

Her heart did a flip-flop. She gathered him into her arms and hugged him hard. "If I didn't know you better, I'd think you were feeling guilty about something."

"I am." He hugged her back, lifting her off the floor and whirling her around. Then he set her down and kissed her. "I've been acting like a jerk all week, and I'm sorry."

"I don't like wondering where you are, or if you're okay." Sandy tried to sound stern.

"I thought you knew I stop off at Linc's most of the time. Sometimes I just need to get out of the apartment. Drive around a little. Get myself squared away, you know? But, tell you what? I promise to call and let you know where I am next time." Cam nuzzled her earlobe and trailed a tickling row of kisses down her neck. He cupped her buttocks with his hands and pulled her hard against him. "Still love me?"

Maybe she should share her niggling suspicions with him now while he was in such a cheerful, upbeat mood. Or maybe she should just enjoy the moment and not ruin it. She probably wasn't pregnant, anyway, and why bring it up if she didn't have to?

"I'll always love you. And I've got your favorite meatloaf in the oven. Want some?"

EVERY DAY that went by without the arrival of her 'friend' left Sandy with a growing jumble of mixed emotions. At the heart of those emotions lurked the inescapable fact that if the once remote chance of pregnancy became a reality, she'd have to tell Cam. Yet every time she brought the subject of babies up, he became evasive and unwilling to pursue the idea, and her misgivings about his reaction increased. But as the days began to add up with no sign of her friend, so did a sense of expectation and secret joy. Cam's baby grew inside her, and she couldn't deny the little thrill of pleasure this thought brought.

When another week passed Sandy decided she really couldn't put off telling Cam any longer. Unable to concentrate anyway, she skipped her last class and hurried home to fix an extra special dinner. Tonight she would tell him. He might be a little shocked. All right, he'd be a lot shocked. But he'd get used to the idea. Cam loved children. She'd seen how he behaved with his nieces and nephews. How could he not love a child of his own?

BARKEEP WASN'T the career Cam's big brother Linc had in mind when he went to college, but it had been a great way to earn money while he studied. Then, after four years of tending bar at night and studying political science during the day, he had decided he preferred the politics of the local pub to those in the halls of government. The decision to hock everything to buy Code Seven when his boss retired had turned out well. Linc made a good living for his wife and kids and, more importantly, he loved what he did. But at the moment, a rare frown clouded his usually cheerful countenance.

Cam watched his brother measure out two shots of whiskey and deliver them to a couple of businessmen sitting at the other end of the bar. Then he glanced down the length of the polished oak surface, and directed a frown at Cam.

He probably thinks I should go home to my wife. Cam glanced away uneasily. *And he'd be right.*

"What'll it be?" Linc grinned at a portly man hiking himself onto a stool two seats away from Cam. The man asked for a gin and tonic, and Linc made it for him.

The click of pool balls came from the back room and a couple off-duty policemen nursed drinks at a corner table, but most of the regulars had gone home. Linc wiped his hands on a towel wrapped around his waist. He came back to lean his elbows on the bar in front of Cam.

"Shouldn't you be headed home, Runt? I imagine that new wife of yours must be worrying where you've gotten to."

Cam made an effort to focus on his watch. Nearly midnight. "She knows where I am. I called her." He shoved his glass forward. "How 'bout one more?"

"How about not?" Linc's frown deepened. "Look, if there's something bothering you, I'm a good listener. " He peered into Cam's eyes.

"Nothing's wrong."

"You aren't fighting with that sweet little thing already, are you?"

"She's studying. And no, we're not fighting."

"Shouldn't you be studying, too?"

Homework is the least of my problems right now. What I need is a fucking beer, damn it! I need sleep and beer guarantees it. But he couldn't say that. He couldn't tell Linc. Not about the nightmares or the guilt. "You're not my keeper, Linc. Now are you going to get me another beer or not?"

"Not." Linc was serious.

Irritated, Cam slid off the stool. "I'm off then." He dug into his pocket and tossed a few bills on the bar.

"Tell me you're not driving, Cam."

"Mind your own fucking business."

Linc lunged across the bar, grabbing Cam by the front of his jacket. "Give me your keys." When Cam didn't answer, Linc's hand tightened on Cam's jacket. He held his other hand out, palm up, waiting.

Cam glared at his brother belligerently. He made no move to hand over his keys.

"I said, hand over your keys, and I mean it." Linc lowered his voice to a whisper. "Or I'll get Haggarty over here to haul your ass to jail."

"You wouldn't."

"I would if it meant keeping you from doing something stupid and getting yourself killed." Linc's gaze held an implacable glint.

"Okay, dammit." Cam fished in his pocket and hauled out the truck keys, then dropped them into his brother's hand.

"I'll take you home." Linc let go of Cam's jacket and pocketed the keys.

"GET A MOVE ON, MARINE!" When a hand roughly shook Cam's shoulder, he surged onto his feet in one swift motion, landing in a crouch looking for his weapon. His mouth tasted like a sewer. His heart thudded painfully and loud. He tried to think.

A pair of sneakers hit the deck in front of him. Slowly, Cam's mind grasped the significance of the sneakers. He was not in the jungles of Vietnam. He hadn't fallen asleep on watch, and he was acting like a frigging idiot.

"You going running or is your head too sore?" Sandy, already dressed in sweats and sneakers, had her arms folded across her chest. A look of censure clouded her usually bright hazel eyes. *She's pissed at me. I don't blame her.*

"I'm going." He straightened the rest of the way. His head thumped excruciatingly, but damned if he was going to admit it. "Give me a minute." He made his bleary way to the bathroom.

Shoving his head under cold water didn't have the beneficial result he'd hoped for, but it did finish the job of waking him up. He thrust his legs into a pair of sweats, dragged a t-shirt over his head, then grabbed a pair of socks and went into the kitchen.

Sandy downed a tall glass of orange juice. "Want any?" She held up the carton.

Cam's stomach lurched. "No, thanks." He sat down to put his sneakers on. This was not going to be a good day.

Sandy set a vigorous pace. Cam forced himself to keep up and prayed he wouldn't throw up. After the second painful mile he staggered to a stop. Bent at the waist, his hands on his knees, he strove to quell the roiling revolt in his stomach.

Sandy circled back to him and jogged in place. "You all right?"

"Fine," he lied, not looking up.

"You don't look fine."

"I will be. Just give me a minute."

Sandy stopped jogging and squatted beside him. "Cam?" Concern colored her voice.

His face felt incredibly cold. As though he might faint. *Come on Cameron, you're a fucking Marine. Suck it up and get moving*

"I told you, I'm fine." He stood up to prove it. The world spun alarmingly, then settled down. *I can do this.*

Sandy reached out to grab his arm.

"Don't!" *If only my stomach would stop doing jumping jacks.*

She jerked her hand back as if she'd been stung.

I am going to be sick. Crap! "Go on ahead. I'll catch up." *I'm going to disgrace myself, and I don't need a witness.*

"We can walk for a bit. Would that help?"

"No, it wouldn't." He swallowed convulsively.

"But . . ."

"Just go, dammit." His mouth flooded with saliva. "Get out of here."

Sandy looked miserable. Obviously torn between hurt at his curt dismissal and worry that she ought to stay with him. Then she spun on her heel and jogged off.

Cam lurched to the curb and retched violently. His eyeballs felt like they were popping out of his head, and sweat ran down his face in rivers. It felt like his insides were coming out.

He clung weakly to a speed limit sign and wiped his arm across his mouth. His legs didn't feel like they were going to be able to carry him home again.

Sandy deserves better than this.

When Cam finally dragged himself home, Sandy had finished her shower and stood in front of her dresser, pulling a sweater over her head. He leaned against the bedroom doorjamb and watched her tousled head pop through the cowl neckline. Besides the sweater, she wore only a very brief pair of panties. The sweater got hung up allowing him a glimpse of one delectably rounded breast reflected in the mirror. He had an instant hard-on.

Jeeze, a few minutes ago I was chucking my brains out and wondering if I would live. Or if I even wanted to. He moved toward the bed and sank down on it before Sandy could notice his condition. The resiliency of the male body astonished him. Definitely not an appropriate response right at the moment.

"I'm sorry."

Sandy spun around, startled. "I didn't hear you come in."

"I'm sorry I yelled at you. I just didn't want you to see me barfing. It wasn't pretty."

"What about last night?" She didn't look ready to forgive him this time.

"I'm sorry about that, too. I promise—"

"Don't Cam. Don't make promises you can't keep. Or won't." She leaned her butt against her dresser and folded her arms beneath her breasts. "Why Cam?"

"Why what?"

"Why do you drink so much?"

He shrugged. "It helps me sleep. "

"Are you wishing we didn't get married? Is that why you don't come home at night?"

Shocked, he blurted. "You know that's not so!"

"How do I know it's not so?" She closed her arms tighter across herself. As if she were protecting herself. From him! "You don't come home until I'm asleep, and you've been sacking out on the sofa for a week."

"I didn't want to disturb you."

"But I want to be disturbed. I want to sleep with you. I want to hear you breathing and feel you touching me." Huge tears welled in her eyes. She blinked hard. "Don't you love me anymore?"

His heart felt like she'd stabbed him. He shot to his feet and reached for her. She eluded him, gulping back a sob, but the tears broke free and ran down her cheeks.

"Of course, I still love you." He ran an anxious hand through his hair. "Please don't cry." He wanted to hold her but she wouldn't let him.

With shaking hands, she pulled on a pair of slacks. She yanked a brush through her damp hair, then shoved her feet into a pair of loafers. She didn't look at him. She grabbed a jacket from the closet and headed toward the door.

"Where are you going?"

"Out."

CAM DESERVED THIS. Sandy had been gone for hours. Hours that he'd spent pacing and worrying. Wishing she'd come home so he could tell her . . . Tell her what? How sorry he was? He'd already said it and she obviously didn't want to hear how he felt. He didn't blame her.

When the door had clicked shut behind her, his first instinct had been to run after her. But then he thought better of it. She'd been angry and upset, and she had a right to be both. If she needed time to cool off, she deserved it. He took a shower instead. A very long shower. Then, he stretched out on the bed, praying the dizziness and nausea would go away, and he'd fallen asleep.

By the time he woke, late afternoon sun slanted across the room, and the apartment was eerily silent.

He scrambled from the bed and checked out every nook in their small apartment, but she hadn't come home.

She couldn't have gone to the beach. The truck is still at the Code Seven, and it's too far to walk. It'll be dark before much longer. Where could she have gone?

He considered calling Natalie, or . . . or who? He suddenly realized he didn't know any of her friends that well. Didn't know beyond the beach or Natalie's dorm room, where she might have gone.

Jesus H. Christ! I'm such a self-centered bastard. I don't even know where my own wife might have gone. I'm so wrapped up in my problems, I haven't really listened to her. Haven't really paid any attention to the things she likes to do unless it's with me. What a selfish bastard I am! I . . .

Maybe she called Linc, and he drove the truck over for her. Alarm surged through him. *What if she's hurt?* That damned truck was old and sometimes had a mind of its own. *What if she ran off the road?* The image of a mangled truck slammed its way into his mind. *Oh, God, please let her be okay. Please bring her home. Please, God.*

Cam paced between the window in the living room overlooking the parking lot and the wall by the kitchen door where the phone hung. Praying like he hadn't prayed in years. The image became more defined and more terrifyingly real. His heart felt like it was being squeezed in a giant vise.

Please, just call me. Let me know where you are. Call so I'll know you're okay. He begged as he stood in the middle of the kitchen staring at the phone. In the next heartbeat, he prayed it wouldn't ring. *It might be someone else with bad news.* He returned to the window.

The front door opened with a soft click. Cam whirled as Sandy came into the living room and dumped her backpack on a chair. Then she looked up and noticed him standing in the gloom.

"Hi Cam." Her usually expressive face gave nothing away. She turned on the lamp by the couch. "What are you doing standing there in the dark?"

Hi? That's all she has to say? Where in God's name have you been? Do you know how sick I've been with worry? How could you leave me here not knowing where you are or even if you're okay? He wanted to shout at her to relieve the tension that had him tied in knots, but he realized he had no right to make such demands. He forced himself to calm down. Then realization came.

Christ! This how she feels when I disappear every night. Worrying about where I am. Imagining disaster. Fighting panic. I go off and say I'll be back soon. Only I never come back soon enough. And more than half the time, I come home stinking drunk.

"I've been worried," he managed to say in a reasonably normal voice.

"Now you know how I feel when you disappear and don't come home." She took off her jacket and hung it in the closet.

"I'm a jerk. I'm sorry." Cam rubbed his forehead with a thumb and forefinger.

Sandy walked across the living room, stopping a couple feet away, her face still unreadable. Even her eyes held no expression. "If I thought you were a jerk, I wouldn't have married you, Cam. I still don't think so. I think you're just so wrapped up in your own misery that you never stop to consider how it makes me feel when you take off." She started to reach out to him, then stopped.

"I know you're not happy, and sometimes I'm afraid it's me you're not happy with. But then I remember the nightmares and whatever else is haunting you. I think you can't or won't talk about it so you drink because it helps you forget. So maybe it never occurred to you that I might be worried, but I don't think you're a jerk."

Cam collapsed onto the couch as if someone had pulled his legs out from under him. "Why didn't you tell me what I was doing to you? Why didn't you yell at me when I came in shitfaced and late?"

Sandy knelt in front of him and put her hands on his knees. "Because you already felt bad enough. Besides . . ." she tipped her head to the side and warmth returned to her eyes. "Reasoning with a drunk isn't possible."

"I'm not a dr—," he started to protest, then shut his mouth as the sickening reality sunk in.

I am a drunk. God help me, she's right. I'm a drunk. And it's got to stop. Right here. Right now. And I pray to God it's not too late.

He put his hands over hers, then closed his fingers around her chilly ones. He felt more ashamed of himself than he'd ever been in his life. "Am I still worth another chance?"

CHAPTER TWENTY-FOUR

Thanksgiving had arrived along with a totally unusual dusting of snow. The aroma of roasting turkey filled Cam's parent's home along with the excited chatter of his nieces and nephews and the amiable conversation of women preparing to put a holiday meal on the table. Sandy loved the feeling of being surrounded by love and acceptance, cozy against the chill of the outdoors and without any of the tension that seemed to haunt her days of late.

Today she would tell Cam about the baby. After dinner, she'd ask him to go for a walk with her. He'd be holding her hand or maybe have his arm about her shoulders, and it would be just the two of them, filled with dinner and contentment. Then they would tell his family. She wished dinner would hurry up and be over. Now that she'd made up her mind the right time had come, she couldn't wait to share her secret.

She lifted the pitcher of ice water she carried just in time to avoid two of Cam's nephews as they raced past. Eric, who she was pretty certain belonged to Beth, whooped like an Indian. George Junior tried to catch him. They wore feathered Indian war bonnets made of brightly colored construction paper on their blonde heads and had, on her arrival, informed Sandy that they were Wawenocks. Sandy smiled and set the water on the table.

"I wonder if I'll ever get them all straight," she muttered to herself.

"Why are you talking to yourself, Aunt Sandy?" Two little girls wearing large white collars and Pilgrim hats had come into the dining room, one carrying a gravy boat and the other a cut-glass bowl of cranberry sauce.

"I just wondered if I would ever remember all your names." Sandy took the gravy boat and found a place for it on the table.

"I'm Gretchen." The cherub bearing cranberry sauce squeezed the dish onto the edge of the table. "I was a flower girl at Aunt Abby's wedding. Dolly was a flower girl, too."

"Now I remember!" Sandy clapped her hand to her forehead. "And you were the prettiest girls in the whole church, too." Dolly and Gretchen beamed with pleasure, then turned and disappeared back into the kitchen.

Sandy looked back at the table. In her mind, she saw white lace and rose petals and the cake created to celebrate her wedding day.

She had been so deliriously happy. How could things have fallen apart so quickly? How could she and Cam have argued so soon? Although she preferred to think of it as a misunderstanding, the uncomfortable truth was that she had cut him off when he tried to explain and walked out on him in a snit.

Maybe if she'd given him half a chance, he might have shared some of his distress with her. But no! She had to get righteous and go off in a huff! Then deliberately stay gone long enough to make sure he would worry about her and feel anxious the way she did when he disappeared. Except that she didn't have a good excuse. Maybe he wouldn't have told her anything, but she could have at least given him the chance. When she had come home she'd made it sound like their tiff was all his fault and he'd been immediately contrite.

He had apologized, taking all the blame, even what should have been hers. When she'd tried to apologize for her temper tantrum, he'd hushed her with a kiss. Then he had made love to her with exquisite gentleness. Her faith that he loved her in spite of the way he sometimes acted had been renewed. She had almost told him about the baby then, but the moment had seemed too fragile.

The quiet self-possession she'd once seen as evidence of confidence and strength wasn't always that at all. Oh, he was strong, certainly, and rigidly self-controlled, but that deceptive calm hid an unbearably deep well of pain. A nightmare place he couldn't or wouldn't share with her. And somewhere along the line, he'd been stripped of his self-confidence and his faith in himself. Maybe even his faith in God. He tried to hide his vulnerability, even from her.

Sandy picked up the little card Linc's eldest daughter had made to mark Cam's place. She fingered the careful lettering that said Uncle Cam. *We're going to make it, Cam. Together, we can get through this.* Her eyes blurred.

"Are you all right, Aunt Sandy?"

"Of course." Sandy pivoted to find another blonde niece staring at her intently. "I'm just admiring the place cards."

"Thank you." The girl smiled self-consciously, then took the card from Sandy and put it back in its place. "Come out to the kitchen and see all the food." She tugged at Sandy's hand.

The Cameron kitchen bustled with activity. All of Cam's siblings had come for dinner along with their spouses and offspring. Cam's mother and his sisters were putting the last of the food into serving bowls with the enthusiastic assistance of four little girls. The eldest of the children had been given the honor of carrying the turkey to the table, and he waited, rather impatiently, while the last minute trimmings were put on it.

"Why don't you go call the men in to dinner, Sandy?" Sandy's mother-in-law tucked a stray wisp of gray hair behind her ear, then wiped her hands on her apron. "I think we're just about ready."

Sandy nodded, and headed to the large den that had been added to the house when the growing brood of Camerons had outgrown the original living room. She found "the men" settled around the television watching football. Cam slouched in the corner of the sofa with Tommy asleep on his lap.

Instead of watching the game, Cam studied the sleeping toddler with an oddly tender look on his face. Sandy's heart jumped into her throat. She thought of the tiny life growing inside her, and pictured Cam holding his own son with just such a look in his eyes.

Cam glanced up and caught her watching him. He smiled, and she returned the smile, imagining the moment when she told him he was going to be a daddy.

With a happy warmth flooding through her, Sandy cleared her throat and made the dinner announcement. The boys scrambled for the other room, jostling past her in their eagerness to get there first.

"Boys." Brian, the Cameron patriarch, didn't have to raise his voice.

"Excuse me," one of the tow-headed lads mumbled.

"Kind of overwhelming, isn't it?" Cam stood beside her, gently jiggling Tommy awake. Tommy whimpered, and Cam tousled the hair on his head. "Time to wake up sport. Don't want to miss dinner, do you?"

Tommy wriggled to get down. Cam put him on his feet, and Sandy watched the toddler scamper off toward the dining room. Cam wrapped his arm about her waist and propelled her toward the sound of scraping chairs and happy chatter. Sandy stalled long enough to go onto her toes and give him a kiss. He seemed so happy and relaxed in spite of the night before.

She had begun to understand why he'd been drinking so much when she realized that when he had enough beer in him he didn't have nightmares. In the week since she'd lost patience and taken off for the day, he'd come home sober and gone to bed that way. And the night-mares had returned.

Last night, she had awakened to find him pawing frantically at the bedclothes as if he were looking for something and swearing crudely at himself. When she called his name to wake him, he'd looked around in confusion. Then he had slowly slumped back onto his heels and covered his face with his hands. She'd thought he might be crying, and then realized he was struggling not to. Finally, he had lain back down and pulled her to him without ever saying a word. She had fallen asleep again with Cam's head cradled against her breast and woke in the early dawn to an empty bed and apprehension in her heart.

Her relief had been immense when Cam came home a half-hour later with a healthy glow to his cheeks and a smile on his face.

"Why so quiet?" Cam nibbled on her ear. "You aren't intimidated by this crew are you?"

She shook her head.

"Good, then let's find our seats before the food is all gone."

"That's hard to believe, even with your family. I've never seen so much food in my life."

The already large dining room table had been augmented by the addition of several smaller tables shoved together. The expanse of crisp white linen extended through the archway and into the living room. And every inch of it was covered with platters and serving bowls.

When everyone had finally found their places and gotten seated, the bird arrived and was placed before Cam's father with a fanfare of trumpet sounds. Brian cleared his throat and held out both hands to those on either side of him. One by one each person took the hands of those seated on either side.

"God, we thank you for another year of blessings, great and small. We thank you for your care of us in our daily lives, for our family, for our home and for the food which we are about to eat. Bless this bounty and bless us to your service." Brian looked up and glanced around the table. "Does anyone have anything they would like to add?"

"Thank you for my new puppy."

"Thank you for my wonderful new wife." Adam spoke up unabashedly. He gazed at Abby with his heart in his eyes.

"And for letting me wear a beautiful princess dress for the wedding." Dolly wriggled in her seat.

"And me, too," echoed Gretchen.

"Thank you for . . ." Cam's brother's widow stopped, swallowed hard, then took a deep breath and went on. "For bringing Cam home safely."

Cam's hand closed convulsively about Sandy's

As a chorus of small amens followed, Sandy felt the tension growing in Cam.

Suddenly he shot to his feet, toppling his chair behind him.

"Nathan." Brian spoke sternly.

"God had nothing to do with it. It was just shit luck. If God cared, He'd have sent Tom home and taken me."

"Nathan!" Brian repeated, getting to his feet. His gaze locked onto his son's with a look of warning.

"Nathan, dear." His mother spoke with gentle firmness. "Please sit down. You don't have to agree, but each of has the right to be thankful in his or her own way."

"God doesn't give a shit."

The children gaped at their uncle with wide, uncertain eyes. Tommy's lip trembled. Linc started to get to his feet as well. Sandy held her breath in dismay.

"Leave the table, Nathan. I will not tolerate disrespectful behavior from any son of mine." Brian Cameron sat down again and picked up his napkin.

Cam turned on his heel and stalked from the room. A moment later the back door slammed and an uneasy silence hung over the table. Abby broke it finally.

"Shouldn't someone go after him?"

"You go, Linc," Barbi urged her husband.

"And miss my dinner?" Linc had begun to take his seat, but he hesitated half way down.

"Nathan can take care of himself. He'll return when he's ready to be civil." Brian's word was law. Linc sat.

Cam's mother lifted a steaming bowl of potatoes and passed it to George. Brian picked up the carving knife and began to slice the turkey. The children wriggled uncomfortably in their seats for a moment longer, then began to reach for the serving bowls nearest to them.

Sandy rose hesitantly to her feet. "I'm sorry, Mr. Cameron. I really should be with my husband."

Her father-in-law nodded his acquiescence.

Abby caught at Sandy's hand as she passed and tugged her down to whisper in her ear. "Look in the old tree house out back."

Sandy gave Abby's hand a squeeze. She felt eyes following her as she made her way past the jumble of chairs. Finally she reached the sanctuary of the kitchen. She had no idea where Cam had put her coat when they'd arrived but she found a row of hooks in the back hall with several jackets layered up on them. She chose the first one she came to and shrugged into it. It smelled like Linc's aftershave. She hoped he wouldn't mind.

Stepping out onto the back porch surprised her. The snow that had been a mere dusting when they arrived had begun to stick. The stairs and the grass were white with it. Carefully she made her way down the stairs, wishing she'd worn boots instead of loafers.

The treehouse perched about eight feet off the ground in a huge old maple tree behind the garage. Large, with a lookout and a narrow deck running along two sides, it must have been a grand place to play as a kid.

"Cam?" Sandy stood at the base of the tree and peered up through the dark hole at the top of the ladder. She got no answer. "Cam?"

After another minute, she took hold of the ladder and began to climb. When she reached the top and stuck her head inside, the odor of old wood and damp leaves filled her nostrils. It took a moment for her eyes to adjust.

CAM SAT against the far wall with his feet drawn up, his knees against his chest, and his face buried in his arms.

"Cam?"

He glanced up. "You should be eating, not chasing after the black sheep." Cam fought against the tide of angry emotions that had suddenly blackened what had started out to be a good day.

Sandy hoisted herself through the hole and crawled toward him "What happened in there?" She slid her chilled fingers into his.

"I acted like an asshole." He didn't meet her gaze as he accepted the comfort her touch offered.

"I didn't mean that."

"But that's what you're thinking."

"No, that's not what I'm thinking. I'm thinking you sounded like a man with something bothering him, and I want to help."

"You wouldn't understand." The anger swirled about him, dragging him down.

"Try me." She squeezed his hand.

"I should've died, not Tom." The words came out harsh. Cam swallowed and tried to soften his tone. "It should have been me, not Tom."

"Why are you so set on this idea that you were meant to be killed? I mean, if you believed that, why on earth did you go in the first place?"

"I thought my patriotic duty demanded it. I thought I was saving the world for democracy." The anger and bitterness were back, and he stopped trying to keep them out of his words. His chest felt tight, and his shoulders ached with tension. "Besides, if I hadn't volunteered, I'd have been drafted anyway."

"Lots of guys went, and whether they were called up or they volunteered most of them came back." Sandy settled herself cross-legged at his feet. She dragged his hand into her lap where she cradled it between both of her own. "Talk to me. Make me understand why you feel the way you do."

He stared at her, taking his time deciding what, if anything, to tell her. What, if anything, she could make sense of. Then he cleared his throat. He couldn't feel any worse, if he tried explaining.

"There was this guy in my father's unit in WWII named Nathan Hale something-or-other. He made a big deal out of the fact that he'd been named after this Revolutionary War dude. And he claimed his father gave it to him so the original Hale fellow would have the second chance he regretted not having when the British were getting ready to hang him. Only problem is, he died, too. Actually, he died saving my father's life."

"And your Dad named you after him."

"Yeah."

There was no comprehension in her face. "I still don't see what that has to do –"

"I told you, you wouldn't understand." Cam yanked his hand out of hers and shoved it into his armpit. He pulled away, shutting her out of his misery. Trying to keep himself from lashing out.

"It's nonsense, Cam."

He closed his eyes and tried to will away the need to smash something.

"Just because you were named after him didn't mean you were supposed to get killed. No one is supposed to get killed."

"Men always get killed in combat." She flinched at his sharp retort. "That's what war is all about."

"But not necessarily you. Not you more than anyone else. It's just a matter of being in the wrong place at the wrong time."

"But that's just it . . ." Cam pulled his hands from his armpits and grabbed her shoulders. His fingers bit into the fabric of the jacket she wore, and she winced. He forced himself to relax his grip. "Tom wasn't supposed to be there at all. He volunteered for a second tour, just like your brother. He made it through his year. He didn't have to go back."

"That was his decision to make, not yours." Sandy wrapped her fingers around Cam's wrists, holding on to him as if he weren't already clutching her like a drowning man. "He chose to go back. I'm sorry he died, but it wasn't your fault. You couldn't have done anything to change the way things happened and you know it."

Cam stared at her for a long time. His eyes burned, and his heart ached. "I never got to say goodbye." He struggled with his emotions. "I tried. Oh, God, I tried. When they told me he was on a medevac chopper I was only two miles from the hospital." Cam swallowed.

"He died before . . ." His voice broke. He dropped his head onto his knees again. "I never got to say goodbye."

"Did you ever cry for him?"

He shook his head. *Marines don't cry.*

"You need to cry, Cam. You need to grieve before you can heal." Her voice was soft but urgent.

"I can't," he insisted stubbornly. He didn't think he'd ever heal. Tears or not.

"You think Tom's wife hasn't cried buckets? Or your mother? Even your father? They probably still do. Why should you be any different?"

"I'm afraid." He bit his lip to stop it from trembling. Felt Sandy's arms go around him in a hard embrace, ignoring his taut resistance. "I'm afraid if I ever start, I'll never stop."

It was the first time he'd ever admitted that to anyone. He was appalled it had slipped out now. But, somehow, the confession eased some of the tension coiled like a snake in his chest. He still couldn't let himself give in to tears, though. *No damned way! I'm not a little kid. I'm a man, and I'll damned well act like one.* He clung to his composure until the snake unwound itself and slithered away.

When the already dim light in the treehouse began to fade into ever deepening shadows Cam realized the sun had set. He straightened up, and Sandy sank back onto her heels.

"I'm cold." Cam's voice sounded almost normal. His emotions were carefully in check once again. His eyes were still dry.

"Not surprising. You forgot your jacket."

Cam peered at her in the gloom. "I hope Linc isn't trying to figure out where he left his."

"I thought this thing smelled like Linc."

Cam rocked himself onto his feet and stood, bent at the waist. "This place shrunk some since the last time I came up here." He stooped, placed a hand on either side of the trap door, then swung his feet through it. "You coming?"

"Thanks for coming after me." Cam waited for Sandy at the foot of the ladder.

"Did you expect me not to?"

Cam shrugged, then shivered again.

"Let's go in where it's warm. You must be starving."

"Now that you mention it." Cam turned and led the way back toward the house.

The kitchen had been completely tidied of its earlier happy confusion. Two plates, heaped with food and covered with plastic wrap, sat on the table. His mother, no doubt.

Wordlessly, they sat down, pealed back the plastic wrap and began to eat. After a while Sandy reached out and touched Cam's arm. He lifted his head and looked at her.

"I love you." She gripped his wrist tighter.

"I love you, too."

When they had finished eating, Cam gathered up their plates and stacked them neatly in the sink. Then he went off to find their coats in the tiny room just off the kitchen that Mary Cameron called her jumble room. He was helping Sandy into hers when his mother came into the kitchen.

"I wish you didn't have to leave so soon."

"I'm sorry for the scene I created, Mom." Cam gave his mother a hug. "I guess I'm just not in the mood for holidaying."

She patted his cheek. "I understand, Nathan. Even if you don't think so." Then she turned to Sandy. "You take care of him for me. Okay?" Mary pressed a container of left-overs into Sandy's hands. "And make him bring you back to see us again, real soon."

He talked about the football game the whole way home without a single reference to his outburst at dinner. It was a far safer topic.

When they arrived at the apartment complex, Cam pulled up in front of the main door and left the engine idling. Sandy looked at him, a question in her expressive hazel eyes.

"Go ahead." He reached across her to open the door.

"Aren't you coming in?"

"In a while." He waited while she got out.

She hesitated, clutching the container of turkey, before finally shutting the door and stepping up onto the curb. Cam put the truck in gear and didn't look back as he pulled back onto the street and drove away.

CHAPTER TWENTY-FIVE

Cam swung his truck into their allotted space in the apartment parking lot, turned the engine off, then gaped in dismay at the clock on the bank across the street. *Shit! How did it get so damned late? Sandy's probably out of her mind with worry.*

He slid out, slammed the door and hurried through the shadows to the rear stairway of the apartment building. He felt tired, but calmer. When he and Sandy left his parent's house, he'd felt like he was coming out of his skin. He had just needed some time alone.

The explosive, on-edge, feeling hadn't been Sandy's fault, though, and the longer he drove around trying to leave it behind, the worse he felt about the way he'd abandoned her, standing on the curb looking distressed and more than a little concerned.

Cam opened the front door soundlessly in case she'd gone to bed and stepped inside their tiny living room. Everything was dark and very quiet. After hanging his jacket on a hook by the door, he tiptoed through the kitchen.

He flipped the light switch in the hall and peered into the bedroom. But the bed hadn't been slept in. He checked the bathroom, then returned to the kitchen. *Where is she?* He stared blankly at the empty room, apprehension building in his chest. "Sandy?"

The phone rang. Cam lunged for it. *Gotta be her.* "Cam, here."

"Christ, Cam. Where the hell have you been?"

Linc not Sandy. Damn it! "Nowhere in particular. Why?"

"I'm at the hospital with your wife."

"Oh, God!" Cam's heart hammered its way into his throat. "What's wrong?"

"Sandy thought she was having a miscarriage is what's wrong. Where the hell were you?" Linc's voice dripped reproach.

Miscarriage! Jesus! How could that be? "Miscarriage? She isn't pregnant!"

"Wrong answer! She *is* pregnant, and she's scared."

"She can't be pregnant. I'd have known." His mind refused to grapple with the unacceptable. It couldn't be true.

"If you stayed home where you belong at night, maybe you would have figured it out. Now get your sorry ass down here." Linc hung up.

Cam tore out of the apartment taking the stairs three at a time. With his mind scrambling for answers, he ran two red lights and ignored three stop signs. *This has to be a mistake. Sandy can't be pregnant. I only forgot to use a condom that one night since we've been married. God, that was only . . .* He counted backwards and decided maybe she could be. His worst nightmare was coming true.

When Cam raced into the emergency room waiting area, he found Linc lounging on an uncomfortable looking vinyl chair watching Johnny Carson on a television set mounted on the wall.

"It's about time." Linc unwound his lanky frame and got to his feet.

"Where's Sandy? Is she going to be okay?" *She was alone and in trouble and where was I? Off feeling sorry for myself as usual.*

"She's fine. The doctor said it was just a false alarm. She's almost past the first trimester and he isn't too worried. Mostly she's just scared."

"The first trimester? What's that mean?"

Linc stared at Cam with a strange expression in his piercing blue eyes. "*It means* she was pregnant when you two got married. I thought you must have known. I thought maybe that was why you rushed into marrying her like you did."

Not possible! Cam's head reeled. *She couldn't have known all this time and not have told me!* He thought back to that night in his room at Delta House. Remembered his dawning horror the morning after when this possibility first occurred to him. The uncomfortable scene in the sheltered garden behind St. Mark's with the old priest.

As he returned Linc's steady gaze, Cam couldn't look away, and he couldn't lie. "She was a . . . She's not that kind of girl and . . ." He stumbled to a stop. Dragged a shaking hand across his stubbled face. "She wouldn't say yes at first. She didn't want to get married just because I felt like we had to, you know? I love her so much, Linc, but I didn't know. I didn't know she was pregnant. His eyes felt watery and dangerously close to giving him away completely. "Why didn't she tell me?"

"You'll have to ask her that," Linc said, his voice gentler than before.

"I'm not meant to be a father. I can't do it." Panic threatened to strangle Cam. *This isn't happening.*

Linc's eyebrows rose at Cam's denial. "Too late, Runt. It's time to pay the piper."

"But—"

"They suggested keeping her overnight, but Sandy wants to go home." Linc retrieved his jacket from the back of the chair. "I'll let you sort that out."

"I'm sorry –"

"Save the apologies for Sandy." Linc gripped his brother's shoulder with one big hand. "And don't be such an ass when you talk to her, Cam. You'll get used to the idea, and you'll make a great daddy."

"I don't . . . You don't understand." *I don't want to be a daddy. Not now. Maybe not ever.*

Linc looked like he was going to say something more, then changed his mind. "Go be with your wife. She needs you." He pointed at a curtain down the hall on the left. "If you want to talk later, you know where to find me." He gave Cam a fierce hug, then turned and walked toward the exit.

As Cam approached the curtained area Linc had indicated, conflicting emotions twisted in his gut. Heartfelt relief that Sandy was okay. Guilt for not being there when she needed him. And terror! He'd gotten her pregnant and there was no going back.

He peered around the curtain shielding the gurney from view. Sandy laid on her side, facing toward him with her eyes shut, the evidence of tears streaking her cheeks. *Asleep maybe? Trying to shut out the world and the scare she just lived through?* He slipped silently into the straight-backed, wooden chair beside the bed.

One slender hand, looking terribly defenseless, lay palm up on the white sheet, a temporary, plastic ID bracelet around her wrist. Cam put his hand over hers. Slowly, her eyes opened. As she focused on him, tears swelled and began to dribble down her cheek.

"I'm sorry, sweetheart." Cam bent forward to kiss her. "I'm sorry I wasn't home when you needed me."

"I was so scared. I thought I was losing our baby." She hiccupped and the tears came faster. The hand clutching his trembled. Tenderness welled up inside him. All the denials and accusations hovering on the tip of his tongue dried up. He pushed a lock of damp blond hair away from her face.

"Why didn't you tell me?" He put his arms about her and hugged her gingerly.

"I was going to tell you today only—"

"Only I didn't give you a chance."

"It wasn't your fault."

"I should never have left you alone when we got home."

"You were upset," Sandy pressed her face into his neck.

"You need to stop excusing my bad behavior." Regret at his churlish dismissal of her pleas not to go off struck him hard. No wonder she hadn't told him she was pregnant. He'd never given her an opportunity. Or a reason to think he would welcome the news.

"I didn't mean to get pregnant. And I guess you aren't too thrilled, but it happened." Sandy pulled away and gazed at him with a pained frown between her brows.

"Sandy?" A new wave of alarm shot through him. He had never seen her in pain before. He didn't know what to do, or say.

Sandy wriggled out of his arms and shoved herself into a sitting position, bare legs dangling over the edge of the narrow bed. "I want to go home." She wiped her tears away with the heels of her hands.

"But if you're in pain—"

"I'm not in pain. I'm just worried.

"If you're worried maybe you should stay overnight?"

"I'm not worried about me or the baby anymore. I'm just worried about what you're thinking. Take me home. Please, Cam? I just need for us to be together." Sandy slid off the bed, and picked up a plastic sack with the name Cameron scribbled in large black letters. She dumped it on the bed, rummaged through her things, then began to dress.

"Linc said the doctor suggested keeping you for the night." Cam didn't know why he argued with her. He just couldn't stop himself. She had good reason to be anxious over what he might say once they got home. The emotions scrambling around inside him were hard to sort out. He couldn't admit he was terrified. Or that he desperately didn't want this baby. What reassurances was he going to offer her?

"The doctor said the baby is fine and I'm fine, and I just want to go home." She stopped buttoning her shirt and looked at him with a nervous expression in her eyes. "Please?"

Cam gave in, his heart constricting in distress. He reached out to finish buttoning her shirt, then took her into his arms again. They stood without speaking for a long time while he held her, rocking her gently. *I don't know what to say to her.*

CHAPTER TWENTY-SIX

Sandy stared up at the ceiling with aching eyes. Cam slept with one arm cradling her against his chest, her head on his shoulder. He had seemed so distant on the way home from the hospital. He apologized for not being there when she needed him. But he hadn't even mentioned the baby. Or asked any questions. Not how long she had known. Not one question about the baby. Like it didn't exist.

But it did.

Their baby wasn't even big enough for her to feel its presence, but she knew it was there, and she loved it.

She glanced at the clock. 3:15. Cam snorted and rolled onto his back, but his embrace didn't relax. His arm still circled her protectively. She snuggled closer, trying to find sleep in the sheer size and warmth of his presence.

The next time Sandy looked at the clock sunlight spilled across the floor and Cam was gone. She sat up and swung her feet over the side of the bed. And then it hit her.

No more delaying telling him. The truth was unavoidably out. It was a relief, in a way. She should have told him weeks ago. But at least, now he knew.

She shoved her feet into a pair of slippers, then padded into the kitchen. An empty juice glass sat on the counter. Beside it sat the morning paper, folded in quarters. Cam must have been reading it while he drank his juice.

Sandy picked the paper up and sank onto a kitchen chair. Under a stark photo of two dun-green helicopters with soldiers, armed to the teeth, deploying out of them into a deserted looking compound of packed dirt and straw huts, the headline read, 'POW camp at Son Tay found empty.'

Was that where her brother might have been? A familiar ache grew in the pit of her stomach. If Tony had been there, he'd been moved before a rescue could bring him out.

All the press seemed to print these days were the failures. Failure to rescue Americans held by North Vietnam. Failure to hold fire bases in the face of increasing infiltration from the north. Failure to meet or even define any understandable goals.

No wonder Cam felt such a hopeless sense of futility and rage over his brother's death.

CAM TOSSED his jacket over a chairback and headed to the bedroom to check on Sandy. But then he saw her, sitting by the table with the morning paper on her lap.

"Shouldn't you be in bed?"

"Why? There's nothing wrong with me." She tossed the paper onto the table.

Cam squatted down and placed his hands on her knees. She reached out to smooth back the unruly swoop of hair that had grown long enough to fall into his face. He needed a haircut. "Are you sure you should be up? What did the doctor say?

"He didn't say anything about staying in bed. He just said to take it easy for a few days. And no sex until I go back to see him."

"Good, God, I should hope not." *How can she even think of that right now?* He gathered her into his arms, stood, and seated himself in the chair with her on his lap. "If anything happened to you . . ." The thought of losing Sandy filled him with panic. It would have been all his fault. For getting her pregnant in the first place. For treating her like shit and ignoring her half the time. "I should have been here."

"You're here now." She pressed her face into his shoulder, and he held her tighter. The shock of last night had worn off and now he felt far too much. Guilt, love, tenderness, confusion and terror. His chest ached with the intensity of it all.

"When were you going to tell me you were pregnant?"

Sandy pulled out of his embrace, twisting her fingers and not looking at him.

"Didn't you think I had a right to know?"

She nodded, but still didn't look at him.

Cam's thoughts scrambled around in his head like a hamster on an exercise wheel. *She's pregnant, and there's no erasing that fact. How in hell am I going to live with this?* His chest felt constricted with the fear that had tied him in knots since his first conscious moment this morning. How had he managed to fall asleep in the first place?

"I was going to tell you yesterday before dinner." She bunched up the tie of her robe, then dropped it back into her lap and smoothed it out, still not looking at him. "I was going to tell you a bunch of times, but it just never seemed like the right moment."

"You should have told me." His voice came out harsher than he'd meant it to be.

Sandy's head jerked up. Tears had formed in her eyes. "I was afraid you'd be angry."

Her admission stabbed him in the gut. "You didn't get pregnant by yourself. If I'm going to be angry, I'd be angry at me. It's not like I don't know where babies come from."

He had known she wanted children. She'd never hidden that from him. He thought she might have been secretly delighted to find herself in this condition, and it shamed him that she'd been afraid to share it with him. If only he could be as happy as she wanted him to be. If only he wasn't terrified by the whole idea.

"But you never wanted to be intimate in the first place." Anguish and guilt hung heavy in every word, and her eyes reflected her shame.

Dousing his own self-centered panic, he hauled her back into his embrace. "I won't lie to you. In my head, I kept telling myself it would be better for both of us if we didn't get it on, but the fact is, I was hot for you." He kissed the top of her head. "If I really meant for it not to go that far, then I should have done something to make sure it didn't."

He rocked her against his chest, remembering the heady way she'd made him feel that night. Remembering thinking he needed to put a brake on things, but making only a half-hearted effort to do so. Remembering the hot, unquenchable need that burned through his loins, and the feel of her hands touching him with such exquisite torment. And letting it happen. He very clearly remembered letting himself fall over the edge into sin and damn the consequences.

And this was the consequence.

"It's more my fault than yours, but we're in this together, now." *Christ how am I going to get through this? How am I going to fake it so she'll never guess how far from wanting this baby I am?* Then another though barged its way into his brain.

He put his fingers under her chin and tipped her face up. The fear had gone. Thank God. But a hint of trepidation still lingered.

"You are happy about it, aren't you? I mean, you wanted a baby, right?"

She nodded slowly. "I wanted us both to be happy about it." She paused, perhaps giving him a chance to agree, but he couldn't bring himself to say it.

Not even for her. He didn't know how he was going to cope with the overwhelming guilt he knew would overshadow everything else. He couldn't lie, but he forced a smile onto his face.

"It isn't the best timing. I mean, I'll just barely graduate before the baby is born. And you haven't even got a job yet. I don't know how we're going to manage the money part. I won't even have insurance once I graduate. I—"

Cam put a finger against her lips to stop the nervous flow of words. "It'll be okay."

Nothing would be okay. Nothing in his life would ever be okay again. He felt himself starting to breathe too fast. Felt the same light-headedness he'd experienced the last time she'd brought up the subject of having a baby. But he had to get control of himself. For Sandy's sake, he had to pull himself together. "We'll be okay."

Sandy gazed up at him with the look of an angel, wide smile, eyes swimming in tears, accepting his assurance. "I love you, Cam. I can't believe how much I love you." She flung her arms about his neck and squeezed hard. "And I love your baby almost as much."

CHAPTER TWENTY-SEVEN

Cam lay on his side, studying the flickering shadows on the bedroom wall. The rising wind howled about the eaves and made the tree outside their window dance. Big, heavy drops of rain began to beat against the panes with sharp splats. The storm mirrored the turmoil in his soul.

Sandy's pregnant! The reality had finally sunk in. The wild panic and his fervent desire to deny that any of it could be real had morphed into acceptance and dread. Dread that sat like a lump of ice in the center of his being. Dread that seemed to freeze him into immobility, unable to respond to Sandy's unspoken plea for him to be excited with her.

He'd caught her staring at him several times during the day with a look of yearning and sadness in her eyes. She wanted him to be happy about this baby, and he couldn't be. He wanted to be, for her sake, but couldn't even manage to fake it convincingly.

Cam rolled over, reaching out for Sandy and pulling her into the curve of his body. She snuggled against him, but didn't wake. He spread his hand over her stomach. His child grew in there, too small yet to be seen, but undeniably there. Dear God, how was he going to cope with this? How could he do it? How could he be the kind of father Sandy wanted for her baby?

"I'm sorry, sweetheart," Cam whispered, nuzzling his face against her neck. "I wish I could be all you want me to be. I wish to God I was all you deserve me to be."

Sandy slept soundly.

He pulled her closer and tried to stop thinking. He concentrated on the wind and the sound of the rain against the window and tried to fall asleep.

SANDY WOKE WITH A START. Cam lay face down, sobbing into his pillow.

"Are you alright Cam?"

"Goddamned fuckin' bastards." He pounded the pillow hard enough to shake the bed.

"Cam, wake up!" Alarm filled her. She'd never seen Cam cry, asleep or not. And he never talked like that either.

"It's my fault." His voice sounded ragged and painful. "I shoulda checked. I shoulda known."

Mindful not to touch him, she leaned closer and spoke louder. "Cam! Wake up. You're having a bad dream."

The sobbing stopped abruptly. Sandy dared to reach out and touch him. She ran her hand over his head, smoothing down the spikes of hair that stuck out at odd angles. She didn't ask what he'd been dreaming, or why he'd been crying. He wouldn't tell her if she did ask. He never explained any of his nocturnal distress. She continued smoothing her hand over his head until she heard his breathing change. Gradually his body relaxed.

What horrible, unspeakable thing had happened that haunted him still, all these months after he'd left hell behind? If anything, Cam's nightmares were getting worse, not better. And guilt continued to torment him, whether he had earned it or not.

Cam rolled onto his side facing away from her. She touched the scars on his back as she considered the guilt he carried around inside him. Snippets of scenes from the news about a massacre flitted through her brain. Had Cam been involved in something like that? Could that be what haunted him?

No! Definitely not that! Not the Cam she knew. He couldn't. He wouldn't. He might refuse to share his experiences with her, but she knew enough about him to know he'd never kill innocent people. But something had happened that haunted his soul. Something he somehow felt he should have been able to stop.

She wrapped her arms around him and hugged him. Not her Cam. Never her Cam.

"HOW DID it go at school today? Today's your first day teaching, right?" Kathleen tossed her coat over the back of a chair, then tugged her sweater down self-consciously. Kathleen's belly had begun to swell into a tight little ball that protruded beneath the waistline of her skirt.

"Well, not exactly. I don't start that until after Christmas. Today was just an introduction. I got to meet the teacher I'll be working with. I was just about to fix myself a cup of coffee. You want one?"

"Have you got any tea?" Kathleen plopped herself into the old rocker Sandy had found at a garage sale when she'd first suspected she might be pregnant. Sandy filled the kettle and put it on the stove to heat. "For some reason, I've lost my taste for coffee lately. Lost my taste for a lot of things, actually."

"Tea it is." Sandy reached for a box of tea bags. She wondered how come she hadn't felt any nausea so far. She thought all pregnant women were supposed to feel nauseated, at least first thing in the morning. But so far she felt terrific. Better than she ever had, in fact. She wanted to confide in Kathleen so she could ask about that and a hundred other things. Cam didn't want to tell his family yet, but Kathleen wasn't family.

"So what's he like? You did say you'd be teaching with a man, right?"

"He seems really nice. The children like him. He's so quiet, he never shouts but the kids all listen up - even on the playground. And they crowd around him like he's a celebrity."

"I'd have given anything to attend public school when I was a kid. The nuns were horrible. They acted like we were all spawns of Satan just looking for ways to be evil."

Sandy laughed. "Well, I had a few not so nice teachers. I guess you don't have to be a nun to be awful. What I always wondered is why people become teachers if they hated kids that much."

The kettle whistled, and Sandy poured water into a pot for Kathleen's tea, then stirred instant coffee into a mug for herself. She carried the mugs to the little table by the rocking chair, and plopped a box of Oreos on the table along with the sugar bowl and the milk.

"I think I'm going to really enjoy working with Alex." Sandy hesitated, considering Cam's reluctance to announce their pregnancy and weighing it against her need to share it with someone. Self-consciously she rubbed a hand over her still very flat stomach and sipped her coffee. Then made up her mind.

"Guess what?"

Kathleen looked up from her mug of tea with eyebrows raised." How many guesses do I get?"

"Three."

"Okay." Kathleen appeared to ponder. "Cam bought you a decent car?"

Sandy shook her head.

"Too bad, that truck is a disaster waiting to happen." She clucked. "You're pregnant."

Sandy felt a rush of color rise up into her face, while a happy warmth filled the rest of her. "How'd you know?"

"You're glowing." Kathleen plunked her mug on the table and launched herself out of the rocker to wrap Sandy in a happy embrace. "Now we can share war stories."

Sandy flinched at the casual use of the term 'war" stories. War stories were Cam's world and they weren't much fun. But she knew what Kathleen meant, and she was bubbling to share her enormous happiness. Kathleen gave her another hug and planted herself back in the rocker.

"What's Cam think?"

Some of the bubbly enjoyment fled. "He doesn't talk much about it."

"Why? I'd have thought he'd be thrilled. Sean goes around with his chest about half a step ahead of the rest of him, just waiting for opportunities to announce his prowess."

"I don't think Cam wants kids right now." *Or ever.*

"He should have thought of that before he got you pregnant, then." Kathleen waggled her eyebrows. "I bet he wanted that part of it well enough."

Sandy got up abruptly and took her half empty mug to the sink. It was one thing to want someone to share her experience with, but another thing entirely to confess her part in the untimely conception. She swallowed hard, then turned back to her friend. "Yeah, he did want that part, sure enough. We both did."

"When are you due?"

"The doctor says the end of May. The eighteenth." Now the timing was out of the bag as well.

Kathleen's mouth formed a little O of comprehension, then she smiled again. "You mean to tell me you've known all this time and you kept it to yourself? Even when you were busily prying my secret out of me?"

"I wanted to tell you. Honest. But I thought I should tell Cam first and somehow I kept waiting for the right time. Only it never seemed to be the right time, and then . . . " The uncertainty and worry she had felt Thanksgiving night, alone and afraid that she might be losing her baby came rushing back. Cam might not want to talk about her pregnancy or their baby, but she needed to. She needed someone to share her worries with. Someone to compare notes with. Someone who would understand.

"I knew Cam would be upset."

"Well you didn't get that why all by yourself." Kathleen made an inelegant sound in her throat. "Men are always up for the sex. They should be ready to take the consequences."

"Cam was always careful about that."

"Not careful enough." Kathleen reached across the table and put her hand on Sandy's arm. "Men like being the center of attention, in case you haven't noticed. Having a baby puts a big cramp in their style in a major hurry. Cam's probably just thinking he's not ready to share you yet."

Sandy hadn't thought of it like that. In fact, she hadn't thought it of from Cam's point of view at all. She flushed with embarrassment at her own selfishness. As the certainty of her pregnancy had grown, she'd only thought of how wonderful it felt to have Cam's baby growing inside her.

"Don't worry." Kathleen squeezed Sandy's wrist. "Before you know it Cam will be acting like it was all his idea." She grinned conspiratorially.

Sandy laughed. It felt like a burden had been lifted and she was glad Kathleen had come by. "You don't know how good it feels to have someone I can talk with. Thanks for ... well just thanks."

"Don't mention it." Kathleen gestured with her mug. "How about a refill? Got anything besides Oreo's. You wouldn't believe how hungry I get lately."

"Oh my God!" Sandy laughed as she turned to rummage in the fridge for something more substantial. "I think I could eat a horse half the time!"

CHAPTER TWENTY-EIGHT

A STACK OF BOOKS AND INDEX CARDS FILLED WITH SANDY'S CAREFUL notes littered the table in their tiny kitchen. The old Smith-Corona portable Linc had loaned them sat in the middle of it all with a fresh sheet of thesis paper reeled under the platen. Untouched, because Sandy was getting ready to head out to the part time job she'd landed to earn a little much needed cash. For the baby.

Cam glared at the closed bedroom door. He didn't like the idea of Sandy working. She had argued that Wellman's paid their seasonal help a more than generous wage and they could use the extra money. And, she got a discount on anything she purchased; she had informed him with a happy little smile on her face. He hadn't asked what the smile was about because Wellman's had a large, well-stocked infant section, and he pretty much knew that was what she had in mind. He didn't like Sandy being gone every other night either. Or bringing in the only income in the family.

He returned his attention to the lined pad of paper in front of him. A blank pad of lined paper. He was supposed to be getting a resume together and sending it to a man his uncle had tipped him to.

'It's a bit of a stretch just starting out, but I know you can handle it. And I'll see you get a couple good recommendations.' Uncle George had said.

And I'll be earning the money for a change! Cam thought as his uncle's promise echoed in his brain.

Footsteps clattered suddenly on the stairs, followed by a timid knock on the door. Cam tossed his pencil down with guilty relief and got up to answer the door.

The man from the downstairs apartment stood in the tiny hall with three of his children gathered about him and a baby in his arms.

"I'm sorry to bother you like this, but I need a really big favor."

"A favor?" Cam glanced at the baby apprehensively.

Kevin Foster, a fireman and former classmate, looked anything but the cool, competent man Cam knew. "Mikey's gone and gashed himself. I've got to take him to the doctor to get it stitched up."

"It hurts." Mikey, the five year old, held his wounded hand up for Cam to see. A thick wad of gauze had been wound around it, but blood had already seeped through. Cam's stomach knotted uncomfortably.

"He was trying to pry a toy open so he could get the plastic jumping beans out," Kevin explained.

"Well, um . . ."

"I hate to ask, Cam, but my wife is out running errands and taking this gang with me— Well, it would be a nightmare."

Cam's knotted stomach did a somersault. "And you have no idea where she went?"

"I think she likes being out of touch and unavailable so *I* have to deal with the kids for a change." Kevin rolled his eyes as if his wife's desire for some time alone was unreasonable. "She didn't expect Mikey to do something stupid and get himself hurt."

"Who's at the door, Cam?" Sandy emerged from the bedroom shoving her arms into her coat. "Oh, hi Kevin." She took in the kids gathered around their father's legs, her gaze returning to Mikey and his bandaged hand. "What happened?"

Kevin explained a second time. "I kinda hoped you could watch the kids for me while I take him to the emergency room. I left my wife a note. She should be home anytime now."

"Of course, we will. Cam why didn't you ask them in?" Sandy gestured for the kids to enter.

Cam felt the walls crowding in on him. Sandy had to go to work, so he knew who would end up watching the kids, and he wished himself far away. "Maybe they won't want to stay if they know you won't be here."

"Nonsense." Sandy reached out to take the baby from Kevin's arms. "No problem. Really. Just do what you gotta do and don't worry about us."

Kevin smiled his relief and lifted Mikey onto his hip. "You boys be good and help with Sarah." He ruffled their hair, then turned and hurried down the stairs.

"But Sandy," Cam protested.

Sandy ignored him as she ushered the children into the living room, then plopped Sarah into his arms. Panic lanced through him. He clutched the baby awkwardly, his heart clicking into overdrive. Sarah shoved her thumb in her mouth and sucked contentedly, her eyelids drooping.

"If Sarah cries, she's probably hungry." Hank, all of six, dumped a bulging pink diaper bag on the floor. "Dad put everything he could think of in here."

"Can I watch Sesame Street?" The four-year-old plopped himself on the sofa.

"It's not on now, stupid."

"Hank called me stupid." Brian's lower lip thrust out ominously.

"I take it back, Squirt." Hank shrugged one thin shoulder and gave Cam a curiously adult look of condescension.

"What'll I do with them?" Cam followed Sandy as she gathered up her purse and her gloves. Then he felt something warm against his side and jerked his head down to find a spreading damp patch on his shirt. He shoved the baby toward his grinning wife.

"I'd guess Sarah needs to be changed, to start with." Sandy consulted her watch. "Then, it looks like its past time for her nap. You can put her on our bed and pile some pillows on either side. She's half asleep already."

"But what about the boys?"

Sandy gave Cam a peck on the cheek, then headed for the door. "You're a guy. You ought to be able to think of some guy thing to do with Brian and Hank." She blew him a kiss and left.

When the door closed behind his wife, Cam peered down into two pairs of identical blue eyes that watched him with somber expressions.

"What's a guy thing?" Hank asked.

"Stuff girls don't like." Cam hunkered down and laid the baby on the floor.

"Like swearing?" Hank plopped down at Cam's side and peered at him hopefully.

Cam choked back a guffaw. Some of his alarm faded.

"Mom doesn't like it when Dad swears. He does it anyway, though." Hank scrunched up one shoulder.

"I don't think that's what Mrs. Cameron had in mind." Cam rummaged in the bulging pink bag, looking for a clean diaper.

"What's a swear?" Brian tugged at Cam's pants.

Cam ran a hand through his hair. He laughed uneasily. He'd have to think of something to do fast before this conversation got completely out of hand. Then he remembered the box of old toys his mother had given him along with his other boyhood treasures.

"Let's get your sister settled down for a nap first. Okay?" With a dozen nieces and nephews, Cam was not a stranger to diapers, but he didn't particularly like dealing with them. Especially not the kind he found when he finally got through all the layers of clothing.

"Yuk." Brian wrinkled up his nose.

"Don't look if you don't like it, Stupid."

"Hank called me stupid," Brian pouted.

"That's what big brothers are for." Cam finished mopping up the mess, then deftly slipped a new diaper under Sarah's chubby pink bottom and pinned it in place. "My big brothers called me Stupid, too. And lots of other things besides."

"Really?" Brian studied Cam's face as if he didn't quite believe him.

"Sure did." Cam ruffled Brian's silky auburn hair. "They also called me Stinky, Pest, Runt, Dumbo . . . I especially didn't like Dumbo."

"Bet you didn't have two big brothers! I have two big brothers and they both call me names."

"I had three." Cam suddenly remembered who had called him Dumbo. He'd give anything in the world to hear Tom call him Dumbo again. He blinked hard at the sudden dampness in his eyes.

"Don't worry about it, Squirt." Cam told the little boy. "It just means they love you."

"Hank calls me squirt, too." Brian glared at his brother.

Cam forced back the flood of memories that threatened to undo him as he snapped the little girl into a dry gown and wrapped a fresh receiving blanket around her. The boys followed him to the bedroom and supervised the arrangements for their sister's nap. Then they followed him back to the living room and stared at Cam with solemn eyes as he opened his box of boyhood memories and sorted through it. They pounced on the tin of toy soldiers.

As Hank spilled the contents of the tin onto the carpet, Cam did his best to squash the feelings that would have spiraled out of control if he let them. The last time he'd seen these tiny green figures he'd been about eight. And he'd been playing with Tom. Now they only made him think of flesh and blood soldiers scattered like discarded toys over the unfriendly battlefields of Vietnam. Don't think about it, he admonished himself. Just don't think about it.

"BOY, am I glad to be home." Sandy shut the door behind herself and sagged against the doorframe. Cam glanced up from where he was sitting, cross-legged in the midst of a vast army of tiny green soldiers.

"Why's it so dark in here?"

A shaft of light slashed across the scene from the archway into the kitchen. An old quilt arranged with rumpled care in the middle of the floor had toy soldiers deployed in its shadowed valleys and folds. Toothpicks outlined a network of roads with miniature Jeeps and troop transports strung along them. Napkins had been arranged like tents with soldiers huddled inside. He stared at the scene as if he hadn't been a part of its creation.

"What's the matter, Cam?"

"Nothing."

"Where'd the toy soldiers come from?" Sandy took her coat off, hung it on a hook, then went to sit on the edge of the sofa.

"They were in the stuff Mum gave me after we got married."

"And you got them out to entertain Hank and Brian. Good thinking. How did it go?"

He shrugged. "It went all right."

"How's Mikey?"

"Okay, I guess."

"So how come you're sitting in the dark?"

Cam opened his hand and stared silently at the broken soldier lying in his palm. After Mrs. Foster had come to collect her kids, he'd knelt to pick up the toy soldiers and return them to their tin. And all the feelings kept so ruthlessly under control while the boys had been around had surged though him with shocking force. As his fist had closed around the soldier he'd been holding, the arms had snapped off.

And the nightmare had raged through him. In the middle of the afternoon. With him wide awake. All the terror of that day in Nam swamped him under an avalanche of helplessness and regret. The echoing sound of the explosion. The smell of blood. The horror of death. The look on Jenkins' face as he stared at the stumps where his arms had been only moments before.

Sandy put her hand on Cam's shoulder. "What's wrong, Cam?"

"Don't mean nothin'."

"Don't tell me it's nothing. I know better." She took the shattered soldier out of Cam's hand.

Cam got to his feet. "You wouldn't understand." Then he walked into the bedroom.

"I might, if you gave me half a chance." Sandy started to follow him.

He shut the door in her face with a soft click.

CHAPTER TWENTY-NINE

SANDY RESTED HER HEAD DROWSILY AGAINST CAM'S CHEST WHILE she watched the television mounted in the corner above the end of the bar at the Code Seven. Linc's establishment was a popular place on New Year's Eve and the hum of activity surrounding her was genial and celebratory. Guy Lombardo, bundled into a heavy woolen overcoat with a long white scarf about his neck and a microphone to his face, was superimposed over the equally festive chaos of Times Square, where the jostling crowd screamed and cheered and craned their necks to see the glittering ball poised against the midnight sky.

Cam, his hip propped against the bar behind Sandy's stool and supporting her against his chest, had one arm draped about her shoulders. His fingers played idly with the silver chain that hung around her neck.

Sandy reached up to touch the little pendant that sported a Celtic design that Cam had told her signified everlasting love. He'd given it to her for Christmas. A clear example of the thoughtful man he could be when he wasn't letting himself be tormented by a past he had no control over. The man she'd fallen head over heals in love with.

"You falling asleep already?" Cam tipped her face up toward his with a hand under her chin. "It's almost midnight." He bent to kiss her.

His lips tasted like beer. He held her captive as he deepened the kiss. He chuckled as his lips left hers. "Happy New Year, sweetheart."

"Happy New Year yourself." She whispered the words against his mouth. "I love you."

"I love you, too." He laughed again and let her go.

Suddenly, Sandy felt oddly alone, sitting on her bar stool in the midst of the cheering crowd as Cam moved about the room, kissing the women and thumping his buddies on the back. He enjoyed this. These were his friends. Friends he'd grown up with, and had probably spent a couple dozen New Years Eves with. Sandy felt like crying and she didn't know why.

Kathleen had warned her that she might have mood swings and crying jags at totally inconvenient times, but Sandy thought there should at least be a reason for them, and at the moment she couldn't think of a reason. Cam looked happy and about ten years younger tonight. He'd only had a couple beers, and the shadows that so often haunted him seemed far away. Just as they'd been at Christmas and in the week since.

Christmas Day at Cam's parents had been everything she always dreamed it would be surrounded by a big boisterous, loving family. In a quiet moment following dinner, Cam had told his parents about the baby.

Of course, they must have known. Linc could never have kept it to himself. Nor could his wife keep it from the rest of the family. But in spite of that, his sisters and mother had swarmed about Sandy, hugging and petting her with a great deal of affection and congratulations.

Cam had gazed across the room at her with an odd expression on his face. She had wanted him to smile as goofily as his brothers and feel as happy as she did. But at least he'd shared their news with his family. And he'd done it on his own, without her urging. And he'd taken the ribbing of his brothers with apparent good grace.

Now Cam caught her gaze from across the room and winked. A few moments later, he was at her side. He peered at her drooping eyelids and suggested it was time to head on home. Gratefully, she slid her arms into the sleeves of her coat and followed him out of the bar.

"You're awfully quiet." Cam glanced across at her as he guided the truck out of the parking lot. "Are you feeling okay?"

"Just tired."

"Did you have a good time tonight?" Cam gunned the engine and made it through an intersection before the light turned red.

"It was fun."

"You don't sound like you had all that much fun."

She shrugged. She had enjoyed herself. She liked getting to know Cam's high school buddies and their wives and hearing stories about him he probably wished she hadn't heard.

"I'm glad we came," Cam offered as he pulled the truck to a stop behind the apartment house and turned the engine off. "You were the most beautiful woman there."

"Right." Sandy chuckled, and the weepy feeling lightened. "Linc's wife is a lot prettier than I am. And what about that red-headed bombshell at the table by the door? The one with half her chest hanging out of her dress?"

"You're the most beautiful woman in the world, to me." Cam replied gallantly and leaned across the seat to kiss her. "No matter who's showing off what."

"Don't tell me you weren't ogling those impossibly big boobs just like every other guy in the bar." Sandy gave him a playful shove, her naturally happy spirits returning in a rush.

"I've ogled Dolly Parton too, but if you ask me, she's got too much of a good thing. Besides, I like yours better." He followed this up with a suggestive leer, as he slipped his hand beneath her coat and fondled her breast. "A perfect handful. What more does a man need?" Then, suddenly, he sat back with a snort. "Hey, we're an old married couple, now. We don't need to neck out here in the truck when there's a cozy warm bed waiting for us inside. C'mon."

He dragged her across the seat and out his side of the truck. With one arm wrapped about her shoulders, he led her up the stairs, fumbled with the key in the dim hallway, then opened the door and ushered her inside.

When the door shut behind them, Cam turned. As he slid her coat down over her shoulders, he bent to nuzzle her neck. Sandy reached up to circle his neck with her arms and leaned back against him, closing her eyes. She felt him shrug himself out of his jacket, then his arms came around her, enclosing her in a strong secure cocoon. He felt so solid and warm. She wanted to feel this sheltered and safe always.

"Have I ever told you how much I love this dress?" His voice sounded husky with desire.

"Thank Natalie." Sandy turned in his embrace.

"What's Natalie got to do with it?" He unzipped the silky pink confection Natalie had given her all those months ago, his fingers still cold from out doors.

"Natalie gave it to me to seduce you with." Sandy worked the knot from Cam's tie and pulled it from his shirt, tossing it in the general direction of the sofa.

"Well, it worked." He chuckled deep in his throat.

THE NEXT MORNING, Sandy stepped from the shower and began toweling herself off. As her reflection in the mirror caught her attention, she paused. Did her boobs seem bigger? Yes. Definitely bigger. The nipples were more prominent, too. She let the towel slide to the floor and cradled her breasts in her palms, feeling the new swell.

Cam liked my boobs best. Just the way they were. A perfect handful. Maybe I shouldn't breast feed the baby. Maybe—

"Is this a private party, or can a husband come too?"

Sandy whirled to see Cam smirking at her, one shoulder propped against the door jam. She yanked her hands away from her body and stooped to grab her towel. Her cheeks burned with chagrin as she hurried to wrap the towel around herself.

Cam shoved himself away from the door jam and advanced on her, the smirk widening into a lecherous gleam. "Don't stop whatever you were doing on my account."

"I wasn't . . ." Wasn't what? How could she explain what she'd been doing? She turned away from him, thoroughly discomfited.

"Wasn't what, sweetheart?" He came up behind her, gathering her into his arms and pulling her against his chest. He nuzzled her neck.

He tugged the towel down and curved his palms warmly around her breasts. "What's not to admire?"

"I wasn't admiring myself."

"Oh?" Laughing sarcasm dripped from his voice.

"I wasn't."

He rubbed his thumbs across her nipples making them stand out even more sharply than they had before he'd come in and caught her gazing at herself. "What were you doing?"

Sandy turned around abruptly and yanked the ends of the towel firmly together, trying to regain some sense of dignity. Cam grinned down at her.

"I was worrying, if you must know."

"Worrying?" His blond brows drew together in puzzlement. "About what?"

"That you will think my breasts are getting too big."

Now the brows shot up into the thick thatch of bangs falling across his forehead. "Are you kidding? I love your breasts."

"But you said you liked them just the way they were. Not big and obnoxious like that woman at the bar last night."

"Your breasts will never be obnoxious. For one thing, you would never wear such an appallingly awful dress. I might have ogled that woman, but I was far from admiring her."

"Weren't you one of the guys placing bets on how long it would be before she fell out of that ridiculous dress?"

He raised his brows and widened his eyes. "I caught you watching me with that little smirk of yours so I deliberately ogled her to make you blush. But I wouldn't have dared to place a bet. Besides, your breasts are perfect."

"But they won't stay that way."

Cam frowned.

"Why won't they?"

"Because I'm pregnant!"

Cam jerked backward as if she'd punched him. He stumbled, banging into the corner of the vanity. "Ouch!"

"Because you hate that I'm pregnant!"

"I don't hate that you're pregnant. I just wish . . ."

"Wish what, Cam? "

"It just isn't the right time for a baby, is all."

"Your family didn't seem to think so! I admit that kind of surprised me, but everyone seems excited about the baby. Everyone but you."

"Well, I'm the one who has to live with it," he blurted. Then he reached for her. "I'm sorry. I didn't mean it that way."

"How did you mean it then?" Her tears that always seemed so close lately, welled up and spilled over. "Why, Cam? Why don't you want to be a father?"

"I don't know how to explain it. And you wouldn't understand if I could."

"How do you know I won't understand?"

Cam glanced at his watch. "Hadn't you better get dressed? We're expected for dinner in half an hour."

"How do you know, I wouldn't understand?" she persisted.

He gazed at her with pain darkening his eyes. "Because I'm not sure I really understand it myself." Then he turned on his heel and fled.

CHAPTER THIRTY

CAM TOOK THE STAIRS TO THEIR APARTMENT TWO AT A TIME, EAGER
to tell Sandy his news. She'd been asking him how the job hunt was
going since before Christmas and urging him to at least talk to the man
his uncle knew. Today, he'd finally gone to see his uncle and found out
the position involved managing an entire construction site. Exactly
what he'd studied for, but didn't think he'd be qualified for without
more on the job experience. He probably wasn't qualified, but he had
an interview scheduled, and that was a start, at least.

Sandy had been patient with all his procrastination, and she
deserved to be the first to know he'd finally pulled himself together
and called the guy. On his way home he'd stopped to buy her flowers.
She deserved them for putting up with him.

What's more, way too much time had passed since New Year's Day,
when he'd bolted from the bathroom just when she needed his reassurance most. And he still hadn't talked about the baby. Hadn't let her
talk about it either.

There were moments when he kept his panic at bay and coped with
his plight like a rational man. Like making up his mind to tell his
parents they were expecting. They had needed to hear it from him, not
just third hand from Linc.

He'd been surprised by the sudden spurt of pride he'd felt. He'd even found himself smiling at the jocular back-pounding he'd gotten from his brothers. Watching Sandy's obvious joy when she'd been the center of his family's solicitous attention had made him feel good. Good that he'd been responsible for giving her that pleasure.

But then he went and blew it, reacting to her bald statement about why her boobs were bigger with his gut instead of his head. His careful composure had all fallen apart. By refusing to talk it through, he'd left her thinking he was as turned off by her growing body as she feared. Which couldn't be farther from the truth. When she couldn't see her toes anymore and her breasts were swollen with impending mother-hood, he'd still think her beautiful. As long as he didn't think about the why.

But he didn't know how to explain what he felt. Didn't know how to explain the irrational, gut-churning fear. Or the overwhelming, para-lyzing feelings of unworthiness. The bloody stumps where Jenkins' arms had been had shocked Cam in those first awful minutes and hours after it had happened more than anything else that he'd experienced in Nam. And the memory of Jenkins' first words would haunt Cam forever. *"I never got to hold my son."* How did he explain that without distressing Sandy for no good reason?

Sandy was such a sensitive woman. Always ready to reach out and help others, giving of herself and anything she had for someone in trouble. What had happened to Jenkins would fill her with horror and grief, and maybe she'd end up with nightmares, too. He simply couldn't do that to her. So he had avoided discussing it all together and that hadn't been fair either. He couldn't undo Jenkins' fate or Sandy's preg-nancy and he owed her better than he'd given so far.

He hurried down the hall, determined to make it up to her. Sandy needed his support. She needed him to get his shit together and face their future like a man.

He opened the door and stepped into their apartment. Then stopped, his heart racing.

A slight Asian man dressed in black slacks and a black sweatshirt sat on his sofa holding the gun Cam had left on the bottom shelf of the coffee table. Alarm slammed through his gut.

The man glanced up, black hair falling loose and straight across his forehead as he stared at Cam out of dark, slanted, unreadable eyes.

Fury boiled up inside Cam, wiping out the instant of puzzled alarm.

"Hi, Cam." Sandy suddenly appeared in the kitchen archway. She crossed the living room toward Cam with a welcoming smile on her face. Cam assessed the likelihood of disarming the other man before he had time to shoot one of them. "This is Tae-Jin Ling. He's a friend of mine from school."

The other man put the gun down, his gaze going to Sandy as he stood.

"Tae-Jin, this is my husband, Cam."

Tae-Jin offered his hand. "I am very pleased to meet you." He spoke with a faint trace of an accent.

In some distant, still reasonable place in his mind, Cam realized that the surge of fury drowning everything else out was misplaced. But reason didn't have a chance against the powerful hostility that thundered deafeningly in his head and made his heart pound with outrage. He didn't take the other man's hand.

"Cam?" Sandy touched Cam's forearm.

"You have an interesting souvenir." Tae-Jin gestured toward the gun on the coffee table.

"Get out," Cam said through gritted teeth.

"Cam, what's the matter with you?" Sandy sounded shocked.

The young man stared questioningly at Cam for a moment, then nodded.

"Certainly." Tae-Jin turned to Sandy. "Where did you put my things?"

"You aren't going anywhere, Tae-Jin. Cam's kidding."

A vision of a half dozen determined, black-pajama-clad men carrying guns just like the one on the table raced through Cam's memory.

"I'm not kidding, Sandy. I don't want him in my home."

"It's my home, too and you are being ridiculous." Sandy jerked at Cam's jacket.

"I really should go," Tae-Jin offered.

Cam could no more subdue the gut-deep hostility that possessed him than he could quell the churning nausea it caused. Obviously this young man was not an enemy. He was a friend of Sandy's. But Cam could barely breathe.

"You are not leaving, Tae-Jin. And if Cam doesn't like it, he can leave."

"But, this is his home, Sandy." Tae-Jin said gently. Then he turned to Cam. "I am sorry to have caused this awkwardness, Mr. Cameron."

Cam forced himself to take deep breath and relax his tightly clamped jaw. Then he looked at Sandy.

She gazed at him with appalled disbelief. Her eyes were no longer warm and welcoming. She looked as though she had lifted a rock and found something revolting under it. With her arms clamped across her chest, she backed away from him.

"Why don't you go back out, Cam? And when you come in again, we'll pretend this never happened."

"No," Tae-Jin interrupted. "I will go."

"Tae-Jin has nowhere to go." Sandy ignored her friend. "A fire destroyed his apartment house this morning, and he needs a place to stay for a couple nights."

Cam swallowed hard. *I've gotta get a grip. This guy isn't VC. He isn't even Vietnamese. Eyes are all wrong.* "Sandy's right. I'm being an ass. Please consider the guest room yours and, as Sandy has suggested, I'll come back when I'm ready to be sociable."

Cam turned on his heel and headed for the door. He remembered the flowers he still held and turned back to thrust them toward his wife. Then he let himself out.

"YOU SHOULD NOT HAVE LET him go," Tae-Jin said in a troubled voice.

"I can't think what got into him. He's just not like that, usually. He loves company." It felt like twenty pounds of lead had lodged where her heart belonged. She couldn't begin to make sense of what had just happened.

"I think I understand."

"Well, I wish you would explain it to me, because I don't."

"You told me he very recently returned from the war in Vietnam. To him, I probably look too much like the men who were his enemy. And I was holding the gun when he came in. Can you not see how that might have appeared to him?"

"I suppose." Sandy sank into a chair, struck by Tae-Jin's logic. "Still, he had no call to be so uncivil. I'm really sorry Tae-Jin."

"You have nothing to be sorry for. Besides, your husband has already apologized."

"He did nothing of the sort."

"I believe calling himself an ass was probably his way of doing so." Tae-Jin reached down to touch Sandy's shoulder. "I did not take his animosity personally."

"It sounded pretty personal to me."

"It is not me he hates, but rather, the men who took the lives of his friends. It is just my misfortune that I look similar, and in that moment, I reminded him of them."

"Well, you're still staying here. No matter what Cam thinks or says." Sandy yanked out the drawer by the telephone and began to thumb through the yellow pages. She felt completely humiliated. "I think I'll call out for pizza. That okay with you?"

"Pizza is fine." Reluctantly, Tae-Jin sat down and picked up the gun again. He took a soft cloth, then polished his fingerprints off the gun before putting it back into its case.

"I CAN'T BELIEVE the way you behaved this afternoon," Sandy said the minute the bedroom door shut behind her.

Cam had returned about an hour after he'd taken himself off at her suggestion. He had a case of beer in his hand and a forbidding, I-don't-want-to-discuss-it look in his eyes. He'd eaten the rest of the already-cold pizza, then settled into his chair and began working on the beer. At least he'd shared the beer with Tae-Jin.

Cam tugged his t-shirt over his head, then sat to untie his sneakers. "I said I was wrong."

"You said you were an ass."

"That too." He shucked his jeans, folded them neatly and laid them on a chair, then stretched out on the bed.

"But you didn't apologize."

Cam folded his arms behind his head. His eyes told her he didn't want to talk about it anymore. "Aren't you coming to bed?"

Maybe Tae-Jin was right. He certainly hadn't acted as though he held Cam's unbelievably rude behavior against him. By the end of the evening, they were both more than a little smashed and cheerfully calling each other names for having opposing views on who should have won the basketball game they were watching. Sandy shook her head. *I'll never understand the way men think.*

She got undressed in what she meant to be a repressive silence. Just because Tae-Jin was ready to forgive and forget, she was not. Just to make her point clearer, she dragged out a huge Boston Red Sox t-shirt and pulled it on. Since her marriage, she'd mostly worn nothing to bed.

Then she climbed in, pulled the covers up to her chin and turned her back on him.

"Mmmm. You smell good." Cam nuzzled her neck.

"I smell like I always do."

"You always smell good." His hand stole about her waist and dragged her up against him. "You feel good, too."

"Don't you even care how embarrassed I felt?" She tried to pull away.

He held her firmly against him. "Of course, I care. I admitted I was out of line."

"No, you didn't."

"C'mon, Sandy, what do you want from me, anyway? I apologized. Can we drop it now?"

He sounded more like he said it just to shut her up than because he really felt any remorse. She didn't want to fight with him, but she didn't want to let it go that easily, either.

She shrugged, trying to ignore her heightened awareness of his way too masculine form curled around her backside. The scent of him wrapped itself around her with equally distracting effect.

"Still love me?" His breath tickled her neck. His fingers tickled the skin just beneath her breasts.

"Damn it, Cam." She rolled over in a rush. "You don't play fair."

CHAPTER THIRTY-ONE

WHEN CAM WOKE WITH A SHAFT OF FEEBLE, EARLY-MORNING SUN across his face Sandy had already left their bed. His eyes hurt the moment he opened them. He'd lost track of how much beer he'd had the night before. Judging by the dry mouth and dull ache behind his eyes, far too many.

Cam rolled over and climbed out of bed. He really had to stop drinking like this. God only knew how many brain cells he fried every time he tied one on. Besides, he was getting tired of waking up feeling like hell with a mouth that tasted like a sewer.

He looked worse. Cam studied his reflection in the bathroom mirror with disgust. Then he shoved his head under the faucet and turned on the cold water.

Five minutes later, he strolled into the kitchen and came up short. His heart threw itself into overdrive at the sight of Tae-Jin's sleek black head bent over the daily paper.

Cam thought he had it all worked out in his mind during the furious walk he'd taken after storming from the apartment yesterday afternoon. Tae-Jin was not the enemy. Nor were any of the hundreds of other Asians he might expect to come across in the course of his life. Maybe his initial reaction to Tae-Jin had been understandable given

227

the circumstances. But he couldn't go through life panicking every time he met someone who looked like Tae-Jin. He'd go crazy.

Except, he couldn't stop his racing heart and suddenly clammy hands.

Cam took a deep breath, unclenched his fists and strode toward the refrigerator.

Tae-Jin twisted in his chair to look at Cam over his shoulder. "Good morning, Cam." "There is coffee if you want it."

"Later." Cam took a carton of juice from the refrigerator. He poured himself a tall glass, then thought better of it and poured the juice back into the container. "On second thought . . ."

The coffee was stronger than he was used to. It scalded his throat, then quickly filled him with soothing warmth. Cam added another spoonful of sugar. The second swallow tasted better than the first.

"Kind of strong, I fear." Tae-Jin grinned. "I am not used to your coffee pot."

"It's probably what I needed after last night, though." Cam lifted the mug to his mouth and took a third swallow, appreciating the bracing strength of the coffee.

"You have a point," Tae-Jin agreed in his careful English.

"Where did you grow up?"

"Suwan. In Korea. It is south of Seoul." If Tae-Jin felt offended by Cam's sudden interest, he didn't show it.

"I wondered how you learned to speak English so well."

"My father worked at the American Embassy. He had employment as a translator. Actually, he spoke several languages. It was his hope that I would follow his example."

"Why did you come to the United States?"

"To go to school, originally. I am hoping to stay. I was fortunate to extend my visa to take graduate courses, but I am not sure if I will be able to remain once they are complete."

Cam got up to refill his mug. This time he added a little extra cream and two teaspoons of sugar. "Perhaps you should find an American woman and make her your wife," Cam suggested, thinking of all the Vietnamese women who had tried to get themselves hitched to an American soldier, thus buying themselves a visa into the U.S.

"I could not marry for such a reason." Tae-Jin's voice took on a sudden chill.

"I didn't mean any offense." Cam turned away from the counter and met Tae-Jin's gaze.

Tae-Jin's eyes were inscrutable, as they had been yesterday when Cam had ordered him to leave the apartment. Then he smiled. "But perhaps I shall be struck by the love bug as you and Sandy were. And if I am very, very fortunate, she will be as lovely as your wife."

"Why thank you, Tae-Jin." Sandy, flushed from her morning run, stepped into the kitchen.

"You are welcome." Tae-Jin got to his feet.

"I hope you're paying attention, Cam. A girl could get used to all this gallantry."

Cam looked from Tae-Jin to Sandy, then back to Tae-Jin. "Sit down before you go giving her ideas I can't live up to." The Korean's manners were impeccable and somehow this annoyed Cam unreasonably. He sat down opposite Tae-Jin, not bothering to kiss Sandy hello.

"Please do," Sandy agreed, tossing her running jacket over the back of a chair. As the jacket slithered to the floor, unnoticed, she glanced at the clock. "I'd love to sit and chat, but I have to get a move on or I'll be late for my first day at school."

SANDY WASN'T LATE, but she was out of breath from running across the parking lot. Timidly, she knocked on the glass panel of the door and waited for the man seated behind the big desk at the front of the empty classroom to look up.

"Yes? Oh, Mrs. Cameron. Come on in."

Alex Kelly got swiftly to his feet. Only a couple inches taller than Sandy, he held himself in such a way that he left the impression of being quite a bit larger. He wore his dark brown hair shorter than the fashion, and he dressed with meticulous neatness. He had a lot in common with her husband. Then he smiled, and his dark eyes warmed, erasing the disquieting similarity.

"Please call me Sandy," she corrected. Back in December when she'd come for orientation, she'd been afraid she'd get teamed up with some old battle axe from the dark ages and had been happily surprised to find that wasn't the case.

"Welcome aboard, Sandy. And I'm Alex, at least when the kids aren't around. Are you ready to face the troops?"

She nodded. "I'm looking forward to it."

"Tell me a little more about yourself. We had so little time to become acquainted at orientation." He gestured to a straight-backed student chair at the side of his desk, then seated himself. His desk, while neatly arranged, wasn't nearly large enough for all the things he'd crowded onto it. But most tellingly, it sported a display of trinkets obviously fashioned by childish hands and presented to a very well liked teacher.

"My father was a teacher, as well." Alex said when Sandy had finished her recitation. "So we have something in common. Now, let me tell you more about the class and what my expectations for your work here will be."

WHEN SANDY FLOPPED INELEGANTLY onto the sofa, Cam looked up from the book he had been reading. "How'd it go?"

"I loved it." She toed off her loafers, then wriggled her toes in the thick shag of their carpet. "Only, I had no idea how exhausting it would be. Especially recess!"

"Recess?" Cam asked the question with only half his mind on the answer. As Sandy slouched down on the couch, hiking her skirt up to reveal almost all of her shapely thighs, his mind, quite naturally, was quickly diverted.

"Alex sent me out to supervise. Either they are always wild or they were just trying to impress the new teacher."

"Probably trying to impress the new teacher." Cam tore his gaze away from the shadowy triangle beneath the hem of her pleated plaid skirt and looked into her face.

Her look told him she knew exactly what he was thinking and what his eyes had been ogling.

Cam waggled his eyebrows at her. "Perhaps, if the little demons have worn you out, you'd like to lie down for a while before supper."

"With or without your assistance?" Sandy waggled her own eyebrows.

"With, of course."

Sandy giggled and slouched further, rucking her skirt up so that nothing was left to his imagination.

"Now, who's not playing fair?" Cam asked as he lunged out of his chair and pinned her beneath him. "I hope you don't behave like this in front of, what's-his-name? Alex?"

Sandy giggled and spread her knees. "I wouldn't dare. He'd give me detention."

SANDY DOZED in Cam's arms with the late afternoon sun casting long shadows across the bedroom. Sated from lovemaking and languid with the remnants of her nap, it was pleasant to just lie there enjoying the feel of Cam's warm body against hers and the sound of his heartbeat beneath her ear. But, finally, the desire to sleep left her, and she opened her eyes.

She stared at the darkening sky outside their bedroom window, thinking about this morning and the pointed questions Cam had asked of Tae-Jin.

Cam kissed the top of her head.

Sandy lifted her head from Cam's chest and looked at him.

"A penny for your thoughts?" He hadn't been sleeping, apparently, and he'd known she was awake again.

"What's with the all the questions you asked Tae-Jin this morning?"

"All what questions?" His bright blue eyes appeared quite dark in the shadowy room.

"All the questions about where Tae-Jin came from and why he's in the United States?"

"I was just interested."

"You sounded more like the INS bent on enforcing immigration laws."

Cam stiffened. "Why did you bring him home, anyway?" A sharp edge tinged his voice.

"I told you. A fire gutted his apartment house. Why are you getting all worked up about it all over again?"

"He makes me feel uncomfortable." Cam frowned.

"You didn't act all that uncomfortable last night."

"I was half in the bag last night."

"More like all in the bag."

"Half in the bag, all in the bag. What's the difference? He makes me feel uncomfortable, and I wish you hadn't brought him home with you."

"It was the Christian thing to do, Cam. He didn't have any place to go. And he's a friend of mine. If he weren't Asian would you be so negative?" Sandy pushed herself onto one elbow and looked down into Cam's face.

"He couldn't have found some bachelor buddy to bunk in with?"

"Probably. I just never thought about it. I ran into him while he was reading notices on the bulletin board. I asked what he was looking for and when he told me, I just figured we had a guest room. Why shouldn't he use it?"

"Sandy to the rescue." Sarcasm laced Cam's words.

"What's that supposed to mean?"

"You always charge in like some damned knight on a white horse."

"I like to help people. What's wrong with that?" They were arguing, and she didn't like the way it felt.

"Nothing, really. Forget I said anything." Cam tried to drag her back down on top of him. Sandy resisted for a moment, then gave in and put her head back on his chest. He put his hand on the side of her face and pushed her hair back, tucking strands of it behind her ear with an absent repeated gesture. "I'm just being grumpy because the guy makes me uncomfortable. I'll get over it."

"Why does Tae-Jin bother you so much?

She felt him shrug beneath her.

"Tae-Jin say's it's probably because he reminds you of the Vietcong."

Cam pulled away from her. "So now you're discussing me with strangers?"

"I was hopping mad when you left here yesterday. Tae-Jin defended you."

Cam rolled off the bed abruptly, dumping Sandy onto the place he'd just been laying. "I don't need him defending me. Not Tae-Jin, or you, or anyone else. I just want to forget about that part of my life and get on with the here and now. Is that so hard for you to understand?"

"The here and now is me, Cam. It's us and our marriage." She felt like crying, but she managed not to. "As for understanding. I get it that you don't want to relive the past, but you didn't act like you were putting it behind you so much yesterday."

Cam grabbed his pants off the chair where he'd left them. He put them on and zipped them up without looking at her. Then he reached for his sweatshirt.

"Please don't go storming off again, Cam."

"I'm not storming off. I just need to go out for awhile."

"If you go, I'm going to feel like you don't care about me."

"Christ, Sandy. You know I care about you."

"Then don't go."

"You don't understand." He slid his feet into his sneakers, then bent to tie the laces.

"What I understand is that every time you don't want to talk about something, you run away."

Cam stood by the door and looked at her for a long time. Then he opened the door, stepped into the hall and closed it behind him. A moment later Sandy heard the sound of the outer door clicking shut. This time, she couldn't stop the flood of tears that ran down her cheeks.

CHAPTER THIRTY-TWO

Cam wasn't really thinking about the paper in front of him. The kitchen around him was quiet, the apartment empty. It should have been easy to get to work, but he felt an incredible lethargy and lack of ambition. He was supposed to be working on a resume to give his prospective employer at the upcoming interview.

Just a few months ago, he would never have believed the ambivalence that clung to him over this job thing. During those sweltering, endless days and nights of humping through triple canopy jungle, all he'd thought about was getting back to the world and getting a real job. A job that had nothing to do with the Marines, or the things they'd taught him to do.

With conscious effort, Cam brought the rough draft of his resume into focus. He couldn't make up his mind about including his military experience. He'd heard that some employers didn't like hiring Vietnam vets. *Like we have a social disease.* Besides, combat experience wasn't exactly what up-and-coming construction firms were looking for. But, if he didn't include the years spent in uniform, how did he explain the gap in his employment history?

He penciled in the dates of his service, the branch and his rank.

Then he added his personal data. Married, no children. *Yet!*

He shrugged off the now familiar feeling of heart-stopping dread and reeled a clean sheet of paper into the typewriter. He typed his name and address at the top, then looked up and gazed out the window.

Light delicate flakes of snow swirled aimlessly past the window. They moved like he felt. Without purpose or destination. He got up and went to stand by the window. He rested his forehead against the icy windowpane and watched while the snow began to collect along the sill.

All of a sudden, he had an urge to go out. It didn't snow all that often in Wilmington, North Carolina and as a kid, he'd been eager to get outside and enjoy every minute there was of it. With more energy than he'd felt all day, he hurried to the row of hooks by the back door, reaching for the leather jacket Sandy had given him for Christmas. For a brief moment he thought he smelled Sandy's perfume. Then he remembered her head resting on his shoulder as they drove home from Sean and Kathleen's. The collar had captured her scent. His heart warmed at the memory as he stepped out into the cold.

The air was sharp and still. He turned his collar up, shoved his hands in his pockets, then strode toward the overgrown lot on the far side of the driveway.

His boots crunched hollowly in the dry grass. He stopped walking and listened for several minutes to the delicate sound of falling snow. The world was so intensely silent that he could actually hear the snow landing on the dead stalks. He'd forgotten the magic of snow.

A smile tugged at the corners of his mouth as he began walking again. Good thing Sandy hadn't taken the truck to work today. He wouldn't have enjoyed the swirl of snow nearly as much if he'd had to worry about her getting home over snow-slicked streets. She was used to plows and sanding trucks as soon as snow appeared, but here in North Carolina folk just pulled over and waited until it melted. Plows and sand were a rarity.

In fact . . . Cam looked at his watch. He'd walk down to the school and surprise her. Things had been kind of strained between them lately. His fault, of course. Tae-Jin no longer slept in their spare room, but Cam had let the tension linger. Selfishly hanging on to his grudge.

"Well, well, well. If it ain't the jarhead war criminal."

Cam jerked around, heart kicking into overdrive, and found Bud Wilson astride a huge black Harley, one foot resting on the curb beside the convenience store. Bud climbed off, kicked the stand down, then swaggered across to the grassy lot.

Cam forced himself to relax and let his eyes wander casually down Bud's leather-clad form. Cam swallowed the ball of anger that threatened to choke him, counted slowly to ten, then looked Bud in the eye. "What's your problem, Bud? You got a hair across your ass?"

"Something about you bothers me." Bud thrust his chin out and glared back.

"And what might that be?" The coolly disinterested sound of his own voice impressed Cam.

"You Marines think you shit vanilla ice cream."

Bud's just trying to pick a fight, but he isn't going to get one. At least not from me. I'm done with fighting.

Gratified to find he no longer felt a burning need to flatten the miserable sonofabitch, Cam stood his ground. Having control of his own reaction to Bud's taunts, he found he almost felt sorry for Bud.

Rumor had it that Bud had flunked out of basket weaving 101 or whatever he'd been taking. With the football season behind him, Bud had been given the bum's rush from college life. Soon he'd be getting an invitation from Uncle Sam and life wouldn't be nearly as pleasant. Cam had also learned, from Tae-Jin in fact, that Bud had once harbored the belief that he would eventually break through Sandy's reserve and get her to go out with him. That is, until Cam had arrived on the scene.

No wonder he hates me!

Cam shrugged. "You ought to give the Corps a try. I hear the Marines are looking for a few good men. You get to do all sorts of fun things, and you even get paid for it."

Bud's fists clenched at his sides as he spat into the snow. Cam took a precautionary step backward.

"I always figured you had no balls," Bud snarled.

"Imagine!" Cam began to enjoy himself. "If they could make a lean mean fighting machine out of a pansy like me, just think what they could do with you?"

Bud's fist slammed in so fast it caught Cam in the midriff, but not before Cam had time to tighten his gut. Bud's other hand swung wild. Cam caught Bud's wrist. With almost laughable ease, he wrenched Bud's arm around and up against his shoulder blade. Bud yelped in shocked frustration.

"See the kind of things they teach you?" Cam whispered into Bud's ear. "You might even like the Corps. But, I guarantee you won't like what happens if you continue to harass me. Or my wife." Cam pressed the wrist higher for emphasis, eliciting another yelp, then dropped it, stepping aside so suddenly that Bud staggered.

"It's been nice chatting. See you around." *Or not, if I'm really lucky.* Cam turned on his heel and began walking. He heard Bud's footsteps closing in from behind, but didn't turn around.

"I wouldn't try it." He used his most intimidating, steel-laced officer's voice. "And remember what I said about the Marines. You just might like it." *Bud would hate every relentless minute of it!* Cam grinned at the mental picture of Bug slogging through the mud of Parris Island, cold, filthy, tired and fuming impotently.

Cam was still grinning when Sandy stepped out the front door of Whitman Elementary School and found him lounging against a sign post in the midst of chattering children waiting for busses.

"What are you doing here?" She walked toward him, managing to avoid being hit by any of the meager snowballs several boys had scraped off the pavement and were flinging at each other.

"I thought you'd be happy to see me." Cam pushed himself away from the post and reached for her book bag.

"I am, but I thought you were going to work on your resume this afternoon?"

"I did. But, I wanted to go for a walk in the snow. Then I thought of meeting you and seeing if you wanted to take in a movie."

"I've got a ton of work." Sandy indicated the bag he had slung over his shoulder.

"All right." He refused to let her puncture his bubble. "How about a pizza then? You gotta eat."

"We can't be eating out all the time, Cam. We ought to be saving money for the baby, not spending it."

He hadn't thought about the coming baby, the job he didn't have yet or his demons since he'd stepped outside into the newly falling snow and felt his heart lighten with unexpected pleasure. But in the space of a heartbeat, it all came crashing back in on him.

"It's just a lousy pizza, Sandy. Not steak and lobster tails."

Sandy frowned, looking regretful. Then the corners of her mouth up and she smiled. "I might be induced to change my mind if we could switch the pizza for a burger and fries, though."

"Burger and fries it is." Cam's good humor returned as he put an arm about her shoulders. "I know a great place for burgers."

SANDY TAPPED CAM'S ARM, dragging his attention away from the television mounted above the bar. "I still have work to get done tonight, Cam."

"In a minute."

"Please, Cam."

Cam murmured an assent, but didn't move. Sandy really did have a project to complete, otherwise she'd have taken him up on the movie. But what drove her at the moment was the nightly news blaring from the television. The war was, as it was far too often, at the center of attention, and tonight featured a platoon of Marines struggling to hang on to some remote outpost in the face of outrageous odds.

Just the kind of thing to give Cam more violent nightmares.

Sandy slid out of the booth, reached for her jacket, and started to put it on. "I'm leaving, Cam. With you or without you. And I'd rather it was with you."

Cam looked up, surprised, as if she hadn't asked several times already. He lurched off the bench. "Sorry." He grabbed his own jacket and put it on.

"Night guys." Linc called out to them as Cam opened the door for her.

"Night Linc," They answered in unison.

Sandy waved then ducked under Cam's arm, and they walked to the truck in silence while Sandy tried to think of a neutral subject to bring up. Cam hadn't had a beer with his burger, but the news had been pretty depressing. She wanted to divert him before they got home, and he grabbed a bottle from the fridge. Followed by a second. And a third. Then he'd withdraw into a silent world of misery where she wasn't allowed to intrude.

They paused at the corner, and Sandy looked up to gaze at the swirling snowflakes turning from green, to yellow, then red in reflected traffic light.

"Isn't it pretty?" Sandy asked

Cam made a noncommittal noise as he watched the halting traffic, then guided Sandy across the street to the truck. He opened the door for her, then hurried around to climb into the driver's seat. He shoved an eight-track into the deck and the Vandellas filled the cab with the rhythmic beat of Nowhere To Run.

How appropriate considering what we just saw on TV.

Sandy stared absently at Cam's fingers drumming in time to the music on the steering wheel as he guided the truck through the light, her mind consumed by the contradiction that was her husband. He seemed so strong and competent, but underneath, his composure was amazingly fragile.

When Cam pulled the truck into their space behind the apartment building, he waited for the tape to end, then shut the engine off. "We're home."

"I noticed." Sandy tried to keep the note of sadness from her voice as she climbed out of the truck.

The snow had finally begun to stick, leaving the driveway slick with slush. Sandy picked her way across it, wishing she had changed into her boots. A car backed out of an adjacent spot, coughed, then lurched forward again. They hurried out of its way.

Suddenly the car backfired with such a loud report that Sandy jumped and almost lost her footing. Cam dove face down into the slush.

"My God, Cam." Sandy reached for him, alarm racing through her veins.

Cam pushed himself onto his knees. He looked at her with a strange expression in his eyes.

Had the car hit him?

"Are you all right?"

"It's nothing."

"What happened?"

"Nothing. I'm fine." Cam stood up and brushed the slush off his jacket. His hands shook.

"Something's the matter." Her alarm grew at his odd behavior.

"It's nothing," he repeated, grabbing her arm and dragging her toward the steps.

She knew better than to argue with that tone of voice. When Cam had unlocked the door to their apartment and ushered her inside, he hung his jacket on the hook, then headed for the bedroom. He shut the door after himself.

Sandy stared at the closed door with a sinking feeling in the pit of her stomach. The backfiring car must have sounded like a gun going off. The sight of her six-foot-plus husband dropping like a stone onto the slush-covered driveway had only startled her, but the frightened, confused look in his eyes and the shaking hands had been deeply disturbing.

What was he thinking, shut up in the bedroom? Was he still shaking? She couldn't even begin to imagine what it must have been like to live through two years of sudden, unexpected gunfire. Gunfire that meant someone was shooting at you. The instinctive dive for safety had followed him home along with the nightmares.

She went to the door and tapped on it. Cam didn't answer. She opened it and went in. He was stretched full length on the bed, clad in clean, dry jeans, one arm folded behind his head.

"Are you okay?"

"I'm fine."

"I was worried."

"You want my stone?"

"Your stone?"

Cam fished in his pocket, then held up the worry stone she'd given him that first night on the beach. She was surprised he still had it.

Surprised and touched. She went to sit on the edge of the bed. She rubbed the pad of her thumb over the smooth surface of the stone, then closed Cam's fingers around it and put her hand over his.

"I was worried because I got to thinking how I would have felt if I was you. I mean, if I thought someone was shooting at me. I'd have been terrified."

"I was embarrassed." He looked up at her as he spoke. His blue eyes were dark with unspoken torment. Then abruptly the shutter went down on the vulnerable expression, and he smiled. "So, did you come to kiss my wounds?"

"Did you hurt yourself?" Sandy backed away to look at the rest of him.

"Nothing a little nookie wouldn't fix." He winked at her.

"You aren't going to tell me, are you?"

"What's to tell? I took a dive in the snow. All that's hurt is my pride."

"Your pride?"

"I feel like an idiot."

"You're not an idiot."

"You going to talk all night, or get undressed?" Cam slid one hand provocatively up her thigh, rumpling the hem of her skirt when it got in the way.

"You can't fix everything by making love."

"There's nothing to fix. Why can't I just want to make love to my wife?" He teased the sensitive flesh of her inner thigh with his thumb.

Sandy got off the bed and moved out of reach. His touch aroused her far too easily, and she didn't want to be sidetracked. "Please, Cam."

"If you don't want to make love, just say so. I can take no for an answer." He put his hand behind his head again.

"I do like making love with you. That's just the problem."

"So, now making love is a problem?" He sat up abruptly. He shoved his feet back into his boots with angry, jerky thrusts, then got to his feet. "I didn't know you considered making love with me a problem."

"That's not what I meant. You're twisting my words."

"Then what did you mean?"

"This stuff that's bothering you has nothing to do with me and nothing to do with sex. When you touch me, I want it to be because you want me, not because you want to forget something else."

Cam dragged a hand over his hair. "For the love of God, Sandy! I always want you! Haven't you figured that out yet? Look at me!" He turned to face her and gestured to the taut bulge in the front of his jeans.

Sandy tried to ignore the evidence of his desire. Just because he was aroused didn't mean he wasn't trying to avoid something. "You can't keep running away. Sooner or later, you'll have to stop running and it's going to catch up with you." Abruptly, she stopped speaking.

Why am I making an issue of this? Why not just make love? Let him feel good and forget?

"I'm not running away, God dammit!"

"Then why won't you talk ab. . ." She bit her tongue rather than finish the question.

"There's nothing to talk about."

"Nothing?" she blurted, unable to stop herself. "You have nightmares nearly every night. You're depressed. You drink too much. You—"

Cam stared at her with hard, unreadable eyes, daring her to go on. So of course, she did.

"You don't want the baby. You don't seem to want a job either. Am I next?"

"I'm just having a hard time getting excited about bringing a son into the world and spending the next twenty years pouring my heart and soul into raising him so some asshole in the Whitehouse can decide he wants to play war and send my son off to fight it for him. And I don't want to see you in tears while you receive a folded flag that is all that's left of your little boy."

"You're not being reasonable." Except that what he'd said *did* make sense. At least to him. *I should shut up right now.* "Men die in war, Cam, and they always will. Until men figure out better ways to settle their differences, which isn't likely to be any time soon. What if the whole world stopped having babies? Pretty soon there wouldn't even be any people left to make peace."

"You don't understand."

"Of course I don't understand, because you won't give me half a chance. Sometimes I feel like the only time I exist for you is when you want to make love."

"So why don't you leave me then? Find some guy who loves talking about himself?"

Sandy felt like she'd been slapped. "I don't want someone else. I want you. I want to help you work this thing out so we can get on with our lives."

"Well, don't hold your breath," Cam spun around and headed for hall.

"Running away again?" Her heart hammered painfully.

"I'm not running away. I'm going out for a little peace and quiet."

"Don't do this to me, Cam."

"To you? Jeezus! You're the one doing all the nagging. You just can't let it be, can you?" Cam came back and stood glaring down at her. "You drink too much, Cam," he mimicked. "When are you going to get a job, Cam? How come you're not excited about the baby? Why don't you ever talk about the war?"

Sandy cowered beneath unexpected onslaught of his anger.

"I don't talk about the war because it hurts too goddamned much. Is that what you wanted to hear? That your lousy excuse for a husband can't hack it without you to rescue him?" For a minute, he just stood there glaring down at her. A pulse throbbed in his temple, and he looked mad enough to hit her. But he didn't.

Abruptly, he spun on his heel and headed for the door. He stormed across the kitchen and wrenched open the door, then slammed it behind him. Sandy heard the sound of his boots on the stairs. Then the lower door shut with almost as much force as the apartment door.

Sandy sagged onto the bed feeling battered. *If I live to be a hundred, the sound of a door slamming is still going to haunt me.* No one had ever told her loving someone could hurt so much. Nor would she have believed it if anyone had suggested Cam could be so deliberately hurtful. He hadn't raised his voice. But then, he hadn't needed to. The words had been steel-edged and cut deep.

Where is the gentle loving man I married? Will I ever find him again beneath the mountain of guilt and anger and misery that is crushing his soul?

CHAPTER THIRTY-THREE

LINC CAMERON RESTED HIS ELBOWS ON THE BAR AND CHATTED WITH an off-duty cop watching Cam out of the corner of his eye. Cam slouched on a stool at the far end of the bar where he'd been for the better part of the night nursing a single beer and feeling disgusted with himself for the way he'd treated his wife.

"Hey Steve, mind the bar, will ya?" Linc pulled the ends of the towel he wore to protect his trousers out of his waistband and tossed it over edge of the sink. He grabbed a couple iced mugs, filled them from the tap, then ducked under the hinged section of the bar and approached Cam.

"This a private party or can anyone join?"

Just what he needed. Another difficult discussion. He could sense it coming considering the determined look in Linc's eyes.

"I've been on my feet for hours, and I'm ready to take a load off. Care to join me?" Linc jerked his head toward a table in the corner. Without waiting to see if Cam would follow, he headed toward the table. He set the mugs down, then flopped onto a chair and stretched his legs out with a theatrical groan.

Cam grabbed the little stone off the bar and got to his feet. He crossed the dimly lit room reluctantly. Turning a chair around, he straddled it and sat, tucking his feet underneath. He reached for one of the frosty mugs, but didn't bring it to his mouth.

Linc pulled his feet back under the table. "You going to tell me what's eating you or am I going to have to beat it out of you?"

Cam didn't answer. With one finger, he traced vertical lines in the sweaty surface of the beer mug, his eyes fixed on the rivulets his finger created. Linc reached across the table and grabbed Cam's wrist to stop the fidgeting. When he did, the worry stone clattered onto the table.

"What's with the rock?" Linc picked it up.

Cam sighed. "It's a worry stone."

"What the hell is a worry stone?"

"It's supposed to be like watching tropical fish."

"Like tropical fish?" Linc frowned.

Cam glanced at his brother briefly, then back at the beer mug in his grip. "You never heard that watching fish is supposed to be relaxing?"

"Yeah, but what's that got to do with a rock?"

"Sandy calls it a worry stone. You're supposed to rub it or something. She says it soothes the soul."

"And does it?" Linc looked at the stone with new respect.

Cam shook his head.

Linc fingered the silky smooth surface of the worry stone one more time, then set it down next to Cam's mug.

"Cam, I don't want to go sticking my nose in where it's not wanted, but I'm here for you if you want to talk."

Linc chugged a couple swallows of beer and waited.

"You ever felt like you were coming apart? I mean, like everything was unraveling, only you couldn't figure out how it got started? Or how to stop it?"

"What, exactly, is coming apart, Cam? Please tell me it isn't your marriage."

"Not my marriage. At least I don't think so, but I wouldn't blame Sandy if it was. I'm talking about me." Cam ran a hand over his hair, then massaged the back of his neck a couple times before going on. "Just when I think I've got my act together again, shit happens, and I find out I don't."

Linc took a deep breath, then exhaled slowly.

"Did you get the Winston job Uncle Bill recommended you for?"

"I didn't ask for it."

"Why the hell not? You're the right guy for it. Besides, old man Winston already likes you."

"It just seems . . . wrong." Cam flipped the stone over several times by pressing down on one side until it rolled away and Linc stopped it, then placed it back on Cam's side of the table.

"Because of Paul?"

Cam nodded. Paul was David Winston's only son. Paul and Cam had been classmates in high school. And Paul was MIA somewhere in Vietnam.

"It's not your fault, you know. Paul volunteered to go, same as you did."

"I know, but if Winston was my boss, I'd feel like, every time he looked at me, he'd be wishing I was Paul. It should be Paul's job."

"And it still will be when Paul gets home. But right now Winston needs someone, and there's no reason that someone shouldn't be you."

"I don't know." This time when Cam flipped the worry stone it skittered noisily across the polished surface of the table.

"Damn it! Stop it with the stone, already." Linc picked the stone up and put it back on Cam's side of the table a second time. Cam pocketed it.

"What about the other job Uncle Bill mentioned?"

Cam shrugged again. "I've got an interview."

"That's good. Isn't it? Or is this all part of what's eating you?"

"I dunno. One minute I feel like everything's fine, and the next I'm losing it again."

"Losing what, for chrissake?"

"There's this guy Sandy knows, named Bud."

"Who the hell is Bud?"

"He's a football jock. Was a football jock. He had or has a thing for Sandy. Something Sandy never encouraged, you understand." Cam made a rude sound in his nose. "Bud decided, the first time I ever saw the asshole, that I would be an amusing target for his idea of a political protest. At first, he really pissed me off, and it was all I could do not to punch him out. Sandy only makes it worse by jumping in the middle of it whenever Bud gets started. Like I'm a candy-ass that has to hide behind a woman's skirts. I felt like killing the son-of-a-bitch. Only, I figured if I let myself touch him, even once, I just might."

"Understandable," Linc muttered sympathetically.

"This afternoon Bud intercepted me on my way to meet Sandy after school. It was more of the usual. Badmouthing the Corps and questioning my intestinal fortitude. Only this time, it didn't get to me like it used to. I felt pretty good about that. And myself. I felt like, maybe, I was finally getting a handle on things.

"Then, after Sandy and I left here, a frigging car backfired in the parking lot behind the apartment. The next thing I know, I'm face down in fucking snow. I felt like a goddammed fool."

"This is what's got you in such a bloody funk?" Linc leaned forward. "Christ, Cam, that's about as normal as you get. It happened to me more than once."

Cam jerked his head up and looked at Linc in astonishment. He'd been seven when Linc was shipped home from Korea with a million-dollar wound. Linc had been his hero. A dashing, decorated hero with a splendid uniform covered with ribbons.

"I never knew that," Cam admitted softly.

"You wouldn't have understood if you had. You were just a kid."

"You have nightmares?"

"That, too. I still have them now and then."

"How come you never told me?"

Linc shrugged. "It didn't come up. It's not the sort of thing a man likes to talk about."

"Tell Sandy that."

"Tell Sandy what? That it's normal for you to have nightmares?"

"That there's nothing wrong with me not wanting to talk about them."

"Maybe you should." Linc suggested quietly.

Cam shook his head, the stubborn resistance surging through him again.

"You know, it's real easy to get the idea that unless someone's been there, there's no way they can understand, so there's no point in discussing it. But by not talking about it, you shut out the people who want to help most. Could help most." Linc leaned forward, resting his weight on his forearms. "What about Sean?"

"He's a flyboy. It's not the same."

"Look, I'm no psychiatrist, but I've worked behind a bar long enough to learn that knowing you aren't alone, that you're not a freak, makes all the difference when you're coping with soul-shattering reality. Obviously, you've been trying to bury the horror you lived through. And maybe a lot of misgivings over the complex, poorly understood reasons you were even there in the first place. Cam, you need to talk it out. Get some perspective."

Cam shrugged. He wasn't convinced.

"You want my advice, Runt?" Linc hurried on without giving Cam a chance to tell him to go to hell. "Go home and climb into bed with that wonderful woman you married, and the next time you wake up screaming, tell her why. Let her share it with you. Things are always easier if you don't have to bear them alone."

"Forget I mentioned it, Linc." Cam stood up abruptly. "What do I owe you for the beer and the couch?" Cam didn't even try to hide the sarcasm in his words.

Linc got to his feet. He met Cam's gaze and held it. "You're not alone, Cam. You're not the only one who feels like you do. I just want to . . ."

"Hey, Linc." Steve called out above the murmur of voices around the bar. "Phone."

Linc gestured with one hand in the air, finger waving to let Steve knew he'd heard. "Don't let it eat at you, Cam."

"Hadn't you better get the phone?" Cam asked as he reached for his jacket.

"Linc!" Steve called out again.

Linc pulled Cam into a quick hard embrace. "I love you, little brother. We all do. And we're proud of you, too. You're never alone, and don't you forget it." Then he dropped his arms and headed for the phone.

CAM PULLED the truck into their slot and shut it off. It hadn't been running long enough to warm up and he was cold, but he was reluctant to go inside. What would he say to Sandy? He couldn't decide if he felt better or worse after talking with Linc. It was a relief to know he wasn't a freak and that his reaction to the car backfiring was more or less normal. On the other hand, he still felt like a fraud. Everyone, from his parents, to Linc to Sandy believed he was a hero. And he wasn't.

If they knew the truth, they would be appalled. And disillusioned. The only heroes Cam had known in Vietnam had come home in coffins. Or missing their arms. He had just been doing his job. What he'd been trained to do. People seemed to think there was something heroic in that, but he knew better. It was a dirty, terrifying, exhausting job, and the only understandable goal had been survival.

Well, he had survived. And he wanted to forget it. Being married to Sandy should have outweighed the burden his soul carried. He'd wanted to believe that, anyway. But unwanted memories weren't so easily forgotten. Especially when your wife kept trying to get you to talk about them.

Cam shivered violently, his teeth chattering. *I can't stay here. And I can't go in.* His angry words echoed hauntingly in his head and, now that the anger had gone, he remembered, all too clearly, the pain in Sandy's eyes when he'd said them.

Why do I do this to her? I love her more than life itself. And she loves me. What makes me behave so unforgivably? I'm not like that. At least I never was. Cam shuddered again. Reluctantly, he got out of the truck. *Sandy would have every right not to let me in.* He made his way up the stairs to their apartment. *I don't know why she puts up with me.*

Cam used his key and let himself into a darkened apartment. As he shucked his boots by the door, he considered sacking out on the sofa and avoiding Sandy altogether. Or the guest room. But he'd still have to face her in the morning, so he headed for the bedroom.

He stripped as silently as he could, tiptoed to the bathroom, peed and brushed his teeth, then returned to the side of their bed. Sandy had fallen asleep with the light on, her book still open across her chest. He bent to remove the book, carefully tucking the flap of the dust jacket in to mark her page. Then he reached to turn the light off and stopped, startled by the realization that something looked different.

With the covers drawn smoothly over it, the new roundness of Sandy's belly struck him hard. How had he not noticed it before? Unthinking, he reached out to touch it, curling his palm to cover the soft little mound. *My baby is in there. The baby we made is growing in there.* His heart seemed to beat harder than usual and his chest felt taut with some unexpected and unknown emotion.

Carefully, he removed his hand, turned out the light, then slid under the covers. When Sandy didn't stir, he reached out to caress her gently rounded belly again. Sliding his hand over the smooth, firm shape beneath her sleep-warm skin, he felt a sense of wonder. *Our baby!* A sudden surge of pride filled his chest, and his fingers tightened with possessiveness. *My son.*

Just as suddenly, a vision of the company corpsman's mutilated body swam before Cam's eyes, and he yanked his hand back as if it had been burned. He stumbled from the bed, all traces of pride swamped beneath a tidal wave of guilt. *I don't deserve a son. I don't deserve Sandy. I don't deserve any of this.*

He bolted from the room, chased by Jenkins' shocked and disbelieving eyes dancing in his memory. Unable to outrun the vision, he lurched to the kitchen sink and braced himself on the icy stainless steel edge while his stomach rid itself of the beer he'd consumed at The Code Seven.

His stomach finally empty, he sank, naked and trembling onto the floor. He hugged his knees against his chest and buried his head in his arms. He felt closer to tears than he'd ever felt in his life. Gut choking tears. Unmanly sobs that once started might never stop.

How am I going to get through these next few months? Hell, never mind the next few months! How am I going to live with myself for the next 18 years? Oh, God, Jenkins. I'm so sorry. I'm so fucking sorry. I wish I was dead.

CHAPTER THIRTY-FOUR

T HE IRRITATING BUZZ OF THE ALARM CLOCK DRAGGED S ANDY FROM a deep sleep. She came to full consciousness reluctantly, feeling like she hadn't slept at all. Her head felt thick, as if she'd been drugged. Cam sprawled next to her, apparently undisturbed by the buzzing alarm.

She didn't remember him coming home and wondered groggily how late it had been when he crawled in next to her. She had vowed not to nag him with any more questions and just let him make love to her. *"Nothing a little nookie couldn't fix,"* he'd said. She'd lain awake for hours, worrying about him, feeling guilty about pestering him and wishing she'd given him the only thing he'd asked for.

She dragged herself out of bed and headed to the bathroom, hoping a hot shower would banish her exhaustion and guilt. Running might have helped to clear the cobwebs, but she wasn't up to it today.

The shower did refresh her, and a cup of hot coffee revived her brain, but neither did anything for the guilt. She gulped down a second cup of java, then glanced at the clock. She needed to get going. Tiptoeing, she went back into the bedroom to check on Cam before she left.

If only she'd known the right thing to say. If she had understood the horrors he lived with better, maybe she would have known what not to say. In any case, if she hadn't been so stupid and kept pushing him, he might never have gone out.

She pictured him before things had gone so wrong, laying stretched out on his back with one arm cocked behind his head, beckoning her with one finger. There had been a mischievous glint in his eye and a seductive smile on his lips. She remembered with a shiver, the feel of his hand sliding up her leg, pushing her skirt aside. She'd wanted to succumb to the tantalizing fire he lit inside her. *Oh, God, why didn't I?*

Why did she have this bee in her bonnet that she could fix whatever was bothering him? Maybe it couldn't be fixed. Maybe she just needed to let him work his way though it in his own way in his own time? Maybe that's what he'd been trying to tell her all along, and she hadn't been listening? Maybe, maybe, maybe . . . Her mind ran in fruitless, self-reproachful circles.

Cam now lay face down across the bed, having moved to take advantage of her unoccupied space, but he still slept deeply. Sandy tugged the comforter up over his shoulders, bent to place a kiss on the back of his head, then with a quick glance at the clock, hurried out again.

Her guilt followed her to school, leaving her distracted and short tempered all morning. A couple times she noticed Alex Kelly looking at her with concern in his dark eyes, but she refused to meet his gaze because she wouldn't know how to respond if he said anything. But even one of her pupils, an engaging little boy with carrot-red hair and a face full of freckles, noticed her moodiness.

The boy had patted her hand, to gain her attention. "Why are you so sad today, Mrs. Cameron?"

Caught off guard by the boy's perception, Sandy didn't know how to respond. "I'm not sad. Well, maybe just a little, but I'm fine now." Sandy gave him a wink. Then, unsettled for having admitted as much to a child, she lowered her voice to a whisper. "You're missing Mrs. Swift's story."

Jennifer Swift, the petite teacher's aide assigned to Mr. Alex Kelly's third grade class, sat cross-legged on the floor in the midst of a group of rapt children. With flashing eyes and extravagant hand gestures, she told the story of George Washington and his ragged army at Valley Forge. The boy turned his attention to the story.

Alex Kelly tapped Jennifer on the shoulder. "You've got a phone call, Jennifer."

Jennifer looked at Sandy, a silent question in her eyes.

"Go on, take the call. I'll finish the story." Sandy moved to take Jennifer's place.

"Thank you." Jennifer said, getting to her feet. "I was just getting to Baron Von Steuben."

"What's a baron?" The tow-headed boy sitting directly in front of Sandy had his hand in the air. Eric was an endless source of questions.

"A baron is an aristocrat," Sandy began and almost before the word aristocrat was out of her mouth, saw Eric getting primed to ask what an aristocrat was. "But more important," Sandy hurried on. "Von Steuben was just what Washington's army needed. The soldiers were cold and hungry, and their clothes were ragged, but they were still anxious to fight. But, back then, our country didn't have places to train their soldiers like they do today."

"Like boot camp?" Eric jumped in. "My father says boot camp is hell."

"Learning to be a soldier is never easy, Eric." Sandy decided to ignore the language. "The Patriots found it especially hard before Baron Von Steuben came to teach them how to drill. But he made a splendid army out of them."

"Like a fire drill?"

"Not exactly." Sandy chuckled, then went on to describe the flamboyant personage of Baron Von Steuben and the long legged dog he had brought with him. Eric's eyes grew round as saucers, and he even forgot to ask questions.

"Thank you, Sandy." Jennifer sank to the floor next to Sandy. "Now where were we?"

AFTER HER YOUNG student's unnervingly observant question, Sandy made a better effort to put the events of the previous night out of her mind. She had a job to do and she'd very well better keep her mind on doing it well. Otherwise, Alex's review of her student teaching assignment would make a note of it and that would hurt her grades.

When she saw how fascinated the children were with the colorful character of Baron Von Steuben, she dredged her memory for other revolutionary heroes they might find equally interesting. An idea formulated in her mind and she decided to mention it to Alex while they kept watch over the playground after lunch.

"I'd like to tell the children about Daniel Morgan."

"Good idea," Alex agreed, smiling. "Morgan is just the sort of hero that will appeal to young boys. Washington, for all his admirable character traits, just doesn't capture the imagination the way a maverick like Morgan does."

"Well, he captured my imagination! I went from hating history to devouring it after I read his story."

"Why don't you talk it over with Jennifer. Dig out a few more interesting people. Include Dolly Pitcher and maybe even Private Robert Shurtleff, a.k.a. Deborah Sampson, so the girls can feel a part of it."

"Shurtleff?" Sandy had not heard that name before.

"An enterprising young woman who disguised herself as a boy and enlisted in the 4th
Massachusetts Foot."

"You're kidding!" Sandy was intrigued. She suspected the children would be, too.

"Sampson got away with it for quite awhile. I believe she'd been wounded a couple times before her sex got revealed. I have a small book I'll loan you. Another . . ." Alex stopped abruptly to field a ball gone astray. He tossed it back toward the group of children playing dodge ball. "Another fellow that might interest them is Nathan Hale."

Sandy's heart lurched at the familiar name. That *was* a story she was familiar with. Too familiar.

"But I'll leave you to choose." The ball escaped again, and Alex reached for it with a laugh. "I'm going to assign a book report from a list of youth fiction I've collected. The books are the kind of adventures kids like, but the history is sound. You might get some ideas there, too. Alex went on to describe a project he had in mind, but Sandy listened with only half an ear. The mention of Nathan Hale had brought Cam and last night crashing back into her consciousness. Cam's misery and her stupidity tugged at her heart. She had wanted him to wake up before she had to leave for school so she could apologize. But he hadn't.

She felt shamed by the accusations she had flung at him. And guilty for badgering him until he couldn't bear to stay home. His voice, mimicking her own, haunted her. Why had she not realized she was just driving a wedge between them with all her nagging?

"Sandy?" Alex raised an eyebrow in an expression of concern. "Is something bothering you?"

"I . . . nothing." She flushed at the lie.

Alex's eyes narrowed for a moment. Then he looked down at his watch and sighed. He shoved two fingers between his lips and gave an ear-splitting whistle. Immediately, the children stopped their game and began running across the playground to line up at the door.

"I'm jealous," Sandy said, glad to change the subject as she strode back toward the school at Alex's side. "I always wished I could whistle like that."

"A sergeant taught me how."

"A sergeant?"

"Back when I first arrived in Vietnam. I met this guy during my in-country orientation. I swear he whistled loud enough Ho Chi Min could hear it all the way up in Hanoi. I got him to teach me how to do it. New lieutenants don't get much respect until they prove themselves. I thought it wouldn't hurt to be able to grab a man's attention so compellingly."

"I didn't know you were in Vietnam?"

Alex didn't respond as they reached the door and followed the children into the building.

Then, about half way down the hall, over the clatter of opening and shutting locker doors, he said, "I finished college just in time for the big build-up and got married two months too late to avoid the draft."

"Oh," Sandy said, preceding Alex into the classroom. "Somehow, I got the impression you weren't married." She blushed again. *Now why did I say that? It's really none of my business.*

Alex suddenly had a distant, unreadable look in his eyes. "My marriage was a casualty of war, I'm afraid."

"I'm sorry." Impulsive as usual, she had stuck her nose into something she shouldn't have. "I didn't mean to pry."

Alex sat down at his desk. He rubbed the bridge of his nose as if his head hurt, then looked up at her. "Don't be. You couldn't have known. Anyway, it's been a few years. I've gotten used to it." Then he pulled out his plan-book.

Sandy stared down at the top of his close-cropped head, wishing she hadn't asked and not sure if she should apologize again. Then she realized Alex had closed the subject and she'd been dismissed.

CHAPTER THIRTY-FIVE

WHEN SANDY ARRIVED HOME, THE DISTURBING CONVERSATION with Alex and his comment about his marriage being a casualty of war still echoed in her head. With her arms full of groceries, she tapped the door with her toe and waited for Cam to open it. When he didn't, she put the groceries down and dug her keys out of her pocket.

The apartment felt depressingly empty. Cam hadn't left a note, either. She dumped the groceries on the kitchen table, dropped her books on a chair, then wandered into the bedroom. Shucking her shoes, she flopped across the bed. Outside the window, the darkening sky added to her disappointment. With a heavy heart, she wondered where Cam had gone this time.

She stretched one arm across Cam's side of the bed, then rolled over and pressed her face into his pillow, inhaling his scent.

Please don't let us be a casualty of war, God. Help me be patient. And help Cam fight his demons. I don't know what he needs, but surely you must.

She didn't know what else to pray for so she let the silence of the room and the smell of Cam seep into her. She drifted on an aimless sea of emotions, hoping for answers. Trying to find some peace.

She rolled onto her side and cupped her belly with one hand. *We need him so much, don't we little one? We need him to love you as much as I do. And please, God, I need him to love me, too.* She felt tears start to form and blinked them back. *That's not true! I know he loves, me. It's just that —*

A sudden noise in the kitchen startled Sandy from her tangled thoughts, and she scrambled to her feet.

"You here sweetheart?" Cam sounded lighthearted, as if last night had never happened. Sandy wiped hastily at her eyes, glanced in the mirror over his dresser to see if her tears showed, then hurried to meet him.

Cam was hanging his overcoat on a hanger. He had on his new suit and a tie. A bright yellow hard-hat sat among the groceries on the kitchen table.

"Hi, Cam." Afraid to ask if the suit and the hard-hat meant what it looked like, Sandy settled on a cheerful greeting.

He turned, and gave her a lopsided smile. "Say hello to the new assistant on-site engineer for the Oak Grove project."

Stunned put Sandy's reaction mildly! Cam had avoided talking about the interview, and she'd begun to think that he'd cancelled it. Suddenly, she was bubbling with hope and momentarily speechless.

"Aren't you going to congratulate me?"

"C-congratulations," she stuttered.

Cam closed the gap between them and swept her into an embrace. "Don't be too impressed." He laughed. "I had an in with the boss."

"I'm impressed anyway." She hugged him around the waist and searched his face, noting the dark circles under his eyes and the lingering haunted look that was so at odds with his behavior. "Let's go out and celebrate?" *Or stay in and celebrate?* The vision of a candlelit dinner appeared and she ransacked her memory for something special she could fix. Something that would be followed by a romantic interlude that ended in the bedroom.

"Did you forget the guys are coming over for poker in an hour?

"Oh!" That meant she wouldn't have him alone for hours. Her heart plummeted. It would seem like an eternity. Sandy pouted, pursing her lips provocatively.

Cam kissed her, as she'd intended. Then he let her go, dug his wallet out and handed her a five-dollar bill. "You and Kathleen can walk down to Friendly's and get an ice cream sundae. Celebrate for me."

"LINC'S GOING to be late for his own funeral," Cam remarked as he grabbed a beer from the fridge and offered one to Tae-Jin and Sean.

Sandy set a bowl of peanuts on the table and made a face at her husband. He liked having friends over, and he clearly looked forward to the evening ahead. Distracted, at least for a while, from the things that haunted him. A distraction she didn't seem able to provide unless they were making love. She really wished they could have had this night to themselves.

Then Cam winked at her, and her heart did its usual somersault, lightening the heavy feeling of disappointment.

"How can a man come late for his own funeral?" Tae-Jin looked puzzled.

Sean laughed at Tae-Jin's confusion. "It's just an expression. Linc is always late for everything. Cam's just pissed because he's feeling lucky, and the man with the real money isn't here yet." Sean stood propped against the kitchen counter with Kathleen leaning against his chest. He had his arms about her and his hands rested possessively over her distended stomach.

"But I am the man with the real money, today." Tae-Jin pulled a thick wad of bills from the pocket of his jeans.

"Christ, Tae-Jin. What'd you do? Rob a bank?" Cam turned a chair around and straddled it with his arms folded across the back.

"Sean teach me good." Tae-Jin grinned. "I play my roommates and I win."

"And I thought you were *my* friend, Sean." Cam made a wry face.

"I tried to pass along my best tips. It's not my fault you're a lousy poker player," Sean protested laughing. "Hey," Sean jerked his hand away from Kathleen's belly and peered down at it. "He kicked me!"

"She, honey. It's a she." Kathleen tipped her head back against Sean's shoulder and grinned up at him.

"Can't be a girl. He's going to be a flyboy like Daddy." Sean bent his head toward Kathleen's stomach. "You want to be fighter pilot just like

Daddy. Right?" He made a plane out of his hand and zoomed in a strafing run over the taut cotton material.

Kathleen caught Sean's hand, giggling at his antics. "Maybe by the time our *daughter*

grows up, the Navy will let girls be pilots too."

"Never happen. Right Cam?" Sean looked for reinforcements.

"You better hope it's a girl. A boy, and you'll spend the next 20 years worrying about your kid going off to fight some God-forsaken war that makes no sense to anybody." Cam brought his bottle of beer to his lips and tipped his head back, but not before Sandy saw the haunted look return to his eyes. She wanted to reach out to him. *This thing about having a son who might get killed in a war really bothers him. What if our baby is a boy? Cam's got to get past this.* She put a hand over her own stomach as if to reassure her baby, if not herself.

The doorbell rang, and Cam got off his chair, set his bottle down, then headed for the door. The bell gave way to impatient knocking. "Hold your horses, Linc. I'm coming, already."

AT THE SOUND of the office door opening, Cam looked up from the blue-prints spread across his desk. A Marine stood just inside the door. A tall, good-looking man. Six feet at least. White-wall haircut, broad shoulders and all muscle beneath the navy blue tunic with captain's bars pinned to the epaulets.

Cam popped to his feet, instinct still strong even after all the years as a civilian. "Can I help you, sir?"

"Nathan Cameron?"

Cam nodded, then came around the desk and offered the captain his hand.

"Your son said I might find you here."

"My son? He's at school." Cam was puzzled.

"Actually your son asked me to come here and see if I could change your mind."

Understanding dawned, and anger replaced Cam's confusion. His son had said something about the Marines two nights ago when his mother had asked which college he was planning to accept. The boy wasn't even eighteen yet.

"You can't have him," Cam growled with barely concealed outrage. The boy

had known Cam would balk at signing the papers so he'd asked the captain to do his begging for him.

"Excuse me?"

"I said you can't have him." Cam's hostility boiled over. "Now, get out of my office and don't go near my son again. He'll be a Marine over my dead body."

The captain stood his ground. "Just a minute. Can't we—"

"Get out!" Cam raised his voice. "Get out of here before I do something we'll both regret."

"He'll be eighteen in six months," the captain pointed out, ignoring Cam's rude dismissal.

"Get out! You can't have him. You . . ."

"WAKE UP, Cam. You're dreaming again." Sandy forgot about not touching Cam and reached out to jostle him out of his nightmare.

Cam lurched to his knees in a flurry of tangled bedclothes, his arm drawing back to strike. Sandy scrambled off the side of the bed. Still half asleep and unseeing, Cam swung toward where she had been only a moment before, smashing his fist through the solid wood panel of the headboard instead.

"Yow!" Cam howled, yanking his hand back and cradling it against his chest.

Sandy flicked on the bedside lamp. Cam's eyes were wide. And terrified. Sandy reached out to comfort him.

Cam shot off the far side of the bed and backed up until he ran into the wall. Sandy rounded the bed and went to Cam, wrapping her arms about his waist.

"It's okay now, Cam. The nightmare's over." *For now at least. Would these nightly demons ever leave him alone?*

Cam stood rigidly in the circle of her arms, his own at his sides. Sandy felt rebuffed.

Uneasily, she leaned away enough to look up at him. He'd come very close to hitting her, but he hadn't meant it. They could talk about that later, but right now, she worried more that he might have hurt himself. "Let me see your hand?"

"My hand's fine."

She took the hand and lifted it to see for herself. He yanked it from her grasp and moved out of her reach.

"I said it's fine!"

Sudden anger boiled up inside her. Irrational, unreasoning anger. All she'd offered was a little honest concern, and he was shutting her out. Again. "I'm not stupid."

"I didn't say you were."

"Then stop treating me as if you think so. You just put your hand through the headboard. It's got to be hurt. You probably need a doctor, but you should put ice on it at least."

Cam shrugged.

Sandy's rare temper soared. "Don't do that."

"Don't do what?" Cam lifted his shoulders again.

"That! That shoulder shrugging thing."

Cam let his shoulders sag back to normal. "I should never have married you."

Sandy felt like he'd struck a knife in her heart. The hand didn't seem to matter so much anymore. How could everything have gone so wrong in six short months? He promised to love her all the rest of their lives, and already he wished he hadn't married her?

"Why?" she squeaked. Tears crowded into her eyes. She blinked to clear them. "Don't you love me any more?"

"I'm making you miserable."

"But you still love me, don't you?" she whispered, feeling a desperate sense of disbelief.

Cam closed his eyes as if in pain. "Yes, I love you."

"Then that's all the matters." A ray of hope steadied her voice.

"No, that's not all that matters." Cam opened his eyes and gazed at her, his lips pressed into a hard line. "I almost smashed my fist into your face. I would have if you hadn't moved fast enough. How loving is that?"

"You didn't mean to hit me. It was the nightmare."

"I'm a basket-case, Sandy."

"Let me help." She reached out to touch him, but he batted her hand away.

"I'm not one of your damned projects." He stalked to the far side of the room.

"Cam," Sandy pleaded, following him.

"It isn't working. Can't you see that? God help, me, I thought it would, but it isn't."

"What's not working?" Sandy struggled to stay calm.

"Us. Me." Cam dragged a hand over his hair. "I thought I could come home and just put it all behind me, but I can't. I thought being married to you would help me get back to where I was before I went, but I'm not the same man anymore."

"You're the same man I fell in love with."

"I can't be the man you want me to be. I can't be the man *I* want me to be. Hell, I don't even know what kind of man I've become."

"What about the baby" Sandy was beginning to feel desperate. This couldn't be happening. He couldn't mean to walk out. Not just like that over a damned nightmare he couldn't help having.

"The baby doesn't need me either." Cam reached for his jeans.

"Of course the baby needs you. He needs his father." Sandy grabbed for his arm. "Don't run away, again."

"If you're smart, *you'll* run away and take the baby with you. You'll both be better off without me." He shrugged her hand away and began dressing. "If you're as smart as you say, you'll pack your bags and be gone when I get back." He shoved his feet into his boots and headed toward the kitchen without even bothering to tie the laces.

Sandy hurried after him and watched in panic as he grabbed his jacket. "But you're coming back. Right? You're not leaving for good. Please, Cam?"

Cam shrugged into his jacket and began rummaging in his jeans pocket for his keys. When he pulled his hand out of his pocket he flung something toward the wastebasket. It ricocheted off the counter, hit the rim of the basket, then bounced down behind it. When he looked at Sandy again, agony was etched into his face. "The sooner you put me behind you, the sooner you can get on with your life."

"But you are my life, Cam."

"I'm a fuck-up. Find yourself a better man, Sandy."

She couldn't believe what she was hearing.

"Find yourself a man who wants a house full of kids. A man who doesn't wake you up every night screaming about things he can't ever change. Someone who has a handle on his emotions and won't put your teeth down your throat."

"I don't want another man. I want you."

"Look Sandy, I'm trying to do something right for a change." He lifted her chin with one finger. "Leave me. Walk away from a bad deal. Don't waste the rest of your life trying to save me from myself. I'm not worth it."

Cam bent and kissed her on the mouth. There was no passion in it, only a frightening sense of finality. Then he turned on his heel, jerked the door open and walked out.

Sandy stared at the door for a long time as painful emotions raced through her, tumbling over each other until she didn't know which hurt most. Loss. Anger. Rejection. Failure. Had her mother felt like this? Had Daddy been like Cam when he came home from his war? Had that been why her mother left them?

Maybe Cam was right, and he'd only break her heart if she stayed. The heartbreak of learning to live with his mercurial mood swings and sudden icy withdrawals. Of not knowing when to laugh and when to leave him be. And never understanding what haunted him. Loving Cam was tearing her apart.

Tears stung her eyes, and she fought to keep them from falling. The ache in her chest grew until her whole body throbbed with it. "Why Cam?" she cried aloud to the empty kitchen. "Why are you doing this to us? Why are you doing this to me?

As her tears gathered strength, she turned and headed for the wastebasket. She tipped it away from the wall and peered down behind it. Her tears made it hard to see. She dragged an arm across her eyes, then looked again.

In the corner, between the wall and the counter, lay the worry stone. The small smooth stone she'd given Cam that long-ago day on the beach. For some inexplicable reason, he'd kept it. But now he'd thrown it away.

A sob rose in her throat, but she swallowed it. Blinking back her tears, she strode into the bedroom. He'd thrown the stone away, just like he was throwing her away.

A silver framed wedding photo stood on Cam's dresser just as a similar photo had stood on her father's dresser. Sandy studied the picture, not her own smiling, naively innocent face, but Cam's.

He had seemed so different then. She'd known he felt a deep loss over his brother's death, but that hadn't seemed so sinister then. Cam had told her he was the happiest man on earth, and she'd believed him. And all the time there had been a self-destructive time bomb ticking away inside him.

Perhaps she should leave. Eventually she'd stop hurting and forget about the pain and the helplessness. Wouldn't she? Maybe even someday the bliss of being in love with Cam would be a distant memory. Perhaps that's what her mother had thought.

But how could she look at their baby and not think of Cam? And not ache for him? How would their child feel growing up without a father?

He doesn't want us. Sandy sniffed back her tears. She tried to whip up the anger that had shut out the pain earlier. *He doesn't want us.* Stooping, she dragged her battered suitcase from beneath the bed. *He'll be happier without me here to nag him all the time. He says he just wants to be left alone. Well, fine! He can have all the time in the world to spend with his demons, but I don't have to stay here and help him enjoy them.*

She yanked open her top drawer, grabbed up fistfuls of underwear and shoved them into the suitcase. She emptied the second drawer and the third. Then she headed toward the closet.

On a shelf next to the closet another photo stopped her in her tracks. A photo of her father just like the one of Cam on her mother-in-law's mantle. Both were of young soldiers outfitted in their dress uniforms, smiling and confident. And both had been taken before those young men had gone away to find out what war was really all about.

Unable to drag her gaze away, Sandy stared at the smiling young officer that had been her father. Another image crowded into her memory. An image of her father looking baffled and hurt. Like a physical blow, the vision left her breathless. She backed away abruptly, two steps, then two more, until the footboard of the bed caught her behind the knees, and she plopped onto the bed.

A rush of memory flooded through her. A memory she hadn't even known she possessed. The memory of a scene she hadn't known she'd witnessed. Something she'd blocked from her mind completely until this moment.

She must have been about four or five when she'd heard her parents arguing. Scared by the raised voices, she'd crept from her bed and tiptoed halfway down the stairs.

Suddenly, as clearly as if they stood in front her, she saw her mother by the front door of the house Sandy had grown up in, a suitcase in one hand, almost no expression on her face. Her father, by contrast, looked desperate and confused and hurt.

"Because you're no fun anymore." Sandy's mother said in a cold brittle voice. "You're not the man I married, and I'm tired of pretending. I have no intention of spending the rest of my life buried here with you and the things you can't or won't forget. I'm sorry for the hurt I've caused you, but you'll get over it. Or better yet, add me to your list of things to mourn. You do mourning very well. It's living you can't seem to handle. Good bye, John."

Then Caroline Marshall had stepped out of their lives forever.

Clinging helplessly to the railing, Sandy had watched her father slump onto the hassock, his broad shoulders shaking. And then, with deep heartbreaking sobs, he had wept. Weeping he didn't even try to control because he hadn't known he had a witness.

Sandy had been petrified. She had been too young to understand the spiteful things her mother had said, but she had seen the disbelief in her father's eyes and heard the gut-wrenching pain in his sobs. As Sandy learned when she was older, Caroline had meant everything to John Marshall, and that awful night he'd lost her forever.

Staring, suddenly dry-eyed, at her father's photo, Sandy finally understood.

She understood why she had always felt compelled to be there for her father. Why she'd always tried so hard to make him laugh when he was sad. Why she had loved him without reservation even when he had done things that had hurt her.

And why she could never leave Cam.

CHAPTER THIRTY-SIX

CAM HAD NEVER FELT SUCH DESPAIR IN HIS LIFE. NOT EVEN WHEN he'd been in Vietnam, surrounded by unthinkable destruction and wasted lives.

He hurried past the old anchor, refusing to look at it or touch it. All the luck in the world couldn't change the mess he'd made of his life or Sandy's. He strode angrily through the dunes and onto the beach, the dreadful ache in his heart almost beyond bearing. He hadn't thought it would hurt this much to let her go. Facing a future without her was just about going to kill him. And if that didn't do it, then the thought of what he had done to her would.

Telling her to leave him had been the hardest thing he'd ever done. It had been all he could manage not to wrap his arms about her when she had leaned into him seeking reassurance. He'd had to hold his intense need for her in check while he told her she would be better off without him. Hope had flickered in her eyes when he had been unable to deny his love for her, but he had swallowed the words that would have undone the damage. He had stifled the desperate cry of his own heart by keeping himself focused on what would be best for her.

Anxiously, he shoved his hand in his pocket, seeking the smooth little worry stone that always made her feel closer. Then he remembered flinging it across the room, and his hand closed around the emptiness that mirrored the void in his heart as he glared out at the ocean, black with faint curls of white here and there as waves crested on their way to the beach.

What would it feel like to slip into those icy waters and just start swimming? How long would it take before the bone-chilling cold sapped the last of my strength and left me floating, numb and uncaring? Would God ever forgive me for committing such a sin? Surely, He would understand.

Staring down at the damp, glistening leather of his boots, his thoughts returned to Sandy. It wasn't God he would hurt the most by committing suicide, but Sandy. She would be devastated. He couldn't do that to her.

Her wonderful hazel eyes, swimming with unshed tears and her tremulous "why?" were indelibly etched in his brain. Maybe she didn't understand. Maybe she'd never understand. God knows, he hardly understood himself. But she'd get over him. She would heal and go on to love again and have half a dozen toe-headed little kids to expend her boundless well of love on. He owed it to her not to make this separation more heartbreaking than it already was.

He'd learn to live without her. He'd managed to survive for twenty-eight years without her until that fateful day last fall. Hard to believe six months could have made such an incredible difference, but they had. The years yawned ahead of him in an endless stretch of nothingness. Years of going to work and coming home. Of eating and sleeping and existing, but without any purpose. Without any hope. Without Sandy.

An hour later. Maybe two. Or even three. He had no idea how long he'd stood there at the edge of the ocean, the cold and wet finally seeped through the leather of his boots, and his feet were numb. He shivered inside the heavy leather bomber jacket. He might as well go home. *She's had plenty of time to be gone by now.*

As Cam strode back toward the truck, he wondered where Sandy would have gone. To Natalie's maybe. Or Sean's. Belatedly, it occurred to him that he should have packed up his own gear and let her stay at the apartment. That would have been the gentlemanly thing to do. He hadn't been thinking very clearly.

Tomorrow he would leave a message at her school letting her know she could have the apartment. They wouldn't be very happy about it, but his parents wouldn't turn him away. He could stay with them or maybe even go back to the frat house.

By the time Cam pulled the truck to a stop, the prospect of their deserted apartment had grown crushingly bleak. Dreading the emptiness, he mounted the stairs and sorted through his keys. He let himself in and shut the door, then leaned wearily against it, trying not to remember how content he'd felt just a few hours ago. Or to recall the things that had brought him to the awful place he was now. The effort proved futile as it all paraded relentlessly through his brain.

The flippant remark he'd made that Sean's baby better be a girl. The nightmare featuring Cam's own son beguiled by a Marine recruiter. And his violence when Sandy woke him from it.

It all came down to that. He could not control his own violence. Sandy was a sensitive, loving woman. She didn't need the turmoil and rage that he'd brought into her life. She needed a man in control of himself and of his life. She needed loving and laughter and babies. She needed stability. A man who would always be there for her. A man who wasn't lost in his own private world of guilt.

He was not that man.

He pushed away from the door, shucked off his jacket and went to hang it on a peg. Sandy's thick wooly parka still hung there. She must have worn her work coat, thinking to come back for the rest of her things later. He buried his face in the thick pile and inhaled the scent of her. Tears sprang into his eyes, and he let them come for a few moments before hauling back in alarm. He dashed his sleeve across his eyes, determined not to break down. Not even in private.

Every muscle in his body cried out for relief. Release from guilt and pent up emotion. Maybe sleep would bring oblivion, at least until the nightmares started again. He needed sleep. God, did he need sleep.

Cam pried his boots off and left them under the row of pegs, then padded into the bedroom. Not until he'd gotten completely naked and was climbing into bed did he realized he wasn't alone after all.

He froze, the covers half pulled up, his heart in his throat. Sandy hadn't gone.

Squashing a surge of unreasoning hope, he reminded himself he didn't know why she hadn't left. There might be half a dozen reasons, none of them permanent. She might not have wanted to wake anyone up in the middle of the night. Or perhaps she'd been afraid to go out at that hour.

And he'd had the truck.

Bastard! Tell her to take off, then leave her no way to do so. What did I expect? That she could blink like Jeannie and just wish herself somewhere else?

He scrambled to his feet again.

"I was afraid you really weren't going to come back this time." Sandy's voice sounded weary, but not clouded with sleep. She'd stayed awake, waiting for him.

"I shouldn't have." There were a million things he shouldn't have done, but breaking Sandy's heart was the worst of them.

Sandy pushed herself to a sitting position, then reached to turn on the bedside lamp. Now he could see the devastation he'd caused. The puffy eyes. The tear streaked cheeks. She reached out and grabbed his hand in both of hers.

"Come back to bed, Cam. You're freezing cold."

"I shouldn't."

"Of course, you should. You belong here." She tugged at his hand.

He wanted desperately to give in to her urging. To let her wrap him in her warmth and forgiveness. "And then what?"

"What do you mean, and then what?" She turned the covers back enlarging on her invitation.

"Nothing's changed, Sandy. I'm still a bastard. It's probably only a matter of time before I do something really unforgiveable.

"The only thing that I would find totally unforgiveable would be you abandoning me and our baby." Her hand tightened around his and her eyes searched his. No longer the bright hazel he loved, but dark pools of uncertainty and distress.

"I thought you wouldn't be here," Cam said, his throat tight.

"I almost wasn't," Sandy admitted softly. "I started to pack but . . .but I changed my mind."

"Why?" he croaked.

"I promised to stand by you. For better or worse. I meant it on our wedding day, and I mean it even more now." Her voice was gentle but firm.

He groaned and even to himself, he sounded like a wounded animal.

"Good Marines don't leave their wounded behind, and neither do I." She squeezed his hand. "If you don't want me, you'll have to say it."

But he couldn't say it.

With every fiber of his being, he wanted her. With every cell in his body, every drop of blood rushing through his veins. God help him, he wanted her despite every good intention. Despite every hurtful thing he'd said or done that brought her grief. That put that pained look in her eyes and the dark circles under them.

He simply couldn't say it.

CAM PEERED through the passenger window of his truck, surveying the run-down building where a group of local veterans ran a soup kitchen. Bricks with the mortar falling out. Windows with broken panes. Peeling paint. Even the sidewalk had cracks. But, used up as it looked, this was the place he needed to be. The place he'd finally realized he needed to seek out.

Linc had told him about this group after the fiasco over Thanksgiving dinner. He had reminded Cam several times on the nights Cam had sat in his bar, anesthetizing himself with beer. But he hadn't been ready then to admit he needed help. What could talking about it do to stop the nightly parade of carnage? If talking could help, then he had Sandy, eager and willing to hear him out. But he had been convinced talking wasn't the answer. He just wanted to forget.

Then he'd erupted into such violence, he'd been forced to admit it.

He needed help.

It didn't matter that he hadn't meant to hit Sandy because that hadn't stopped him from swinging. Only her fast reaction had saved her from serious injury. An injury he would never have forgiven himself for.

And what if he did nothing and this whole thing continued to escalate out of control? What about when the baby arrived? Would he abuse his own child next? He broke out in a sweat just thinking about the possibility.

Convincing Sandy to leave him hadn't worked in spite of all the harsh things he'd said to her. No telling how he'd have ended up if she had gone, but at least Sandy and the baby would have been safe, and she'd have been able to create a better life for the two of them. Except Sandy refused to abandon him. She had the courage and tenacity of a whole company of Marines.

More courage than he'd shown so far. She'd been willing to face whatever problems he had straight on, and all he'd done was hide from them, or pretend they didn't exist. Coward that he was, it had taken him almost a week just to call Linc and ask for the address. And another four days making his mind up to attend a meeting. All kinds of excuses kept popping into his mind: getting time off from his new job, being the most convenient.

But every time he looked at Sandy, her words came back to him. 'Good Marines don't leave their wounded behind and neither do I.'

He was wounded.

It wasn't easy to admit. Not something he wanted to admit, but there were parts of him that were broken. Just as he'd told Sandy the night he'd proposed, something inside him had been broken. How on earth had he thought he could be a decent husband or father when he wasn't even a whole man?

You're a worthless bastard, Cameron. A fucking disaster. What in God's name Sandy finds to love in you is a mystery.

But calling himself names didn't fix the problem. He needed help. Wounded, broken men don't get better all by themselves.

So, here he sat. Listening to his truck engine tink as it cooled, trying to screw up his courage to join the meeting that would begin upstairs in the next few minutes.

Cam got out of the truck, walked around the front and crossed the sidewalk to the front door of the building. Inside, he could see rows of folding tables and neatly stacked chairs. Painted onto the window beside the door were the hours meals were served. Not for another three hours. The door was shut tight.

Cam leaned away and looked up, then noticed another door beyond the big storefront window. Tucked a foot back from the front of the building, it had a discrete little sign that read, "Nam Vets Welcome."

Cam turned the knob and pushed the door open. A tiny foyer tiled in cracked but spotlessly clean black and white greeted him. A row of four mail slots adorned the wall. Above them a cardboard arrow pointed up the stairs.

Cam recognized the hand painted rectangle of yellow, with red and green vertical stripes. He had a matching campaign pin in a box buried in his sock drawer. He sucked in a ragged breath, squared his shoulders, then started up the stairs.

CHAPTER THIRTY-SEVEN

FEBRUARY 15

They waited for him to speak, but his throat ached and nothing came out. Silent patience, punctuated by the ticking of the clock on the wall. Cigarette smoke hung heavy in the air. Cam considered bumming a butt from the wiry, little, chain-smoker they all called Wiz. But he'd probably choke on that, too.

"It's Okay, LT. You don't have to talk tonight if you're not ready."

Cam hadn't been ready for the three weeks he'd been attending these meetings. He might never be ready, but talking was the reason he'd come. To talk about the nightmares and the flashbacks. And the guilt. And the violence. The unforgivable, uncontrolled violence. Otherwise he might as well go for that swim he'd been contemplating the night it had all blown up in his face.

"Man, it was months before I shared anything more than my name," Giff, a round-faced man dressed in a battered field jacket offered Cam an excuse for delaying.

"Now we can't shut you up," the smoker sitting next to Cam retorted.

"But you love me like a brother anyway, right?"

. . .

FEBRUARY 23

"Drinkin' to forget is somethin' we've all tried. Sometimes it works, most times not." A tall, skinny, black man, aptly nicknamed Stilt, opined complacently through a lazy curl of pot smoke. Seemed like he'd found his opiate.

"I only drink to stop the nightmares," Cam insisted. "Forgetting isn't going to happen ever, I don't think."

"The nightmares'll fade. Eventually." The older man had been a sergeant in Korea. In Chosin. Now that had been a living hell, and if the Sarge said the nightmares would get less horrific, maybe there was hope.

"You talk to your wife about 'em?" Wiz asked.

"NO!" Cam blurted.

"She doesn't want to hear about it, I suppose."

"That's not the reason. I . . ." Cam swallowed his protest.

"Oughta try it. Might help."

MARCH 1

"My wife's pregnant," Cam announced hesitantly.

"Hey, congratulations, man."

"But . . ."

"But it's not your kid?" Giff shook his head sadly.

"Of course, it's my kid." Cam felt a surge of outrage at the suggestion.

"So, what's the problem, LT? You don't like kids?"

"I like kids fine. I just don't deserve . . ." The familiar suffocating guilt rose up and swallowed the rest of the sentence.

"Something happened in Nam? Something sickening that happened to a kid?" Sarge asked gently.

Cam shook his head. "To his father. To the kid's father. And it was my fault."

MARCH 8

"This nightmare— It's always the same? Always about this corpsman, this kid named Jenkins who lost his arms?" Wiz had decided to put Cam on the spot. Provoke him into telling more than just the bits and pieces he'd been getting away with so far.

Cam stared past the chain-smoker, focusing instead on a tattered poster advertising a movie, *Dirty Harry,* that hung on the far wall.

"Most of the time it's about Jenkins. Not always about the booby trap, but most always about Jenkins. Sometimes—" Cam swallowed a mouthful of saliva. "Sometimes, he's just showing me this photograph of his new baby, see? And he's always saying how much he wants to hold the kid. How much he missed being there when his son was born."

"Must have been thousands of kids born while their daddies were off chasing Charlie around the jungle."

"Of course, there were, but . . ." Cam broke off, remembering with a familiar sinking sense of horror, how Jenkins had folded his arms and pretended to rock a baby in them.

And then he didn't have any arms.

MARCH *15*

"The wounded guy was rigged. The VC knew we'd try to help him."

"I saw a man cut in half by a Bouncing Betty. It wasn't pretty."

"But that wasn't your fault," Cam argued.

"Jenkins wasn't your fault either. How long did you say he'd been there?"

"Too long. A day too long."

"Long enough to know about booby traps as well as you did."

"But he was just a kid."

"We were all kids."

Cam looked at Giff, the kid with the perpetually cherubic face who looked like he belonged in junior high. "I was the old man. Older than any of them. I shoulda known.

Stilt took a drag on his joint. "We were all kids. Even you."

MARCH *22*

"We were so fucking tired. Everyone just wanted to get back to base, and I didn't —" Cam shut up abruptly, his heart racing. Sweat beaded on his forehead, and he suddenly had difficulty breathing. "I should never have called the corpsman up. I shoulda checked first."

Cam saw the corpsman reaching to turn the wounded soldier over. He opened his mouth as if to scream a warning. Then he did scream. In horror. In fury. In agony. He flung his folding metal chair crashing into the wall. A couple of the men ducked. But they didn't retreat. And they didn't let him run either.

"Let it out, man. Just let it all out."

Cam stopped screaming and stood panting, fists bunched at his sides. The rage left him in a rush. Sobs worked their way past his armor, and he sank onto the floor like a broken doll. Bawling into his hands. Chest heaving. The pain unbearable. The only sound in the room the gut-wrenching noise coming out of his own throat.

One by one, the vets joined him on the floor. An arm circled his shoulders. A hand gripped his knee. Another pressed warmly against his back. A hand laid on his head as if in benediction. Hands on his neck and on his arms. A solid circle of support and understanding as the tears continued to pour down his face like they might never stop.

APRIL 5

"When's the kid due?"

"In a month."

"You gonna be ready?"

"I put the crib up the other day."

"That's not what I meant."

"I know what you meant." Cam ran a hand over his face. "Sandy was so happy. She was all over me, but it was just a lousy crib, for Christ's sake. It's not like . . . I just don't know."

"Well, you still got time."

APRIL 12

Cam was running out of time. He'd had five months to get used to the idea and he still got a panicky feeling in the pit of his stomach most of the time.

"We started Lamaze classes last week." All those grinning, eager fathers-to-be huffing and puffing, making jokes, comparing notes. Cam had wanted to bolt.

"Fuck! You're really gonna be in there when the kid gets born?"

"I promised her." Cold sweat began to trickle down Cam's sides. He'd reeked of his own sweat after the Lamaze class. But, after everything Sandy had done for him, he owed her this. She would be the one suffering through the labor. What happened to Jenkins might not be entirely Cam's fault, maybe none of his fault, but Sandy being pregnant with his baby most definitely was his doing. Fuck yeah, he owed her!

"I promised her," he repeated.

"Ya want, I could wait outside, LT. Ya know, in case ya need . . ." Wiz didn't finish his offer, but Cam knew he meant it.

These guys had been here for him every week for the last three months. They'd be there for him whenever he needed them. Especially this little, loud-mouth, runt of a guy who poked and prodded every time Cam tried to back away from something he didn't want to face.

Cam looked at the man, then around the circle of now familiar faces and realized he felt as close to these men as he had to any of the men he'd served with. Closer. Together they'd faced demons as frightening as anything they'd experienced in the cauldron of war. They'd wept and cursed and held each other up. They'd carried Cam through the worst of it when he couldn't make it alone.

"Thanks. That means a lot to me, but this is something I've gotta do on my own."

APRIL 19

"A couple a nights ago, Sandy grabbed my hand and put it on her stomach. The kid was having basketball practice or something." It hadn't been the first time Cam had felt his baby moving, but the wonder of it caught him by surprise anyway. And he'd been grinning like a jack-o-lantern.

"Amazing thing, isn't it?" Sarge asked in his usual gentle voice.

"Yeah, it was. But then . . ."

"Then?" Wiz prodded.

"Then I remembered Jenkins."

"And . . .?"

"Jenkins never got to feel his kid move at all. At first I felt like I was gonna puke again. But then—"

"But then you didn't. And a good thing, too. About time you got your head screwed on right." The little guy tipped his head back and blew a cloud of smoke into the air. Then looked directly at Cam. "This guy Jenkins? You really think he'd want you tied up in knots over you being able to hold your kid just because he didn't get the chance? You said he mooned over that photo and loved that little boy of his, right? Don't you s'pose he'd want you to love your kid that way? And hold him every chance you got?"

"Of course, he would, but it doesn't seem fair—"

"War ain't fair!" Stilt dropped his chair back onto all four legs with a thud. "Ain't nothing ever been fair about war. Not what happened to Jenkins or any of the other guys who came back in pieces. Not what happened to your brother. Or your wife's brother. Or any of the kids who came home in metal boxes or so screwed up in their heads they'll never get it together. But you can't hold yourself responsible for all of it. You did the best job you could and from what I've been hearing all these weeks, you did it a damned sight better than any of the Louies I ever had to report to."

"Wasn't fair to any of us. Ever consider that, LT? This war wasn't fair to you neither!"

MAY 3

"We picked out names."

"What are you hoping for? Boy or girl?"

Cam shrugged. As recently as a month ago, he'd been praying for a girl. A daughter he figured would be easier. Now he didn't care. "Either." He smiled and it felt genuine. Easy, contented and genuine.

"So, if it's a boy, you naming him after his daddy?"

Cam shook his head. "We're not naming him after anyone. I don't want him to have to live up to anyone else's expectations."

"It sure as hell is good to see you smiling, LT. Right guys?" Wiz glanced around the circle, and everyone nodded, agreeing with him. "Good chance we won't be seeing you for a week or three, but you sure as hell better bring some cigars by."

CHAPTER THIRTY-EIGHT

SANDY CLUNG TO CAM'S HAND AS IF SHE THOUGHT HE'D BOLT FROM the delivery room at the last minute. All the huffing and puffing done, and in another moment, the doctor would be urging her to bear down again. Her face was flushed and sweaty. Her hair hung in damp tendrils around her face. But she smiled in eager anticipation. And she was still the most beautiful woman in the world.

"What time is—" She broke off abruptly as another contraction caught her up in its iron grip.

"Push," the doctor ordered from his seat at the foot of the table.

"Push," Cam parroted. His heart raced at about a thousand miles an hour. He glanced at the clock. Two minutes past twelve. "Push, sweetheart, it's past midnight. This'll be the best mother's day present you'll ever get.

Sandy grunted and did as she'd been told.

"Hey, I can see hair! Lots of it! It's —" Cam broke off as the head emerged. His baby. Eyes screwed shut, face as red as Sandy's. Cam gaped in awe.

"One more big push," the doctor ordered as he turned the infant's face and eased the shoulders out.

Suddenly the doctor held a baby in his hands. A baby boy. A son. A beautiful baby son. Tears surged into Cams eyes.

Sandy fell back onto the pillows gasping for breath. Cam tore his gaze away from the infant and glanced toward her.

"Cam! What's wrong?" Alarm sounded sharply in her voice.

"It's a boy," he told her. "A beautiful little boy. He's . . . he's perfect."

"About as perfect as they get," the doctor echoed, then placed the squalling newborn on Sandy's stomach.

Sandy let go of Cam's hand and reached to touch her son with trembling fingers. Then she looked back at Cam and smiled. "He looks like his daddy."

Cam bent to kiss her. "I love you," he whispered, his throat aching with emotion.

"Do you want to hold him for a few minutes before they take him to the nursery?" The nurse scooped the wailing baby up in a receiving blanket and thrust him toward Cam.

"I don't — I'm not —" Cam gulped, then with infinite care, he took his son into his arms.

The bundle felt warm and unbelievably tiny. As Cam gazed down at him in wonder, the infant stopped howling and opened his eyes. He returned Cam's gaze with solemn blue eyes and made a puckered little O of his mouth. Tears streamed down Cam's face and he didn't care who saw them. His heart thundered with pride and an immeasurable amount of love. He tried to swallow past the lump in his throat and blinked fiercely at the tears that made his son's face waver.

"Welcome to the world Philip Bowie Cameron." Then Cam buried his face in the infant's blanket and rocked his son close against his chest. "This is for you Jenkins. For you and for me."

CHAPTER THIRTY-NINE

January 2014

CAM TURNED AWAY from the window in the surgical waiting room and paced back to the sofa for the thousandth time. He fidgeted with the tiny stone in his pocket and paced back to the window again, guilt and fear eating at him. The doctor still hadn't reappeared and every minute Sandy remained on the operating table felt like an eternity.

Why? Why had he let her go out to do *his* errand? Why hadn't she told him it was icy? That Buick of hers had no traction on anything but dry roads. *Please, God. Please let her live.*

"Sit down, Dad. You're wearing a path in the rug." Cam's daughter, Kate, patted the sofa next to her.

She looked so much like her mother. A fact that usually filled him with pleasure, but just now, made him feel more like crying. Kate had her mother's patience, too. And calm, good sense.

Cam lowered himself onto the sofa, but couldn't relax the taut muscles cramping his shoulders and back. He continued to finger the worry stone in his pocket. Sandy's first gift to him all those years ago.

"Mom's tough." Kate gave him a reassuring hug. She smelled like Sandy, too. His eyes watered alarmingly, and he blinked back the tears.

"How long will it take the twins to get here?" A handsome Marine asked, turning away from the counter with a fresh cup of coffee in his hand. Philip, Cam and Sandy's eldest son, looked just like his father. He had his father's height and sky-blue eyes and his mother's impatient enthusiasm for life. He'd been born on Mother's Day, and had fulfilled every dream either of his parents had ever had, including the one Cam had feared most.

After years of skinned knees, homework, soccer games and laughter, Philip had graduated from high school one sunny June afternoon. The next day, he hugged his parents goodbye and boarded a bus bound for Parris Island to begin basic training. He'd only been seventeen at the time, and Cam had been tracked down in his office to be talked into giving his permission.

It's ironic how things work out, the thought settled into Cam's consciousness as he studied the square set of his son's broad shoulders and the insignia of a gunnery sergeant on his uniform. Philip had first seen action when he was still in his teens. Since then he'd been to Somalia and Iraq, and in two weeks time he'd be leaving the relative safety of Camp Lejeune to report for duty in Afghanistan. He'd been decorated twice for risking his own skin to save the life of a buddy. He was everything a Marine was meant to be and had made the Corps his career. And Cam couldn't have been prouder.

Every time he said goodbye to his son, he knew it might be the last, but he'd come to terms with that. He embraced his son with unabashed candor, told him he loved him often and left his life in God's hands. Just as Sandy's had been for the past four hours.

God, please let that doctor come out and tell us Sandy's going to be okay.

Cam glanced past his eldest son, to his youngest. The black sheep. At least that's what Jake tended to call himself when he stacked himself up against his siblings. Cam had never seen Jake in that light and was as proud of him as he was of any of his kids.

Jake had made the youthful mistake of getting his high school sweetheart pregnant and had paid for it by giving up his college ambitions, going to work for his old man and becoming a breadwinner. And he'd gotten his heart broken when Marsha got tired of being a mom and wife and took off, leaving Jake to bring up his three daughters on his own. But, instead of being bitter about any of it, Jake had grown up fast, and remained the cheerful, generous person he'd always been. He was a terrific dad, one of the best construction site managers Cam had ever had in his employ, and he still found time to join the local volunteer fire department and care for his ailing mother-in-law.

Jake turned suddenly and gazed across at his father. His eyes echoed the worry and fear pounding in Cam's own heart. "She'll be okay." Cam read the words on Jake's lips and wondered which of them Jake was trying to convince.

"We got here as fast as we could, Dad." A disheveled, blue-eyed man almost as tall as his father burst into the room. His identical twin rushed in behind him.

"Will got stopped for speeding. Good thing he's a state trooper or we'd still be waiting for Sheriff Nicholson's new deputy to finish writing a ticket," Ben said breathlessly as he flung himself into the chair opposite Cam. "How's Mom? Is she still in surgery?"

Cam nodded, reaching out to hug Ben. Then he got to his feet and enfolded Will in a quick embrace, as well.

"How's the dog-whisper?" Philip set his coffee cup on the table and sat down on the arm of Ben's chair, resting one hand on Ben's shoulder.

"Been busy," Ben answered distractedly. "You heard anything yet?"

"Nada," Kate answered calmly. "The doctor will brief us as soon as Mom is out of surgery."

"You make it sound like a press conference, Kate." Will sank onto a chair next to his twin.

Kate looked at the anxious males seated all around her. "You guys are likely to make it feel like one, if I know you. You'll all be talking at once, demanding answers before the poor man has half a chance to say anything."

"It's a she," Cam corrected his daughter. "Dr. Danielle Jorgenson."

Kate shrugged with a hint of a smile tugging the corners of her mouth. "In that case, the doctor will survive."

The squeak of sneakers sounded in the hall outside, and a tired looking woman in bloodstained scrubs stepped into the room. Cam's heart lurched into his throat, and his fist closed so hard around the worry stone that pain shot up his arm. Dr. Jorgenson pushed the green scrub hat off her short brown curls and wiped a slender hand across her eyes. Then she smiled.

"Mr. Cameron . . ."

Five men leapt to their feet and advanced on the tired-looking woman. The doctor's gaze scanned them all, but settled on Cam. "Your wife is going to be fine."

Thank God. Cam's knees went weak.

"When can I see her?"

"You can sit with her in recovery if you want to. It may be a while. She was on the table a long time, and we had to . . ."

He didn't hear the rest of Dr. Jorgenson's report. Kate would fill him in on the details later. He strode out of the huddle with the worry stone still balled in his fist, ignoring tears of relief he couldn't hide, not even from his Marine-tough son, his no-nonsense daughter, the twins who had never seen their father cry or Jake, whose eyes weren't dry either. He couldn't wait a moment longer to be with the most important person in his life.

Acknowledgements

When the men and women who fought in Vietnam first returned from their tour in Southeast Asia, they were not welcomed home as they should have been. Their sacrifices were ignored as our country struggled to come to terms with an unpopular war. My brother, CPT J. Scotty Parker, was one of those men and some of his experiences, related to me in the wee hours of the night when he couldn't sleep were the inspiration for this book.

I also have to thank Paul Solotaroff who published *The House of Purple Hearts* in 1995 – the story of a shelter created in Boston for men who were struggling to find their way back after coming home from war; men with broken marriages, broken lives, broken families and broken hearts. Men filled with anguish, and yet courageous in their fight to rebuild their lives.

I owe a huge debt of gratitude to Nancy Quatrano who encouraged me to publish this book, Elizabeth Sinclair, who read and critiqued as I wrote, my daughter Lori, who took on the daunting task of copy editing, and everyone who has ever supported me in my writing and encouraged me along the way. And of course, my brother who read this book long before it arrived in your hands and helped me keep it real.

AUTHOR'S NOTE

If you enjoyed this book, the author would appreciate a review on
Amazon, B&N, Bookbub or Goodreads.

ABOUT THE AUTHOR

Skye Taylor, mother, grandmother and returned Peace Corps Volunteer, loves adventure and lives in St Augustine Florida where she enjoys the history and ambiance of America's oldest city and its beautiful beaches. She posts a sometimes-weekly blog and sends out a monthly newsletter, volunteers with the USO, and is currently working on a new mystery series. Her published work includes: *The Candidate, Falling for Zoe, Loving Meg, Trusting Will, Healing a Hero, Iain's Plaid* and *Keeping His Promise.* Short stories: *Loving Ben, Mike's Wager and Saving Just One* and non-fiction essays of her experiences in the Peace Corps (Available on her website: www.Skye-writer.com.) She has a page on her website featuring short stories, some set in Tide's Way. She is a member of Romance Writers of America, Women's Fiction Writer's Association, Florida Writer's Association and Sisters in Crime. She loves hearing from her readers at Skye@Skye-writer.com You can also request to be added to her newsletter mailing list.

www.ingramcontent.com/pod-product-compliance
Lightning Source LLC
Chambersburg PA
CBHW071542110726
47908CB00007B/1966